About the Author

Mark Hayden is the nom de guerre of Adrian Attwood. He lives in Westmorland with his wife, Anne.

He has had a varied career working for a brewery, teaching English and being the Town Clerk in Carnforth, Lancs. He is now a part-time writer and part-time assistant in Anne's craft projects.

He is also proud to be the Mad Unky to his Great Nieces & Great Nephew.

Also by Mark Hayden

The King's Watch – Conrad Clarke

The 13th Witch
The Twelve Dragons of Albion
The Eleventh Hour
Tenfold
Nine of Wands
Eight Kings
The Seventh Star
Six Furlongs

Operation Jigsaw
(Conrad Clarke & Tom Morton – prequels to the King's Watch)

A Piece of Blue Sky
Green for Danger
In the Red Corner

Tom Morton Crime
(following Operation Jigsaw)

A Serpent in Paradise
Another Place to Die

All available from Paw Press

Tales from the Watch

The First Four King's Watch Novellas

MARK HAYDEN

PAW PRESS

www.pawpress.co.uk

First Published Worldwide in 2021 by Paw Press
Paperback Edition Published
January 01 2021

Individual Stories Copyright © 2019, 2020 Paw Press
All Rights Reserved

Cover Design – Rachel Lawston
Design Copyright © 2020 Lawston Design
www.lawstondesign.com
Cover images © Shutterstock

Paw Press – Independent publishing in Westmorland, UK.
www.pawpress.co.uk

ISBN:
ISBN-13: 978-1-914145-01-8
ISBN-10: 1-914145-01-1

For Ian Forsdike

Who has given a lot to help others.

Including me.

Contents

Phantom Stag   9

Wings over Water   71

Ring of Troth   123

French Leave   195

A Note from Vicky

There's a whole load of stuff in these stories that Conrad doesn't know about. Yet. He's bound to find out sooner or later, but don't be in a rush to tell him. Alright?

I don't know about you, but I have real trouble keeping track of everyone. Especially when I've never actually met them. That's why Mr Hayden put together a list of all the people, good and bad, who've crossed our paths. You can find them here:

www.pawpress.co.uk

Cheers,
Vicky.

Phantom Stag

This story was originally published in February 2019. The action takes place about one third of the way through **Tenfold**, *the Fourth Book of the King's Watch.*

Mark Hayden

Prologue

The Hunter

It had been a clear night. A cold one, too. Over the Hunter's shoulder, the stars in the east were dimming as the sun limbered up to replace them. Another half an hour and it would all end in failure, ignominy and recriminations. Unless...

There. A light in the trees. Two lights. Maybe three.

The Hunter didn't take his eyes off the leading light as he picked up his bow and straightened up, his knees creaking just a little from squatting on the damp grass. He touched the Artefact on his chest and felt the threads and patterns of the Charm come alive under his fingers. He drew some Lux and wove the net of magick that would hide him from the onrushing deer. They were nearly at the edge of the forest, and he would soon have a clear shot. So would the enemy, the other Hunter who must be chasing them – deer wouldn't break cover like this unless they felt in danger. He took an arrow and notched it to the bow.

The first deer broke through the bushes at the edge of the forest, and the Hunter started to draw the bow and take a bead on the stag...

Just in time, he saw it. That was no stag: it was a doe, heavy in calf and clearly in distress. He shuddered at the thought of what would happen if he'd brought her down. Then the second deer broke through and he saw them gleaming against the black trees – the curving, elegant points of silver antlers, the crowning glory of a Phantom Stag. The arrow was in the air before his head knew what his hand was doing. When the arrow struck the beast, an enormous flash of Lux burst across the meadow, blinding him and sending a horrible shiver up his spine.

The doe had disappeared into Home Wood before his eyes cleared, and the Hunter placed his bow carefully down before jogging a little unsteadily over the grass to finish the job.

He reached for his knife as he approached the beast, a few spots of light still cartwheeling around his mundane and magickal sight. And then he stopped, hand on his knife, jaw hanging slack at what lay on the ground before him.

With an enormous shudder, he took out not his knife but the short hunting horn.

The Priestess

She hadn't moved for over an hour, and wouldn't move until Bríd showed her face over the hills and brought the hunt to an end, perhaps with a smile, more likely with a frown at the horrible incompetence of the so-called Hunters. Eight hours they'd had to find the Phantom Stag. Nothing. They were a disgrace to the Foresters.

She had been looking at the main part of the forest, rising gently across the valley. The flash of Lux over to the left took her by surprise, and she gasped. *So much magick*. That could not be a good omen.

She turned to look at the source, well away to the south west and somewhere near Home Wood. She opened her Sight and saw a rising plume of Lux, a spirit dissipating and blowing away. That was some Stag indeed.

And then she heard the horn. Not the notes of a clean kill but the repeated blasts of distress. On and on they blared.

By her side, Tanya struggled to her feet. The Priestess turned to her handmaiden and said, 'Quickly. Get me there as fast you can.'

Tanya lifted her skirts and jumped on to the quad bike, fumbling off her gloves as she reached for the ignition. The engine was roaring into life as the Priestess climbed more sedately onto the pillion. Neither woman bothered with helmets. Tanya flicked on the headlamps and set off across the field.

The lights picked out one of the Hunters in the meadow between Home Wood and the edge of the forest. The Priestess rose a little in her seat to peer over Tanya's shoulder as they approached the scene. The Hunter was standing slack and slumped, the silent horn now lowered, and staring at something by his feet. Something large.

Something human. With a hunting arrow sticking out of its chest.

Tanya slowed and stopped. The Witches dismounted and stared. Not *its* chest – *his* chest. The dead man was heavily camouflaged, but there was no mistaking him. The standing Hunter was Colwyn, and at his feet was one of his rivals in tonight's Royal Hunt. Ioan. The Priestess's great nephew.

Tanya let out a whimper, chewing her knuckles.

'What happened?' snapped the Priestess to Colwyn.

'The Stag,' said Colwyn, half in a daze. 'I shot the Phantom Stag.'

'Clearly you didn't.'

She heard a noise from the edge of the forest and saw a light bobbing towards them. She waited until the third Hunter, Aaron, had arrived.

'In the name of Bríd, what's happened?' said Aaron when he'd seen the body.

'The Stag,' repeated Colwyn. 'I shot the Phantom Stag.'

Tanya and Aaron looked at the Priestess. What happened next was up to her. She knelt down and touched Ioan's body before turning to Tanya. 'Get my phone and switch it on. It's in the bag.'

'Are you going out of the Circle?' said Aaron.

'Of course. If the Foresters are going to survive this, we need someone else to investigate. I'm calling in the Witchfinders.'

'The King's Watch? But Mack's left the country. They'll send Rick James. The Foresters will never speak to him.'

'They'll send the Dragonslayer,' said the Priestess as she accepted the phone.

'Why? How?' said Tanya.

'Because he's a friend of my son, that's the *Why*. The *How* is more difficult. The cost to me is going to be very high.'

She found a number in her phone and stabbed the green icon. *Calling Chris* appeared on the screen.

1

Captain Victoria Robson FGW MC KW RMP

At least, that's what I think happened out in the Forest of Arden this morning. That's what people told me happened. I wasn't there. I was thirty miles away in Clerkswell and fast asleep in me bed.

I am not a morning person. Never have been, probably never will be. Besides, five o'clock isn't *morning* in my book. More like the middle of the flipping night, though I do understand that other people think differently. One of them is Myfanwy.

I didn't hear the hammering on the door. I didn't hear her shouting my name. I didn't hear anything until she came in and shook me. Credit her, she tried to be gentle.

'Vicky! Wake up!'

'Umngrr.'

'Vicky! Wake up! I've got the Constable on the phone.'

By the gods, is that a huge pink bunny holding a phone?

'Mngggrrr! Wha?'

'Hannah. The Constable. Your boss.'

At that point, my conscious reflexes took over from my automatic ones, and I sort-of woke up. Sort of. The large fluffy shape by the bed turned into a blonde Druid and not a huge rabbit. She was still pink though. That dressing gown…

'I knaa who she is, Myvvy.'

'Yes, and she's on the phone.'

'No.'

'Yes. Here.'

'What time is it?'

'Half past five.'

She held out her iPhone. At least she'd put call on mute. With some reluctance, I took it from her.

'Put the kettle on, pet,' I said, struggling to sit up. 'And why did you wake me? Why not his lordship? And what was she doing ringing you in the first place?'

'She said I wasn't to wake Conrad until I'd given you the phone, and she called me because she knew you'd sleep through it if she rang you. I'll be in the kitchen.'

I rubbed my eyes and unmuted the phone. 'Ma'am?'

'At last! I hope you feel like shit, because I do at this time in the morning.'

Good old Hannah. When it comes to suffering, she's very much an equal opportunities employer.

'Is everything all right, ma'am?'

'No, and I'll tell you why. You know that Cora's only just come out of hospital?'

'Aye. She's not relapsed again, has she?'

'I wouldn't blame her if she did. Her poor husband is sleeping in the spare room and had her phone. He gets a call and has to wake her up. She rang me and now I'm passing it on to you.'

'Right.'

I had no idea what she was on about. *Cora* is Cora Hardisty, Dean of the Invisible College and a Very Important Magickal Person. Also a very *injured* magickal person. I should know – I had held her hand while we waited for the ambulance and we had both tried not to stare at the metal spike sticking out of her abdomen. My mind wanders at the best of times. Half past five in the morning is not the best of times.

Hannah dragged me back to the present. 'There's been an incident in the Forest of Arden. One of the Foresters is dead and they've called us in to investigate.'

I sat up straight. 'No way! They hate the King's Watch. They still call us the Witchfinders, or so I've heard.'

'They do. They tolerated Mack McKeever, but now he's gone, and the Priestess has called in a favour.'

'Oh?'

'Yes. She called her son.'

I had no idea who the Priestess of the Arden Foresters might be, still less who her son was, and how come he had the Dean's private mobile number.

'Who's he when he's at home?'

'Chris Kelly.'

'Aah. I see.' Chris Kelly is the Earth Master, professor of Geomancy and one of the big cheeses at Salomon's House. He's a really nice bloke, but sooo boring. He's also a friend of Conrad's.

Hannah gave a big sigh. 'I doubt you do see, Vicky,' she said. 'Chris and his mother haven't seen each other for years.'

I had no idea. Why should I?

'Is that because she's a Witch and he's a professor of Quantum Magick?' I asked.

'They got over that years ago, and got over him changing his name. No, it's his wife. His mother can't stand her, and the feeling's mutual.'

'Ouch.'

'Exactly,' said Hannah. 'I'll text Conrad the location. Don't hang about. You can have breakfast when you get there. Oh, and don't let him mess it up.'

'Am I not capable of messing it up on me own, ma'am?'

I was wasting my breath. She'd disconnected.

There was a light tap on the door.

'Vic?' said Conrad. 'What's all the racket, and why have I got a set of co-ordinates on my phone?'

'Come in,' I sighed.

I don't mind Conrad seeing me with bed hair and no make-up. He's seen me when I was both naked and dead, and you don't get much more exposed than that.

He stuck his head round the door, and the rest of his great lanky body followed behind when he'd seen that I wasn't armed. I have been known to attack people who disturb my beauty sleep.

'We've got a case,' I said. 'In the Forest of Arden. We need to get a shift on.'

Conrad pulled his lip. It's not so much that he's a morning person, it's more that he's an ever-ready person. He was in the RAF for so long that he can switch himself on at a moment's notice, day or night.

He nodded. 'It's nearly freezing outside, but it's going to be hot later. I'd suggest layers.'

'Yes, Uncle Conrad. Shall I lay me clothes out on the bed for you to check?'

He pulled his lip again. 'I think I can trust you to get dressed on your own. I'll go away now, shall I?'

If it wasn't so early, I'd have chucked a pillow at him.

'Swap?' said Myfanwy when I got to the kitchen. She held out a slice of toast and a travel mug full of tea, and I swapped them for her phone.

Conrad had been down long enough to slurp an espresso and get a nicotine hit before I appeared. Men. They have it easy. He had a big map spread over the table and was staring at his phone. Other people, normal people, would have been staring at a map *on* their phone, but not Conrad. His phone doesn't have GPS, or the Internet, or a camera. It doesn't even do emojis when I text him. He says it's to stop people tracking him. I'm not so sure.

'Got it,' he said. 'Right. Let's go.'

He folded the map carefully and slipped it in one of the enormous pockets of his Barbour, picked up his own travel mug and said goodbye to Myfanwy. He was out the door and expecting me to follow before I'd finished chewing one mouthful of toast.

Myfanwy gave me a kiss. 'Take care, Vicky, love.' Then she gave me a gentle push towards the door. Who needs enemies when you've got housemates like Myfanwy and Conrad? He already had the engine running and was de-misting the windows when I got round the front of the house. His house.

It's a very nice house, of course. Big and old and comfy, and all that, but it's not *my* house, nor even my parents' house, and Conrad is my work partner, not my uncle. Myfanwy may be a friend, but she's also part-prisoner and part-housekeeper. Neither of us are living in Conrad's house by choice.

If it wasn't so early, I'd start to wonder how I ended up in a guest bedroom in the middle of nowhere. Instead, I shivered. Conrad was right: it was bloody freezing out here.

'What we got, Vic?' he asked when we were racing along the A46 and I'd finished my toast. And a granola bar from the stash in the glove box.

I took a moment to relay what Hannah had told me about the death. I was keeping the business about Chris Kelly to myself for now.

'That's it?' he said. 'A death? That's all we've got to go on?'

'Aye. Obviously it's suspicious, or they wouldn't have called us in.'

He grunted. 'What should I know about the Arden Foresters?'

'It was started by a breakaway group from the Daughters of the Goddess sometime in the 1840s. It was one of the first Circles to admit men and women equally. Before that, all the mixed Circles had the men in charge. The Foresters were different from day one, and they've always been run by a Priestess with a man as her second in command. They thought it reflected ancient practices.'

He looked over at me. 'And?'

'And what?'

'Is that all you know about them?'

Conrad thinks I keep things from him. I might have done, once, but not now. Not now it's my life on the line, too.

'Howay, man, they're a closed group. You have to sign up to get in. I never met Mack McKeever before he tittled off to America, so how could I know anything about them unless I lived in the Esoteric Library? I know they're very big in the Midlands, but that's about it.'

'Oh.'

'And I know that they don't like the Watch.'

'Who does like the Watch? Don't answer that, you might depress me with how short the list is.'

'I know something else, too. The Priestess is your pal Chris's mam.'

'Chris Kelly?' he asked, bemused.

'Who else? She's why we're on the case. I don't think she sees eye to eye with her son, though. Something to do with her daughter-in-law.'

There. Done. I thought I slipped that in quite subtly for me. He slowed down for a second, then raced past a milk tanker. It was the first thing we'd come across on the road, and at this speed we'd be there in … I hadn't a clue. We were in the countryside, south of Birmingham, and that's about all I could tell you. Conrad used to fly helicopters without an autopilot and can tell which way North is without a compass. Sometimes that skill is actually useful. I shut up and let him drive.

We bumped over a cattle grid, and Conrad pulled up next to a pair of black 4x4s. Definitely Mages.

'Showtime, Vic. I'll get my gear,' he said.

I got out, too, and while Conrad fiddled with his arsenal in the back of the car, I soaked up the atmosphere. It wasn't quite as cold out here, and the countryside was already giving off those smells that everyone gets so worked up about: cowshit, mostly. And then I stared.

I stared down the hill, where wisps of mist were hiding from the sun and a small stream cut through the grass like a bread knife through a warm cob. I stared across the grass, and I saw it. I saw the Forest of Arden. Wow.

Think of the greenest grass you can think of. Think of the perfect, pillowy shape of an oak tree in spring and multiply it by a thousand, by a hundred thousand oaks, ash, beech and elm, and every tree of an Old English forest, spreading away across the gentle hills. I let out a sigh.

'What's up, Vic?'

'I never thought it could be so … perfect. Thanks for this, Conrad.'

He gave me that What have you been taking? look.

'The forest,' I said. 'It's beautiful.'

He turned and looked away from the forest and pointed at a scrappy piece of woodland on our side of the field. 'That?' he said. 'That's the Forest of Arden?'

I had a horrible feeling. I knew exactly what was coming next. I made a mighty effort to work it out: the sun was behind us, so that's east. The forest must be…

'Can you not see it?' I asked. 'Over there, to the north, running for miles.'

He sucked air through his teeth. 'Nope. All I'm getting is a variety of arable fields and pastures, with some horticulture thrown in. Mostly arable, though. I take it there's magick involved.'

Damn. This was going to be very complicated.

I lifted my arms in a gesture of defeat, just as a wisp of mist blew away and a group of Mages came into view. They were all clustered around something and arguing. The Forest of Arden could wait.

'Come on,' I said. 'They've seen us.'

The Arden Foresters had set up base at a big black quad bike. There was even a camping stove on the go. The body was further along. I tried not to look. Yet.

There were six of them, and it didn't take long to work out who was in charge, and not just because she was obviously Chris Kelly's mam, based on her height.

She was wearing ceremonial robes of undyed wool, hitched away from the wet grass by a leather belt. The front of the topcoat was beautifully embroidered with an oak tree, acorns picked out in gold and surmounted by a small gold crown. Slightly more worrying were the small creatures flying around the tree. They were little sprites, not something you find in mundane nature. Another thing to worry about later.

Underneath the robes she wore leggings and walking shoes with thick socks. Sensible woman. Her hair, as you'd expect, was plaited into a Goddess Braid. So was mine, but there the similarity ends. The Priestess had obviously been out all night, yet looked fresh as the morning dew. Then again, she'd got dressed up first and not been dragged out of bed at half past five like I had. She looked a healthy, glowing sixty and her face was pointed, almost triangular. Handsome, you'd say. Scary is what I'd call her.

Standing behind the Priestess was a young woman, even younger than me, and also in robes. Her oak tree didn't have the acorns or the crown. Or the sprites. She looked scared half to death, poor bairn. On either side of the Priestess were two couples, and I started to guess what this might be all about. The men were in camouflage hunting gear, all browns and greens and even camo paint on their faces. Two bows were propped against the bike.

The couple on the Priestess's left were very much an item. She had her arm through his, both clutching him for support and acting as a shield; their faces were closed, defensive and aggressive at the same time.

The other couple were standing apart and showing very different emotions. The man was staring at the ground, slump-shouldered and in despair; the woman was bottling up a murderous amount of anger. Her arms were folded, and only just kept her from exploding. I could see her jaw quivering with rage well before we got close enough to speak. Even when everyone else turned to look at us, she never took her eyes off the lovers.

The Priestess lifted her chin and stepped forward to meet us. Conrad took the opportunity to put his foot straight in it. He's good at that.

'Ms Kelly,' he said with a bow (he got that bit right). 'I'm...'

'I know who you are,' said the Priestess with an air of disappointment. 'I am not anything *Kelly*, let alone *Ms*. You may address me as *Oma*.'

His mouth twitched. Just enough for me to know that he'd come up with a joke. I held my breath.

'Yes, Oma,' he said, bowing again. I breathed out. 'This is Watch Officer Robson, and I take it that this was no hunting accident?'

The Priestess made a face and turned to her flock. 'Wait here while I talk to the Witchfinder ... I mean, while I talk to the Dragonslayer.'

It's great to feel wanted, isn't it? I joined the King's Watch especially for these moments of abuse, hostility and alienation.

She strode towards the body, robes swirling in a breeze she'd created for herself. When we'd crossed the thirty metres distance, she stopped and raised her arms. With a flick of her wrist, she wove a Work of magick and the dawn chorus died. Funny that, I hadn't even noticed what a racket the birds were making until they stopped. Oma had put a Silence around us, and from the colour of the weave it looked like a ring – it blocked sound in and out, but we could still talk to each other. That's hard. No way could I do a Work like that, and she barely broke sweat to do it.

I touched Conrad's arm, and whispered, 'Did you feel it?' He shook his head. 'We're under a Silence.' He nodded a quick nod, and we couldn't put it off any longer. It was time to look at him. The dead guy.

'This is Ioan, my sister's daughter's child,' said Oma.

'We're sorry for your loss,' said Conrad. We all looked down. I'm glad she'd said his name. Much better than *dead guy*.

Ioan was dressed in camouflage gear, too, and there was another of those hunting bows tangled up with his arms in a heap. It was hard to tell under the black paste on his face, but he looked younger than the two men over by the quad bike. I'm telling you that because I'm trying to avoid talking about the bloody great arrow sticking out of his chest. I forced myself to look at it. Yes, it was an arrow. I looked away.

'Tell us what happened,' said Conrad. 'Your presence suggests that this was more than just a bit of sport. Assume we know nothing about your Circle.'

'Which you clearly don't,' said the Priestess. She looked at the Mages. 'We need a new ... King. Chief. Male leader. Call him what you will, but we haven't had one for a few years now. We choose our King in the Royal Hunt. It was nearly over when this happened.' She paused, and Conrad let her pause.

She pointed to the man on his own, the one who looked to be in shock. 'That is Colwyn. The other Hunter is Aaron. Colwyn took up a waiting position, down there by the bushes. Three quarters of an hour before dawn, he saw a doe and the Royal Stag coming out of the forest, or he thought he did. When the shot hit, a huge Charm burst. I was on the hill, way over there, and I could see the flare of Lux clearly, so there's no question about that.

'We drove over as fast as we could, and when we got here we found Colwyn standing over Ioan. Someone had made a complex Charm and put it on Ioan, and did it so well that Colwyn really believed he was aiming at the Stag. The question is *who*.'

It was obvious that Ioan was lying where he'd fallen. I think someone had closed his eyes, but that's it. Conrad turned round slowly, then said, 'And where was Colwyn's position?'

Oma pointed to a large bush, just behind the quad bike. 'There.'

Conrad stared at the bush, and pointed to the scrappy woodland. 'But the forest would have been behind him? That doesn't stack up.'

He might have been talking RAF for all the Priestess understood him. I sighed both, inwardly and out loud.

'I think there might be a problem, Oma,' I said. 'Watch Captain Clarke has a bit of a blind spot. He can't see the forest.'

She looked at me as if I were insane. 'Are you mad?' she asked.

See? I told you she thought I was insane. Conrad was looking very confused. It was going to get worse.

'I'm afraid not, ma'am. His strengths are more towards Geomancy than Sorcery.'

He grinned at the Priestess. 'Yes, I'm no great Mage. Can we skip the abuse and move on? What's this forest you're both on about, assuming it's not the nice little coppice over there?'

She wasn't going to skip anything. 'You can't see the Forest of Arden when you're standing next to it? How did you manage to slay a Dragon? That's if it really was you.' She turned to me. 'Did you kill it and let the man take the credit?'

'Oh no, ma'am. I was in an ambulance. He did that all on his own.'

'With a lot of help in advance,' said Conrad, smiling. 'From your son. I couldn't have done it without him.'

Damn. I'd hoped he'd forgotten about that.

The Priestess grunted, to show she'd heard him and wasn't going to rise to the bait.

Conrad's eyes flicked up the hill. There's nothing wrong with his mundane vision. 'We've got more company.'

He was right. Half a dozen more cars had arrived, and the occupants were getting out and doing a lot of pointing. At the quad bike, yes, but mostly at us.

'The forest can wait,' said the Priestess. 'We must return Ioan to his family, so do what you have to quickly.'

'Vic?' said Conrad.

'Aye?'

He frowned. 'Do your thing. With the sPad.'

Oh dear. He was going to be in for more disappointment very soon. To keep him happy, I bent down, got my Focus out of my bag and turned it on.

He calls it my sPad – Sorcerer's iPad, I think he means. It's my Focus, the Artefact I use to enhance my magickal sight, and it's not much use on a dead body. Conrad thinks it's some sort of Dr Who sonic screwdriver. I glanced at my sPad. Ooh. There was an email from my flatmate in Camden. She had forwarded the electric bill and wanted to know if I was OK, and was I ever coming back? I think that was her way of saying that she missed me. And my financial input.

I did look at the body, quickly, then I put out my hand for Conrad to help me up. 'Cause of death was penetration by a sharp object,' I said. 'Probably the arrow sticking out his chest.'

'Have a little respect!' said the Priestess.

Conrad ignored her. I blushed. It was a bit tactless, I suppose, but I get like that near violent death. 'Sorry,' I muttered.

'Nothing else?' he said.

'The Work on him disintegrated when it was struck by the enchanted arrow,' I explained. 'I can't even see any residue of his Imprint. There's not a trace of Lux anywhere.'

We really did have company now. More than two dozen Mages had formed a circle around us, and they'd been joined by the young Witch in robes and the angry woman. That left Colwyn, Aaron and his partner over by the bike.

How do Mages know that we're the King's Watch? We carry an enchanted Badge of Office that's impossible to forge. Unfortunately, Conrad's is stamped into the stock of a handgun. Drawing a gun on a crowd of Mages is not a good idea, even if it's just to prove your identity, something Conrad didn't need me to tell him.

'I think you'd better vouch for us,' he said to the Priestess. 'But first, who were the women with you when we arrived?'

Oma pointed to the young Witch. 'That's Tanya, my handmaiden. She was with me all night. Over there, holding on to Aaron is his fiancée, Judith. The other one is Erin. She's a friend and ally of Ioan. Was a friend. Erin and Judith were the boys' sponsors. They saw them off into the forest at different locations and waited. They came here when they felt Ioan's passing.'

'Didn't Colwyn have a sponsor?' we asked.

'Karina. No sign of her. She's not answering her phone, either.'

The crowd was waiting. They had formed a loose circle, at a respectful distance. The circle was made of groups – friendship groups and family groups of two, three or four. Two women had already begun to comfort Erin. The Priestess checked her Braid and lowered her skirts to the ground, re-fastening the belt and adjusting her robes. She had an athletic top on underneath, and pushed up its sleeves out of sight. Finally, she raised her arms and cancelled the Silence.

We all took a couple of steps away from Ioan, and Oma spoke.

'My children,' she said, arms still raised. Her voice, freed from the damping effects of the Silence, boomed round the field.

There was a pause. A few of the Mages dropped to their knees. Tanya was the first. One by one the others followed. Oma didn't repeat herself; she just waited. In the end, only Erin was left standing. That she was itching to speak was obvious.

The pause stretched out. How the Priestess kept her arms up like that, I don't know.

Erin let out a low moan and dropped her head. Without looking up, she wheeled round and started running up the hill towards the gate and the parked cars.

I had to fight to stay standing myself. In situations like this, the Goddess Braid weighs heavily. I was wearing it as a mark of respect. Every other woman in the field was wearing it as a mark of dedication and worship.

Conrad didn't kneel. He once told me that the King's Watch only kneels for the King – or one of his family.

When Erin was away up the hill, Oma spoke again. 'Blessings of the Goddess upon us. As she wills it, so mote it be.'

'So mote it be,' echoed the Circle.

'This is a tragedy,' she continued. 'I did not see who did this, nor has the Goddess vouchsafed an answer to me. I will not have us torn apart. I will not settle this in blood. Here is the Dragonslayer. He has been touched by Odin and the Goddess both, and you can see that his partner wears the Braid. Let them pass in peace and be vessels of the Goddess, to take this burden from us as she wills it.'

No one spoke. No one got up either. Oma took that as a good sign and turned to us, lowering her voice to a whisper. 'Go about your business. If you can.' She raised her voice. 'Tanya will be my voice and ears.'

The young Witch flinched, bringing her hand up to her mouth and staring at a woman behind us, on the other side of the circle. I turned to look and saw that not everyone had knelt. A heavily pregnant black woman was resting her hand on a man's shoulder. Her bump was so huge that if she'd knelt down, it would have needed a team to get her up again.

'Go, child,' said the mother-to-be. She smiled. 'There may be running involved, and I'm not doing that right now.'

Tanya got up and backed away from the circle, leaving a gap. That was our cue. Conrad turned and bowed to Oma.

'Send someone you trust to search for Karina,' he whispered. 'She may be in danger.'

Oma nodded, and we followed Tanya out of the circle.

2

Conrad's long legs quickly caught up with Tanya. I still can't get used to how quickly he can move when he wants to, because most of the time he half limps. Today must be a good day for his bad leg, and I had to jog to catch up, and when I did, I unzipped my fleece. The sun was over the trees and Conrad was right. It would be a hot day.

'How did they get here so quickly, and all together?' he said to Tanya.

We were well away from the circle now. Tanya had led us in an arc, so we were out of earshot of the group by the quad bike, too. I glanced behind and saw that the circle had contracted until they were shoulder to shoulder around Oma and Ioan.

Tanya stopped and pushed some loose strands of hair away from her face. On closer inspection, she didn't just seem younger than me (I'm twenty-three, in case you'd forgotten), she seemed barely out of adolescence. About nineteen. I was still an Aspirant to magick at her age.

'Everyone was waiting at the Grove,' she said. 'It's just west of Henley in Arden. They were waiting to acclaim the new King. Erin sent a message to say what had happened. Oma tried to stop her, but …'

'Mmm,' said Conrad, pulling his lip. He was getting nicotine withdrawal. I could guess what was coming next. 'Any chance of a cuppa? I think Colwyn could definitely do with one. And food if you've got it.'

Tanya smiled nervously and looked over at the Circle. 'Do you mind if I take these off, sir?' she said, pointing to her robes. She looked scared of him. I don't blame her.

I moved over and felt the fabric. Thick wool, soft and heavy. 'You must be boiling in there, pet,' I said. 'Sort yourself out and we'll take a minute.' I leaned in. 'And don't call him *sir* unless you're in the Army. You're not in the Army are you?'

She snorted with laughter. That's better.

We left her to sort herself out and get the stove going, and we drew back a bit. Conrad checked the breeze and stood downwind to light a cigarette. Colwyn, the one who'd shot Ioan, had slumped to the ground and was sitting hunched up, head in his hands. It was only then I realised that Judith had disappeared. I looked around frantically.

'She's coming back,' said Conrad. 'She's been up to her car for something.'

He was right. Judith was up at the vehicles, talking to a man who was sitting astride a big motorbike and fastening a crash helmet. He'd be the search party for Karina. Judith touched him on the shoulder and he started the engine.

She jogged down the slope and handed a package to Aaron. He opened it and started to wipe the camouflage paint off his face. She had another packet of wipes with her, and she moved slowly over to Colwyn.

'Do we think she's going to get her story straight?' said Conrad.

'Why no, man. You've got such a suspicious mind. She's just trying to be nice.'

'Hmph. We'll see.'

Judith tapped Colwyn on the shoulder and said something. He looked up and shook his head. She pointed at us and opened the packet of wipes. When Colwyn didn't move, she steadied his head and started cleaning his face for him. They'd been an item once, I reckoned, and Aaron didn't look too happy about it.

When she'd finished, she went back to Aaron, and he put his arm round her and kissed the top of her head. Men. Always trying to mark out their territory.

Tanya held up two plastic mugs and said, 'Sugar?'

'Not for us. Put two in Colwyn's. He needs it.'

She spooned the sugar and added, 'This is all I've got. Two giant Mars Bars.'

'We'll share one,' said Conrad. 'Give the other one to Colwyn with his tea.'

We blew the steam off the top of our mugs and took a sip. Boy, that was good. Conrad doesn't have much of a sweet tooth and handed me the Mars Bar. 'Enjoy.'

'Cheers,' I said and ripped the top off with my teeth. I was starving.

Conrad looked at Aaron and pointed to the hunting bows. 'Which one's yours?' he asked.

'The black one,' said Aaron.

'Thanks. You can sit over there, on that hillock. It looks dry and warm.'

Aaron and Judith moved away, and Conrad said, 'Check the other bow, Vic, and tell me if there's any magick in it. When you've finished chewing.'

Aaron's bow – the black one – was all carbon fibre and flame detailing. It looked very similar to the one lying under Ioan. Probably top of the range in hunting circles. Colwyn's looked a lot older and had more natural wood in it. I touched the string and ran my fingers down the curve of … 'What's this bit called?' I asked.

'The stave,' said Conrad.

'Right. Nothing on the string, and I'm not going to get much out of the stave. This has been sealed with a blessing. To get at the Works underneath, I'd have to unpick it.'

'Fair enough. Right, let's do it.'

He took the map out of his pocket and added his Barbour to the growing pile of clothes over the bike seat. I did the same with my fleece, and we crossed to Colwyn.

Judith had left him the packet of wipes and he'd finished the job himself before eating his Mars Bar. He looked up at us, and Conrad extended a hand. 'Up you get, Colwyn.'

The Warlock accepted the hand and Conrad hauled him to his feet. Colwyn was definitely the oldest of the three Hunters, and looked the same age as Conrad (who's thirty-seven). Conrad bent down and picked up the mug of tea. He handed it to Colwyn and said, 'Watch Captain Clarke and Watch Officer Robson, here on the King's Business and with the support of your Circle leader.'

Colwyn nodded and drank some tea.

Conrad continued. 'Tell us everything that happened from the time you left the Grove last night until we got here. Take your time.'

Colwyn looked around, and quickly turned his eyes from the Circle of Mages. They were now holding hands, and the sound of prayers drifted over the grass. He turned to face the gate and said, 'Is Karina here?'

'Not yet. The guy on the bike's gone to look for her.'

Colwyn nodded again. His voice had squeaked a bit when he spoke, and he cleared his throat. 'The Hunters – Ioan, Aaron and me – we'd been on vigil in the Grove from dawn yesterday. We'd placed our bows on the altar at sunrise and waited all day. Long day it was. The Three and our sponsors came just before sunset.'

'Three what?' said Conrad. Oh no. Not again.

Colwyn gave him the look; I've seen it twice already today. It's the look where the Mage is saying: *how can you be a Watch Captain and not know that?*

'Oma, Eliza and Tanya,' said Colwyn. 'Who else would they be?'

I leaned up to whisper in Conrad's ear. 'It's traditional. Oma is the old woman and Tanya's the maiden. Eliza must be the pregnant lass who spoke up before.'

'Right! Mother, maiden and crone,' he said. 'The Three. Got you.'

He scratched his nose and turned round. 'Tanya!'

She jumped up from where she'd been leaning on the bike. 'Yes, sir? I mean, yes, Dragonslayer?'

'Nip over there and pull Eliza out, if you can. Ask her if any members of the Circle were missing when the news came through this morning.'

She looked nervously at the circle and set off slowly. Eliza looked like a nice woman. I'm sure she wouldn't mind being interrupted. I couldn't swear for the others, though. Tanya could look on it as a learning experience.

Colwyn pressed on with his story. 'Our sponsors vouched for us before the Goddess and the Three blessed our bows as the sun went down. We split up then, and I got changed in the car. As soon as we could, Karina dropped me off, and I crossed into the forest.'

'But not near here,' said Conrad, avoiding the issue of the forest being invisible to him.

'No. The last thing we did in the Grove was draw lots. The Goddess sent me to the Spernall station and way-marker.'

Conrad took out the map and unfolded it. 'Show me where you were, and the others, if you don't mind.'

Colwyn stared at the map as if it were in hieroglyphics. 'Where are we now?'

'Here. Just off the Wootton to Morton Bagot road.'

'Haven't you got a map of the forest? It's easier to work out.'

'Do your best.'

With Conrad's help, Colwyn worked out four places on the map: the three stations for the Hunters and the viewing point where Tanya and Oma had waited. I didn't pay much attention. Maps are Conrad's department; I focused on the interaction between Tanya and Eliza.

I couldn't hear, of course, but I could see Eliza put her arm round Tanya's shoulder and whisper in her ear. Tanya said something back, and Eliza looked round the Circle. She thought for a moment, then said something that Tanya didn't believe. I know that because she shook her head. Eliza said it again and shooed Tanya back in our direction. Tanya gave us a wide berth for now and started making tea for Aaron and Judith.

'Good,' said Conrad when they'd finished with the map. 'This is Home Wood behind us, isn't it?' Colwyn nodded. 'You were actually the furthest from Home Wood at the start. Why did you come here?'

'I'd always planned to. It's called Home Wood for a reason. If the Stag crosses that stream, they're home free.' He gave that rueful smile that blokes give when they've started to realise they're not as young as they used to be. 'I'm not the greatest Hunter, nor the fastest, and I haven't got the stamina of the other two. But I am the best shot and I am the most patient. I reckoned that if I waited here, there was a good chance one of the others would flush him out.'

'Him?'

'The Stag. And it worked. Or so I thought.' He sighed. I wondered for a second if he had the strength to go on. The poor bloke was starting to sway. I'd have sat him down, but Conrad just waited for him to continue with the story or fall over.

Colwyn took a deep breath. 'About three quarters of an hour before dawn, I saw two lights in the forest. I waited until they broke cover and came towards me. I drew a bead on the first, then just in time I saw it was a doe. Pregnant. I nearly fired.' He shuddered. He was showing more remorse at nearly shooting the doe than for actually shooting his comrade. 'Then the Stag came out. It blazed. Magnificent. I've seen one before, you know, but even with all my Sight, I couldn't tell that it wasn't the real Stag.'

'How did you know it wasn't a big doe?'

Colwyn gave him the look again. 'The antlers. What else would it be?'

It was Conrad's turn to give Colwyn the look. 'It's May. Stags don't have antlers in May.'

'No, of course not, but we were hunting the Phantom Stag. A regular deer anointed by the Prince.'

I drew a sharp breath and interrupted. 'The Prince of Arden?'

'Yes,' said Colwyn patiently.

I grabbed Conrad's arm, something I rarely do. Usually I kick him to get his attention. 'I think we should let Colwyn rest,' I said. 'Perhaps we can talk to Tanya next.'

'Just one more question,' said Conrad. 'Has any Hunter ever died in the Royal Hunt before today?'

Colwyn shook his head. The weight of his answer overbalanced him, and I let go of Conrad to catch Colwyn as he fell.

We put Colwyn in the recovery position and left him. 'We need to talk to Tanya before we talk to Aaron,' I said, 'and I don't think you're gonna like what we hear.'

'I haven't liked very much at all so far. I'm not sure it can get much worse.'

'Believe me, it can.'

We glanced at the Circle. They were kneeling now, except for Oma and Eliza, who stood together in the centre. Right where Ioan was lying.

'Do you want another cuppa?' said Tanya.

I shook my head. 'Maybe in a bit. Could you help us out, pet? We're struggling here. We had no notice of this, obviously, otherwise we'd have done our ... what did you call it, Conrad?'

'Due diligence.'

'Aye. Due diligence.'

Tanya looked impressed. She looked more impressed by Conrad than she did by me. She's not the first.

'How can I help?' she said, nodding enthusiastically.

'Tell us about the relationship between the Foresters and the Fae.'

Conrad has a good poker face. Mostly. I've known him long enough to work out his tells: when he needs a fag and he's stressed, he pulls his lip; when he's gobsmacked, he scratches his left ear. When I said the word *Fae*, he started going at his ear like he had fleas.

The Fae look human, sometimes act human, and most of the time pretend to be human, but they're not human. Not at all. They lay eggs, for one thing. For another, they have wings when they hatch. They are also very powerful, and one of them was involved in a plot to blow us up not long ago. We've no idea who.

'It's mutually beneficial,' said Tanya. What's the betting she didn't come up with that line on her own. 'There's been a coven of Witches here since forever.' That sounded more like Tanya. 'Until the business with Shakespeare and the Witchfinders.'

'Shakespeare?' said Conrad.

Tanya blushed. 'It's a long story.' She looked at me. 'I bet you were told differently in Solomon's House.'

'Aye, we were. Shall we stick to when the Foresters came on the scene?'

'Yes. Of course. When the railways came, the forest was really under threat. The founding Foresters came down from Oxford and Glastonbury and made a treaty with the Prince of Arden. We act as conservators of the forest; in return, the Prince supports our Grove and blesses us with stuff. I mean, he anoints the Stags, for one thing. And during the Hunt, they keep the other animals out of the way.'

'Other animals?'

'Wild boar. The Fae love to hunt them. They also have a few Particulars. A talking lion. That sort of thing.'

Conrad was looking worried. I was probably looking worried, too. The Prince of Arden's sídhe (his nest/mansion) was far too close to Conrad's house for comfort. Then again, we had absolutely no evidence that this Fae was the one who'd tried to blow us up. Conrad was leaving this to me, and my gut said that what had happened last night in the forest was more human than Fae. Still, best to be sure.

'Was the Prince or one of his nobles active in the Royal Hunt?' I asked.

Tanya shook her head. 'Only in anointing the Phantom Stag. After that, he retires underground and leaves the Hunters to it.'

I could hear Conrad breathe a sigh of relief, and he half turned to go and speak to Aaron. I wasn't so sure we were ready. 'Let's get this straight, Tanya,' I said. Conrad turned back. 'Tell us why you have the Royal Hunt and what it means.'

'Oh. Right. You don't know?'

Conrad gave one of his smiles. 'I'm more at home with Gnomes, Dwarves and Dragons. Underground stuff.'

'I've never met one of the underground races,' said Tanya. 'Not sure I'd want to meet a Dragon, though.'

'You wouldn't.'

She made a vague gesture at the Circle. 'Oma and Eliza are in charge of the group.'

'And you, surely,' said Conrad. 'You're one of the Three, aren't you?'

She blushed again. 'In theory. The handmaiden doesn't always get listened to, especially in her first year, and I've only been doing it since the Equinox.

Less than two months.' She smiled quickly. 'Handmaidens serve for three years, and you have to have been one to sponsor a Hunter.'

'So Judith, Erin and Karina have all done it?'

'That's right.'

Conrad rubbed his jaw. He'd somehow managed to shave before we left. Blokes really do have it easy in an emergency. 'So where does the King fit into the Circle, and why has there been a vacancy? How long?'

Tanya started to look uncomfortable. Our antennae started to twitch.

'The last King died ages ago, before I was admitted to the Circle. When there's no King, Oma appoints a Champion, but there can only be a change to our charter if there's a King and he agrees to it. Oma said it was checks and ladders.'

'Balances,' I said. 'Checks and balances.'

'Oh, yeah. Sorry.'

'So why is there a Hunt now, and who wants to change the rules?' I said. Conrad nodded.

Tanya looked down. 'I can't say. Oma and Eliza wouldn't talk to me about it. I do know that we had the Hunt now because Colwyn petitioned for it and two thirds of the Circle voted in favour.'

We looked down at Colwyn. The poor bloke had gone to sleep. We wouldn't get owt from him for a while.

'Thank you, Tanya,' said Conrad. 'You've been most helpful.' He looked at his watch. I checked my phone. It was a quarter past seven in the morning and it felt like mid-afternoon. My stomach made a huge rumble.

'They're moving,' said Tanya.

The circle had broken up. Three men and a woman had picked up Ioan's body and were carrying it up the slope towards the cars.

'What now?' I asked.

'They'll take him to the Grove and lay him out for the funeral. The actual cremation won't be for a couple of days. We have to choose a tree and chop it down first. Oh, I forgot. You asked me to find out who was missing at the Grove. Eliza said that the only one missing was my mum, only she's not here either, so it can't be her.'

Conrad and I looked at each other. 'What's her name?' he asked gently.

'Alexandra. Everyone calls her Alex except me. She was Mother to the Circle before Eliza.'

She looked down when she said her mother's name. 'Have you been in touch?' I asked.

'Yeah. I tried texting her, but she hasn't answered. Should I stay here or go with the Circle?'

Conrad took out a business card. 'Text me Alexandra's contact details. I think we should all go to the Grove. Can you bring sleeping beauty with you?'

'Who?'

'Colwyn.'

She looked at the Warlock and her hand went up to her mouth. 'How can he sleep after ... after what happened?'

'Shock. Comes out in funny ways. We'll follow behind Judith.'

Judith and Aaron were already on their feet and coming towards us. They were about to kick up a stink until Conrad said we were all going to Henley. Judith said she'd wait until all the other cars were gone, then lead the way. Aaron said something to her, and she unhooked a small Artefact from the chain round her neck.

'You'll need this,' she said. 'You won't get through the Wards otherwise.'

I was expecting an oak tree, as worn by the Three on their robes. No. It was a little golden arrow. I couldn't work out whether that was interesting or not.

Before we left to follow the Circle, Conrad lit a cigarette and said, 'I know it's been a couple of hours, but there's one thing I need to know. Could you track the deer?'

'I don't know. Why is it important?'

'Why was Ioan chasing it? He wouldn't chase a doe, would he? I need to know if Colwyn's telling the truth. Ioan could have been chasing the real Phantom Stag, in which case Colwyn is our killer. If Ioan wasn't chasing the real Stag, then we're looking at two substantial illusions: one on Ioan and one on the doe. Even then, it could still be Colwyn.'

I hadn't thought of that. That's why we're a good team. Conrad is basically a sneaky sod; that's the sort of thing he'd think of.

I looked at the sun and I looked at Home Wood. 'Sorry, Conrad. Too late.'

He carefully put out his cigarette and went to pick up our coats. 'You know the real reason I want to get to their Grove?'

He was smiling when he said it. That was a big clue. 'You reckon they've got a feast there, don't you?'

'If I was going to be acclaimed King of the Arden Foresters, I'd expect a decent breakfast, wouldn't you?'

3

We spent most of the journey updating the Boss on what had happened. Well, I did. Conrad focused on following Judith. Hannah's advice was that we should be careful. I'll give her this: she doesn't interfere. Before I knew it, we were following Judith's Land Rover down a farm track.

'Watch out for Wards,' I said. 'I can feel the magick building.'

Conrad slowed the car, and the little Artefact started to pulse as we approached a pair of trees.

On the way down the lane, I'd seen a farmhouse and barn ahead of us. When we passed the trees, everything went dark for a second, then lit up again, and the farmhouse was replaced by a beautiful old manor house with a wood behind it. A large area in front of the house was already filled with vehicles.

'Remind you of anything?' said Conrad.

'Miss Marple? Midsomer Murders?'

'Have you never been to Stratford on Avon, Mary Arden's House in particular?'

'I'm guessing this has to do with Shakespeare, but no, never been to Stratford. Who's Mary Arden when she's at home?'

'She was Shakespeare's mother. We used to go every year from school. The half-timbering looks authentic enough to be from the period.'

'Half-whatty?'

'Half-timbering. All those bits of wood in the walls, see? That's one way to build a house when you can't afford bricks – put a wooden frame up and fill it with something cheaper. You'll find them all over Germany.'

'Wouldn't know. Never been.'

Aaron was waiting, on his own in front of an open gate, and walked towards us when we'd parked up. I lowered the window. He looked the middle in age of the three Hunters (with Ioan being dead, it was hard to tell). He was wiry and built for speed rather than strength. Not my type, usually. Colwyn would have been worth a second look when he was younger, though.

Aaron looked shattered. 'I'm denied the Grove, for some reason,' he said. 'Eliza told me it was a technicality. She asked me to take you into the hall and wait for them to finish the laying out. Same for Tanya and Colwyn.'

We followed him through the nail-studded front doors and straight into a big open space that went all the way to the roof. Very impressive. The same timbers that Conrad had been obsessed about featured on the upper walls inside (and were holding up the roof), but the bottom two metres of the inside was covered in dark panelling, just like great chunks of the Invisible College. Unlike the Receiving Room at Salomon's House, this wasn't enchanted, so you didn't have the sense of carved animals watching you all the time.

What their great hall lacked in creepy enchanted carvings, it made up for with heraldry. All round the wall hung coats of arms. Some were on shields, and mostly included stags, sometimes with lions, roses and other devices. They would be the Kings. The rest of the heraldry was on upright diamond shapes. If I remembered right, they would be the women's arms, a line of Omas going back to Queen Victoria's time. The building might be older than Shakespeare, but the Foresters were less than two hundred years old. Even the King's Watch is older than that. A lot older.

One end wall had a gallery with a staircase up and doors underneath. The opposite end had an elaborate tapestry. I was going to study it further until my eyes were dragged away by my nose. A big, rough table filled the middle of the room and, aye, there was food. All three of us swallowed heavily as we salivated like a pack of Pavlov's dogs. 'I am so sorry,' said Aaron. 'I can't offer you hospitality yet. Come through to the solar.'

'Solar?'

'Early modern conservatory,' said Conrad, 'but without the chintz furniture.'

Aaron managed a smile. 'Sorry to disappoint. Up here.'

He led us up the staircase and through the minstrels' gallery. Stools and instruments for proper minstrels were lying ready for music-making. Witches do like to party. The staircase carried up a bit further, into the top of the building and an open space with very non-Shakespearean Velux windows. And chintz. Lots of chintz. There wasn't any heraldry up here, but there was a collection of quilts pinned up on the blank spaces. The lights weren't on, so that put them in shadow, and I didn't get to look at them properly. You can tell a lot about a group by its quilts, or that's what me Granny says. Aaron collapsed on to a sofa and closed his eyes.

'It's a good job this isn't a listed building,' said Conrad. 'You'd have to take those windows out for starters.' Typical home-owner. More worried about the building than the view. Me? I was already looking out at the wood.

The sacred Grove of the Arden Foresters was formed out of the very top end of the forest itself. I felt the window frames – magick. There was something in the timbers that enhanced the view of the Forest of Arden. Conrad had joined me. 'Is that south?' I asked.

'Yes. In Odin's name, how is that possible?'

'You can see it?'

'I can. Just. It comes and goes.'

The Hall was at the top of a slope. As far as the eye could see, trees flowed away across the landscape we'd crossed on the way here – a landscape covered with fields, not a bloody great forest.

'Do you remember me telling you that there is only one universe?' I said, not taking my eyes off the sight in front of us.

'Yes.'

'You need to speak to your pal Chris about this. It's one of the many strings to his bow.'

'Vic! Poor choice of metaphor in the circumstances.'

'Sorry.' I waved my arm. 'All these trees, they exist in the same physical space as the farmland, but they have a different energy level. Like ultra-violet light. They're both real and not real at the same time.'

Conrad gave me a raised eyebrow. 'Very helpful.'

'I don't really understand the theory.'

'Do they have any physical reality? Do they soak up water, for example?'

'A bit. A tiny bit. They definitely need sunshine. A Fae forest is a huge Collector. It filters Lux out of sunlight. This is the biggest in England. No human could create anything like this.'

Conrad glanced over his shoulder. 'This is fascinating, but we'd better take Aaron's statement before he falls asleep.'

We sat down opposite the Hunter, and he reluctantly opened his eyes. 'You do realise I haven't slept for twenty-four hours?' he said.

'We do,' said Conrad. 'We'll be brief. Did you see any other Hunter, any other human, any Fae or any enchanted deer last night?'

He shook his head. 'No. Or not that I know of. I did see a few does, but now I've heard Colwyn's story, I can't be sure I didn't see the Stag in disguise, can I?'

Aaron had a pronounced Birmingham accent, more than any of the others we'd spoken to. Tanya had one, but much milder.

'I was on the trail, though,' he added. 'Towards the end, I finally picked up the trail. The Phantom stag leaves a trail of Fae dust behind it, and I was on the trail when I heard the distress horn. I ran straight towards it, and when I got there, Oma and Tanya had already arrived. That's it.'

'Thank you,' said Conrad. 'Just for my notes, if you'd become King, would you have vetoed the changes?'

Aaron struggled upright. 'You what? It's me and Judith who want it changed. Who told you that?'

Interesting. Very interesting. Before Conrad could ask what the changes were, Tanya's voice came up the stairs.

'Dragonslayer? Aaron? Are you up there?'

'We are.'

There was a stumbling and staggering on the staircase, and Colwyn weaved unsteadily into the room. He'd already taken his boots off and made a beeline for a dark corner where he collapsed onto a day bed. He was asleep before Tanya could get up the stairs. She was carrying two pillows, and put one carefully under Colwyn's head. She offered the other one to Aaron, who took it gratefully and started unlacing his boots.

'Any sign of Erin or Karina?' he asked.

Tanya shook her head. Aaron grunted and lay down. I pity Judith: by the time we'd got back to the great hall, both Colwyn *and* Aaron were snoring. Poor bairn must be forced to sleep under a Silence. I've done it meself once or twice. I didn't say that out loud, or Conrad would have started on about my love life again.

Tanya stood in front of the big table. Conrad, for some weird reason, looked underneath. 'This is the original board,' he said.

'You sound like your dad,' I replied. Alfred Clarke used to be an antiques dealer. Likes to pretend he still is when Mary isn't around. Tanya just looked mystified.

'Look, Vicky, trestles. When you're not entertaining, you can collapse the table and put the board to one side.'

'Looks like a load of planks to me.'

'We get so many expressions from this set up,' he continued. 'Bed and board, chairman of the board, board and...' I kicked him then. On his good leg.

See? I can be merciful.

'Ow! What?'

'I think Tanya has something to say.'

'Erm, are you hungry?' said the young Witch, not taking her eyes off Conrad.

'You have no idea,' I said.

'Then eat and be welcome in our hall, as the Goddess wishes. I'd take your food through to Oma's sitting room, if I were you, before the rest of the Circle come back.'

I left Conrad to issue the formal thanks and do the bowing thing. I already had the covers off half the plates before he'd finished. There was no hot food, but it all looked delicious: home cured ham, game pie, curried boiled eggs, potato salad, chunks of fresh bread. Lots of protein and carbs. Even thinking about it now makes me mouth water. I was on me second sausage roll before we got to the sitting room.

Conrad was much happier in Oma's sitting room: no chintz. Tanya nipped out while I was still singing the praises of the game pie and feeling the depth of the cushions.

'It's a good job there's no fire in here, or I'd be joining Aaron and Colwyn in the land of Nod,' I said. 'As it is, I may have to pop the button on me trousers.'

We both jumped when Tanya opened the door to the hall. A flood of sound washed in, a flood that had been held in check by an adapted Silence on the door. Handy when you've got work to do. Or private discussions to be held. Tanya had a big pot of coffee and three cups. 'Oma will be with you shortly,' she announced.

'Time for a break,' said Conrad, pouring himself half a cup of coffee and heading outside for a smoke. For half a second, I considered joining him. It was only the thought of standing up that put me off. Tanya followed him out and closed the door behind her.

If Conrad were in here, he'd be up and mooching around the pictures, opening the cupboards and sticking his nose into the nooks and crannies. Me, not so much. I closed my eyes instead.

'Aah, the sleep of youth.'

'Mnnh?'

I blinked and saw Oma leaning against the fireplace. How did she come in without me hearing?

'Sorry, ma'am. Would you like coffee?'

Conrad and I had avoided the big armchair next to the fireplace. The embroidered cover with the Foresters' sign and the gold crown was a bit of a giveaway. Oma lowered herself into it carefully and took a moment. 'Yes please. That would be kind. It should be me offering to help, but … that was the worst thing I've had to do. Laying out one of our own when someone from the Circle has taken his life is not something that should happen.'

I poured her coffee, and one for myself. Conrad reappeared and topped up his own. When he came through the door, he'd started limping. That's the only way you know he's getting tired. He thanked Oma for the hospitality and made himself as comfy as he could, rubbing his leg and grimacing. When he does that, I try not to think of the scars.

He has a very good memory, does Conrad, so the notebook he got out was for effect. He made a couple of notes and said, 'Tanya … Eliza … and? Are you Iris or Alice?'

What's he on about now?

Oma said nothing. Conrad smiled at her. 'Vicky doesn't speak German, so she doesn't know that *Oma* means *Grandma*. My grandmothers were Iris and Alice.'

'Bridget,' said Oma. 'My given name was Bridget.' She fixed Conrad with a look. 'You're going to ask, aren't you? About my son? And about the changes to the charter.'

'Yes to the charter.'

'They're connected. My son's given name was Ruaidhrí. He should have learnt his Art here, not Salomon's House.'

We waited. Oma moved a cushion behind her back. Then she stood up and said, 'Excuse me.' With a shuffle and shake, she worked off her robes and placed them on a window seat. She was suddenly a lot thinner and had an even stronger resemblance to Chris Kelly. She sat back down and drained her coffee. 'That's better. I hear you've been to the Grove at Lunar Hall. Both of you.'

'We have.'

'Mmm. Have you heard of Arianism?'

Conrad looked at me. I shrugged.

'It was a heresy in the early Christian church. Very popular for centuries, especially in northern Europe. It left a legacy in the world of magick: Materianism. You won't win any friends by talking about it. According to Ruaidhrí ... I mean, Chris.' She rubbed her temples. 'According to *my son*, the texts on Materianism in the Esoteric Library are locked away. You need special permission to get at them.'

I shrugged again. Never heard of it.

'In the world of magick, there was a group who believed that Mary was an aspect of the Great Goddess, and that Jesus was her son. They are the Materianists.'

'Aah,' said Conrad.

Eh?

He turned to me. 'Do you remember that statue in the Grove at Lunar Hall?'

'Aye. Athene, wasn't it?'

'On the surface. In the first moments after the Battle of Lunar Hall, when you were still outside the grounds, I saw it stripped of magick. Underneath, it was a statue of the Virgin Mary.'

'And you didn't think to mention that before now?'

It was his turn to shrug. 'We weren't proper partners then, and it was their secret.'

Fair enough, I suppose.

'Quite,' said Oma. 'Materianists were doubly hounded – for being Witches and for denying the doctrines of Christianity. Very few survived. The founding Foresters included a group of Irish Materianists, from which I am descended, as is Aaron. Judith is a convert.'

'But not Chris?' said Conrad.

She shook her head. 'This is all linked. I promise you. Ruaidhrí's father was from another Circle. Ruaidhrí knew that James Kelly was his father from day one. James gave Ruaidhrí his second name – Chris. When he was a teenager, there was a big falling out. In a fit of teenage rebellion, he applied to the Invisible College and started calling himself *Chris Kelly*. He was perfectly entitled to do so, of course.'

'I'm sorry to hear that,' I said. 'It must have hurt.'

'It did. I'm glad he went through with it, though. He fits in to Salomon's House in ways he never would have here. I am very proud of my son, no matter what he calls himself. Except for one thing.'

'Your daughter in law?'

'Precisely. I'd rather not talk about her, if you don't mind.'

That was a relief.

'I stopped being a Materianist when I became Circle Mother,' said Oma. 'It's in the charter, and I was happy to let it go. That's not enough for the younger generation. That and the rule on joining out.'

This time I actually knew what she was talking about. 'I'll tell you later,' I said to Conrad. I did not want to have a discussion on the mating habits of Witches in front of Oma. He nodded.

'To cut a long story short, Judith and Aaron want to allow joining in, and for the Circle Mother to have freedom of conscience. They have support. In due course, Aaron would have become King because he's very, very good. I think that Colwyn forced the Royal Hunt before he got too old to do it.'

This time, Conrad made notes like he meant it. I leaned over to have a look, and this is what he'd written:

- Aaron – Materianist. Powerful Warlock.
- Judith – freedom of choice???
- Colwyn
- Ioan
- Erin
- Karina
- (Alex??)

Instead of asking Oma to fill in the list, he started on a tangent. 'You said that Ioan is your great nephew. Are your sister and niece here?'

'They are both Daughters, not Foresters, with a coven in Scotland. They, too, rejected Materianism, and wanted some distance.' She looked hard at Conrad. 'And yes, my sister may have wanted some distance from me.'

'I know the feeling,' he said.

'Mmm. Ioan was the first Warlock in our family for generations and couldn't stay with the Daughters once he'd reached puberty. He's been here since he was eleven years old. It was his twenty-first birthday last month. I called my sister to break the news straight after I'd spoken to my son to ask for your assistance. Shall we go outside? It should be a bit quieter out there now.'

The thought of leaving Oma's sofa was a challenge, but Conrad was on his feet and offering me a hand up before I could argue. 'Can I …?' I said.

'Through the door to the left of the staircase,' said Oma.

It *was* quiet in the hall. Eliza was sitting at the head of the table, in one of the few proper chairs. Everyone else had had to use benches. Tanya and another Witch were carrying stuff through to the kitchens, and that was it. Everyone else had gone. Eliza waited until I'd been to the Ladies before calling me over.

African hair does not go into a Goddess Braid easily. There's a whole mountain of anger in the world of magick on that very topic. Eliza's hair was defiantly, extravagantly big and bushy, but she'd pulled it back with an undyed woollen skein, and what is wool, if not sheep's hair? It was enchanted to mimic the patterns in a human Braid, and that's why I'd not noticed when the Circle first arrived at the meadow this morning. It was a way of fitting in without compromising your identity.

My BFF, Desirée Haynes, is also of Afro-Caribbean heritage and she has her hair short or in cornrows. Then again, she is a confirmed Christian, not a Goddess-worshipper.

The Foresters have a special set of robes for their Circle Mother when she's expecting. Eliza had put them on for the laying out ceremony and had taken them off after eating. They were folded neatly on the bench next to her; she looked hot enough without them, so goodness knows they must have been like a sweat box. Her dress was loose and green; at some point it had matched her eye shadow. Not so much any more.

'I love your Braid, Mother,' I said.

'Thank you, child,' she responded. 'You look as tired as I feel. Oma and the Dragonslayer have gone outside; I think she's going to have a relapse and cadge a cigarette from him, so I'd take the weight off your feet and join me until they're done.'

Her accent matched her features – part Caribbean, part Birmingham. I pulled up a bench and sat down.

She sat back in her chair and rested her hands on her bump. There wasn't really anywhere else to put them. She rested her eyes on me. I could feel her magickal Sight drifting over me, like butterfly wings.

To check me out like that would be considered beyond rude in the Invisible College and in every Circle I've visited, unless there were pressing reasons. Simple curiosity is not a pressing reason. I could have resisted, but I was intrigued.

'There's a gap,' she said. 'There's a gap in your soul where you left the world for a moment. What brought you back?'

Interesting. She could see that I'd died – that my heart had been stopped by a homicidal Druid. Instead of asking how I'd died, she wanted to know how I'd come back.

'He brought me back,' I said, pointing outside. 'With help, obviously.'

She chuckled. 'Of course. He couldn't have done it on his own, now could he?'

'He's full of surprises, is Uncle Conrad.'

Her eyes flicked outside and back again. Even more interesting. Either she hadn't scoped out Conrad or she hadn't been able to see his Imprint well enough to realise that we we're not really related.

The smile on her face died a little. 'You share a lot, don't you?' I took that as rhetorical. 'Has anyone heard from Alexandra yet?'

What an odd question. Of all the things going on in the Circle, she picks on that.

'No, Mother. Are you worried about her?'

'It's a bit more selfish than that. She's my midwife, and I'm going to need her very soon.' She patted her bump. 'This boy's already been trouble and he's not going to make life easy for me. They should be finished with their smoking.'

I haven't been dismissed like that in a long time. She didn't actually say *run along now*, but you could hear it in her voice.

What I didn't hear until I was nearly out of the door was a blessing. 'Peace of the Goddess be on you, child.'

Conrad would have given her the benefit of the doubt. I didn't. You don't bless someone's back.

The main path from the hall led straight to a wood – a real wood with real trees that was also part of the Forest of Arden. I wasn't going to attempt to explain that to Conrad; his poor little head would burst.

The Foresters' Grove would be in the middle, and in the middle of that would be Ioan. Conrad and Oma were coming out of a walled garden off to the side.

Before they got to me, they stopped and Conrad bowed to Oma. She gathered him in and kissed his cheek. He stayed put and she strode towards me. 'There's been a development,' she said, grim faced. 'Conrad will explain it all. If you decide to go ahead, you do so with my full support.'

Go ahead with what?

Before I could ask out loud, she reached forward and took my hands in hers. Her fingers were colder than I expected. Instead of a spoken blessing, calling on the Goddess, I got a quick burst of Lux and a picture in my head – a picture of two ash trees, their canopies mingling to form an arch. What's that all about?

'I'm sorry,' she said, letting go of my hands. She quick-stepped back into the hall, and Conrad limped up to me.

He pointed to the walled garden. 'Myfanwy would love to see their herbal garden. I wonder if Elvenham House will end up like that when she's finished? This way.'

Before I could ask what was going on, he was heading round the side of the building and over to the car. When we'd got in, he shoved the key in the ignition and said, 'Let's get off the premises, shall we?'

Before he felt it was safe enough to talk, we weren't just off the premises, we'd gone into Henley in Arden and parked up at the little railway station .

'We have a problem,' he said.

'Really? I'd never have guessed.'

'The Countess of Stratford called Bridget while she was showing me the gardens.'

Countess of Stratford? Where have I heard that name before? He saw the look on my face. 'Oma said that she's a Fae: the most powerful noble in the court of Arden. After the Prince, of course.'

This did not sound good. The Fae are quite happy with modern technology, when it suits them, but for a Countess to make a personal call, something must be wrong.

Conrad drummed his fingers on the wheel. 'Apparently, this has never happened before – an incomplete Hunt. Right now, there is an anointed Stag running round the forest. The Countess pointed out, politely but firmly, that the Hunters are still considered blessed, and the Prince expects them to finish the job. Tonight.'

'Bugger me.'

'Precisely. Can you help me see the forest?'

I could see where this was heading. 'Perhaps. At night. With a suitable Artefact. And some practice.'

'That would be a No, then.'

'Sorry.'

'Are you ready for this? On your own?'

'Whaaat? You want me to go in there?'

'You're not a Watch Captain. You don't have to.'

He left it there. Left it for me to come to my own decision. The Royal Hunt Part Two was tonight. We could probably get Rick James up here from Wells. He'd sort it out. If we didn't, there could be further bloodshed, and the killer might get away with it.

'Shall we call Rick?' I said.

He shook his head. 'Not an option, I'm afraid. The Circle don't trust him, for some reason.'

Oh. Come on, Victoria, I said to myself. It's not as if it's underground, is it?

Sometimes, when I can't sleep, I imagine that Conrad has gone underground. Into the Old Network, down to a Dwarven Hall, something like that. And I imagine having to go down alone to rescue him, but I can't. I literally can't imagine putting one foot in front of the other and going through the opening.

'Aye. I'll do it. On one condition.'

'You want me to cook you breakfast in the morning?'

'Hell, no. That's a given. I want you to give me your word. I want you to promise not to charge into the forest if you get worried. At night, with a Hunt on, the forest will be at its most powerful. For you, it would be like ... running out of an Antarctic research station in your budgie smugglers. You're gonna die, it's just a question of how long it takes.'

'I don't possess any budgie smugglers. Is it really that bad?'

'Worse. In Antarctica, it would be quick and fairly painless. In the forest...'

'Really?'

'Really.'

'Mmm. So, what's "joining out"?'

'You wanna know that now?'

'I want to know what's at stake. Religious differences easily lead to violence, but I want the whole picture.'

I watched a pair of pensioners walking towards the footbridge to the other platform where they could catch their train to Birmingham and go for a nice day's shopping in the Bull Ring. What a lovely thought. Wandering and mooching. I could pop the car door open and follow them...

My subconscious brain agreed, and I moved in the seat, half turning to the door. When I moved, I rustled. Too much quick-dry artificial fibre clothing and (almost) no makeup. I could not go shopping like this. When I die, tonight, in the forest, I will tell myself that it is a better fate than being caught on camera in rugged outdoor wear.

I sighed and got back on track. 'You remember that fuss about Abbi Sayer's dad?'

'Deborah conceived by anonymous sperm donor. Yes, I remember. Oh, I see: *joining* as in coupling. Mating.'

I blushed. Well? So would you. 'Aye. Witches want children, and there aren't many Warlocks to go round. It happens almost everywhere. In mixed Circles, the *joining out* rule stops the men turning the Witches into a harem.'

Conrad looked appalled. 'Is there no marriage in these places? No wonder Chris Kelly went to the Invisible College.'

'Of course there's marriage in the Circles, just not for the office holders.'

'Right.'

'So now you've got the big picture, what do you think?'

'I think I'm glad I met Mina before all this magick business came along. Fair enough, Vic. I give you my word. I won't enter the forest on my own. Now, what are our objectives, and what are the challenges?'

I hate it when he puts me on the spot like this. At least we didn't have an audience. To keep him quiet, I said, 'Stay alive is number one.'

'Good. Glad to hear it.'

He opened the window and saw the look on my face. Rather than light up in the car, he got out and stretched his back. I had a minute to think this through before he leaned through the window and asked me again.

When he did, I was ready. 'We've got a dead Mage. We have to find who put the Work of magick on those bows.'

'We do,' he replied. 'I asked Oma Bridget, and she said that none of the Circle could have done it. They simply don't have any Artificers who are that good. Someone brought those bows in, though, and used them.'

'Right. We have three Witches unaccounted for: Erin, Karina and Alexandra. I spoke to Eliza, and she said that Alex is a midwife. I can't see her being involved.'

'I can't see her as an actor, but she could be the Author.'

'Eh?'

'Someone cooked up this plan. I'm going to call them the Author. They may have used others as actors, but we have to find the Author, the one who dreamed it all up.'

'I see what you mean.' I paused to think that through. 'Are there any of them you'd rule out?'

He crushed out his cigarette. 'Erin. I think she's a loose cannon, but you can't fake that sort of rage. She defied Oma rather than shut up.'

'Aye. That means any of them could be involved. Aaron, Judith, Colwyn, Karina, Alex... Plus any or all of the Mages who weren't in the forest last night.'

He got back in the car. 'Yes. I trust Oma, though. Completely.'

'So do I.'

'And I trust her to keep everyone else out of the forest. That will leave you in pole position to sort out who's behind this.'

'Good. What's the plan?'

He started the engine. 'Back to Clerkswell for some sleep. We're both too tired to make plans.'

4

'Why am I starting here?' I asked.

The sun was kissing the tops of the trees to our right. The Hunt would begin as soon as it disappeared. Ahead of me, a small stone in the verge glowed silver. This was one of the entrances to the Forest of Arden, something that Conrad still couldn't get his head round.

'You tell me why we're standing here,' he said. 'That looks like an impenetrable hawthorn hedge to me.'

'No. Leave that to me. Why am I miles away from the action, not going in next to one of the other Hunters?'

He gave me a look. 'Because it's all downhill from here, and if you do what I said, you'll sweep the area and won't risk the action taking place behind you.'

'Any last minute advice?'

'Be very careful of men with asses' heads.'

'Howay, man. What are you on about?'

'Doesn't matter. This is your world, Vic, and you know what you're doing. Trust yourself.'

It wasn't my world at all. If anything, it was the Fae's world, but I didn't argue. The sun was behind the trees now, and I shivered. Conrad had made me bring extra layers and insisted on a rucksack. I'm glad. It was going to get very cold very quickly in there. Rather that than rain, though.

'You'd better go,' I said.

'I'll be waiting.'

Instead of a hug or a kiss, he saluted. It seemed right, somehow. I saluted back, and he turned away. When the rattle of the Volvo's engine disappeared round the bend, it went very quiet. Above the trees, Venus was winking at me. Time to begin.

So, you'll be wondering, how *do* you walk through an impenetrable hawthorn hedge? Or dry stone walls? Or cross roads with traffic without getting run over?

Simple: magick.

Less simple: Quantum Topology.

Totally not simple: solid matter is 99.9999999999996% empty space. You change the resonance of your atoms and just walk. It helps that a Fae forest has these enchanted way-markers.

I reached down and opened my magickal Sight. The glittering rock grew into a column of stone as real as the gateposts on Conrad's house, except that Uncle C's gateposts don't glow like lighthouses. Starting at the bottom, I ran my hands up the marker, feeling the magick tingle through me as the light got stronger.

If any of you have noticed a phallic element in this procedure, you'd be spot on. That's the Fae for you.

When I got to the top, the sparkling lights had spread up my arms and washed over my body. They were so bright that I couldn't see anything except the marker stone. I let go and the light subsided. Instead of an impenetrable hawthorn hedge behind the stone, there was a pathway into the trees. A pathway into the Forest of Arden.

I jumped over the small ditch that marks the boundary of the forest and took a few steps down the path. It's best not to linger too close to the edge: the Work that put me in harmony with the forest can wear off quite quickly, and it's dangerous to do it twice.

Another question Conrad asked when I was telling him about it was, 'How come you can see it from a distance but need to use these way-markers to go in?'

'No idea,' had been my answer. 'Didn't get that bit of the course, and it wasn't part of the practical test.'

There is another way to get in to the forest – through a conjoined wood, like the Foresters' sacred Grove. That wasn't an option today.

I've been in enchanted woods before. The Daughters have one as part of their complex at Glastonbury, but it's not on this scale. What does it look like? Like a mundane forest under very strong moonlight but even brighter.

We had a plan. Of sorts. This is what Conrad had written in his notebook after talking to Oma in the walled garden:

- *Aaron – Materialist. Powerful Warlock.*
- *Judith – Freedom of choice??? Average Witch.*
- *Colwyn – Ambitious. Most powerful Mage of the whole group. Not noted for politics.*
- *Ioan – Eager. The outsider. Was not expected to win the Royal Hunt. Lots of raw talent.*
- *Erin – A close friend of Ioan. Aaron's ex-girlfriend, supplanted by Judith. They broke up when Aaron became more religious. Wants to keep joining out as the policy. Explicitly blames Judith for what happened. Likely to be out for revenge. An apprentice Enscriber.*
- *Karina – Colwyn's younger sister. Very, very quiet. Took a sabbatical after being handmaiden. Has performed little magick recently.*
- *Alex??) – Oma can't believe she's involved. Healer and midwife. Much loved by the women of the Circle, even Materialists. Has suggested that Materialists should leave and form their own Circle, but only as a way to avoid conflict. Tipped to replace Bridget as Oma.*

'I think Karina's either in on it with Colwyn or she saw something and is in hiding,' I had said after studying the notes. 'My money is on Aaron, though. I think he knew perfectly well that there would be a re-run tonight. I think he got rid of Ioan to level the playing field.'

'You could be right,' said Conrad. He stared at the notebook again. 'That would explain why it feels wrong – you'd think that Colwyn or Aaron himself would be the target otherwise. You know, Vic, I can't help feeling that we're missing something.'

'We probably are. I can cheat, you know. I can find the Stag using Sorcery in ways they're not allowed to.'

He raised his eyebrows. 'How do you know that?'

'I texted Desirée before I crashed out. There's a copy of the Foresters' charter in the Esoteric Library. I got her to look it up for me.'

'Excellent. Sounds like a plan, then.'

And that was it: find the Stag and hope for the best. And try not to get killed. That's always part of the plan.

Two stations further round the perimeter, Aaron would now be on his way into the forest. Judith was being watched by the guy on the motorbike to make sure she didn't cross over. He is the former Champion of the Foresters and completely loyal to Oma.

With Judith under watch, there could be as many as five Mages in the forest with me: Aaron and Colwyn for sure, and any or all of Erin, Karina and Alex. Plus the normal forest dwellers, something I realised when I saw a gleam of golden light through the trees.

It's always risky to leave the paths in an enchanted wood, but last night's evil had been done off the path, and off the path I went. Very carefully.

Fae magick is silver, with rainbow highlights. Human magick is mostly primary colours, and Gnomes have a coppery tint. Gold means way up or way down. Dwarves give off a golden glow, but Dwarves do not hang around enchanted woods. That golden glow over there meant non-material: in other words, a Spirit.

I used the trees for cover, working slowly towards the glow; Conrad would have been proud of me, coming over all boy scout like that. I was about to peek round a huge oak when the Spirit moved, and I could see it clearly through a gap in the trees.

It looked human, or about as human as you can get when you're wearing a monk's habit with the hood up. Dæmons can look human, when they want to, but not when they think no one's looking. That narrowed it down, but not by much. I tried to get a clearer view: *monk's habit* is a bit generic. If I could see a sign or emblem, it might narrow it down further.

From somewhere out of my sight, he picked up a golden rake and started to draw it over the ground. What on earth? I couldn't see them at first, but the tines on his rake collected small leaves of Lux, mostly silver, but other colours mixed in. I stepped round the tree to extend my Sight. Naturally, he spotted me straight away.

The golden monk stopped and turned to face me. He put the rake down and lifted his hands (normal fingers) and lowered the hood. I let out a deep breath when a normal looking old man stared back at me. He smiled, and beckoned me over. For the first time tonight, I asked myself *what would Conrad do?*

I could almost hear his posh voice in me head: *I'd ask you what the Spirit was and proceed accordingly*. He was right. I should have this.

Conrad had called the person behind all this madness *The Author*. This glowing figure was not going to be the Author. It just felt wrong. Whatever had led to Ioan's death had *human* stamped all over it. This Spirit had once been human, but wasn't now.

He beckoned again, and I came out from behind the security blanket of the oak tree and went up to him. He was shorter than I'd realised, and was about my height. He didn't just look *old*: he looked like he'd had a hard life and that he wasn't having an easy afterlife, either. Closer still, and I saw a cross hanging from a rope around his neck.

'Well met, father,' I said.

The monk pulled his robe further away from his neck, and I saw a gleaming silver chain, fine and delicate round his neck. Ooh. Nasty.

Enslavement of humans by magick has been illegal since the Dark Ages. Enslavement of Spirits is not illegal, and something the Fae have a bad rep for. I'm sure they also enslave humans when they can get away with it.

The monk opened and closed his mouth in silence, then pointed to the chain again. Worse and worse – the Fae had taken away his voice as well as his freedom. Not my business, not really, but this guy could be a witness. He touched his mouth with his hand and pointed at me, then held out his hands. He wanted me to give him a voice.

I made stag's horn gestures with my fingers on my head and pointed around the forest. He nodded eagerly and smiled. No wonder he looked hard done by – the poor bloke only had half a dozen teeth.

'I may regret this,' I muttered. I closed the gap and knelt in front of him. He placed his hands on my shoulders and ...

'*Ave Maria, gratia plena,*
'*Dominus tecum.*
'*Benedicta tu in mulieribus,*
'*et benedictus fructus ventris tui...*

The words flooded out of my mouth like a torrent. I couldn't stop saying Hail Marys as fast as my lips would form them. I bucked and tried to break away, but his spectral hands pressed on the nerves in my shoulder and I couldn't move. I felt it coming: the panic that takes over me when I'm underground or locked in a room with a spider...

'*Ave Maria, gratia plena...*'

My head was bowed. I stopped trying to fight the words and let them flow for a second. There was peace in the rhythm, and the pressure on my nerves slackened enough for me to lift my head. The Spirit monk had his eyes closed, and he wasn't using his Sight, either. Around his neck, the wooden cross had gone from a generic gold to jet black. Except at the edges. The arms of the cross had a brighter etching on them, as if someone were colouring them in. Another Hail Mary finished, and one more line was etched in.

I put two and two together and came up with an even bigger slice of evil. This monk had passed out of the mortal world on a promise: the Fae had promised him something in return for his service. This wasn't slavery – it was bondage, and I bet the monk couldn't tell the difference. And his service would last until he'd said a few thousands of Hail Marys and filled in the whole of his cross with etchings.

When you're a Spirit, that's no biggie. And then the Fae took his voice away.

'*Ave Maria, gratia plena...*'

I don't know much Latin. Enough to recognise a few key words of magick. What I needed was a three syllable word, preferably a name. Of course: Diana, goddess of the hunt.

'*Ave Diana, gratia plena...*'

He didn't notice the first time round. The next time, I said *Diana* a bit more forcefully, and he staggered back, letting go of my shoulders. Pain and sorrow washed over his face.

I moved towards him and lifted my hand. He flinched and covered his face, expecting me to strike.

'Easy, father,' I said. 'I just want to bridge the collar. It won't hurt.'

He backed into a tree. When I didn't attack him, he slowly lowered his hands and gave me a pitiful look. I reached out and ran my finger over the Fae collar. There was no way I could take it off, nor would I want to (the Fae would not take kindly to that), but I could bridge it. I put my thumb below the collar and my forefinger above it, then I let the Lux flow up and down.

'Try to speak,' I said.

'*Ave Maria, gratia plena...*'

I took my hand away and shook my head firmly. The pleading look came back, and he held up five fingers. I shook my head again and held up one. We compromised on two.

When he'd said his two Hail Marys, he went quiet.

'Father?' I said. 'Have you seen the Stag? Did you see the Royal Hunt last night?'

He spoke. I'd tell you what he said, but I don't speak mediæval Gaelic at all. Great. An Irish monk. Of course, in the last six hundred years, no one's talked to him, so he hasn't had a chance to pick up modern English.

I dropped my hand and started to play charades. Five minutes later, I figured out that, yes, he'd seen the Stag, but no, he'd run away from the Hunters. Marvellous.

I was about to head off when he came forward and touched my arm. He grabbed his rake and quickly heaped up a pile of leaves of Lux. I have no idea why the Fae wanted him wandering their forest doing this. It could be a crucial part of the magickal ecosystem, or it could be a pointless joke. That's the Fae for you.

He rummaged in the pile and separated a few tiny silver acorns. He made the horns of a deer and pointed to the magickal seeds. Now that was worth knowing. He passed me the acorns and lifted his hand in blessing.

All the shenanigans with Father Patrick (which may or may not be his name) had cost me a lot of time. The Hunters would be well into the woods by now. I went back to the path and looked around. Father Patrick had mimed being frightened of the Hunters, and that gave me a clue. He wouldn't be lingering in this part of the forest if the Hunt were nearby, so I made an executive decision: I was going much further in before I started a proper search. I shoved the silver acorns in my pocket and started a gentle jog through the wood. Don't tell Conrad I was running; he might make me do it more often.

It was about this time that I realised that it was actually very quiet in here, compared to most forests (real or enchanted). I hoped that the Fae had remembered to round up the wild boar before sunset.

The path sloped down a bit, then twisted sharp left round a dense bit of matted undergrowth and tangled brambles. I'll bet that corresponded to a mundane structure – a lambing shed or something rural. Because of the bend, I got no warning of what was round the corner.

She was sitting on a tree stump right next to the path, in a pool of silver light cast by her own hair. That's just showing off, that is.

I've met the Fae in person before. There are always a couple knocking round Salomon's House, for one thing, and they're very popular as party guests, if you like seriously wild parties. Again, don't tell Conrad, but everything you've heard about Fae anatomy is true. That was different. They were guests. On their best behaviour. Bound by the rules of hospitality. Not here, they're not. This is their wood, their rules.

'My lady,' I said, bowing.

She giggled. 'Well met by moonlight, my dear.' She said it in a funny way, as if it meant something. No idea what.

I straightened up and took a good look (she was taking just as good a look at me). Her glowing, fine-spun hair was long, but not too long, and it managed to be both blond and silver at the same time. It was blond if you looked at the whole creature, silver if you looked at the hair. Her dress was one shouldered, long, and effortlessly satin in the way it clung where it needed to and draped where it didn't. Her legs were crossed, and diamante strapped sandals showing off perfect toes completed her outfit. She was holding her knee with long, slender arms. I shivered all down my spine at the thought of exposed flesh on a night like this. Seeing a Fae on their home turf reminds you that they don't feel the cold: they are the cold.

'I am so loving the rambler-chic look that all the girls are going for tonight,' she said with a toss of her hair. 'Though I must say, it would have been nice to meet the Dragonslayer.' As the light from her locks spread behind, I got a glimpse of a stocky male figure carrying a sword. That meant she was at least a couple of rungs up the hierarchy. Even more reason to be on my guard.

I ignored the comment about my appearance. I've heard a lot, lot worse. When she didn't get a rise out of me, or a comment about Conrad's absence, she stood up and rested her chin on her fingers. Her fingernails were blood red and pointed.

'I am sent by our Prince,' she announced. 'The anointed of Nimue are welcome here, and we wish you well in your journey.'

The Fae will not utter the words *The King's Watch*. They don't accept our authority, but they don't reject it either. To them, the Watch is the bodyguard of a Nymph called Nimue and not a police force.

In one sense, we are bodyguards, actually. Long story. Doesn't matter. The Prince had gone out of his way to make it known that I had a free hand in here, and that was a relief.

'Thank you, my lady,' I said with another bow.

'I also have a message for Oma Bridget. If this Stag is not taken by a Hunter tonight, there will be no Royal Hunt until the turn of another winter. We are not pleased by this.'

'My lady.'

She considered me again. 'You'd better hurry along before you miss the fun. Fare you well.'

I backed off and turned round. Then I ran.

I'd gotten off lightly back there. Only one insult, no dangerous illusions and no sexual propositions: just a message. She must have been under strict instructions, and she couldn't have been more accommodating, which meant that the Prince wants this business over with as quickly as possible, and that holding me up wouldn't have helped.

I kept jogging (again, the presence of the Fae Lady meant no Stag nearby), and what stopped me was a vibration on the thigh. Eh?

I pulled out my phone and checked. An enchanted wood is about as dead a dead zone as you can get for modern technology, so what was happening? On the screen was a message from Conrad: *Can you get this? Any news?*

It seems like years since the Battle of Lunar Hall. Just before the battle, I'd entangled our phones, and when he brought me back from the dead, we developed a magickal bond of some sort. Clearly, the bond was strong enough for his message to get through, somehow, because I was getting no mundane signal at all. I took a minute to text back: *No luck so far. Met a Fae and got a free pass. They want it over tonight. No more Hunts for a year if not.*

Conrad has an aversion to wishes of good luck. He text back: *All quiet here.* And that was it. Time to move things on.

'Ow,' I said when I put my phone back in my pocket: it had dug the silver acorns into my hip. Sharp little buggers. I took them out and was going to move them to a different pocket when I had an idea.

I left the path and found a space. With great care, I placed the five acorns at the points of a pentacle and took out my pick. Conrad's Badge of Office is on a handgun; mine is on a little golden pickaxe, in honour of me dad's time down the pit (and his father, and his father's father etc.). What I was about to do was something I hadn't tried since I took my final examination at the Invisible College.

I stood in the middle of the acorns and touched the pick to one of them. The golden pick trailed a thread of silver, like a spider's web (ick), and I drew it from acorn to acorn, creating a pentacle of silver light. I wouldn't have tried this without the Prince's all clear – I was piggybacking off Fae magick here. That Lady and every other Fae who cared to look would know exactly what I was doing. I hope they're impressed. I was.

When the pentacle was complete, I closed my eyes and let like call to like.

Little lights lit up around me, like stars in a dark sky. Crowns of them – ripening acorns on the branches of enchanted oaks, and carpets of them underneath. I turned round slowly to get a feel for the scale of the vision.

There were gaps, huge gaps of nothing then clusters of spectral oaks. I nearly turned round too quickly and forgot where I'd been, but one of the oaks had an extra glow. That was the tree these acorns had fallen from, so that was the way I'd come in. Turn round again and ... Over there, to the right. A big group of oaks.

The Phantom Stag starts out as a real flesh-and-blood ruminant until the ghostly antlers lift it into the realm of the forest, like the way-marker had done for me, and a spectral animal needs sustenance. I imagine the acorns tasted delicious, and that cluster of oaks down there is exactly where a Stag would go looking for food.

The lights winked out. I'd overloaded the acorns and they'd evaporated, so I'd better not forget which way the oaks were. With a spring in my step, I set off up the slope of a hill in search of the Hunters or their prey. Either would do.

5

There wasn't much to see until I got to the top of the hill and had to catch my breath. I'd been a bit keen up that hill, not that it was much of a hill by Conrad's standards. I did get a better view from the top, though.

The Work I'd done with the acorns had given me enough of a sense of the oaks to try looking on my own now that I was closer. There. Down the other side of the hill. I was about to set off when a human figure appeared below me. A mortal, Witch-shaped human figure, coming in from the right. Erin. Shit. I put on a Silence and started to run.

Erin was heading towards the cluster of oak trees and trying to look sneaky. She looked about as home in the woods as I did. With the Silence on me, she had no idea I was coming until I was nearly on top of her. She swung round ... and lifted a shotgun.

I couldn't help it. I hit the deck and rolled to the side. It was only when I hit a tree and the Silence broke that I cringed: not with fear, but mortal shame. My Ancile would have stopped the gun. Wait till Conrad hears about this. She didn't even fire it.

Beyond the screen of oaks, I felt rather than heard the Stag take fright and run off. I got up just as Aaron detached himself from a tree. Bloody hell, I'd run right past him, and Erin had missed him, too. Not now, though. She'd been tracking me with the shotgun barrel; when Aaron appeared, she switched targets and brought the gun up to her shoulder. Aaron had no Ancile. Not allowed on hunts.

'Stop!' she shouted, but he was off in pursuit of the Stag, the stupid bloke. Who does that when there's a mad woman with a shotgun? His only hope was for me to get between him and Erin.

I sprinted ahead and made it just in time for an arrow to whack into my Ancile from the left. What the hell?

Erin screamed, a roar of frustration, and charged after Aaron. I was right in the way, of course. She lifted the shotgun and went to take a swipe at me. My adrenaline was going now. I didn't flinch this time. I used my magick to send a blast of air along the floor. It blew her feet from under her and sent her sprawling. The gun had a soft landing and didn't go off, but it did fly out of her hand. Mine, I think.

'Leave it,' said a woman behind me.

A high-pitched voice. Totally unfamiliar to me, but not to Erin. 'Karina!' she said.

I did leave the gun, but I moved to put myself between Erin and the weapon before I turned round. The missing Witch, Colwyn's sister and sponsor, was all in tight black combat gear and carried another of those bows with red flames licking along the stave. She was thin and wiry, her face almost gaunt with prominent cheekbones. She'd pulled her Braid right back, too, making her face look even tighter.

'Who do you think you are, pet?' I said. 'Katniss Everdeen?'

Why did I have a go at her? She'd just tried to shoot me, that's why. Conrad and I have that in common. We tend to get sarky when people shoot at us. She did look good, mind, if you go for that sort of thing, and a lot of blokes do.

'I will have that Stag,' she said. With the grace of a ballerina, she dropped to a squat and placed the bow gently on the ground. In one silky movement, she stood up, drew a knife and came at me.

I gave her the same blast that had floored Erin.

And it swept past her. Bugger. Hunters aren't supposed to wear Anciles. They're not supposed to be women, either. I started to retreat. Quickly.

The biggest danger was a tree root, and I swerved right to avoid it. Karina didn't look as confident with the knife as she clearly was with the bow, and she knew that I had enough magick to fight back when she got close. If she didn't kill me first. She got ready to take a run at me, moving to a half-crouch. I set myself to defend as if I knew what I was doing. We were both focused so hard on each other, we'd forgotten about Erin. And the gun.

Erin had put a Silence on herself, and must have used a Glamour, because neither Karina nor I knew she was there until she appeared at my side. The gun was pointing at Karina. 'You bastard,' said Erin. 'You sneaky bastard. You killed Ioan.'

Karina went white (no camouflage makeup for her). She looked totally stricken.

'This is gonna take some sorting out,' I said and turned to my left. Conrad's always on about priorities. 'Give me the gun, Erin, before you make things worse.'

'Ioan?' squeaked Karina. 'Ioan's dead? He can't be. I've just seen him!'

I ignored her and tried to channel my inner Vera Stanhope. 'Erin? Let the Watch deal with this. C'mon, pet, give us the gun.'

We hadn't got a good look at Erin when we arrived at the field this morning. She'd been wrapped up against the cold, and hadn't stayed to be interviewed. She had a pleasant face, not striking or stunning, just open and wide-eyed with lovely fine blond hair. Much more my type, if I were into women, not that she looked very pleasant right now. She wasn't holding the gun properly, and might break her wrist if she fired it. I saw the black smudges on her hands from her work as an Enscriber and shuddered. Last month, an Enscriber had tried to kill us. Several times. I'd bashed her head in with a metal crutch. That image still gives me the shakes. I forced myself to focus on the present.

'Look at your fingers, Erin,' I said. 'Ink stains, not blood stains. Hand it over and help me out, eh?'

She held the gun out to me and looked away. I took it from her, and her shoulders slumped. It was my turn to stare at the gun. Conrad has run me through the basics of shotguns, just in case, but his shotguns are breech loaders. This was a pump action. 'Is this even loaded?' I said to Erin.

She perked up a bit. 'Of course. And there's one in the chamber. What are you going to do about her?'

We looked at Karina. She was wiping away tears. 'Is Ioan really dead?' she said.

'Aye, he is. Colwyn shot him. That's why we're here.'

'Who are you, anyway?'

'A Witchfinder,' said Erin. 'There's another one somewhere.'

'Hey, less of that,' I said as sharply as I could. 'Oma called in the King's Watch, and we'll sort this out.'

Karina looked appalled. 'No. No, no, no.' She started backing away from us. From me. 'I didn't shoot to kill you. I was only going to tie you up.'

She was so light on her feet, she almost danced back to where she'd left her bow. There was no point trying to grab her, or shoot her. She fumbled her dagger, trying to sheathe it, and dropped it. She cursed and picked up her bow. Then she was off, a ghost slipping through the trees.

'That bow,' said Erin. 'It was blessed.'

'Eh?'

'It had the same blessing as the other bows. Colwyn's and Aaron's. And Ioan's.'

'And it was identical to Aaron and Ioan's.'

'That model is one of the best for carrying on foot.'

A horrible thought ran through my head. Had we been set up by Oma? 'Who did the blessing?' I asked.

'Eliza.'

'Then Aaron is in serious danger. Serious, serious danger.'

'Not now you've got the gun,' said Erin. 'I've failed Ioan, and Aaron will get away with it.'

'It wasn't Aaron you numpty. Or Judith. She's under guard. It was Eliza and Colwyn, and maybe Karina, too.'

'How come?'

'Who else could have blessed Karina's bow, and put a Work onto Ioan's to make him *look* like the Stag. The reason Colwyn was in shock this morning was that he was expecting to have killed Aaron, not Ioan. Something must have gone wrong.'

'Really?'

'Yes, really. Now, are you gonna help me or do I have to spend ten minutes tying you up?'

'I'm no hunter. You probably noticed.'

'Aye, well, neither am I, but I know someone who is.' I put the gun down and got out my phone.

'Wow!' said Erin. 'Does that work?'

I started typing and said, 'It only works to Watch Captain Clarke's phone. He … he's outside the forest.' I finished typing and sent this message: *Karina has bow. Eliza cursed Ioans. Colwyn wants Aaron dead. Where would Stag hide?*

Erin had picked up Karina's dagger. 'Do you want this?'

'Shove it in my backpack for now. Never use another Mage's weapons. King's Watch 101.'

While Erin loosened the strings and stowed the knife, Conrad got back to me: *A stag would hide in a dense thicket. Will also try to mask scent, or magick equivalent. I'll look for Colwyn.*

'Right, Erin. Time to be useful,' I said. 'There must be lots of mundane buildings under this wood.'

She nodded. 'Yes.'

'We want a big building that's also a door to the Prince of Arden's sídhe.'

'Erm. Right. There's half a dozen. Why?'

'Because if the Stag gets in there, it'll take ages for a human to flush it out.'

We needed some way to whittle down the options. 'Forget about the ones near the way-markers. How many does that leave?'

She thought. 'Three.'

Still too many. We needed better local knowledge. Perhaps Conrad could talk to Oma… No. He didn't need to. She'd already given me a clue. 'Does one of them have two ash trees bent to form a canopy?'

'Yes! That's the Countess of Stratford's Door. How did you know?'

'Never mind. Which way? And don't tell me you're lost.'

'No. I love walking the forest. It's about half a mile that way.'

I picked up the gun. 'Does this thing have a safety catch?'

Erin knew that much. She locked it and we jogged through the forest.

I'll admit it. We didn't run very far. Both of us were out of breath pretty quick, so we settled for a brisk walk. I blame the stout outdoor walking shoes that Conrad made me buy: warm and rugged, but no good for running. Definitely the shoes. And the chafing. I will admit that there was chafing.

'How close are Colwyn and Karina to each other?' I asked, with lots of pauses to breathe. Erin was the same. We kept going, though.

'Not very. Not until she came back from her sabbatical. He's twenty years older than her, for one thing. Same father, different mother. They've definitely been hanging out more, lately. She's so shy, though, it's hard to tell who she's close to.'

'Where was her sabbatical?'

'She never said. Down south, somewhere. May even have been abroad.'

'And what's with the midnight huntress thing? She's not going to be King, no matter how many Stags she kills, is she?'

'I have no idea what she's up to, Watch Officer. Sorry. I don't know your name.'

'Robson. Vicky Robson.'

'Sorry. Not everyone likes the Hunt. Some want it banned. Could be loads of agendas.'

'Much further?'

Erin stopped and looked around. She squinted through the trees. 'Down there, see? A blockage. That's the back edge.'

'Right. You stay here.'

'What? With no Ancile and wait to get picked off? No chance. And you've got the gun, so I'm no threat. I can watch your back.'

For the second time, I asked myself *what would Conrad do? Would he tie her up or let her tag along?* I'm sure I could hear him answer: *Do you trust her?* The thing that made my mind up was a bit less noble than Conrad's question: I just didn't fancy doing this on me own.

'Come on, then,' I said. 'Keep quiet, keep down and keep your eyes open. We'll skirt the thicket and look for traces of the hunters.'

'Right. Gotcha.'

We crept up to the thick tangle of brambles and … rhododendrons? I don't know. Whatever they were, they were big, bushy and in the way. I turned right and said, 'You use your Sight, and I'll watch for movement.'

Without thinking, Erin reached out to hold on to my arm. I nearly swung the gun at her, until I realised she'd closed her eyes and needed me to lead her. I moved off, scanning all round.

We'd got about a hundred yards (this thing was *big*) when she tightened her grip and pulled me to a stop.

'Here,' she said. 'The Stag went in here. The trail has almost been washed away by Fae magick.'

We both used all our senses to scope the open woods and into the thicket. Nothing. No Hunter had followed the Stag into the undergrowth.

'Do you fancy going in there? I don't,' said Erin. I had to agree with her.

'Let's cheat,' I said. 'If we work together, I reckon we can set a trap.'

'How?'

'Follow the Stag's trail back a bit, then make a false one round to the front. We can meet them there.'

She looked at me blankly. 'How do we do that?'

'It's not real scent, is it? It's magick, and what can be analysed can be copied.'

'Oh. Right. Did you learn that at Salomon's House?'

'Not as such. Let's do it.'

PHANTOM STAG

Erin showed me the trail. It was easy enough to blow it away as we moved back into the main part of the forest. When we came to a fork, I stopped and we bent down to have a closer look at the trail of the Stag. We both opened our Sight and discovered something very quickly.

'Eurgh,' said Erin. 'That stinks of wee. If you can duplicate that, you're very weird.'

'How is that possible? It should be a simple magickal echo.'

We looked up at the same moment and spoke at the same time. 'The Fae.'

Erin sighed. 'What now, Officer Robson?'

'Get that dagger out of me backpack, and call me Vicky.' She fumbled behind me and got out Erin's knife. 'There's no Goddess death magick on that, is there?'

Erin looked at the dagger. 'Not that I can see, besides, there's no such thing as Goddess death magick.'

Despite rumours to the contrary, there is no such thing as blood magick, either. That's not to say that blood isn't magickal, though. It is. One of the first practical classes at Salomon's House is *How to Draw Blood Safely*. 'Cut me,' I said to Erin.

'Are you sure?'

'Aye. Get a nice bladeful and smear it round. Then follow me.'

Now that we'd spoken a bit more, I reckoned that Erin was older than me. Twenty-five or six, perhaps. They must teach the same lessons in the Circles, because she drew blood from my left arm with practised ease and scooped a load on to the blade. I left her to it and jogged round the thicket, making sure I was dripping as I went. It sounds gross, I know, but being underground is far, far worse. To me, anyway.

I stopped when I saw the twin ash trees. The main track through the forest ran up to them, and through the arch I could see a silver path that would lead to the Fae door. Perfect. I dripped up to the trees and squeezed the wound closed. We also had classes on *Stopping the Flow*.

Erin caught up with me. 'Let's get behind the ash tree,' I said. 'We'll have the drop on them.'

We moved into position. 'Where's the gun?' I said.

'You had it.'

I pointed to my arm. 'I couldn't carry it. I left it for you to bring.'

Erin didn't answer. There was no point. Shit and damnation. Bugger. Arse.

'Get ready to run,' I said.

'Why are you in here on your own?' said Erin. I was beginning to wonder that myself. She deserved an answer, though.

'Because Conrad can't see the forest, that's why.'

'Oh.'

Erin went up in my estimation then, because a lot of people would have run screaming at that point. She did give me a look though.

We didn't have long to wait.

Aaron had done the same thing as us – found the thicket and worked his way round, but he'd done it clockwise and came up from the left at the same moment that Karina followed the trail of my blood from the opposite direction. She'd also found the gun. Erin and I stood up as the two Hunters faced off.

'Shall we try again?' I said.

We made a triangle, about twenty metres a side, with Karina at one corner, Aaron another and Erin huddling next to me at the third.

'Karina?' said Aaron. 'It is you. What the hell are you doing here, and what happened to Ioan?'

'Let me...' I tried to get the initiative, but they weren't listening.

'See?' said Karina, holding out the shotgun. 'Empty. And useless.' She dropped the weapon and took out her bow. She notched an arrow and aimed at Aaron. He echoed her movements.

'Aaron,' I said. 'She's got an Ancile.'

'What?'

'She's right,' said Karina. 'Put down the bow, Aaron, and break it. I'll leave then.'

'Just so that your dead beat brother can cheat and win the Hunt? No chance.'

'Not Colwyn,' said Karina. 'Me. That Stag is mine.'

With slow precision, she drew back and loosed an arrow. I couldn't follow it in flight, I just heard the low *whoosh* as it thudded into the ground between and behind Aaron's feet, having passed through his legs on the way. It made me shiver, and I'm not a man. An arrow that close to their dangly bits would have made most men wince. There was another arrow in her bow before we could look up. 'I mean it,' said Karina. 'Time is passing.'

Erin shoved me in the back and whispered, 'You have to get between them.'

I started forwards.

'Stop there,' said Karina, 'or he gets it now.'

Aaron was showing no signs of backing down. Idiot. Was he expecting me to pull a rabbit out of the hat? Fine. I spoke up. 'Erin, go and knock on the Prince's door. The Fae won't be happy about this. They may not sort out these two, but they'll pull the Hunt.'

Karina looked beside herself. 'Don't move, Erin. If you leave her side, I'll have to stop you.' She flashed the bow from Erin to Aaron. She could shoot both of them easily.

It was time to pass the buck to Conrad. In a manner of speaking. I took out my pickaxe and smeared it with some of my blood. Most Anciles are personal. With my blood, Erin should be able to work it. I took it from round my neck and gave it to her.

'She's going,' I said. 'And then I'm coming to arrest you. If you shoot me, you'll have to answer to my partner. He's waiting outside. You really don't want that.'

'So?' said Karina.

Aaron finally lowered his bow. He didn't drop it and break it, but it was a start.

'You won't know this,' said Aaron, 'but her boss is the Dragonslayer. If you hurt Officer Robson, he'll track you down to the ends of the earth.'

'Partner, not boss,' I said. 'He's also a psycho. Dragonslaying is only part of it. The Allfather was once his patron. I wouldn't put it past him to revive the Blood Eagle.'

'No!' said Erin, aghast. The Blood Eagle is so gruesome I'm not going into it here. You can look it up if you want.

'I think he would,' said Aaron.

'I'll take my chances,' said Karina. 'If Erin moves, you two will be dead and I'll be after the Stag before the Fae have answered the door.'

Was she bluffing?

I'll admit it: my nerve failed at that point. I was about to order Aaron to stand down when he heard something and looked away from us, deeper into the forest. Then Karina heard it, too. Finally, I picked out the sound of desperate running heading towards us. Surely that couldn't be Conrad?

No. The approaching figure was definitely female. She ran into the space between Aaron and Karina then stopped, out of breath and leaning over to rest her hands on her knees. She had on a long parka, leggings and white sneakers. When she straightened up and turned to face me, her coat flapped back. Underneath was the royal blue of a nurse's tunic. Oh.

'Mutti!' said Erin.

'Alexandra, I presume.' That was me.

'Yes.' She turned to Karina. 'Stop it. Stop it now. You're not going to shoot a Circle Mother, and you know you aren't. In the name of the Goddess, desist.'

'And you, Aaron,' I said. 'In the name of the King, put down your weapon or answer to the Cloister Court.'

Aaron put the arrow back in its quiver. As he unstrung his bow, he said, 'Has it come to this, in Arden, that the word of the Witchfinders has more power than the Goddess?'

Karina let out a scream of frustration, anger and stress. She turned and aimed through the arch of trees, drew back her bow and fired. I jumped when a bass *thud* rumbled through the forest floor. 'I'm coming back,' she shouted at the archway. 'Do you hear?'

I took my pickaxe back and moved quickly to Karina, but not as quickly as Alex. In seconds, Karina was sobbing on her shoulder.

'Where've you been?' I said to Alex. I know, I know. Priorities. That wasn't the most important question, but I couldn't help myself.

'Delivering a baby. In Stratford on Avon. There were complications, and my phone battery died. My patient didn't have a compatible charger. I only finished an hour ago, and Tanya told me what had happened.'

That was a pretty good alibi.

'We'll need to question Karina,' I said.

'Not now,' said Alex. 'She's fragile. I'll look after her and bring her to you at the Foresters' hall. In the name of the Goddess, I promise it.'

'So mote it be,' I replied, 'but we'll need the bow. It's evidence.'

Karina was out of it. Alex lowered her to the ground, taking the bow from her in the process. She handed the bow to me and put her arms round Karina. 'Evidence of what?' she said.

'Of Eliza's involvement in this mess. She's the Author of this. Her and Colwyn.'

Alex looked down; Erin looked away. Neither disagreed with me, and that was pretty telling. It was Aaron who spoke up. 'And now Colwyn will claim the Stag, become King and no one will be able to argue.'

'I'll be arguing,' I said.

'He'll be exempt,' said Erin. 'Oma, the Mother and the King are exempt from justice in the Cloister Court. The King can only be tried by combat.'

I felt my phone vibrate and checked the message. 'That's moot,' I said. 'Watch Captain Clarke has Colwyn under arrest. Oh, and the Stag made it to Home Wood alive. Which is the quickest way out of here?'

6

It was all kicking off when we got back to the Foresters' hall.

The car park was lit with a pair of halogen floodlights mounted on the hall; another feature that would upset Heritage England if they could see it. I got a tinge of magick – those floodlights were helping keep up the Occulting Works surrounding us. Clever, that. I made a mental note to tell the Royal Occulter about it.

The car park wasn't nearly as full as this morning, and right next to the doors of the great hall was our trusty Volvo. Conrad had beaten us to it, and Colwyn was tied up in a corner inside. No one had been to dress his bloody nose or split lip. In the opposite corner, Judith was being guarded by the guy on the motorbike. I never did learn his name.

The hall looked even more spectacular at night. It was lit with Lightsticks placed in the roof beams and supplemented by a few round the wall. The light that came off them was warm and mellow, and echoed by a small fire burning in a huge fireplace. Eh? Where had that come from? Oh. The tapestry had been there this morning.

The hall has two sets of doors, one pair facing the car park where I'd just entered and the other pair leading to the wood, their sacred Grove and into the forest of Arden. Oma was standing in front of them, arms folded and wearing her robes and a look of thunder. About a dozen of the Circle were scattered around the room in groups.

I'd waited in the car park with Erin until first Aaron, then Alex and Karina had appeared. Karina looked stricken, as you might expect, but she'd recovered from total collapse. I led the way, and was about to say something when I heard a cry from upstairs that turned into a moan.

'Eliza!' said Alex. She dashed up the stairs towards the solar, leaving Karina to fend for herself.

'Erin?' I said, 'Put Karina in that corner and keep an eye on her. Get someone to make her hot, sweet tea.'

'Right.'

I left them to it and followed Alex up the stairs.

Eliza was in labour, and Tanya was holding her hand. Alex already had her coat off and was wiping her hands with sanitiser when I got there. Less expected was Conrad.

I've not been round many women in labour. Make that none, to be exact. I was starting to panic when Conrad got up and came over.

'It's early days, yet. Contractions have barely started,' he said. 'Are you OK?'

'Aye. Since when are you an obstetrician?'

'Twice in Helmand. Once in the back of my helicopter, would you believe. There's a little boy in Afghanistan whose middle name is Conrad.'

'Poor bairn.'

'Take me to the Grove!' shouted Eliza. 'I will not be denied.'

I waved my hand around generally. 'Why are we still here?'

'When I arrived, Oma had already barred Eliza from leaving. Probably because of the text I sent her. Once Tanya heard that her mother was on her way back, the sensible thing was to wait for the real expert to turn up. And you, with the evidence.'

Alex finished her examination and came over. 'She can't stay here much longer. This is going to be difficult. She needs attention, in hospital or in the Grove.'

'Let's get her downstairs while we can,' said Conrad. He stood well back while Alex and her daughter helped Eliza to her feet.

He bent down and lowered his voice. 'Eliza admitted supplying Karina with a blessed bow, and putting a curse on Ioan's. She says she had four bows on the altar and messed it up. Ioan's bow should have gone to Aaron. She's blaming Colwyn for coming up with the idea, though he had no idea about what his sister was up to regarding the Hunt. We can sort the rest out later.'

'What now?'

'Let's see.'

Oma hadn't moved from the door. A chair had been put in front of her, and Eliza had been lowered into it.

'I demand the Grove,' said Eliza, eyes locked on Oma. 'I have confessed and will let the Goddess judge me.'

'Watch Captain?' said Oma. 'Are you content?'

Conrad shook his head. 'That's not for me to say. Eliza is out of my jurisdiction, but will *you* be content if she doesn't say who enchanted those bows? She may have blessed them, but someone else performed the curses and other magick. The King's Watch is very interested in knowing who.'

'Name them,' said Oma. 'Name them and I will stand aside.'

'Would you turn me away?' said Eliza. 'No Oma has ever turned away a Mother from the Grove.'

'And no Mother has ever killed one of the Circle. Name them or go. Forever.'

'I will sit here until you let me pass or I die. Will you do that?'

Alexandra gripped Eliza's shoulder. 'Your child will die first. In your womb. I won't let that happen. You were born to be a mother, so let the Goddess guide you.'

Eliza stared at Oma, and Oma stared back until Eliza was racked by a pain.

'Take me,' said Eliza.

Alexandra lifted Eliza out of the chair and said, 'Someone get my coat from upstairs.'

'Is it far to the maternity unit?' I asked.

'Alexandra Hospital in Redditch. Fifteen minutes max. We'll be fine. Tanya? Go and get the car open. You're driving.'

Alex's daughter ran out. A Forester brought Alex's coat. She shrugged it on and led Eliza outside. A couple of the Foresters got up to see them out. Through the open doors, I could hear Alex on the phone to the hospital.

'Close the doors,' said Oma. 'Get out the board and let's sit down.'

The Foresters moved with practised ease to get that table in place. OK, alright, *the board*. One of them handed out mugs of tea. Boy did that taste good. Conrad asked for a break and almost dragged me outside. While I went through what had happened in the forest, he smoked a cigarette.

'What about you?' I said. 'Did Colwyn put up a fight?'

'Stupid arse thought I wouldn't use my gun on him and came at me. I whacked him with it.'

'How did you find him?'

'I thought about it. His strategy last night was basically good. Why wouldn't he repeat it? I got Tanya to take me to Home Wood on her quad bike and there he was. We'd better get back inside.'

The Foresters were sitting at the board now, apart from Colwyn and Karina in their opposite corners. Seats had been left for Conrad and me next to Oma. She'd been sitting with her head in her hands, and looked up when we got back in. The strain on her face was there for everyone to see. 'How did it come to this?' she said. No one spoke, but a few of them looked as if they'd have plenty to say when the time was right. 'I know you're thinking it,' she continued. 'And yes, a lot of it has to be down to me. That's for the future. When we're alone. First, we have to decide what to do with Colwyn and Karina.'

'And me,' said Erin, in a very small voice.

'The Watch has no interest in Erin,' said Conrad. 'Though we have confiscated her shotgun.'

'It's mine,' said Aaron. 'She took it without my permission.'

Oma waved him away with her hand. 'Bring Colwyn here, Aaron.'

The Hunter dragged his rival over and shoved him into a chair off to the side.

'Why, Colwyn?' said Oma.

The Forester licked blood off his lip but said nothing.

'Jealousy,' said Conrad. 'Jealousy of Aaron, I think. And Eliza worked on that. She wanted Aaron dead.'

'How was that going to work?' said one of the female Foresters.

'Eliza played them both,' I said. 'I'm guessing that she knew about Karina's ambitions to be a Hunter, and she played her by giving her a bow and getting her in the forest. She would have needed a sponsor to help disguise the four bows on the altar and the switch she made. I've seen the bow staves now, and there was a double curse, I reckon. One made the Hunter with the cursed bow think that all deer were Stags, and the other made him look like a Stag to everyone else. It only went pear shaped because she mixed up the bows.'

'Is that right?' said Oma. Colwyn said nothing. Oma sighed. 'Then let the Cloister Court decide. I…'

Colwyn sat up. 'I confess and ask for service in the forest to repay my crimes.' The words tumbled out of his mouth in a rush, to stop Oma finishing what she was going to say.

'Eh?' I said.

Oma looked at Conrad. 'He has that right. We will hand him over to the Fae, and they will put him to work. Thirty-two years he'll be in there.' She shuddered at the thought.

'Better than the Undercroft,' said Colwyn.

'Say hello to Father Patrick,' I said. 'If you're nice to him, you might get time off for good behaviour.'

'Put him in the store room,' said Oma, 'and bring Karina forward.'

Karina was brought to the chair that Colwyn had just vacated. Her glossy black outfit looked right out of place in the homespun surroundings of the Foresters' hall, and she made a half-hearted attempt to undo a webbing harness. When she couldn't manage the fastenings with her shaking hands, she dropped into the chair.

Oma softened a little. She clearly trusted her current handmaiden, Tanya, implicitly, and her attitude to the former holders of the office was quite revealing. She had little patience with Erin, that was clear, and I can imagine that Erin would make a great friend but a terrible officer. Judith, she treated with a wary respect. Don't forget, Judith had dumped Colwyn and displaced Erin in Aaron's bed. Then she'd converted to Materialism. I wouldn't trust her either.

Karina was different. She looked at her like you'd expect a granny to look at their favourite, most indulged granddaughter. She tentatively reached out a hand, then pulled it back when she saw me staring at her.

'What were you trying to achieve, my dear?' she said. 'You need to tell me, and I'm afraid that Officers Clarke and Robson need to hear it. Victoria risked her life tonight.'

Karina sniffed. Erin reached into her pocket, found a clean tissue and passed it over. Whatever deadly weapons the midnight huntress had in her pouches, a hankie clearly hadn't been part of the kit.

'Equality,' she said. 'For women *and* men. This is the twenty-first century, Oma. Women should be allowed on the Hunt, and men shouldn't be forced to win the Hunt to become King.'

The other Foresters couldn't stay quiet any longer. One of the women (I think she'd had a small child with her this morning) said, 'We shouldn't be doing the Hunt at all.'

Another woman said, 'At least she doesn't want the men eligible to become Oma.'

'Enough!' said the current Oma.

It may be the twenty-first century outside, but large parts of the world of magick have barely moved on from the 1300s.

Oma turned to me. 'Was Karina's arrow aimed at you, Officer Robson?'

'Conrad's the ballistics expert, Oma, but it struck my Ancile quite high up. I've seen what a good shot she is, so no, I reckon it was aimed to scare me. We don't know if she'd have killed me later though. She did threaten to do it. And Erin.'

'Karina?'

The young Witch dropped her gaze and fiddled with the tissue. 'I don't know what came over me, Oma. I don't know.'

'I think I do,' said Erin. 'I think she would have shot Vicky, and me, but I also think she sniffed a bit too much Fae dust.'

Karina didn't look happy at that, but she didn't argue.

Oma nodded. She looked round her flock and gauged the mood. Finally, she drew herself up and said, 'You have lost your way, my child, and you have lost touch with the Goddess. I want you to go on a pilgrimage to reconnect with her. On foot. From Glastonbury to Bríd's Well in Ireland. If you return, I will welcome you with open arms. Your key, please.' When she finished speaking, there were no murmurs of dissent.

Karina, with shaking hands, removed the small golden arrow from round her neck. Oh, that reminds me. I got out the one I'd been given and passed it over. Oma slid my key back to Judith, its rightful owner, while we waited for Karina to come to a decision.

She held up the little golden arrow and placed it carefully on the board. 'As the Goddess wishes. I will leave at the next new moon.'

Conrad had been sitting very still up to now. Always a dangerous sign. He coughed and reached into his pocket to pull out a badge. Oh no.

'Take this,' he said, offering the badge to Karina. She was so shell-shocked, she took it. On one side is this logo:

MERLYN'S TOWER IRREGULARS

And on the other side is Conrad's mobile number. And mine. 'When you've finished your pilgrimage, you could join the King's Watch,' he said with a smile. 'We have full equality.'

Erin had been leaning over to look. 'Ooh, can I have one?' she said. 'Not that I want to join the Watch or anything.'

Conrad put on a stern face. 'Can you play cricket?'

'I have no idea. Why?'

'Clerkswell Ladies is recruiting. If you fancy it, give me a call.' He gave her a smile and handed over a badge.

Oma cleared her throat. During the nonsense with Conrad and Erin, Karina had pocketed her badge. Interesting.

Oma gave me Karina's key. 'And you should have this, Officer Robson. You are welcome here, should you wish.'

'In the name of the Goddess, thank you,' I said. That was generous of her.

'And I shall remit a fee to the Constable. Thank you, both of you, for this service. The Arden Foresters are very grateful. Sadly, Watch Captain Clarke, I cannot extend the same gift to you.'

'Can I ask a question?' said Karina, in the tiniest of voices. She was looking at Conrad. Oma nodded.

'Watch Captain Clarke,' said Karina, 'your partner said you might inflict the Blood Eagle on me if I hurt her. Is that true?'

Conrad shook his head. 'The Peculier Constable has a policy: the King's Watch is part of the solution, not part of the problem. I can't enforce the occult law if I break it, and performing the Blood Eagle would be huge breach, no matter how much you deserved it.' Karina looked a little disappointed at that, which was quite alarming, but Conrad hadn't finished. 'What I'd do is this: I'd come down to your cell in the Undercroft every day and watch you disintegrate. With a bit of luck, I'd be there on the day you took your own life.'

Karina looked down and swallowed hard. I heard a couple of coughs from round the board.

'And on that note...' said Oma. She stood up, and we all followed. All except Karina. 'Erin, the doors please.'

Oma escorted us to the threshold.

'There is one thing,' said Conrad. 'If you would truly do me a service.'

'I can't deny you, after this,' said Oma.

'Then see your son.'

She snorted. 'As you wish. May the Goddess guide you. Travel well.'

We bowed, and she returned to face the company of Foresters. Conrad went to the car, but I lingered when Erin waved me over as she closed the doors.

'Is Conrad the coach of this cricket team?' she asked with a nervous glance at our car.

Bloody typical. You can't take him anywhere for Witches (and stable girls) hitting on him.

'Assistant coach,' I said. 'His girlfriend is in the team, too. So's his housekeeper. She's a Druid. I think you'd like her.'

'What, a real Druid Mage?'

'Aye. A good one, too.'

'What's she doing in Gloucestershire, then, and why is she his housekeeper.'

'That's her story to tell. Ask her yourself.'

'I might just do that. See you, Vicky.'

'G'night, Erin.'

She closed the doors and I headed for the car.

7

'Well done Vicky,' said Conrad, as soon as we'd driven through the Wards around Foresters' Hall. 'You did a superb job in that forest. You should be proud of yourself.'

'I am. I suppose. It was nice to be above ground for a change, but I'm not so keen to have another encounter with the Fae.'

'Was it that bad?'

'No, and that's the worrying thing. She was under orders to be nice. There has to have been another agenda going on there. Talking of agendas, what the hell do you think Eliza was up to? She never expected to get away with that, surely?'

'You'd think not. Talk it through, Vic, what was her preferred outcome?'

'Aaron gets killed and Karina shoots the Stag.'

'Which creates all sorts of chaos in the Circle, doesn't it? Would Oma Bridget have called in the Watch if it hadn't her nephew who got killed?'

I thought that one through. 'She's a bit harsh, but I didn't see her playing favourites.'

'Don't forget, Aaron was very unpopular in some quarters. A lot would have been glad to see him dead, and Oma Bridget was more concerned to be impartial *because* Ioan was her nephew. She couldn't have pointed the finger at anyone without being accused of bias by someone else. And we shouldn't underestimate the chaos that would have been caused if Karina had killed the Stag. Your Fae friends would not be at all amused. If we hadn't been called in, there would have been too many suspects for Eliza to be proved guilty beyond reasonable doubt.'

'I suppose. We learnt a lot from Karina, didn't we? And if she'd succeeded in killing the Stag, her testimony would never have come out.'

'Yes. And there's something else.'

I waited for him to go on, and when he didn't, I looked up. It was starting to get light out there, and Conrad looked a bit troubled. 'What's up Uncle C?'

'While you were in the forest, I talked to Tanya about all sorts of things, just trying to get gossip, really. She said that Eliza was a week overdue. I think that giving birth in the Grove was a top priority for her, but I'm scared to ask why.'

I sighed. 'It can go on our list of unanswered questions, but I've a horrible feeling you're right: I doubt we've heard the last from the Arden Foresters.'

It was almost dawn when we finally reached Clerkswell. I was dead on me feet, but I wasn't going to let Conrad get away lightly. I was also famished, and he owed me a cooked breakfast. The noise of the car woke up Myfanwy, and she wasn't going to miss a fry-up, either.

'You know what I think you two should do,' said Conrad when he'd tied on his apron.

'Go on.'

'Myvvy should pour Vicky a large glass of wine and you should both go through to the drawing room while I cook. Put your voice recorder on, Vic, and tell Myfanwy all about it. You can turn it into a story later. After all, you're going to have to write the report.'

'Fine. Can't argue with that. C'mon, Myfanwy.'

And that's why I've been telling you this story, not Conrad. He hasn't seen what I've written, but I'm sure he'd want you to know that his cooked breakfasts are worth staying awake for.

I started typing it up a week later, and I'd just begun when he passed by and dropped a tatty old book on the table.

'That might help,' he said.

I lowered the lid on my laptop (to stop him peeking), and looked at the book. *A Midsummer Night's Dream*. 'Eh?'

'My GCSE English set book. It's got all my annotations in. Don't worry, I had to rub out the obscene ones before the exam.'

'Eurgh. Why will this help?'

He gave me his especially annoying smile, the one where he knows something that I don't. 'Read it and see.'

'Nah. I'll Google it later.'

I pushed the book away and he left me to it. The phone rang shortly after, and I never did get round to Googling the play, and now I've finished typing this up, it doesn't seem worthwhile.

Mark Hayden

Wings over Water

This novella is dedicated to Ian Sherry,

Conrad's first public fan and

Proud Citizen of God's Own County.

It was originally published in July 2019. The action takes place about one quarter of the way through **Nine of Wands**, *the Fifth Book of the King's Watch.*

At the time, Conrad is in Shropshire re-qualifying as a helicopter pilot and Mina is away visiting her dying mother in India.

Mark Hayden

Prologue — A Visitor

There are a lot of officers in the RAF. Far more than in the Army or the Royal Navy. You can draw your own conclusions about this, and plenty have – you can read their comments online. As I'm an RAF officer myself, I shall maintain a dignified silence. Given the proliferation of stripes and braids, it shouldn't have made the hairs on the back of my neck tingle when one of them walked into the mess. But it did.

I was finishing my supper at RAF Shawbury and minding my own business in a corner of the communal mess. I'm only a humble student at the moment, taking a refresher course on flying helicopters, and I'm in a class of one, so there aren't even any fellow students to moan at. A couple of diners nodded to me, then ignored me when I sat on my own and got out my phone to Whatsapp my girlfriend.

I finished the message, and seconds later the screen said that Mina had read it. Mission accomplished. If you're interested, the message was *sleep well*, because she's in India, and it was past her bed-time. I began to think about taking a coffee outside to go with a cigarette, until the air moved ever so slightly, and those hairs started to tingle. I looked up and saw a female officer in full uniform, carrying a case and staring at me from the doorway. It could have been my survival instinct that told me she was there, or she could be a Mage. When we made eye contact, she started walking nervously over to my table.

Out of habit, I checked out her uniform first. She was a flight lieutenant in the RAF Police (motto: Let there be Justice. Nickname: the Arctic Monkeys). My first thought was *what have I done wrong*? Then I remembered that I'm on the right side of the law for these days, and my second thought was panic: *has there been an accident to Mum and Dad in Spain? Or Rachael in London?*

She gave me a hesitant smile. No one smiles when they're doing a death knock. I noticed the visitor's badge, and then I noticed the person wearing it. Before I could look too closely, she was at my table and saluting. I saluted back.

'Squadron Leader Clarke?' she said. I nodded. 'Could I have a word, sir?'

'Get us some coffee and you can have a whole conversation. Black, please.'

She put her case down and went for coffee. I took a proper look at her as she crossed the mess. She was slightly under average height for RAF women, and looked a little square in her uniform, an impression that came from strong shoulders. Her hair was fair, what little of it I could see that wasn't stuffed into her cap. When she turned round to bring the coffee back, she concentrated hard on carrying the cups and there was a determined set to her jaw.

She put the drinks down and offered her hand. 'I'm Roberta Woodhouse, sir. Everyone calls me Woody, except my wife. She calls me Bobbi.'

That was a rather loaded introduction, and had too much information for a military visit. The determination in her face was tempered with nerves and a hesitant smile.

'Have a seat, please,' I said, 'and call me Conrad. Where are you based?'

'I'm in the reserves.'

That would explain the crisp uniform and the personal nickname. Regular officers in the RAF Police don't have printable nicknames. Or first names, come to that, and she'd told me her status, but not her base of operations.

'So what are you doing stalking a humble chopper pilot in Shropshire?'

By way of an answer, she took out a business card. 'I have the worst job title in the world. Here.'

The card had her name, rank and phone number on one side. I turned it over and found a coat of arms with the caption *Peculier Necromancer*. I could see her point: definitely a dodgy job title. I put the card down.

'How come I've never heard of you?'

'I don't work for the King's Watch, not that I wouldn't love to, if I could. I work for Historic Royal Palaces.'

I was confused. 'Your lot look after the Tower of London, and you're a Mage, but not in the Watch. You're RAF, like me, but Hannah's never mentioned you.'

She shifted uncomfortably, picked up her coffee and put it down again. 'I try to keep a low profile. It's much easier to do my job if I don't get involved in magickal politics.'

I grunted. 'If only I could do the same. What is your job, precisely?'

'It used to be called *Royal Exorcist*. My predecessors dealt with unquiet Spirits on royal property.'

'Oh. That's a job and a half. Did one of them have to deal with the Princes in the Tower?'

She smiled. 'Who knows? The records were mostly destroyed during the Reformation, and it's not something they'd have written down anyway. When the Invisible College was set up, they changed the name to Peculier Necromancer and it became a post in the Army. We shifted to the RAF after World War Two.'

'Aah. Because of Bomber Command?'

'Yes, sir. Sorry. Yes, Conrad. In 1945, there were a lot of haunted airfields. Not so much, any more, which is why I'm only in the Reserves, not full time.'

'And how did you get the job?'

'Born to it, in a way. My dad was an officer in the Engineers, so I was an Army brat. Until I started having the visions, that is.'

I had wondered about her accent: vaguely southern, vaguely public school. Growing up on military bases is not an easy life. To combine that with incipient magickal powers would be potentially devastating. Now I'd had a chance to look closely, I reckoned that she was about thirty years old. She must have been doing this a while, and I made a mental note to Google *Toy Story*. I wonder how old she was when she picked up *Woody* as a nickname?

'And what brings you to Shawbury?'

'It's a long story. If you give the Constable a ring, she'll explain, but she wants you to help me.'

'I'll call her in a minute. Help with what?'

'I've spoken to the base commander. He's happy to let you fly as PIC to RAF Leeming tomorrow night. I'll pick you up and explain everything then.'

I'm sure you're wondering: *PIC* is short for *Pilot in Command* – what they call *Captain* on holiday jets. It would be my first time as PIC since before the crash that shattered my leg. I nodded my head slowly as I took it in. 'You've come a long way to tell me that.'

She shrugged. A very stiff shrug. 'I needed to see the CO, and I knew it would be much easier for you to believe if you saw me in person. And vice versa. I need you in Yorkshire on Friday.'

'Oh? Why?'

'New moon. The Spirits will be easier to see.'

That wasn't the most inviting incentive I've ever heard, but definitely intriguing. 'I can't wait. I'll text you my ETA before we take off. I'll try not to crash on the way over.'

'Thanks, Conrad, and don't forget to pack your dress uniform.' She saluted and left me to finish my coffee.

I waited until she'd left the mess and took the coffee outside, along with my fags and my phone. I called Hannah Rothman, my boss and the commanding officer of the King's Watch. She answered on the first ring.

'You've met Woody, then?' she said.

'I have. How come you decided that now was a good time for me to meet her?'

'She asked for your help. Your reputation spreads by the day, it seems.' Hannah is as dry as the white wine she slurps.

'It's a good job I have you to keep me modest, ma'am.'

'Quite right, too. What do you make of her?'

'More to the point, what can you tell me about her?'

'She's legit. Not up to me to say more than that. I can't order you to help her, you know.'

'Would it make your life awkward if I said no?'

Hannah laughed and finished the call by saying, 'You make my life awkward just by breathing, but several people will owe us a favour if you agree to help.'

'Then count me in. I'll keep you posted, ma'am.'

'Good. And take care, Conrad.'

1 — *Soft Landings*

It was a bit of an exaggeration to call it *night flying*. The sun had barely gone down, and it was definitely light enough to see any obstacles. Far too easy for my training officer. 'We'll go via Snowdon,' he announced. 'And just to make it interesting, you can touch down on top of Cader Idris.'

His definition of *interesting* clearly came from a different dictionary to mine. Putting a three tonne helicopter down on top of a mountain in the dark was under *daft, see scary* in my dictionary. It would be good practice, though. If we lived.

He flew as second pilot, and one of the next generation lurked in the back. She would be sitting in his seat when they dropped me off. I calculated the route and flying time before sending Woody a text, much to the training officer's disgust. 'Would you like to me to whistle *Yankee Doodle Dandy* while we manoeuvre?' I said.

'Shut up and get in, before I call it off and go home to my bed.'

The trouble with flying so fast (over 150mph) is that you can run into weather. The cold front that was going to rain off the weekend's cricket was already crossing the Irish Sea as we passed over Snowdonia, and Cader Idris has commanding views of the waves. During the day, of course.

Right now, it was getting distinctly blowy and the TO was swallowing nervously. He'd added the glory landing because he could, and because he didn't often get to boss a squadron leader around. Now that he could feel the chopper pitching, he was having second thoughts.

You can't actually land on the summit. I selected a flattish area just east that looked big enough on the map, provided I missed the plunge on either side down to a watery grave. I flew over the site, barely visible under the clouds, and said, 'Will that do?'

He swallowed hard. 'If you think it's safe.'

I took the Jupiter round in a big arc. You can't just plonk a helicopter on a sixpence: they take a long time to slow down. It was time to find out if my magickally augmented sense of direction would work under pressure.

Yes, is the answer. I let the skids touch the grass for a second before putting on the power and rising over the trig point on the actual summit.

'How did you do that without the ground display?' said the training officer with a squeak.

'Practice. Can we go to Leeming now?'

He shut up after that.

Woody found me lurking behind one of the hangars, sneaking a cigarette, and she tried not to let the disapproval show on her face. She looked much more human in civvies, with her hair in a ponytail and jeans instead of the uniform skirt.

'Good flight?' she asked.

'It was interesting. Are we going far?'

'Malton, north east of York. We're staying at the Talbot, and I've already checked us both in.'

That was a good job, because we wouldn't be there until well after one in the morning.

She pointed to the car park. 'That's mine.'

I peered into the dark. All I could see was a dumpster. 'Where?'

'There. The Yaris Hybrid.'

Oh. Not a dumpster. It just looked like one. 'Why don't you have a 4x4 or a sports car like normal Mages?'

Woody had stopped underneath a light. She looked at the car while she answered. 'Frances cycles everywhere or gets the train. I can't. She wanted me to get an all-electric car, but I have to dash all over the country at short notice. You can't do that in an EV, so this was the compromise. It does 80 miles to the gallon.'

'I'm sure it does. So long as I can fit in.'

By way of an answer, she clicked the remote and the hazards flashed. I had to put my kit bag on the back seat, because the "boot" was already full of wellingtons, waterproofs and a rucksack. I didn't ask where she kept her AK47. Perhaps it's just me that drives around with a small arsenal.

It took so long for me to adjust the seat to a position where my neck wasn't going to break that we were well out of the base before I surfaced. 'So what's this all about, Woody? If we're both at the hotel, I take it you don't live nearby.'

'Cambridge,' she said, as if that explained everything. When she glanced at my face and saw that it didn't, she shuffled in the driving seat. 'Most of the old airfields are around East Anglia and Lincolnshire, so I settled there. It's where I met Frances, too.'

'Your wife?'

'Yes. She's a Reader in English at the University. Malbranche College. You're from Gloucestershire, aren't you?'

'I suspect you know a lot more about me than that.'

'Only the magickal stuff. And that you're in a relationship.'

'I am. She's in India at the moment, visiting family. She'll be getting up soon.' We got on to the A170 and she put her foot down, or as far down as the Toyota would let her. 'Talking of getting up, what time are we on parade in the morning?'

'No rush. We're meeting some people at eleven, and it's not far from the hotel.'

I was getting tired of this. 'What people?'

She hemmed and checked the satnav. 'Archaeologists. They're doing a dig at former RAF Draxholt.'

'Never heard of it.'

'It was only in use for a short while, towards the end of the war. Not much more than a cleared airstrip and a few huts.'

'So they're not military archaeologists. What do they want and why are we seeing them? Why am *I* seeing them?'

'You can pretend to be my supervisor.' She said it with a laugh. 'That's why I asked you to bring your parade uniform.'

'Pretend?'

'Everyone needs a supervisor. You know, when you ring the call centre and get grief off them, you ask to speak to a supervisor. It isn't really a supervisor, it's their mate at the next desk. They say the same thing, so you ask to speak to the manager, but the manager's busy and they'll ring you tomorrow.'

'That makes me your mate at the next desk, then. What are we saying "no" to?'

'I want them to suspend the dig and clear the site from 12:00 tomorrow until 14:00 on Saturday, but they're not happy. There's a bunch of undergrads coming from ULIST for the weekend, and they don't want them going down the pub and getting wrecked.'

'Fine. Why do you want them off site? Presumably for magickal reasons.'

'I'm notified of all digs on Crown property and try to check them out first. They normally go home on Saturday nights, so I did my visit last weekend. We need them off-site tomorrow night.'

She went quiet. That didn't sound good.

'What happened last Saturday?'

'It's a bit complicated. I'd rather show you.'

She'd gone too far now. Any situation involving magick could put my life in danger as quickly as snapping your fingers. Even quicker without a proper briefing.

'Come on. Why show me when you're sitting here with nothing else to do but follow the Satnav?'

She drew a short breath through her nose and her arms went rigid on the steering wheel. Even in the dark, I could tell that she was blushing.

'It's because I'm not sure, sir. It's not dangerous, but it's all very unexpected. I'd say it was all old wives' tales, if I didn't talk to Spirits on a regular basis and if I wasn't banned from using the expression. Frances doesn't like it.'

I eased off a bit on the mission. She was clearly happier talking about her private life than her professional one. 'And what does Frances think of the world of magick? I take it she's not a natural.'

Woody barked a laugh. 'You could say that. If I'm honest, she doesn't want to believe at all, but she's got no choice. She just pretends it's not there and treats my life like it's a form of social work.' She hesitated. 'What does your girlfriend think of it? I take it she knows.'

'She doesn't just know, she was present at a manifestation of the Morrigan. And she's met the Allfather.'

'Wow! Frances's head would explode if that happened.' The undertone of jealousy was clear. 'What's her name, if you don't mind me asking?'

'Mina. Mina Desai. It's a shame you're so far away in Cambridge, or she'd recruit you for the women's cricket team.'

'She'd be disappointed if she did. Strictly women's rugby, me. Haven't played for ages.'

'Were you any good?'

'Not for me to say. I never had problems getting a game, though.'

'Then you should take coaching badges. There's a tremendous shortage of female sports coaches. That's why I'm the bowling coach for Clerkswell Ladies.'

She nodded. 'That's a good idea.'

She was being polite. Either she had no desire to get back into sport, or it was simply not in her life-plan at the moment. Or perhaps it wasn't in *Frances's* life-plan. At least we'd established a bit of common ground. I moved back to the important stuff.

'I get that you don't want to pre-judge the case. Can you at least tell me why you called me in for the magickal elements? I know what people say about me, and I don't mean the Dragonslayer bit.'

She glanced at me and grinned. 'And what do you *think* they say? I'll let you know how accurate it is.'

I reached into the back and ran my fingers over the gun lying on top of my open kit bag. A ripple of magick flowed through the car. 'Did you feel that?'

'Yes. It was your Badge of Office, wasn't it?'

'It was, and it's stamped into a SIG P226 handgun. The Dwarf who made it gave it a name: *The Hammer*. People talk about me in the same way – "When your only tool is a hammer, you see all problems as nails." I get sent into situations where there's a likelihood of lethal force.'

She opened her mouth to say something and changed her mind. She swallowed and said, 'I called you in because of the Annex of Westphalia.'

This is a magickal pledge that every Mage is supposed to make: *to abjure the wars of Popes and Princes*. In other words, not to take your magick into a mundane battle. 'Go on.'

'Because of the Annex, and because you came late to magick, you're the only Mage I've ever come across with actual, mundane combat experience. And in the RAF, too. You know what these guys have been through.'

'Apart from the dying part. I hope never to have the experience of dying in an aircraft.'

'Most of the Spirits don't either. Or not the ones I deal with. They're more recent deaths, and they haunt the airfields for all sorts of reasons. They miss it, I think.'

'This isn't your first case, obviously, so why do you need me?'

She sighed. 'This lot are different. The Peculier Necromancer before me had done it for decades. She was the first woman to hold a senior post in the magickal hierarchy, even if it is pretty much under the radar. So to speak. Her childhood sweetheart died in a Lancaster Bomber and came back to be with her in Spirit. They were a team. Quite sweet, really.'

I thought it was downright creepy, not to mention bizarre and dangerous that a royal officer had formed a team with the ghost of her late boyfriend. Clearly Necromancers see this world (and the next) rather differently to you and me. Unless you are a Necromancer, and in that case, I shall try to be more understanding.

The Satnav interrupted, telling her to *take care on steep hill*. It was a good warning, and I shut up while she negotiated Sutton Bank. When she'd finished, I said, 'Just tell me why this one's different, and I'll change the subject.'

'These Spirits only really manifested when the archaeological dig started. There's something funny about them. I'm not sure they're real. That's all.'

It took me a couple of seconds to pick up on the word *real*, which proves how deeply my perspectives have been warped by magick. Very little of this was real in any sense of the word. 'Real ghosts? Real airmen? Real what?'

'I don't want to pre-judge things. Sorry. I'm not trying to be a pain, but it's hard to put into words. Do you mind?'

I did mind. I minded a lot, but Hannah had told me that people would owe the Watch a favour if I helped out. I moved position, as best I could, and said, 'So, did you go to Salomon's House or one of the Circles to get your magickal training?'

She flicked a glance over and gave me a rueful smile that surely came from her father: I've seen it on the faces of so many technical officers over the years that she must have learnt it from him. 'I was hoping for something on a completely non-magickal subject,' she said. 'Like, "Do you prefer Strictly Come Dancing or I'm a Celebrity?" Something like that. I prefer Strictly, by the way.'

'And I prefer the beer in the Inkwell to both of those. I'm surprised that Frances goes in for such things.' As soon as the words were out of my mouth, I realised what I'd said. 'Sorry. I'm tired. I didn't mean it that way.'

"Salright. She pretends to look down on Strictly, but she loves it really. I know that because she watches it when I'm out on business – like last weekend – and then she watches it again the next day with me, and she can't stop herself giving spoilers away because she gets so worked up.' She spoke with a mixture of affection and secret triumph. She clearly loved Frances a lot, no question. There was also no question that their relationship had issues.

'I'll give you a choice,' I said. 'Helicopters, cricket, Spanish villas or Dragons. That's all I'm up for tonight.'

'You gave a seminar on Dragons at Newton's House, didn't you?'

'I did.'

'So you don't mind talking about it?'

'Not at bit. It all started with an egg…'

And I was still talking when we got to Malton.

It's a sleepy little town at the best of times, and at one in the morning there really wasn't a lot going on. We passed a whole stack of substantial houses on the way in, and the town centre was just coming into view when we arrived at the four-square Georgian block of the Talbot Hotel. Woody slowed right down and the electric motor took over. Her Yaris was so quiet that it didn't even wake the night porter.

I extracted myself from the cramped car with some difficulty and picked up my bag. Woody handed over a room key and manila envelope while I grabbed a quick ciggie.

'See you in the morning, Conrad. Sleep well.'

'And you.'

We made our way through the silent corridors of the substantial old inn and parted with a wave. The room was in an odd corner, but finished to a very high standard. I summoned the energy to get undressed and forced myself to Google one item before sending home a request. I collapsed on to the bed, and my last act before plunging into sleep was to send Mina a WhatsApp.

Arrived safe. No idea what the hell's going on. Love you. Conrad. XXX.

I didn't get a reply.

2 — *Lessons of the Past*

Woody looked a bit dishevelled at breakfast. 'What?' she said when I stood looking at her.

'Don't tell me you're going in civvies,' I said. 'Last time I checked, a Cambridge sweatshirt was not Parade Uniform.'

'No point getting jam down it. I'll change after breakfast. Have some of my tea, if you want.'

I sat down and put the unopened manila envelope on the table. A waitress offered me a menu, and I said, 'I know what I want, thanks. More tea, toast and the full English, please. One fried egg.'

'Of course, sir,' she said smoothly. She turned my teacup the right way up pulled out her notepad. Customer service is very good at the Talbot.

Woody had noticed the sealed envelope but was too nervous to say anything. I poured myself some of her tea and sat back. 'How's Dr Eder this morning? I presume you've been in touch. Is she looking forward to her lecture on Christina Rossetti?'

She flinched back, alarmed. 'Why have you been checking up on me?'

'To level the playing field a bit. I told you last night that Myfanwy the Druid is doing time as my housekeeper, and she gets up very early. Before I crashed out last night, I asked her to track down any Frances she could find at Malbranche College. Is that where you met?'

Woody went bright red. When she'd avoided the question about her magickal education, she'd also avoided saying that she'd started at Cambridge as a mundane undergraduate before transferring to Salomon's House as a late developing Mage. Dr Frances Eder is a dozen years older than "Bobbi" and was already established at Malbranche College when Woody matriculated. Frances was also married (to a man) and had a child. That child would now be fourteen.

The arrival of my food gave her a chance to gather her dignity. 'Frances is a professional,' she said. 'I started on philosophy, not English, so yes, I knew who she was, but we didn't start dating until after I'd left and gone to Salomon's House. Satisfied?' I lifted my knife and fork in a gesture of surrender and carried on chewing. She pointed to the envelope. 'Why haven't you opened that? Too busy checking up on me?'

I swallowed. 'Partly. And partly I wanted a cigarette. What's in it?'

'Open it and see.'

I was tempted to play the naughty boy and say no, but my professional instinct kicked in. I was supposed to be the senior officer, after all. Spearing the last of the sausage, I wiped my hands and ripped open the envelope.

It hadn't been very thick to start with, and most of the contents was a printout from the Department of Archaeology at University of Lancashire Institute of Science and Technology. It was a proposal for a dig, and meant nothing to me. I flicked through the pages to the end, where I found maps. Now those I could understand.

Or not. According to one of the maps, I was eating breakfast under Lake Pickering. I looked at the ceiling, and it was dry. I looked back at the map and saw an annotation: *Limit of glacial ice*. Not a contemporary map, then. Something tickled the back of my memory, but I was keen to get on solid ground and shuffled the sheet to the back. The other map was a good old Ordnance Survey printout, marked to show former RAF Draxholt.

I poured more tea and ran my fingers along the contour lines to get a feeling for the area. Bomber Command had chosen a perfectly flat area north east of the village of Sherburn, in a typically wet place. I could see all the drainage channels running into the river Derwent. Unlike Suffolk, the airmen would at least have had a *view* of some hills. 'I wonder why they put it there?' I said, without realising I was talking out loud.

'Bribery,' said Woody.

'Sorry?'

'The landowner was fed up with labour shortages and he bribed the Air Ministry to build there. He was compensated. They only ever really used it as a relief landing strip – when those big raids limped home, they were always short of fuel and needed as many safe places as possible. It wasn't uncommon for exhausted pilots to fluff the landing and break the undercarriage, blocking the runway for those behind.'

'I know how they felt. Been there. Any fatalities?'

'None recorded.'

There was one other annotation, in the top corner, pointing north east and saying *To Star Carr*. 'What's that?'

'It's in the bid.'

I folded the OS map and put it in my pocket; the others I replaced in the envelope. 'I'll read it while you get changed. How far away is it?'

'Half an hour. I'll see you outside at ten thirty.'

She got up and I cadged a mug of coffee from the obliging staff that I could take to one of the outside tables. I was going to make the most of the morning sun because the weather forecast was not good for later.

I was lighting a cigarette when a large black luxury saloon pulled in. The chauffeur, in matching black, nipped smartly out of the front and opened the rear door. A suit got out of the back and headed into the hotel with barely a nod in the direction of the man who'd safely brought him here. The chauffeur's shoulders relaxed as the tension left him and he looked around. I saw his right hand move to his jacket pocket in the unconscious gesture of a fellow smoker before he realised that he couldn't leave the car where it was. A mad idea came into my head, and I nipped back into the hotel.

When he'd disposed of his vehicle, the chauffeur reappeared at the same time as a waitress with a pot of coffee for him. The sheer joy in his eyes turned to suspicion when she told him that the RAF guy had paid for it.

'Not that I'm not grateful, sir,' he said, 'but I don't know anything about why he's here, if you're after information.' He pointedly hadn't touched the coffee.

'I don't know who he is, nor do I care. It's you I'm interested in. Go ahead. You look like you need it. Here.' I offered him a cigarette and he poured himself a cup, adding cream and sugar.

He took a slurp and tilted his head. 'Go on then.'

'It's like this…'

The Audi's suspension took the field in its stride, and the chauffeur ignored the line of parked cars to take us to a gazebo on the edge of a series of marked zones that signalled the start of the dig. I waited for him to get out and open the door, enjoying the look on Woody's face as she emerged from the gazebo to receive me.

I got out of the car and said, 'Thank you. An hour should be ample.'

'Sir.'

Woody saluted and turned puce, all in one clockwork motion. I saluted back. 'Good morning, Flight Lieutenant Woodhouse.'

'Morning, sir,' she said out loud. She lowered her arm and her voice to whisper, 'How the fuck did you pull that off? I thought you'd gone and left me in the lurch. Sir.'

I leaned down. 'I said I'd arrive in the manner befitting your CO, and I did. Your toy car is not befitting. You want your CO to look important, don't you?' I straightened up and raised my voice. 'Good work. Let's get started, shall we?'

We had an audience. Three archaeologists, clutching enamel mugs, had come out of the gazebo to watch, and another half-dozen had stopped work in the trenches to see what was going on. I nodded to everyone and held out my arm, ushering Woody to make introductions. She jumped to.

'Sir, this is Professor Cargill, and Doctors Rice and Gardner, all of ULIST. This is Squadron Leader Clarke.'

There was a shaking of hands and I got a good look at them. They were all dressed in variations of technical fabrics – boots, quick-dry trousers and aerobic tops, as much of a uniform as the light blue that Woody and I were sporting. I felt the calluses on their hands as we shook, and I noted the sun damage on their skin. I felt especially sorry for Dr Rice, the female member of the trio, who looked a lot older than the age given in her profile. Perhaps she'd lied.

'ULIST,' I said. 'That's in Cairndale, isn't it?'

Woody gave me an odd look.

'Yes,' said Professor Cargill. He was 48 and wore a floppy hat to protect his bald head.

I looked over at the digging. When the trio turned to look with me, the lesser diggers stopped staring and went back to work. 'What are you hoping to find under here?' I said.

Woody's odd look turned to alarm. 'It was all in the proposal document, sir,' she said hastily.

'Was it? Didn't get that far,' I said. 'I'm sure that Professor Cargill would prefer to show me and explain things in person, wouldn't you, Professor?'

Cargill was taken aback. 'Now you're here, it wouldn't hurt.' He led me to a virgin piece of grass, roped off but as yet undisturbed. The others fell into step behind. 'Do you know much about the late Mesolithic … erm, sorry, I didn't catch your first name?'

'It's Conrad. Isn't that the stone age?'

He waved his hand. The universal gesture of an academic forced to use terms he's not happy with. 'You could say that. It makes more sense if I say *hunter-gatherers*. After them came the farmers who built Stonehenge, amongst other things.'

'Right.'

He pointed north east. 'Just over there, near Scarborough, is Star Carr, the best preserved Mesolithic site in Britain. It was preserved because the site was next to a lake, and the lake filled with peat. To cut a long story short, we're doing an exploratory dig here, hoping to find something similar.'

'Or better,' I said, with a smile.

Cargill turned his head sharply. He was a professor, an academic. They can be as ruthless as the businessman whose car I'd commandeered. More so.

'Quite,' said Cargill. 'I don't suppose you've heard of the Storegga Slide?'

I shook my head. I could have made a joke about water slides at the North Yorkshire Water Park down the road at Wykeham, but that would have been crass. I was aiming slightly higher than that.

'Around eight thousand years ago – 6200BCE – a huge chunk of underwater cliff collapsed. Near Norway. It was huge. The cliff was as big as Iceland, and it slid down into the deep Atlantic Basin. The tabloid newspapers said it caused "The First Brexit."'

'Let's keep Brexit out of things, shall we? What happened?'

'A tsunami is what happened. One of the biggest to leave evidence. A wall of water washed all the way up to Stirling in Scotland. It also submerged the land bridge that made Britain a peninsula. That tsunami turned us into an island people.'

'And it washed up here?'

'It did. We've done some computer modelling, and we think that the Moors may have deflected some of the energy.'

I'd been right about the outlook – flat as a pancake. Cargill gestured to the distant hills. 'This would have been devastated, all right, but if the waves were lower, evidence of Mesolithic life might have been preserved.'

'Interesting. How are things going?'

He led us over to the dig area that was being worked. I glanced behind us and saw that Woody was giving me a furious look. Doctors Rice and Gardner were looking bemused. Good.

The worked area was the size of a tennis court. A tennis court that had been attacked by weird cubic moles. There was a small digger in the corner of the field, and it had been used to scrape away the top two feet of earth, now sitting in a heap at a distance from the dig.

The rectangular hole had then been levelled to a perfect flat surface, and four seemingly random holes about the size of a grave had been excavated, none of them perpendicular to the main dig. It did nothing for my sense of order to see them at odd angles like that.

Cargill didn't explain, but I'm guessing that the flat base layer was a reference point, down from which these grave holes would be measured. Each hole had a pair of diggers, one down and one sifting. Wheelbarrows and planks marked the track to the spoil heap.

'We're time-travelling,' said Cargill. 'Every day we travel further into the past.' It was a well-rehearsed introduction. I cut it short.

'Found anything yet?'

'We're still working through the alluvial deposits. The river has been putting down soil here for thousands of years.'

'Why this spot? Why not over there?'

Cargill grinned. 'I'd like to say that we used aerial photographs and ground-penetrating radar, but our target zone is too deep to show up. I chose this spot because it was near the road, but not too near. Would you like to go down?'

'You've been most kind, but I think I've seen enough. I don't want to hold you up, not when things are going to stop in half an hour anyway.'

He froze to the spot. 'Shall we discuss that over some fresh coffee?' he said to the whole company.

'Good idea,' said Woody. 'Sir, could I have a word first?'

She held out her hand to drag me away from the archaeologists. Her fingers stopped moving when they hit the magnetic field around my sleeve. There isn't a real magnetic field, of course, it's just that she realised she was about to lay hands on a senior officer. She drew it back and pursed her lips. I pointed to her car and we walked over.

She waited until we were well out of earshot before speaking. There was definitely steam coming out of her ears. 'What's with the Prince Andrew impersonation? Sir. You've made me look a right plank.'

'No, I haven't. I've softened them up, and now I have a plan.'

She stopped walking. 'What plan? Tell me.'

'No. I'd stop for a cigarette, but that would be grounds for a charge, so we'll go back and wrap this up, shall we?'

I turned and strode back to the gazebo. I'm six foot four and wearing trousers; Woody wisely chose not to keep up with me. Walking away like that was a cheap shot, I admit. I'll live with the guilt.

I took one of the chairs in the shade and took my cap off. There were five assorted camp and cottage chairs around a remarkably sturdy set of conference tables. They must have been fastened together underneath, and the stains and scratches testified to a life more used to sorting dirty finds than hosting meetings.

Cargill sat down and kept his hat on. Dr Gardner put a battered Manchester United mug in front of me, and Woody sat down to my left. 'No coffee, thanks,' she said. I took a sip from the mug. She'd made the right choice: it was too hot, bitter and thin.

Cargill took a slurp. He must have an asbestos mouth, and it left him free to speak first. 'Where have you come from, Conrad? I can't imagine it was round the corner.'

I put the mug down. As far from me as possible. 'I stayed at the Talbot in Malton last night. Thoroughly recommended. Are you all sleeping in those tents?'

'I am,' said Dr Gardner, speaking for the first time. 'We get a fee and it's up to us how we spend it.'

'And I'm too old for tents,' said Dr Rice. 'Look, Mr Clarke, are you going to give us any idea of what's going on? We've been very patient. I think Professor Cargill was trying to be polite, but I'm too old for that as well.' She leaned on the sturdy table. 'You want us to lose valuable excavation time and disrupt the site experience visit. Fine. The rain might do that for you tomorrow anyway. But Ms Woodhouse won't say what the problem is, and you've waltzed around here without saying who you really are or what's going on.'

'I really am Squadron Leader Clarke. Do you want to see my ID or call my CO?'

'Just get on with it,' said Rice. She was clearly bad cop.

I reached into my jacket and pulled out the top of a green form. The royal coat of arms was just visible. I tapped the paper and said, 'This is an order under the Protection of Military Remains Act 1986. It'll stop you doing anything in this field for a long time.'

It was actually my expenses form, but they wouldn't know that. This was a poker game, so were they going to call my bluff?

'But we checked,' said Cargill. 'There are no military interests here.'

'There was a confusion over the paperwork. Bureaucracy and all that. You can appeal if you want. I presume ULIST can afford an appeal.' I slid the paper back, out of view. 'This is a University dig, isn't it?'

'Of course,' snapped Cargill. 'We wouldn't be bringing undergraduates to an unlicensed operation.'

It was my turn to lean forward. 'And the funding? According to the committee minutes, funding was only given for the dig at the Trough of Bowland. Not this one.'

Gardner looked nonplussed. Rice looked at the table. Cargill did a good dying fish impersonation. I finished him off.

'Where did the money come from, Professor?' I leaned back. He was skewered.

I turned to Dr Rice. 'Can I let you into a state secret? On a fully deniable basis, of course.'

She nodded rather than commit herself to an answer. It was good enough for me.

'Flight Lieutenant Woodhouse has done an excellent job under difficult circumstances. It was my decision not to bring her into the loop, and I regret it now, which is why I've come up here myself. Before we go any further, am I right in thinking that there is nothing you want down to a depth of one metre?'

Dr Rice's eyes narrowed, and Cargill tuned back in. 'No…' said Rice.

'Good. If you clear off at noon, we'll do our bit and be gone. There may be a hole left behind. I personally guarantee not to go deeper than one metre.'

They weren't going to let go like that. They're professionally curious. 'What on earth for?' said Rice.

I took my hat off the floor and brushed some grass off the brim. 'A lot of things were buried after the war. Sometimes literally. Bad decisions were airbrushed away. Accidents were covered up.' I placed my cap in front of me, the RAF badge pointing squarely at Dr Rice. 'In July 1943, the city of Hull was bombed by Germany. That's only 30 miles away. Twenty people were killed, and that was only the latest operation.' She nodded as I was confirming something she already knew. 'Later that month, the Allies bombed Hamburg.'

'It was terrible,' said Gardner. 'A war crime.'

Oops. I'd have to watch my step if he'd heard of it. 'Possibly, Dr Gardner. Personally, I disagree, but what happened here was unquestionably a crime.'

They all looked at me. 'The second night of the Hamburg raid was curtailed by storm. A lot of the bombers turned back, and one of them got properly lost. It flew over Hull, and the ground defences shot at it. They thought it was a German plane. The crew bailed out. Most of them. The pilot managed to limp on to here and crashed. That wasn't the crime, though. The crime happened after the crash.'

I paused long enough for what I'd said to sink in, but not so long that they felt like they could ask questions. 'Unfortunately, the officer in charge of RAF Draxholt decided the best way to avoid awkward questions was to burn the evidence, along with the British anti-aircraft shells inside it. They dragged the pilot out and rushed him to hospital. He was unconscious. He couldn't tell them that the poor sod on the radio was injured, not dead. They burnt him. Alive. And when they took the wreckage apart, they found him, buried him and denied it all.'

Rice couldn't bear it any longer. 'How did this come out? Where did they bury him? Why isn't this in the records?'

I turned my cap around so that the badge faced me. 'When the pilot woke up in hospital, it all came out. The base commander was quietly dealt with, but he never said where the body was. We only discovered that in a deathbed confession after the war.' I sighed. 'Leading Aircraftman Tomkins wasn't married. His mother died in the London Blitz. His brother was told that he'd landed in the sea and that his body was never found. Someone – I really have no idea who – decided that Tomkins should rest where he was, and the documents were never added to the file.' I patted my pocket. 'They can be added now, if you want, and I'll serve the Military Remains order. Or you can let us get on with it tonight. The result will be the same, either way. It's your choice, Professor Cargill.'

'We'll down tools,' said Cargill, before Rice or Gardner could interrupt. 'Early finish for everyone. I'll get on to the department and arrange for the minibus to go to Scarborough tomorrow instead of here. We'll show them round Star Carr in the morning. It's a useful opportunity.'

A purr from the field announced the return of my temporary chauffeur. I put my cap on and shook hands. 'I am very grateful to you all.' I didn't want to linger now that I'd won the point, and I'd be back soon enough to have a good look round.

Woody walked with me to the waiting car. Her face was a blank. 'Can you make sure they clear off and join me for lunch in the Talbot?'

'Yes, sir.' When she saluted, her face was still giving nothing away.

3 — *Teamwork*

'I don't know whether to thank you or send you back to Shawbury,' said Woody when she found me at the pub, changed out of my uniform and enjoying a drink. 'Mostly I want to shout at you. That was outrageous, dangerous and embarrassing.'

'Go and get changed,' I said. 'That's an order.'

She looked a lot more comfortable when she came back. Even angrier, but more comfortable. I didn't offer to buy her a drink.

'Do you know what they really say about you, sir?' was her opening gambit.

'I'm sure you're going to tell me.'

'Put it this way: I was advised to pack a long spoon.'

In other words, I was the Devil. 'I'm sure Hannah didn't say that. She's Jewish, if you didn't know.'

'Stop patronising me! She said, "Keep him on a tight leash," if you must know.'

'And you can stop patronising me. You've dragged me off a course doing something I love to get you out of a hole. You – and you're not the first Mage to do this – you treated me like a spade. Something useful, but not too clever, and something you need to wash your hands after using.'

'Frances was right. You're a typical man: you think you know best and the little woman gets pushed to the side.'

I was so tempted to say *not so little*. So tempted. Instead, I took a deep breath. 'You told me you wanted them off site. You didn't say how I should do it.'

'Negotiate. I said they had to stay away until 14:00 tomorrow so that you'd have room to give them a concession and let them in earlier. Instead, you created a ticking bomb. When they realise it was all a load of bullshit you gave them, it could easily explode in our faces. My face, in particular.'

'You mean that I was supposed to negotiate with them, but you weren't going to negotiate with me. Why didn't you tell me your plan? It wouldn't have worked, by the way.'

'I was going to tell you on the way over, then you pulled that stunt with the chauffeur and blindsided me. That was outrageous, by the way, but my plan would have worked.'

'No it wouldn't. Why would the diggers go off site? Where would they go?'

'I usually bung them a couple of hundred in disruption expenses.'

I threw my hands in the air. 'And you didn't tell me that, either! I hope you really do need me tonight, or I'm catching the next train to Cheltenham. I'll make sure you get a military funeral.'

'What the fuck are you on about now?'

'You missed it, didn't you? You're too trusting, that's your problem.' I pulled up. If I didn't defuse things, we could end up falling out properly. She was about to come back. 'Let me finish, then you can tell me to fuck off if you want.'

She folded her arms and sat back in her chair.

I moved my drink and the ashtray to the edge of the table, clearing the way between us. 'I did do my homework. I looked at the proposal and said to myself *this should not be happening*. Cargill's proposal had no evidence to justify it. Nothing. He has a good reputation. So does Dr Rice. Why would he pitch a no-hope proposal to the University unless he knew something?'

I left it as a question to draw her back in to the conversation. She didn't unfold her arms, but she did say, 'What do you mean?'

'The ULIST committee passed his methodology, his health and safety and his risk assessments, but they wouldn't give him any money. He must have known that. He spent hours – days – on that proposal, and the only reason he'd do that was if he had a private sponsor lined up. He went very quiet when I asked him about it.'

This time she unfolded her arms. 'I did notice that, and I also noticed that you didn't press him on it.'

'The main objective was to get them off site. Their sponsor is a can of worms we can open later, when we've got more of an idea what the magickal implications of all this are.'

She leaned forward and didn't object to my use of *we*. 'You don't think there's a Mage behind the dig, do you?'

'Very possibly. I don't believe in coincidences like that. Why did they choose *that* field to dig in? There's no archaeological reason – he sidestepped my questions about aerial photography because they were going to dig there, and only there. And this one-horse landing strip suddenly becomes haunted? Not a coincidence. I didn't get any sense of magick at the dig, but I wouldn't. Did you?'

'No, but you're right about the coincidence. Is that what you meant about getting me a military funeral?'

'Yes. I don't think we'll be alone at Draxholt tonight, and I don't mean the ghosts. We could have very human company. And that really is one of the problems of bringing me on board.'

'Eh?'

'As you said, I'm quite well known. When Cargill tells his paymaster that *Squadron Leader Clarke* was there, they will either go into hiding or bring reinforcements.'

'Good point. What do you suggest we do?'

I looked at the sky. We should be good for a few hours before it rained. 'Have a decent lunch, then prepare to spend the rest of the day at Draxholt. I want Maddy to have a look at it.'

'Who?'

I took an Egyptian Tube out of my case and removed the cap. I shook out a few inches of willow wand. 'This is my dowsing rod. It contains some form of a Spirit called Madeleine.' Woody already had her hand stretched out. 'It might not be safe to touch,' I said.

She hovered her fingers. 'Where did you get that?'

I replaced the cap on the tube. 'I'll tell you over lunch, and we can work out a proper plan. With contingencies. How does that sound?'

'Good.' She looked down and rested the tips of her fingers on the weatherbeaten wood of the table. 'I'm so used to working on my own. I don't like relying on other people.'

I seized the olive branch. 'And I do like pulling rabbits out of the hat. It would have been better if we'd discussed my performance first.'

'Full disclosure?' she said with a smile.

'Full disclosure,' I replied. 'And talking of which, it would have been even better if I'd had the RAF file on Draxholt. I could have added some convincing details. Have you got a copy?'

She shook her head. 'Only the digital version, and I got that from Professor Cargill. I asked the Ministry of Defence, but they said they couldn't find it. It's probably in transit somewhere after they made a copy for ULIST.'

'Doesn't surprise me. Drink?'

She nodded and looked up. 'White wine spritzer, please.'

I came back with the menus, her drink and a coffee for me. One pint is enough at lunchtime.

'Cheers, Conrad.' She lifted her drink and took a sip. 'You had me believing that story about poor Aircraftman Tomkins. Where did it come from? Some thriller?'

'In a way. I adapted it from something that I was once involved with. In those days, you really did have to use a long spoon to sup with me.' I lit a cigarette. 'So what made you want to study philosophy?'

'We'd better dig a grave,' I said. 'Just in case someone asks.'

'The whole place feels like a grave,' said Woody. She gave an appropriate shiver to go with her comment. That could be her sensitivity to Spirits, or it could be the wind that was blowing down the Vale of Pickering. Being an insensitive sort of chap, I zipped up my fleece. Definitely the wind. It was a cold, wet westerly wind. It could be a lot worse: when the wind blows *up* the Vale, off the North Sea, then you definitely need a lot of extra layers.

She was right about general atmosphere. Bereft of archaeologists, Draxholt had reverted to being a field with holes and tents. A very flat field in a notoriously hilly county. Yorkshire should be sweeping Dales, heathery moors and terraced houses climbing cobbled streets, not hedgeless fields and intensive agriculture. Then again, Yorkshire is a very big place.

In fact, one of the things which made Draxholt stand out from the surrounding nameless fields was that it *did* have a hedge. A thick one. Another was its size: as big as three fields and long enough for heavy bombers to land (but not take off). That gave me a question to answer when I walked round it.

'Can you use a digger?' I asked, in what I hoped was a neutral and non-patronising way.

She grinned. 'As it happens, I can. That's what growing up with a father in the RE does for you.'

'Good. You can dig a nice hole when I've finished.'

'What do you want me to do while you do your thing with the rod?'

'Sit by the gate and keep watch. Catch up on emails. Play Candy Crush. Whatever, so long as you don't fall asleep.'

'Angry Birds,' she said. 'Definitely Angry Birds. I'll commandeer a comfy chair. You're going to be a while, aren't you?'

I looked at the field again. My bad leg twinged in anticipation. 'Yes.'

Woody set herself up by the gate and I got Maddy's tube out. I've found that I get the best results going anti-clockwise and working inwards from the edge, and the archaeological diggings were to the left of the gate. I went to the right, leaving them until last, and got myself ready.

I have two magickal talents. Very minor ones. Just enough for me to count as a Mage. One is being a Navigator, a life-saving talent in itself but something you're born with, so not recognised as having any importance in the world of magick. My other talent is Geomancy – sensing the flow and direction of Lux, the mysterious force that causes magickal effects. If I went to the Invisible College as an undergraduate, the only module I'd pass would be basic Geomancy. Basic. Advanced Geomancers don't just sense Ley lines, they create and repair them.

I opened the Egyptian Tube, closed my eyes and shook the willow wand into my hand.

Water. Trickling water running over granite stones and bubbling happily in the sunshine. I always get water when I meet Maddy, and I've no idea why. Usually it stops with a sense of water, and a sense of her presence nearby. In places of great power, it turns into something visible. I've had the sea, lakes and a river. With a jolt, memories turned into perceptions, and there she was.

'Who's that gel?'

Madeleine died during the Edwardian period, and dresses appropriately. Today was something floaty and white. Perfect for a picnic. She also has an unmoderated upper class drawl, hence *gel* for *girl*. She was staring at Woody, and Woody was staring back.

'Well?' said Maddy. 'Are you going to stand there like a broken statue, or are you going to introduce us? And mind your feet.'

Ermmm? What? I looked down. Water was flowing towards me over the grass. Literally over the grass, as if the field were made of tiles, not dry soil and thirsty plants. This did not look good. In visions with Maddy, water means Lux, and Lux is power. That much power meant a serious injury. I stepped back, but it was gathering speed.

'Shut her down!' shouted Woody. 'Now!'

I still had the Egyptian Tube in my left hand, and rammed the willow rod into it.

'NOOOOO!' screeched Maddy.

Her scream nearly pierced my ears. She made a grab for my hand as I fumbled for the cap. Ice water fingers gripped my arm. It was the first time we'd touched, and her Spirit fingers were colder than a burial at sea in Arctic waters. My arm was frozen in place and I could feel crystals of frost forming on my skin.

Woody jumped out of her chair and started to run towards us. The growing lake of Lux-water was in the way, and she was going to run right through it. 'Please, Maddy,' I said, trying to force the nerves in my fingers to listen to the screaming in my brain and close the tube.

Maddy glanced up. 'Stay back, stupid girl,' she said.

She slackened her grip enough for the signal to get through, and my fingers closed the cap on the tube. I twisted the magickal seal and everything went grey. Then black.

Is that coffee I smell? Real coffee?

'C'mon, Conrad. Wake up. Please.' Woody sounded upset about something.

'Coffee,' I mumbled.

'What?'

'I smell the coffee, therefore I must wake up. That's wrong. I should wake up *then* smell the coffee.'

'What are you on about?'

I risked opening my eyes, and saw an ant. An ant-sized ant, on a blade of grass. Woody had put me in the recovery position. I groaned loudly, just to reassure her that I was alive, then started to move things. They all worked. 'Give me a hand to sit up, will you?'

Woody eased me into a sitting position. 'Look at my finger,' she said, holding up a digit in front of my nose.

Aah. A concussion test. I did what I was told.

When she'd finished, and decided I didn't need an ambulance, she rocked back on her heels and asked what a normal person would ask. 'Are you okay?'

'I don't know. Could I have some water and an actual cup of coffee. A chair would be good, too.'

'Yeah. Hang on.'

She scampered off, and I lifted my right sleeve. My arm was bruised and burnt in four small places, where Maddy's delicate, ghostly fingers had gripped it. When Woody came back with a chair and bottle of water, I showed it to her.

'Ouch. How bad is it?'

I drank deeply. 'I think it looks worse than it is. I'll try to get up, if my leg will let me.'

Woody looked down at my leg and shuffled uncomfortably. 'I saw it. You thrashed around at first, and your trouser leg rolled up. I thought Maddy had done it to you, then I realised it was an old wound.'

I gripped the camp chair and levered myself into a half-stand before flopping on to the seat. 'The wound may be old, but the pain is new every morning.' I reached into my pocket. 'You deserve this.'

I held out the specially printed *Merlyn's Tower Irregulars* badge. She took it dubiously and turned it over in her hand. 'What is it?'

'You ran towards the danger. You might have been destroyed when you hit the river of Lux. Telling me to shut Maddy down saved my life. It's just a token.'

She looked at it again. 'Nice picture, ugly badge. What the hell happened there?'

'I was going to ask you the same thing. Maddy has never appeared before without enough Lux around to light up the sky. A Dwarven Hall or something. There's nothing like that here.'

She looked away, towards the centre of the field. 'I'll get us some coffee and bring my chair over.' We had brought three flasks of decent coffee with us. As she walked towards the gazebo, she put the Merlyn's Tower Irregulars badge in her pocket without thinking.

My arm was starting to throb a little when she got back. Getting at the first aid kit would be my first job when I stood up. After coffee. And a cigarette.

'I think it might be me,' said Woody. 'I think I may have given Maddy a window.'

'A window?'

She let out a deep breath. 'When I spoke to the Constable, I asked if you'd had any experience with Spirits. She told me about your Great-Something-Grandfather.'

'Spectre Thomas. He haunted the family home for nearly four hundred years. I've also met Helen of Troy.'

Her head jerked up. 'Helen? And you survived intact?'

'Yes. Another time, Woody.'

'Right. Well, in the world of Spirits, Helen is at the top of the tree, and Spectre Thomas is – was – about half way down. Thomas did a physical manifestation, didn't he?'

'He did. He also drank my single malt whisky.'

She nodded. 'And that's the difference. Thomas retained *all* his memories, and all the physical elements of his earthly life. Most don't.'

'What do you mean?'

'The Spirits I deal with aren't all there. They *think* they remember the taste of whisky, but they don't. They can just remember liking it. There's a big difference. No matter how much Lux was available, your average ghost couldn't manifest physically as a complete person.'

'Right.'

'And that's where I come in. What do you know about the different planes of existence?'

I remembered standing by a hedge outside a golf course in Warwickshire. I remembered my partner in the Watch, Vicky Robson, drawing Lux from a magickal post and disappearing in front of me. According to Vicky, she then walked through the hedge as if it wasn't there, and when she was inside the golf course, she entered the Realm of the Fae. I said as much to Woody.

She nodded, calibrating my levels of ignorance. 'I studied at Salomon's House, and they use different terms there, but I'll stick to the old ones. A Necromancer can open a window between the Spirit world and this one. It allows Spirits to see and be seen, and to interact more easily.'

'Sounds dangerous.'

'It can be. All magick can be dangerous, but you're right, bringing another entity into the equation makes it inherently unpredictable. The real Art of Necromancy is dealing with them after you've found them.'

'You seem to be making a good job of it.'

'Thanks. Every Spirit wants something different, of course, but nearly all ghosts want to be at peace. They're not happy where they are. My job is to find out what's causing the problem and to smooth it over. Sometimes I pass on messages, or promise to. Sometimes I offer reassurance.' She looked down at her coffee. 'And sometimes I have to intervene. Sometimes I have to unravel them. Exorcise them. Destroy them. Call it what you like, but it's not easy.'

I gave her a moment. 'When I met Helen of Troy, she'd been brought in by a Summoner. What's the difference?'

'What's the difference between you and a murderer?'

Ouch. Where did that come from? The surprise – and hurt – must have shown in my face. And maybe a little guilt, too.

She bit her lip. 'Sorry. That was meant to be more theoretical than it sounded.'

'It's hard not to take something like that personally, Woody. Go on, you did just save my life.'

She scratched her arm to get rid of a sudden heat rush. 'It's down to intent, is what I was trying to say. Being a Necromancer is just like learning Urdu or Polish: it allows you to deal directly with the Spirit world instead of having to go through translators, but a Summoner wants to get something out of a Spirit, either by bribery or force. And yes, before you say anything, some of what I do uses the same techniques that Summoners use.'

It was time to risk standing up. I held on to the back of the chair and steadied myself. Everything appeared to be in working order. 'What about Maddy?' I said. 'Can you tell me anything?'

'She's not a complete Spirit, I can tell you that much. There are chunks missing. Not many, but some. They may have been in the wand, anchoring her to it, or they may have gone forever. I'm in no rush to find out.'

'Can we try again, and can you suspend your talents for the duration?'

'Yeah. No problem.' She picked up her chair. 'Oh. One thing. What did you mean by *river of Lux*?'

'That great sheet of power that looked like water flowing over the grass. You nearly trod in it, and I dread to think what would have happened if you had.'

She stared at the grass. It was green again and posed no threat. 'I didn't see that at all,' she said, 'and I have no idea what it was or where it came from.'

'I'll be careful then.'

Woody retreated, and I psyched myself up for a second encounter with Madeleine, after a quick application of burn-cream from the first aid box. I closed my eyes and opened the tube.

The water bubbled and rose. I gripped the wand tighter and tried to exert some sort of control over her manifestation. I might as well have tried plaiting the sea. I was not the one in control here.

I felt her presence growing near me. Growing, but not growing more solid. It was just a sense that she was with me, in the field but not in the field. If you see what I mean. No? Not surprising. I'll try again.

Instead of being *next* to Maddy, it felt like my personal space had expanded and that I was *sharing* it with her. A sort of blindfold psychic three-legged race. There. That's as close as I can get to explaining it.

I still had the sense of water, of course. I've shared an ocean liner with Maddy, and a canoe. This time the water was near, but not underneath us. Like a picnic on the shore of a lake. I caught a phantom image of her in the white muslin dress, lifting a glass of something. Memory? Vision? A bit of both, I think.

The first few steps, still with my eyes closed, were a set of stumbles and near-misses. The field was flat enough to land a bomber, but not billiard-table flat. I found a rhythm and walked slowly forward, expanding my Sight to look for Lux. Specifically, to look for a Ley line or something similar. A flow of Lux.

Nothing. Magickally, Draxholt was as mundane as the field next to it. So far.

Now that I've done a fair bit of dowsing, I'm learning to open half an eye as I walk. Saves bumping into hedges. I parted my right eyelids and saw that I'd wandered towards the middle rather than the edge. I corrected my course and moved steadily east. I was looking for something agricultural as well as magickal, some sign that the Draxholt field had once been subdivided.

Every other field was bounded by land drains or ditches. This one had never had them. Why not? Why increase the chances of flooding? The drains were put in long before tractors, so there was no mechanical advantage from a bigger field. Was this important? No idea.

My leg was aching before I got to the first corner. It was really aching by the second, and still nothing. I paused for a few moments to shake it out, closing my eyes and trying to work out something nagging at the back of my mind. Maddy was still in picnic mode next to me, and could I smell her scent, or something from the lake where she'd had her fun? Something floral? It reminded me of something, as smells often do. Before I could capture the memory, it was blown away by a wet, salt wind with the smell of the sea, which was odd. We were miles from the sea, and then the cold winds of Pickering snatched the ghost fragrances away, and I moved on.

The last corner was in sight, as were the tents and the dig site. I was staggering from the pain in my leg. Not only did it throb, it had started to burn. I desperately wanted to put the wand down and scratch. I resisted, and made it past the tents. Ahead of me, Woody got up and moved out of the way.

The circuit was complete, and I'm 100% sure that no Ley lines ran in or out of Draxholt. I didn't dare stop again, and I turned sharp left to take me back into the field and towards the dig location. I got to the edge and fell in. Of course I did.

'Conrad! You OK?' shouted Woody.

The grave-sized holes had tempted me to fall into them, but I'd resisted, landing on compressed dirt and rolling to avoid a crash landing. Maddy interjected an audible *Oomph* when I hit the deck.

'I'm good,' I said, desperate to keep Woody at bay. I heaved myself up and closed my eyes. There was something here. Something trickling. Faintly. No, not here. Over there.

The twinge in my willow wand was pointing to the cordoned off second-dig area, a good fifty metres closer to the middle of the field. I let Maddy guide me towards it.

My leg hurt too much to climb over the rope barrier, so I just blundered through it like a robot. *So sweet*, came a thought. Where from? No idea. And not sweet like sugar, or sweet like a child's smile: sweet like a morning breeze over water. Sweet like freesias and nicotiana after the rain, tickling the back of your nose and making you ...

Achoo!

The spell was broken. Maddy was still there, but there was no life in the dowsing rod. I sat down and felt the earth under the grass dampen my trousers. I closed my eyes and let my senses drift down through the earth. Under the grass, under the topsoil, under the compacted alluvium, there was something. A spark of heat, a spark of Lux. So deeply buried that I couldn't tell how big it was or whether it was moving; I just knew it was there.

More water fell, running down my neck.

My neck? Shit. That wasn't magick, that was rain. I was about to get soaked. I closed my eyes and said *Thank you, Madeleine. I hope we meet again soon.* My nose tickled again, but no more. I stowed the wand and got to my feet. Woody had already moved under the gazebo, out of the rain. She held up the Thermos and waved me over.

4 — The Big Guns

'Well?' she said.

'There's something out there, all right. Oh, cheers.' I took the mug of coffee and lit up. 'And it's under the second dig site. Deep, but definitely under there, and before you ask, I have no idea what it is.'

'Right.' She stared through the rain, across the grass. Her eyes had widened a touch, and her lips had pursed just a fraction. She was worried. So was I.

'How did you know about the bribery?' I asked.

'Sorry?'

'How did you know that the landowner bribed the air ministry?'

'I put two and two together. There was a letter in the file gushing about the quality of the site. There's nothing special about it that I can see, so I assumed the civil servant who wrote it had been given a back-hander.' She grinned. 'Who knows – perhaps it was a homage to Sir George Cayley.'

'Is he local?'

She pointed up the road, and over the river Derwent. 'He's buried two miles up there, in Brompton.'

I turned and lifted my hat, as every RAF officer should. Sir George is truly the father of aviation, and worked out the physics of flight decades before the internal combustion engine made it practical.

'If you're listening, Sir George, all help would be gratefully received.' I nodded slowly. 'I'm not saying you're wrong about the bribery, it's just that there might be other factors at play. Do you know Vicky Robson?'

'By reputation. We've not met.'

'She's got a great future in the Watch, I reckon, and that's because she's learnt to think outside the circle. Most Mages think they see the world more clearly, and that blinds them to other things. They're rubbish at cyber-security, for example.'

She grinned. 'It's a good job you're not after me, then.'

'But someone else might be. Think about it.'

'Oh.'

'Anyway, ignoring magick, what can you tell me about this field?'

She got up and went to the edge of the gazebo. She looked around for a minute before shrugging. 'It's quite big, I suppose.'

'It is, and it's always been big. They dug the drains around it for some reason, and have a look at the levels.'

'What do you mean?'

'Every other field is level with or below the road. This one is a good three inches higher.'

'That's nothing.'

I shook my head. 'Three inches means a lot to water. In a real deluge, this would be one of the very last fields to flood along here. Why? I have no idea except that it's yet another coincidence.' I checked my watch. It was three o'clock on a Friday afternoon. I'd have to be quick. 'I'm going to call Ruth Kaplan.'

'Who's she?'

'I thought you knew. She's Hannah's twin, and our contact in the police. If I'm in luck, she's still at work.'

Inspector Ruth Kaplan of the City of London Police was still at work. Good. I sweet talked her into checking the ownership history of Draxholt, and she said she'd get back to me.

'What did you say at the end?' said Woody when I'd disconnected.

'*Ah gutten Erev Shabbos*. It's Friday night, or it will be. Talking of which, shall we go to the pub and come back later? The sun doesn't set until 21:35.'

She shook her head. 'You go if you want. It's much better for me to just be here. There's no law that says Spirits appear after sunset or at midnight, and don't forget British Summer Time: actual midnight isn't until 1am. It's just that the later it is, the more likely they are to appear. Ditto for the time I spend in contemplation.'

The rain was getting heavier, and I checked the forecast. It wasn't due to ease up for ages. 'I could do with extra layers, and I'll try and bribe the landlord for sandwiches. Do you want anything?'

She laughed. 'I'm used to this. In fact, it's a real luxury to have portable toilets.'

'Right. I'll try not to think about that. I won't be long.'

The Talbot is a lovely hotel. It's also beyond the normal limit of expenses and half an hour from Draxholt. Too far. We'd checked out this morning and moved to an inn near Sherburn with the unusual name of "The Heavy Gunner." The signboard showed a substantial artilleryman next to an equally substantial piece of ordnance. England is full of oddly named pubs.

The landlord agreed to provide sandwiches (at a price), and I nipped upstairs to get some extra layers. Ruth called while I was putting on thicker socks.

'I shall start calling you the Bloodhound,' she began. 'You can sniff out trouble from a hundred miles.'

'I've had worse nicknames. Tell me.'

'It belonged to the Brompton estate, as in the Earls of Brompton. They owned a big chunk of the Vale of Pickering. When the last earl died in the war, the estate was broken up into farm-sized parcels and sold off. Except for that one field.'

One sock was on. I dropped the other and grabbed my notebook. 'Who owns it now and which war are we talking about?'

'World War 2. He had no brothers and two daughters, and mere women can't inherit, can they?'

'Definitely not. That wouldn't be good at all.'

'If I didn't know you better, I'd say you meant that. Come to think of it, do you?'

'Ask my sister. Who owns the land now?'

'It went into a trust, and that's where it becomes opaque. I can't start looking into it until Monday morning. Will that be too late?'

'I hope so. In a good way. I think I can guess who benefits from the trust. Did the Earls of Brompton have a suitable stately home?'

'They did. It was converted into apartments in the 1970s. None of the current registered owners have the family surname.'

'Great. Thanks.'

'Anything else before I shut down my computer and apologise to Moshe for being late starting the dinner?' There was a distinct warning in her voice. I'd used up my Brownie points for today.

'No. Tell your husband it's all my fault. He'll forgive you and blame Hannah. And tell her I haven't upset too many people yet.'

'Tell her yourself. Ah gutten Erev Shabbos, Conrad.'

'And you, Ruth.'

My laptop was charging quietly in the corner. Should I take a risk and look up the Earls of Brompton, or get back to Woody? Much as I fancied sitting in the warm, dry pub, the call of duty was ringing over the fields. I closed my notebook and picked up the other sock.

The landlord had our evening picnic ready when I got downstairs. 'Room all right, squadron leader?' he said.

'Fine, thanks.'

He went to the till. 'Good job you suspended digging at Draxholt, or you'd be sharing with your colleague. She got Dr Rice's room. Our best.'

'Oh. Has she gone?'

'As you were wanting the room, I let her have a refund. She's gone home to Clitheroe. There's your change.'

'Must have been a nice boost to trade,' I said, stuffing the money away. Anything to give me an excuse not to go back into the rain.

He grinned. 'Thirsty work, all that digging. Are you there to look for the bodies?'

He didn't see my hand stop in mid air. I smoothed down my pocket and gave him my best conspiratorial grin. 'What bodies would those be?'

He grinned back. 'The Germans, of course. My dad called them *the Krauts*, but we're supposed to be friends now, aren't we? Brexit notwithstanding.'

I made myself comfortable. The bar was empty, just that bit too early for the post-work crowd. 'Scotch, please, and one for yourself.' I got my wallet back out.

He put my drink down and stowed the ten pound note in the till. I gave the scotch a sniff and left it. 'What did your dad tell you?'

'That yarn you span to the diggers,' he said. 'The one about Aircraftman Tomkins. Just enough truth in it to give you some cover.'

'I'd hoped they'd keep it secret,' I muttered.

'No one gossips like professors. My great uncle was the one who saw it, if you can believe a word he said. My granddad was away with the war, and his little brother was too young to be called up in '42. He had to register though, and he had to do Home Guard duty. Proper Dad's Army it were, too, until the Jerrys crashed, but you'll know all about that, won't you?'

The look on his face said that he didn't expect me to know anything. The door slammed and a pair of young women stamped their feet noisily in the foyer, complaining loudly about the rain. One of them came through and headed for the bar.

The landlord moved away to serve his new customer. 'Heinkel He 111,' he said. 'Crew of five, normally. There's one in the churchyard, and the POW van took another one away from Staxton Hall. I'm sure you can count. Right, Thea, what can I get you?'

I left my scotch on the bar, untouched. It was only blended. No great waste.

The Peculier Necromancer had not been idle while I collected dry clothes. A very neat hole had now appeared in the Draxholt grass, well away from either of the dig areas. A trail of muddy tracks led back to the mini-digger.

'Good job, Woody,' I said. 'Did you get bored?'

'A bit. And I thought the digger might get bogged down if it carries on raining. Everything okay? You look a bit ... preoccupied?'

I hadn't been going to tell her (or you), but we had another four and a half hours until sunset, and I couldn't share it with anyone else. 'It's Mina. I can't get hold of her to talk to. I think she's up to something.'

'Oh. I'm sorry. Do you mean ... ?'

'Do I mean another man? No, I don't. I trust Mina completely. It's her family I'm not sure about. And talking of family, I think we may encounter a Brompton before we're finished.'

I told her about the late Earl, about the trust and about the old tale told to me by the landlord of the Heavy Gunner. 'Was it coincidence that the story I dreamed up was similar, do you think?'

'I know you don't like coincidences, Conrad, but they do happen. You had to come up with a story that wasn't in the records, and there aren't many variants with dead bodies in them. I should know, I've looked into enough similar cases. The thing that intrigues me is that he said the POW van went to Staxton Hall, not Draxholt Airfield. There might be something in it, or like I said, it might be all an old wives' tale. I'm more intrigued by the trust that owns the land now.'

'What's the betting that one of the Earl's daughters was involved in the world of magick?'

'Or his wife. Shall I look up how he died? What are the odds on him being in the RAF, I wonder? Fancy a bet?'

'Go on. If he wasn't in the RAF, I get your room. It's much nicer. What do you want if you're right?'

She was going to laugh it off, then she paused. 'Do you see much of Dean Cora Hardisty?'

'Now and then. I have a lot of time for her, especially after what she's been through.'

She nodded thoughtfully. 'If the last Earl of Brompton died in an aircraft, I bags a social meeting with Dean Cora.'

'Deal. I'll invite you both for dinner.' I took out my room key and slapped it on the table. 'Go on then.'

Woody got her phone out. It didn't take her long. 'Damn. He died in a tank during the D-Day campaign.' She looked up. 'Why were you so certain?'

'It's fashionable for royalty to join the RAF these days, but back then, no member of the aristocracy would be seen dead in light blue. We're too meritocratic. Imagine the scandal if they failed their aircrew tests? I bet he was in one of the old cavalry regiments.'

She looked at her phone again. 'The 8th King's Royal Irish Hussars. Damn. I should have thought of that. Dad will laugh his socks off when I tell him.' She took out her room key and swapped them over. I took it for now (a bet's a bet, after all). Whether I gave it back later would depend on how the evening went. I looked out at the rain. It was going to be a long and miserable one, with a chance of violent death later.

I shoved the key in my pocket. 'Are you close, you and your dad?'

'Yeah. Despite him not being entangled.' She meant that he wasn't involved in the world of magick.

'How did he take it when you came out? If you don't mind me asking.'

She gave the square shrug again. I thought it was her uniform that made her do that, but there's some tension in those shoulders. 'He was great. In his head, it's all tied up with the visions. I started my magickal education at the same time as I came out, so when I stopped acting like a nutcase, he put it down to having repressed my true nature for years. He blames himself for that, of course, no matter how much I tell him otherwise. He's great about it, though he is checking his watch and wondering when the grandkids are coming along.'

The curtain of rain dripping off the four sides of the gazebo was like the walls of a confessional. We'd both said things we wouldn't outside it, and it was Woody who'd brought the subject up. 'What about you?' I said gently. 'Is your biological clock ticking?'

She made a face. 'I asked for that, didn't I? We're ready for kids, but there's a problem with the sperm donor.'

I had no idea what to say to that. Woody didn't notice my lack of response. She was looking out at the rain, thinking of Cambridge.

'I'd like a Mage, or the chance of one,' she said. 'Frances is adamant that is has to be a gay donor. What about you, Conrad?'

'Mina and I are both old fashioned. We want to get married first.'

'So? I'll help you down on one knee, if you're leg's hurting.'

'I shall bear that offer in mind. My leg isn't the problem, it's the Nāgin, the snake-woman.'

She sat up straight. 'You're having me on!'

'I wish I was. I'll tell you about it.'

That's how we passed the next three hours. It's amazing how much you feel you can get to know someone when you're shut away like that.

And then, we weren't alone any more. We looked up and seven men were standing round the gazebo looking very unhappy.

'Oh shit,' said Woody. That was my thought exactly.

5 — Defence of the Realm

'Let me do the talking,' said Woody. I was more than happy with that, and nodded mutely in agreement.

It was nowhere near night-time yet, but the gloom of the cloud and rain made the light murky, and shadows from another world flickered over the men's faces. The aircrew's faces.

All seven wore overalls under heavy sheepskin flying jackets. Leather helmets distorted the shape of some of their heads, as if they weren't creepy enough already. The rain wasn't getting them wet, nor was it passing through them like a hologram. It just seemed to stop when it got to their space. Their faces were swarthy, sunburned and battle hardened.

They were beyond the gazebo, standing in a group between us and the second dig site. Four of them were in a rough line, with two slightly behind and one slightly in front. Woody had already sprung out of her seat and taken a step towards them. I don't spring out of chairs any more. I got up as steadily as I could and moved to stand behind her and to the right.

Woody cleared her throat. 'Please forgive us for trespassing in your domain. We are honoured to meet you.'

She followed her words with a bow. I came to attention and saluted. It seemed like the right thing to do. The airman at the front wasn't wearing a helmet. A flat cap, just like mine, adorned his head. An officer. The Pilot in Command. He returned my salute and turned his focus back to Woody. I may outrank her on the parade ground, but these veterans knew that she was the one in charge of this operation. He straightened his cap and blinked. In the gloom, his eyes shone a vibrant blue, completely at odds with the heavy stubble and a skin tone that matched the others behind him.

'You've come again,' he said, with an accent I'd never heard before. The words *come again* sounded like *hom agayin*. Not Polish, not French. The RAF did cast its net wide during WW2.

'We're here to help you,' said Woody. 'I can be your bridge to the world. I can answer your questions.' She paused, lifting and opening her arms. 'I can help you fly your final mission. Into the next life.'

She wasn't winging it – this was something she'd said before. It came across as confident, reassuring and exactly what a lost soul would want to hear. The crew were not interested.

'It is not for you to help,' said the pilot. 'Make your offering if you wish, and go in peace.'

That was a stumper, and no mistake. Their script didn't sound like any ghost I've ever heard of. Woody's head tilted back a fraction as she absorbed the message.

'Your vigil must be a lonely one,' she said, 'with nothing but the stars for company.' She paused again. 'We share your motto. *Per ardua ad astra*. Through struggle we reach the stars. I can help you reach the stars and rejoin those you've left behind.'

One of the two guys at the back looked up at the rain and muttered to his comrade. I had no idea what he said, but my money's on *no fucking stars out tonight*. When he spoke, a breeze drifted under the awning, carrying that scent of wildflowers again, and the ozone tang of the sea, just like it did when I'd been dowsing with Maddy. I grasped at the memory. Nearly there.

The second airman looked up, too, a wry smile on his face. It froze there. He pointed at the sky and shouted something in an alien tongue. What the...?

The pilot pivoted and pushed his comrades aside to look up. Woody stepped forward and turned to scan the scene. I grabbed her arm. 'Woody. The gate. Someone's here.'

There was a shadow at the entrance, the bulky shadow of a squat 4x4. A woman was getting out of the front. 'You see to her,' said Woody. She strode out of the gazebo to join the aircrew, all of whom were now staring and pointing at the sky.

I paused to grab the Anvil, my Gnomish sword, and slung it over my shoulder. The woman pulled the hood of her Barbour over her head and climbed the gate. I was half way to meet her when she jumped into the field and picked up a sword of her own. She must have chucked it over while I was talking to Woody, and lingering hope that this wasn't a Mage disappeared in a puff of smoke.

She lifted her gaze and the hood slid back a fraction, enough for me to see pale skin, fair hair and a triumphant smile. I couldn't stand it any longer, and risked a glance up and back. I stopped still and slowly turned to get a proper look.

There was a light in the clouds. A point of light like a giant LED torch being held by the god of thunder. It got brighter, closer to the edge of the clouds, and then it emerged. A black figure came first, a little mannequin born out of the mist. It was followed by the light, and the light became the glowing canopy of a parachute. A paratrooper from Heaven? I knew it was nonsense (Heaven is not up in the sky, apparently), but the thought thrust itself into my head anyway. The clouds were so low that it wouldn't take the newcomer long to land, and he or she was heading for the roped off area of the second dig. The aircrew shouted and charged towards the drop zone.

'I've waited a long time for this,' said a cultured voice next to me. I hadn't heard her come up, and flinched away. Her hood was lowered, and an aristocratic woman about Woody's age smiled at me. 'My grandmother,

Patience,' she said, pointing to the parachutist. 'Or her Spectre to be precise, Mr Clarke. I'm Eleanor Brampton, as you've probably guessed. Come on, or they'll start without us.'

I could have stopped her. Probably. At least slowed her down. I chose not to. For one thing, she hadn't broken any laws. This was her land, and that was her grandmother. She jogged towards the brewing confrontation; I gritted my teeth and jogged after her.

The parachutist executed a perfect landing and roll in the dead centre of the dig site and bounced back to her feet. I was getting closer, and it was definitely a woman. Behind her, the canopy, still glowing, subsided to the ground and put her face in shadow. The aircrew had given her a wide berth on the way down, but now they hopped over the ropes and surrounded her. The pilot stopped about twenty feet in front of her, with Woody catching up.

The pilot barked something in that strange language, full of Xs and Chs and K sounds. The Spectre of Patience Brompton just smiled at them and hit the quick-release on her harness. She shrugged it off and it sank into the earth; behind her the silk canopy did the same, leaving a glow to spread across the grass and light up everyone's faces. Patience pulled off her leather helmet and shook out her hair into a long bob. Now that I could see her properly, the resemblance to Eleanor was clear.

Her granddaughter vaulted the sagging rope and dashed between two airmen. She stopped at a respectful distance and bent the knee, bowing her head and lifting her long coat in a curtsy to Patience. I caught up with the group, and Woody turned to look at me. Her face was a picture of appalled confusion and a fair bit of terror. That made two of us.

As soon as I joined her inside the square, that smell came again, the purest chill of spring flowers. It was so familiar…

Eleanor turned to the pilot and bowed. 'It is time for what was hidden to be revealed,' she said.

'No, no,' said Woody. 'Not here.' She might as well not have bothered for all they cared.

'It is not for you to do this,' said the pilot. 'You are not of the blood. For you, the mystery will remain.'

Patience took a step forward and spoke out. The sharp vowels and clipped consonants of the upper class cut through the rain. 'This sacrifice I make willingly. I offer my whole self on her altar. Let what is hidden be revealed.' She took another step and prostrated herself on the grass, spreading her arms. Eleanor moved to her side and drew the sword from its scabbard.

The nearest airman made a grab for Eleanor. Sparks glittered from his hand and trailed behind him. With the speed of an Olympic fencer, Eleanor whipped round the sword and sliced off the airman's hand in a burst of Lux.

We all staggered back from the explosion of magickal power. Even Eleanor was rocked back on her heels.

The airmen regrouped, readying themselves. They all took off their headgear, except for the pilot, and they all shook out long, black hair. What? Not only was hair like that strictly against regulations, it shouldn't have fitted under their caps. And that wasn't the only change. Their eyes glowed even more brightly blue, and the clean-cut jaws sprouted straggly black beards. They were reverting to whatever their true essence might be, and I'm betting they've never seen the inside of a Lancaster bomber for real.

Their leader kept his shape and kept his cap on. He barked a couple of incomprehensible orders and drew his personal weapon. From the holster at his side came an axe. With a stone head. The rest of his crew crouched down and felt in the long grass. As one team, they stood up and had spears in their hands. The odds didn't look good for the Bramptons.

'In the name of the Goddess, stop this,' said Woody. She turned to me, pleading in her eyes. I felt for my own personal weapon and made the biggest mistake of my magickal career.

6 — *In Her Name*

I've been told by a Dwarf that the magickal rounds in my gun would work against some varieties of Spirit. They would definitely work against Eleanor Brampton, but shooting her was the last thing on my mind. What I wanted was protection from those spears if the guardians decided to chuck one at me.

The Hammer has two Works of magick stamped into the butt. One is my Ancile, my magickal shield, and it would protect me from any magickal or mundane missiles. A spear, for example.

I gripped the gun and activated the Ancile. On the other side of the butt is my Badge of Office, a gold stamp of Caledfwlch, the sign of the Watch. It was put there in the presence of a nymph called Nimue, and a little of her essence is woven through the Work. My fingers brushed the Badge, and I remembered what the smell of wildflowers was all about.

Lux flowed from my fingers into the Badge, and it acted like a lens, spreading magick across the square. And down, into the ground. The smell of cold, fresh mornings cut through the evening drizzle and soaked into our clothes, into our skin, and into our blood.

'Conrad, what have you done?' said Woody. The panic in her eyes was gone; it had been replaced by the naked fear of imminent death. All the actors had stopped to stare at me, too, until the leader of the guardians looked down at his feet. They were sinking into the ground.

I felt a piercing cold run through my muscles and my organs, into my bones. I breathed a raw breath of ice and started to choke as water filled my mouth. I was standing in the open air, and I was going to drown from the inside out.

I doubled up and pitched forward on to the grass. And through it. The ground did not stop my fall, and I disappeared into the soil with a flash of light.

Can't breathe. Choking. Floating. Darkness everywhere. My insides heaved and I felt like I was expelling water from my nose and mouth. My poor lungs rebelled and forced me to take a breath, even though I knew it was death. Cold pierced my ribs. Stars flashed in my eyes. I thrashed in mid-air and screamed.

The sound of my own voice made me stop. I caught another breath. Another. I was breathing. I blinked a couple of times, and the fireworks faded, as did the smell of flowers. Black turned to grey and I knew that I was falling slowly down. I braced myself for a crash, and rolled when the ground hit me. Right into Woody.

'Mngrah,' she said groggily.

I levered myself up and blinked again. To my right was a light, and it was growing brighter. I looked up and saw impossible stars gleaming brightly in a clear sky, all the clouds and all the pollution gone. I sat up straight and closed my eyes to let my magickal senses feel around. North was still north and I knew with absolute certainty that I was now twenty metres down from where I'd been when I touched my gun. Oh dear.

I nudged Woody. 'Roberta. Are you okay?'

'Eurgh. Oh fuck my head hurts,' she said, clutching it with her hands.

I couldn't stand. Not yet. I looked towards the light and saw Eleanor Brampton trying to get to her knees. Behind her was a big rock. A very big rock. A very big glowing rock, with something taking shape in the light above it. I scanned for a sign of the guardians or of Patience. There were shimmers here and there, points of light floating down and swirling.

It made sense. The kind of sense that sends you screaming to a warm beach in the sunshine to get away from the bonkers. Magickal sense, in other words. We had all shifted to a different level of existence. We had entered the Spirit world.

The discipline of the Invisible College is adamant: there is only one universe, and we all share it. The reason you don't bump into ghosts, gods and Dæmons on Oxford Street is that their essence operates at a different frequency. They can pass through us and we can pass through them. To move from one to the other requires Lux. Lots of Lux. Enough Lux to allow Woody, Eleanor and I to move around twenty metres underground, on the site of a pre-historic temple, because that's what it was. A temple to Nimue, and those impostor airmen were her ghostly guardians. They'd be along in a minute, and so would she.

A thought nudged my consciousness: *What if you change back? You're underground. Instant burial.* I batted that thought firmly away and focused on things I could affect, like Woody. Like standing up.

She was still clutching her head. I put my hand on her neck. It was wet, as was her hair. I don't have that problem. For some reason the Spirit drowning hadn't penetrated my waterproofs, and I was no wetter than I'd been in the rain.

'Breathe, Woody. Breathe in … breathe out.'

'Shut up, you mad fucker. I'm not hyperventilating. I've got a headache. Owwww.'

'Good. I'd give you aspirin if they weren't seventy feet up in the air, so sit up and tell me how the hell we're going to get out of here.'

She was still gripping her head. 'Please tell me we're not really underground.'

'Sorry. We're underground and under all that ground water, too. Nimue used it as a conduit to bring us down here.'

She moaned. 'Why did you do it? Why did you summon that mad creature?'

'Later. Her guardians are rejoining the party. Come on, Woodhouse. Up you get.'

I put everything I had into getting up. I must have looked like a baby giraffe, all legs and falling over. When I had a semblance of upright, I grabbed her arm and pulled. By Odin, she was heavy. Solid. I gave up when I'd got her into a sitting position, because I heard voices.

The RAF flying suits were gone, but not the spears. All seven guardians were clothed in neatly sewn animal hides and wore furs around their shoulders. Black hair sprouted all over the visible parts of their bodies, and their faces looked ... different. Not just different from their RAF faces, different from anyone. As their bodies became completely solid, all trace of ghostly shimmer left them, and they brought with them the smell of the sea, of iodine and ozone, and of the taste of salty lips. The final pieces of the puzzle clicked into place, and I kicked myself for a fool.

I've tasted Nimue's well in Merlyn's Tower, and water from one of her springs in the Lakes. It's cold, fresh and has floral notes. I hadn't recognised it here because the salt had distorted my palate, and the salt had come from the tsunami, triggered by the Storegga Slide. The cataclysmic event that excited Professor Cargill had washed over this place and wiped out whole communities, including the men who were guarding the altar. Magick, perhaps Nimue herself, had transported them to the Spirit world and they've watched ever since.

And why did they look so odd? Because our Mesolithic ancestors aren't really our ancestors. They were erased from the record, first by the farmers and then by the workers in bronze. Not just culturally, but genetically. No wonder they weren't keen to accept Patience Brampton as one of their people. The lady herself had appeared, looking none too healthy and clinging to her granddaughter. At least they were both upright. They were also surrounded by spears.

I looked around for my sword, and felt for the Hammer. Neither were here, and Eleanor had realised the same thing about her weapon. The guardian on the right was holding his spear one-handed, the other being a mangled stump. He looked really, really unhappy.

There was a tinkle of running water, a burst of light and a welling up of violets. Nimue rose from the altar.

She is a true water nymph, made entirely of water and naked, like a melting ice sculpture. Droplets cascade from her hair and she has no feet – her ankles rise from the water like a fountain. Her face, though, is sharply defined by refracted light and is as beautiful as water can be, and anyone who's seen dawn rise over Grasmere will tell you that water can be very, very beautiful.

I reached down and grabbed Woody's hand, hauling her to her feet so that we could all bow as low as possible. This was Nimue's show, now.

When I straightened up after my deep bow, I had to blink to make sure I wasn't seeing things. Nimue's left hand was leaking. I've seen her twice, and she always has perfect definition, as I said, like an ice sculpture.

Not this time. Her left hand looked like it was continually melting and re-forming, with water flowing out of it. And it was getting worse, moving slowly up her left arm. In this place, Nimue was not as stable as she could be, perhaps a legacy of the tsunami. If she started to disintegrate, how the hell would the living members of her congregation get back to the surface?

She spoke, her voice barely rising above the sound of running water that seemed to haunt this place. 'Too long. I have been too long from here.' She looked at the leader of the guardians. 'Xhaliyaha?' It sounded like his name, and he responded in that long-lost language.

He made three short statements, each one preceded by a gesture. The first gesture pointed to Patience Brampton, the second to Eleanor and the third to Woody. Nimue stared blankly at us for a second, then lifted a liquid finger and pointed, not to Woody, but to me. 'Welcome, Watch Captain. How fares the realm?'

'Troubled, my lady, as it ever was. We...'

She cut me off by saying something to Xhaliyaha. I think she was telling him that we were the good guys. I hope she was.

Eleanor Brampton's face showed a mixture of triumph and wonder. Despite our traumatic descent into a dangerous realm, she was lapping it up. Her granny was less happy. Patience Brampton was a scared woman. Above ground, she had offered her neck to the sword gladly, the fulfilment of some wish or the end of a mission. Down here, she was frightened. Very frightened. When Eleanor whispered something in her ear, she forced a smile to hide her terror, then Nimue looked at her, and the smile died on her lips.

'Spirit, you should not have come here,' said the Nymph. 'You have much guilt upon you that you cannot wash away with your sacrifice, but I will be merciful and accept it anyway. Your child's child can add to it with her own sacrifice.' She turned to Eleanor. 'I am not a doll to be played with, mortal. You have insulted me and your presence defiles my sacred place. Xhaliyaha, take them to the lake.'

'No...'

Patience screamed first, and dashed towards the altar. Two spears thrust towards her, one of them piercing her leather jacket and drawing blood. She staggered back, and Eleanor caught her.

'My lady...,' said Eleanor, but she was talking to an empty space. Nimue had dissolved back into water and there was nothing but a pool in a depression on top of the rock to show that she'd ever been here.

Xhaliyaha barked an order, and the guardians moved like lightning. Four of them dropped their spears and dived at the women. Patience whipped up her hand to try magick, but it was too late. They collapsed in a heap of flailing brown arms and grunts. In seconds, each Brampton had been forced to their knees and been pinioned by one of the guardians.

I'd stepped forward when the action started, and stopped dead when Xhaliyaha turned and raised his stone axe. It was all over before I could get his measure, and now one of the guardians was facing us. I stepped back. He waved the axe, and the guardians started dragging the Bramptons away to the south. Woody and I started to track them.

'Conrad, do something,' said Woody. 'You can't let this happen.'

So long as we got to the surface, I was quite happy to let it happen. These guardians were elite hunters. They had weapons. They had orders. What did I have?

'Any suggestions gratefully received,' I said.

Woody put on a spurt and moved in front of the group. 'In the name of peace, let them go,' she said. 'You have seen the world. The days of blood speaking to blood are over.'

Xhaliyaha had been given his orders in English, and clearly understood them. He understood Woody, too, and gave her a predatory grin. 'Blood will always speak. Listen.' He put two crooked fingers in his mouth and whistled. He paused and whistled again, modulating the clear note into a minor key that sounded very wrong to my ears.

I looked round and realised that we were heading towards a secondary light source, about two hundred metres away, if distance works the same down here. Three shadows formed, silhouettes against the light, and moving towards us. Xhaliyaha waited, looking at the figures as they came closer.

'Oh shit,' I said.

'What?' said Woody. 'I can't see anything. Oh. Right. Shit.'

The three shadows resolved themselves into young men. Young airmen, and these were the real thing. Their leather coats were barely visible under the combined lifejacket and parachute that all aircrew wore, and those leather coats were neater, squarer and longer than the shaggy sheepskins that the RAF wore. That's because they weren't RAF, they were Luftwaffe, and they were all staring at Patience.

Their eyes were feral, hungry and eager. One of them bared his teeth. '*Guten tag, mutti.*'

'What'd he say?' whispered Woody.

'*Hello, mum.* I'm sensing irony. And bloodlust.'

Xhaliyaha spoke, and the guardian holding Patience released her with a forward shove. She staggered and grimaced, bringing up a hand to hold the wound in her side. Blood was flowing through her fingers. Once a mother, always a mother, or so I've been told. Patience used every ounce of strength to turn to Xhaliyaha. 'I will go. Spare my child's child. She is innocent. Foolish, but innocent. This is my sin to remit.'

I don't think Xhaliyaha's English was good enough to understand remission of sins. He got the gist, though, and shook his head. 'Both of you. It has been spoken.' He didn't look thrilled about it, and turned himself fractionally away from Eleanor.

The living Brampton had turned white. 'Patience, what have you done? Tell me it's not true. I thought…'

'*Nimm sie weg,*' said the leading German airman. *Take her away.* Patience bowed her head, and the other two grabbed her arms. Their leader looked at Eleanor. She whimpered.

To the right, towards the growing light, I glimpsed another shadow, little more than a flicker, and I knew who it was. It would have been good if the Allfather had chosen this moment to drop in, but this was not his turf. There would be a raven watching from an underwater tree, no doubt, but this phantom was from my past, and just to complete the party, he was an airman too. He once supped with me, and used no spoon at all. My actions cost him his life, and much of what I've done since then has been overshadowed by that.

I looked back at Eleanor. I wouldn't throw my life away for her, nor would I offer to exchange it for hers. But I would definitely risk it. I owed her that.

There was only one way to save Eleanor Brampton: Xhaliyaha's orders would have to be rescinded, and only one person, one being could do that. I had one chance, and I needed some help. 'Woody, buy me some time,' I said, and then I legged it.

I ran away from the group, which most of the guardians found very amusing. Woody looked appalled until she realised where I was going, then she turned back to intervene. My leg throbbed as I put on a spurt. I had to get to the altar before it was too late.

The rock wasn't glowing like it had done, and barely any water was left in the pool on the top. Blood does call to blood, but Nimue was literally bloodless. I needed water.

When I'd patted my pockets earlier, I'd discovered that not every magickal Artefact had stayed on the surface. I pulled the Egyptian tube out of my coat and snapped off the cap. *Mina, if this is the end, I hope you know how much I love you.* The thought ran quickly through my head, almost unbidden, and then I grabbed the willow wand, pulled it out and plunged the end into the shallow basin. The electric shock blew me back at least five feet and thunder rolled across the underground grass.

7 — *Patience*

Screams. Women's screams, high pitched and piercing my ears. Got to get up. Got to. No chance.

A jerk on the arm. 'Oww. Careful.'

'Conrad, quick.' A breathless Woody pulled me again, and I rolled with it and let her broad shoulders pull me up.

Nimue was back, her left arm no longer dripping. At the foot of the rock, the diminutive form of Madeleine was staring up at her.

This version of Maddy was older than the other one, closer to her real age when she died, and her figure was slightly more rounded, but she was infinitely more beautiful because she was alive and fizzing with anger.

'No more,' she said. 'You gave your word, my lady. No more to go unwillingly into the water.'

Nimue danced on her glittering column. 'Did I? It's so easy to forget, especially here.' She stilled herself. 'Especially when Hans, Kurt and Willi were sent unwillingly to me. I'm just following Lady Brampton's lead.'

'And she will go, as she must. But not the little one. Remember *my* sacrifice. I gave you my life for my daughter's. There can be an end, my lady, if you show the same grace.'

By Odin's eye, so *that's* why Maddy and water go together: she drowned herself to save her daughter. That answered one of my questions, even if it raised a boatload more, the most obvious being, *if she drowned in Windermere, how did her Spirit end up in a tree at Lunar Hall?*

That question was for later. Right now, all eyes (including Xhaliyaha's) were on Nimue.

She wavered a little, as if blown by a breeze, and more violets wafted across the grass. She looked up at the stars. 'I remember you, Madeleine, and I remember your sacrifice. You have given me shape again in this place, and for that I thank you. Eleanor Brampton can live, if she promises to make amends. Xhaliyaha, bring her to me.'

I scanned the crowd. The three Luftwaffe boys were keeping their distance, well away from the altar. Two of them were still holding Patience. Xhaliyaha ordered his men to bring Eleanor forward.

'You will plant a grove in this place,' said Nimue, 'and bring my children to it that they may make offerings, and so it will be until you join me underneath. That is the price for your freedom.'

Eleanor bowed her head. 'I will serve you properly, as I did not before. You have my word until death and beyond.'

'So mote it be,' said Nimue. She ran a critical eye over Woody. 'You are a seer and a guide. You may be of service.'

Woody looked very worried and blurted out, 'My lady.'

The nymph turned to her guardians and spoke in their language before pointing to the German boys. The guardians looked at each other. Instead of putting their hands up, three of them volunteered by touching their thumbs to their chests. One did so quickly, one slowly, and the third after a word from Xhaliyaha. They all looked happy, whatever it was they'd signed up for. They planted their spears in the ground and walked towards an even more worried Woody.

'Hans, Kurt and Willi will join my guard,' said Nimue to Woody, 'and you will lead these three away across the field to their last rest. Xhaliyaha will help you return to what lies above when you are done.' It was my turn next. 'We will meet again, Watch Captain. Guard the realm well.'

The higher up the Spirit chain you are, the shorter are the goodbyes. Nimue spread her arms, spoke three words in Mesolithic and dissolved back into the water.

As she did so, the altar dimmed and so did Maddy, losing the bloom of life. She reached her hand towards me. 'Conny, I ...'

She, too, dispersed, flowing back into the willow wand that had been flung across the grass. I stepped over and scooped it into the Egyptian tube. Behind me, things moved quickly.

'Patience!' said Eleanor, moving towards her grandmother. Xhaliyaha put out his arm to block Eleanor's path, and the Luftwaffe boys led her grandmother towards the lake, now glowing brighter than ever. She looked over her shoulder once before they disappeared, and gave her granddaughter a sad nod.

Xhaliyaha took Eleanor's arm, gently but firmly, and pulled her to me. 'Join hands,' he said. 'All hands. And do not let go.'

We put our four hands together and gripped. He moved a few fingers until he was satisfied. 'Close eyes. Deep breath. Deeper. Now go.'

Our arms were yanked upwards, a violent wrench that lasted for a second until I felt water around me again and the weight was taken off a little. I kept my eyes firmly closed and my lips sealed against the freezing chill that shocked me. A few seconds later, I heard a gargled scream and Eleanor pulled against my grip.

I opened my eyes and saw panic. Shapes moved around us, and Eleanor had lost it. I had only one option: hold tighter and think about the surface. She bucked and fought, trying to get away, and bubbles escaped her mouth. I pulled her in, closer to me, and she kicked my bad leg. I spasmed and nearly let go.

With a kick up the backside, we flopped onto wet grass under a black sky. I coughed out water and Eleanor started to choke. I let go of her hands and went into resuscitation mode.

Eleanor was lucky. Again. There wasn't enough water in her lungs to stop her breathing, and I quickly put her in the recovery position. 'Don't move,' I said. As she groaned and coughed again, I realised that the rain had eased a little. With no moon, it was still pretty black out in the field.

I squatted next to Eleanor and scanned the area. A few bits of metal glinted on the grass. There were a lot of magickal and twenty-first century artefacts scattered around. I tried to add my Sight to the search, and felt the powerful signature of my sword, the Anvil, nearby. It was a start. I stood up, groaned and grabbed the Anvil. I stumbled across the field, trying to get my circulation going again, and retrieved an LED lantern and torch from the gazebo. Armed with some light, I went back to Eleanor and started collecting stuff, scanning around for Woody. How long does it take to exorcise Mesolithic ghosts, I wonder?

Eleanor was breathing more easily, and now at risk of hypothermia. 'Come on, let's get you under cover. I'll help you up.'

She staggered a little, and I supported her arm until she nodded and said, 'Thanks. I think I can make it now.'

I left the lantern in the field and escorted Eleanor to shelter. She slumped into a chair and rubbed her face with her hands. Her hair was soaked, plastered to her head in rats tails. I grabbed a beanie for my own poor denuded bonce and gave her a towel. I broke into the third flask and poured us both some hot coffee. I unzipped a waterproof pocket in my coat and pulled out a dry pack of cigarettes. 'Smoke?'

'Yeah.'

'Did Patience really sacrifice those boys, do you think?'

She nodded mutely.

'Why?'

'She was trying to make a link between our ground level and the altar below. She didn't know about the Storegga slide or the tsunami. She didn't realise that Nimue was damaged here. Now I know why she was so keen to sacrifice herself in remission.' She shook her head. 'I always knew that the story going round the village had some truth in it, and Patience told me that they were too injured for medical help. I was too keen to believe her.'

'And what did you do to upset Nimue?'

'Did you notice a trailer in the layby down the road?'

'The low loader with the huge piece of rock on it?'

'Yes. I was going to put it in here as a new altar. I'd already started the rituals when the guardian showed up, but that's not what upset our lady. I was using a ritual that would have bound me to the altar as priestess. Nimue likes to choose her own acolytes.'

'Why did you sponsor the dig? You must have known that the altar was way too deep to come to the surface.'

'I think I know,' said Woody. I nearly jumped out of my skin.

'Bloody hell, where did you spring from? Are you okay?'

She pointed to the road. 'That way. I'm fine, but I need some coffee.'

I poured and she inhaled the aroma before taking a gulp. 'Boy that's good. Mmm.' She closed her eyes for a second. 'Where did you hear about me, Eleanor?'

'Patience told me about the Peculier Necromancer. Your predecessor came here in the 1950s. Patience had to work quickly to cover her tracks, but she did a good job. My grandmother was ten times the Mage I am or ever will be. Once I knew there was such a thing as the Peculier Necromancer, it wasn't difficult to find out who you were and set things up.'

This didn't make sense to me, and I said so.

'She lured me here,' said Woody. 'She got the archaeologists on site so that I'd have to take an official interest, and once I was here, she knew I'd open a window. She and Patience planned to jump through.'

'We weren't expecting there to be so many,' said Eleanor. 'I only saw the leader, not the whole crew. Neither did we expect someone with such a close bond to Nimue to be here or to have her essence on his person.' She gave me a grim smile.

'See?' I said to Woody. 'I'm not just the weapon of last resort. And do you know what the best thing about tonight is?'

'Go on.'

'I don't have to write the report. I just have to call the Boss on Sunday.'

'Sunday?'

I checked my watch. It was well after one in the morning. 'It's now Shabbos. I'm only allowed to disturb her if lives are at stake. Time to wrap things up and go to bed, I think.'

'You're not joking,' said Woody. 'What needs doing?'

I gave Woody her phone, her keys and a small leather box. 'Did you lose anything else?'

'No. That's all.'

'Have you got far to walk?' I said to Eleanor.

'It's alright. I can drive.'

'Not without a car, you can't. You can collect your little number from RAF Shawbury on Monday. I'll leave your sword in the boot and your keys at reception.'

Woody snorted into her coffee. Eleanor looked outraged, but bit her lip.

'You conspired to use an officer of the crown for your own ends,' I told her. 'Count yourself lucky I'm not arresting you. You don't want me to arrest her, do you Flight Lieutenant Woodhouse?'

'Tempting, but no. Nimue's dispensed enough justice for one day.'

'Good. Here you go.' I gave Eleanor her phone. 'You can message the archaeologists and tell them to backfill their holes when they pack up and leave later today. You can call a taxi, too, if you want.'

She shook her head. 'I'll call my boyfriend. He can be here in half an hour.' She attempted a smile. 'I'll use the time to reflect.' She looked up. 'Thank you, Watch Captain. I hate you for what you did, but I'll be grateful for ever that you saved me from being sacrificed.'

'Don't thank me, thank Madeleine.'

She lowered her eyes. 'I do. Please tell her. If she remembers.'

I started packing things away. When I'd finished, Woody joined me as I went to retrieve the lantern. 'What made you change your mind?' she said.

'About what?'

'About saving Eleanor. You were going to leave her.'

'The thirteenth spirit.'

She did some calculations. 'There were only twelve, unless you're counting Nimue.'

'I'm not. You didn't see him, but he was there. Here's your room key back.'

'Are you sure?'

'I'm too tired to swap rooms. I'll see you for breakfast. They stop serving at ten.'

'Then I'll see you at five to. Goodnight, Conrad. Sleep well.'

8 — A Day of Rest

Timing is everything, in breakfast as much as in life. We arrived in the bar at the right moment to get all the leftovers, and our Full English plates were heaped higher than an American at an all-you-can-eat buffet. Woody and I dived in and didn't surface until our plates were clean.

'You're dying to take that coffee outside for a smoke, aren't you?' she said. She followed up this insight with a rather loud and most un-officer like belch.

'Yes.'

'I'll join you. Not for a ciggie, but I need to stand up before I burst.'

It was still drizzling outside, and I took refuge in the covered smoking shelter round the back.

'Eleanor got home safely,' said Woody. 'I know you'll be pleased to hear that.'

I took a few seconds to think about. 'Actually, I am. I'd hate to think she did something stupid after getting a second chance that I risked my life for.'

'Thought so. You're all heart, Conrad. I'm seeing her this afternoon, just to tie up some loose ends and make a few plans. And to get something in writing.'

'Do you need me?'

She shook her head. 'I'll email you the draft report when I'm done. Are you going straight back?'

'To what? A single room in Shawbury? It's too far to Cheltenham, and I don't think I'm fit for a long journey today. I thought I'd have a drive round. It's lovely here. Might work my way up to Scarborough and stay there tonight.'

'Sounds good. Any word from Mina?'

'Only a Whatsapp. She's on her way to see her father's family. Says she'll talk when she gets there.'

'You're welcome to drop in on us if you're ever in Cambridge.'

'Ditto for Gloucestershire. And I've got something for you.' I passed her a folded piece of paper with a mobile number on it. 'Do you remember the story of the Thirteenth Witch?'

'I still can't believe you said no to Helen of Troy.'

'It was tough. I hope I don't meet her again. That's the telephone number of an Artificer in Brighton. He was – is – Abbi's biological father, and he's gay. He'll take a bit of persuading, but he's had one Mage child by donor.'

She looked appalled and touched in equal measure. 'I can't just call him up.'

'Yes you can. If you really want it, you'll find a way.'

She stared at the paper before folding it carefully and putting it in her bag. She leaned up and gave me a kiss. 'Thanks, Conrad. Consider yourself invited to the Naming Ceremony, if there is one.'

'It would be an honour and a pleasure.'

She shivered and looked north, towards Draxholt. We both took a moment to reflect on last night, then she patted her handbag, gave me a smile and walked back towards the warmth of the pub.

Author's Note

Wings over Water came from a suggestion by Ian Sherry (formerly of the Heavy Artillery) that not enough stories are set in the remarkably beautiful but little known part of Yorkshire that lies east of York. That seed was planted in the fertile soil of our ancient history and watered by some of the tales my father told me about his wartime service as a Navigator on Lancaster bombers.

I'm afraid that you won't be able to visit Nimue's shrine at Draxholt (invitation only), but you can definitely explore the discoveries at Star Carr, and there is plenty of information around about the Storegga Slide tsunami and its impact.

Some things you can't make up, and the *Daily Mail* did indeed call the Slide "The first Brexit".

Ring of Troth

This story was originally published in December 2019.

*The action takes place during **Eight Kings**, the Sixth Book of the King's Watch. At the time of this story, Conrad is embroiled in the events of the King of Wessex election – after the treaty but before the murder of Lord Mowbray.*

Mark Hayden

1 — *The God of Beginnings*

Was I pleased that Conrad had proposed to me? Of course I was.

When he got down on one knee (with an alarming *crack* from his joints), I was the happiest girl in the world. I still am. I'm sure that he's the happiest man in the world, too, even if he doesn't show it by dancing in the streets. Or dancing at all, come to that. Which is probably for the best. I have seen him dancing, and you have not, so believe me when I tell you that it is not a pretty sight.

His proposal also caused our first serious argument. Really serious, as in he almost asked me for the ring back.

The row happened after we got back from the temple in south London and a visit to my favourite priest, Mr Joshi. It was only right and proper that when I asked for Ganesh's blessing on our engagement – our betrothal, to use the old word – that we should make that prayer with Mr Joshi to help us.

Mr Joshi did not know it, but there was far more at stake than a ritual blessing. Every time I think back to that night at the Clarke's Well when Conrad proposed, I think about how my heart wanted to burst. And then the shadow falls. The shadow of Pramiti. A long, low snake shaped shadow, slithering around our feet.

Ganesh has many Spirits who serve him. One of them was a Nāgin, a snake-woman called Pramiti, and it was her who opened a door for me: literally opened a door. She used magick on my friend's cell when I was banged up in prison, and that open door may have saved my life. For that service, a debt is owed. A debt that became due the moment that Conrad got down on one knee and proposed to me. If I want Ganesh's blessing on my marriage and on our children, that debt must be paid.

It started just after we got back to the flat in Notting Hill. I had worn suitable Indian dress to visit the temple and I was half way through getting changed for a more English night out when Conrad said, 'Do you think Ganesh will pass on the message to Pramiti?'

I do not have Pramiti's number, and neither does Conrad. 'I'm sure he will. Ganesh is most meticulous when it comes to balance sheets. He is the god of accountants as well as artists. I'm sure that he adopted mobile technology years before your Allfather.' I was rambling deliberately because I had no top on. I could see an argument coming and didn't want to start at a disadvantage. 'Is this kurti too long for the pub?'

'No. It's fine. Isn't it a bit heavy?'

He was right. The weather was unusually warm – by the standards of an English bank holiday weekend. Our favourite gastro-pub would be heaving tonight and we hadn't reserved a table because we were supposed to be going to visit someone. They had cancelled, but I am getting ahead of myself and trying to avoid what happened next. I slipped off the kurti and replaced it with a red cotton dress. 'Better?'

'Gorgeous. Like you.'

He does talk rubbish sometimes.

I put my hair in an Alice band and went through to the living room. 'Ganesh will give the message to Pramiti, Conrad, but Pramiti will be in touch with me, not you.'

'Eh?'

We were coming to the crux of the matter. 'It is me who owes the debt to her, Conrad, not you. It is me that must repay it.'

He was shaking his head before I'd finished speaking. 'She made it very clear that she was going to collect from me. You weren't there, remember?'

'Yes. I was in prison. I'm not going to forget that, am I? It doesn't change anything. I prayed for help. I was given help. It is me who owes the debt, not you.'

'Technically, I suppose. It doesn't matter, though. So long as it's paid.'

I went to stand nearer the open window to get some air. 'Pramiti has been told in no uncertain terms that she deals with me. Not you.'

'How? When? If you don't have her number…'

'I met her. Remember?'

Earlier in the summer, the Mages of Salomon's House had conducted a summoning at the well. They had been after Conrad's ancestor, Thomas Clarke, and their Summoner, Li Cheng, got Pramiti as a bonus.

Before that day, when the slippery Nāgin had doorstepped Conrad, she was attacked by a dog and seriously wounded. She had taken refuge in the well and reappeared when that poor man had used all of his magickal energy to summon Spectre Thomas. See what I mean? Pramiti stole his energy to heal the wound in her side. It took Li Cheng days to recover.

'Of course I remember,' said Conrad. 'You gave her a piece of your mind and threatened dire consequences if anything happened to me.'

I nodded my head. 'Mmm. About that.'

He narrowed his eyes. That's the first warning sign with Conrad.

'What about that?' he said. And that was the second sign: his voice goes flat. The third warning sign is that his hands go to his sides, within easy reach of his guns.

'I spoke to Pramiti in Gujarati and Hindi. I may not have translated it accurately.' When you are trying to get him used to a new idea, it's best to take it slowly.

'So what did you really say?'

'I told her that she was to deal with me and only me, and that I would tie her in a sack with a giant mongoose if she tried to contact you.'

'A giant mongoose.'

'Yes. I know that you've heard of Rikki-Tikki-Tavi, so don't pretend you haven't.'

Keep him off balance. Also a good idea. Unfortunately, he showed last week that he can still ride horses and fly helicopters. His sense of balance is not so easily disturbed.

'And where would you get a giant mongoose? In snake form, Pramiti is fifteen feet long. Even Rikki-Tikki-Tavi would baulk at that.'

'Import one from India. If there are giant snakes, there must be giant mongooses. Mongeese. Whatever.'

He nodded slowly. 'Quick thinking, love. I'm all in favour of extravagant threats.' He isn't. I've never known him make a threat that he wouldn't happily carry out. He smiled in a brave attempt to disarm what he was about to say. 'You lied to me.'

And that was the real problem.

Before he ever became involved in the world of magick, I made Conrad promise never to lie to me. I had good reasons at the time. Honestly. And because his family motto is *A Clarke's Word is Binding*, he has stuck to it.

Now that we are betrothed, I am beginning to see that such a one-sided arrangement isn't necessarily a good thing for the long term, and I am a firm believer in the long term. I could make the same promise myself, but I'd never keep it.

'I had a good reason to lie,' I said. 'You had just learnt that your ancestor was part of terrible events that are causing even more trouble four centuries later. You didn't need any more problems.'

He pulled his lip. That's usually a sign of moral uncertainty. 'I proposed to you because I was ready to take on Pramiti. If you'd told me the truth, I might not have proposed at all, and I definitely wouldn't have proposed without talking it through first.'

Damn. He was being reasonable. I hate it when he does that. I nodded my *I agree with you* nod. 'I was going to talk it over with you next week,' I lied. 'Before we go back to Pellacombe for the royal election. You took me by surprise. It was a beautiful surprise. I didn't want to spoil it.'

He turned away and his hands reached for his pocket. Not his gun, the pocket with his cigarettes in. Then he remembered that he couldn't smoke in here. This was to my advantage. 'Things have changed,' he said. 'You have your Ancile now. We'll take it on together.'

I took a deep breath. 'No. This is something I have to do on my own.' His eyes narrowed again. I didn't give him a chance to respond. 'This is my debt in every sense, Conrad. I cannot have you risk your life over it. Or your reputation.'

'My reputation?' He'd swallowed the bait. Good.

'If we were dealing with a Dragon or an angry Mage, I would stay well away and leave you to it, but we are not. We are dealing with a serpent. The lowest snake. An Indian cobra.'

'What's Pramiti's ethnicity got to do with anything? In particular, what has it got to do with my reputation?'

'It has everything to do with your reputation. You swallowed that story she gave you hook line and sinker.'

Pramiti is missing a jewel. A special jewel. She told Conrad that it was stolen from her while she slept. Hah.

'Why would she lie? Vicky said that she was seriously weakened.'

The jewel is crucial to a Nāgin's life-cycle. 'I don't deny that she has lost her Mānik,' I replied. 'What do you know about them? How much research have you done?' He shrugged. 'I thought so. I have been looking into the race of Nāgin for weeks now, with help from Dr Somerton. You cannot steal a Mānik, any more than you can steal someone's liver. I think she gave it away or traded it.'

'What? You can't be serious.'

'I can. I may need to steal it back. You cannot be involved in that.'

'Nor can you! You've only just been given an appointment with the magickal court. If you get arrested for theft, you'll be fired and lose everything you've worked for.'

'I might. I wouldn't lose you, though. You cannot risk getting involved with Pramiti.'

He pulled his lip. 'It's too dangerous. I know you've got your Ancile, but you have no other magick at all. I barely get by as it is, but at least I can do *some* magick.'

I planted my feet apart and put my hand on my hip. '*Too dangerous*! Says the man who took on a Dragon single handed. What's sauce for you is sauce for me, Conrad. I may be short, but I am no one's little woman.'

'I know. Believe me, I know. You're worth more than I am. If you try to go after the Mānik on your own, I'll withdraw my proposal.'

Damn. I wasn't expecting that. 'What if I don't want to live together? What if I want marriage?'

His head drooped. 'Then I'd let you go. I'd rather lose you than see you hurt trying to marry me. I'm not worth it.'

Double damn. My heart surged with love and my shoulders slumped with despair. All at once. To add to my misery, Scout appeared from the spare room. He whined and sat next to Conrad, who naturally bent down to comfort him. Since Conrad's bond with his Familiar was upgraded, that dog knows far too much about our business.

I tried to look positive and open. 'But I won't be alone. Vicky has agreed to help me.'

'Oh no you don't. You can't drag Vic into this.'

'I am not dragging her anywhere. She jumped at the chance to get involved. You trained her too well, Conrad. She is a Watch Captain in her own right now and she can make her own judgements.'

He gave one of his mega-shrugs, and his hand reached to his cigarettes again. It was time to go in for the kill.

'Ganesh is the god of beginnings,' I said. 'This is the beginning of our future. I promise two things, Conrad. First is to listen to Vicky. If she tells me, at any point, that it's too dangerous, then I will withdraw. Second is this: if we return to Clerkswell with Ganesh's blessing, I will release you from your promise not to lie to me.'

He blinked. 'Where did that come from?'

'It would be wrong to start our betrothal like this. You should not be under a one-sided obligation, and I cannot be restricted in choosing what to do.'

'I'm not going to stop you, am I?'

'Not this time. Not any time.'

'Then give me a kiss.'

We kissed. We kissed for a long time. 'I'd better go and do my makeup,' I finally said. 'If we don't go out soon, there will be no room left at the pub.'

2 — A Snake in her Lair

Pramiti sent me a message on Sunday afternoon: *About time he proposed. Come round and see me later.*

The message arrived just after Dean Hardisty's barbecue, and we were about to leave for an important cricket match in Clerkswell on the bank holiday Monday. I replied: *Sorry. I'm busy tonight. How about Thursday afternoon? Text me your address.*

All I got back was one word: *Fine.* The address didn't arrive until Thursday, and was a mews house in Chelsea, which is a long way from the Tower of London and was very annoying: I had been round the corner from Pramiti's house most of the day for an important shopping expedition with Conrad's new little sister, Sofía. I had to take her back to the Tower so that he could escort her to Salomon's House and so that I could rendezvous with Vicky.

Vicky was the one who introduced me to the world of magick. I like her a lot, even if she can be a bit gloomy sometimes. I blame it on the northern winters. Growing up in Newcastle not only gives you a most strange accent, I'm sure it gives you the voice of doom. I base this on a scientific sample of one: Vicky is the first Geordie I've known properly.

'Are you sure you're ready for this?' I asked when we had settled ourselves into the Uber. Vicky has only just returned to duties after suffering a punctured lung in the line of duty. The enforced rest made her a very grumpy housemate sometimes. On the plus side, she used the time constructively to address important issues such as leg waxing and eyebrow plucking. If you think I am being superficial, bear in mind that you didn't see the *before* version. The thing I miss most about prison is 24/7 access to qualified hairdressers.

Vicky grinned. 'Aye. I'm champion, thanks. Are *you* sure you're up for it?'

I nodded. There was no more to be said.

Vicky was there when Pramiti first appeared. She had a good look at her, and nothing I've learnt since has made Vicky think any differently about the creature. Now that we're on our way to meet her, it's time I let you know a bit more of what we're dealing with.

One of Conrad's allies at the Invisible College is the Keeper of the Queen's Esoteric Library, Dr Francesca Somerton. She is a very wise old woman and has the history of magick at her disposal, and I took every opportunity I could to pump her for information. The first thing I learnt was the right name. The mundane world knows these creatures as *shapeshifters*. That is not only inaccurate but considered insulting. The correct term is *dual natured*.

Like their mundane counterparts, werewolves have been extinct in England for centuries, and much of what Dr Somerton told me related to them rather than the Nāgin. The principle is the same, though, and the same magick applies to the dual natured wherever you find them.

I have not seen Pramiti change with my own eyes. When she stops being a fifteen foot Indian cobra and becomes a woman, she sprouts arms and legs and all the other parts of a human and slowly rears into an upright position. It is similar in reverse. So where does the snake go when it becomes a woman?

I cannot do magick, but I can understand the theory. For all its craziness, magick obeys the law of conservation of mass: where does twenty stone of snake come from and go to? The answer is *another plane of existence*. Vicky has been to the Forest of Arden, which exists in the middle of the Warwickshire countryside. All the oaks and other trees exist on a different plane of energy, and you have to change your own energy state to get there. It is the same with Pramiti.

She has two bodies, one human body and one serpent body. They both occupy the same physical space but have different energy levels. The Mānik is a crucial magickal Artefact for swapping between bodies. If you want to be pedantic, you could say *swapping your consciousness between bodies and changing the bodies' energy states*.

Some of you will be scratching your heads and saying, 'But how do you exchange consciousness? And how does she drag the other body around with her?' I know you will be asking those questions because I asked them, too. This is what Dr Somerton said. 'The bodies each have their own cerebellum, but the rest of the brain is singular. It's more a question of plugging a different body into the same brain. As for moving two bodies around, we haven't got time for that, dear. It involves manipulating the Higgs Boson.'

Fine. I left it at that.

I got the Uber driver to drop us off round the corner from Pramiti's house. It had been raining when we left the Tower. The rain itself had stopped, but the clouds were low and grey. I could see Vicky's hair visibly going into a frizz. Mine would not dare.

I adjusted my bangles and my smoothed out my dress. Vicky hitched up her jeans. We were ready for action.

We walked up the close and Vicky stared around at the converted coach houses, now known as mews. She is househunting at the moment and asked the obvious question. 'How much do you think these are worth?'

'I checked. That one over there, the one that looks like it needs new windows, it went for £3.5 million in February.'

'Nooo! You're kidding me.'

'I wish I was. Would you swap that for three Elvenham Houses?'

'I'd like to have the choice. Is Pramiti renting?'

'Yes. It's that one, with the blue doors.'

'Nice. It's got three storeys, too. After you.'

I rang the bell and stood back. I assumed that Pramiti would keep us waiting on principle, but the door was opened straight away by a thin young woman of South East Asian heritage. She barely looked up enough to see who was at the door before lowering her head and standing back. She was wearing a cheap black shift and leggings and had no makeup on. That would be a deliberate policy, I assumed: Pramiti would not want the help looking more glamorous than her.

The mews house may have been high, but it wasn't very deep. There was room for a small kitchen on the left, with a cloakroom, then you were straight into the living room, which also included the staircase.

The underlying decor was still a tasteful mix of water themed blues and whites, just visible if you looked beyond the riot of colours that Pramiti had dumped all over the furniture and walls. Vibrant red and green throws covered the sofas with gold cushions on top. Two mosaics with scenes from the Hindu epics in metallic tiles glittered in the lamplight. Crammed into a corner and sitting on top of a chest was an altar to Ganesh. As you might expect, our hostess was absent.

'Sit down, please,' said the maid. 'I make tea.'

'Bit gloomy in here,' said Vicky. 'What's wrong with daylight, eh?'

I made Namaste to Ganesh and chose one end of the larger sofa. Vicky took the other. While we waited, I asked where she had been looking for houses. A safe topic. We both knew that Pramiti would be listening – we could hear her moving about upstairs and even opening drawers. She waited until the maid had finished bringing in the tea before she descended the staircase. We both stood to greet her and give her the respect she is owed as a creature of my lord. She deserves that much. She will have to earn the rest.

'You will not believe how hard it is to get servants in London,' said Pramiti. 'No men will work inside at all except eunuchs, and no Indian girl will do it either. I had to have this Cambodian or a Bengali. It took me a week to show her how to make tea properly. Sit down, please. You may pour now.'

Vicky leaned in to whisper, 'Eunuchs? Seriously?'

'I'll tell you later.'

We made ourselves comfortable again, and while the maid was serving, I took a good look at our hostess. Pramiti should not be considered human, because she isn't. When she visited Elvenham, she turned into a snake because that is her natural form, and the Wards protecting the house made her change. I had to force myself to remember this when I looked at the image from a temple carving made flesh and sitting opposite me.

She is taller than me, but not much, and Conrad was being very polite when he described her as *curvy*. That doesn't do justice to her figure, and I have seen her naked so I speak from experience. The word I would choose is *ripe*. Her breasts are large and defy gravity, her hips are broad and well padded, and her waist is pinched. No real woman ever looked like that without spending an epic amount of time under the knife of a deranged cosmetic surgeon.

The most galling thing about her is that despite the improbable body shape, she looks completely natural. Next to her, I look like undeveloped child. Unfinished. I don't know how Vicky feels because I am scared to ask.

The maid finished serving, and Pramiti dismissed her. 'Do not disturb us,' she said. My arm throbbed with magick and the servant brought her hand to her chest. 'I have put a Silence on her,' said Pramiti. 'We can talk freely now. Please, enjoy your tea.'

The maid had served proper Indian tea: milky, sweet, strong and spicy. And hot. Vicky burnt her mouth on the first sip and looked at the glass as if it contained poison. Chai can be an acquired taste; I do not serve it to the others at Clerkswell.

Our hostess was dressed in the most expensive, luxurious sari, more extravagant than most Indian women would dream of for their weddings. Silk, of course, and bright red, with gold embroidery. She adjusted it and switched to Hindi to address me.

I kept a straight face and turned to Vicky. 'Pramiti has asked when the man is going to arrive.'

Vicky laughed her big Geordie laugh and said to Pramiti, 'That depends on whether you ordered one, pet. What time do they normally deliver men in Knightsbridge?'

Pramiti's face darkened like approaching thunder. I quickly stepped in. 'Perhaps it would be quicker if we stuck to English, Pramiti-ji. I am sure that you have been practising a lot.'

Very powerful people, or snakes, will never acknowledge criticism. She did, however, stick to English. 'Where is Conrad?'

I bowed my head. 'Watch Captain Robson has graciously agreed to assist me. I am very lucky to have such a powerful Mage on my side.'

'I don't want her, I want the Dragonslayer, as they all call him.'

I had warned Vicky not to rise to the bait. She kept her lips pressed together and only opened them to drink more tea.

'Conrad is unfortunately detained elsewhere,' I said. 'He sends his apologies and begs your forgiveness.'

'That is very kind of him, I'm sure.'

'Perhaps we could focus on your Mānik, Pramiti-ji. How was it you came to lose it?'

'It was stolen from me. By an English Mage.'

I nodded. 'A very powerful English Mage. More powerful than any that I have heard of to have been able to perform the … what did you call it, Vicky?'

'The biplanar disentanglement.'

'Aah. That's it. Human Mages have never succeeded in this before. You must have been very unlucky that the first one to do so was wandering along the Ganges while you slept.'

Pramiti's chest flushed almost as red as her sari. 'What are you saying?'

'I am saying that we cannot help you unless we have a clearer idea of what happened.'

Pramiti stared at Vicky. Hard.

Vicky finished her tea and put the glass down. 'Cheers for that. I'll tell you what, there's so much sugar in there that you don't need biscuits, do you?'

Pramiti turned back to me and sniffed. Her hair is huge, bouncy and wavy and flows about her like a cloak. I would love to have my hair like that. And enough time in the day to do it. Or magick. She shifted some of the locks away from her arms and said, 'My English has improved a lot since I first came here. Especially after I spent so long in that well of Conrad's. It stank of those creatures. Thomas-ji told me that the English word for them is *Fae*.'

I blinked, but Vicky couldn't control herself. She took a sharp inbreath and then swore. 'In *India*? There's no Fae in India.'

'And for that we must be thankful,' said Pramiti gracefully. 'It also explains why one of them was able to trick me.'

'What was she even doing there in the first place?'

'He. It was most definitely a he, and don't start to quibble with me. I know a man when I see one.'

This is not the place for a long detour into the sex life of the Fae. 'No one would know better, Pramiti-ji,' I said. 'The other question is still one that troubles me: what was one Fae doing in India?'

'Have you heard of the Delhi Durbar of 1903, little one?' she asked me, naturally assuming that Vicky hadn't heard of it.

I bowed my head. 'There is a photograph in my father's house of Paradaada-ji attending the Durbar. I saw it earlier this year. It is still there.'

'Gujarat, isn't it?' said Pramiti.

'North west of Vadodara. Not far from the river Mahi.'

She bowed her head in acknowledgement. 'I have never been.' She looked at Vicky and then at me. 'Tell her. It will save time.'

I spoke rapidly. 'When Edward the Seventh became king of England, he also became Emperor of India. There was a mega ceremony to proclaim him in Delhi. It was massive. The Governor was very upset that Edward didn't turn up himself.'

Pramiti took over. 'He sent his younger brother, Arthur, Duke of Connaught.'

Vicky's eyes lit up. 'Didn't he have a spell as Duke of Albion?'

'I wouldn't know,' said Pramiti. 'Or care. If he did, he had abdicated by 1903. The actual Duke of Albion came along with him and there was a parallel, magickal Prana-Durbar. I attended as one of Lord Ganesh's agents.'

Vicky and I looked at each other and smiled. *Agent* was a word that could cover a multitude of sins. Pramiti pretended not to notice.

'One of the aristocrats from England was the Earl of Kerry. His son was Lord Butler.' She paused.

'Nope,' said Vicky.

'I am afraid that I have never heard of either of them,' I said.

'No matter. The son was a changeling. A Fae Count. I believe that's the correct term.'

'A Count?' said Vicky. Pramiti nodded. A Fae Count is a noble in their world. He/She serves a Fae Prince.

'Yes. He said that his lord was considering setting up a sídhe in India, and had sent him out to explore the possibilities.'

'Ooh,' said Vicky. 'That's a bit naughty.'

'The British Empire in India is history for you. I lived through it. I saw much, much worse.'

'Sorry,' said Vicky.

Pramiti nodded to show that she accepted the apology and moved on. 'I have met several of the Fae here in London. They are all much the same. Thomas-ji said the English expression was *They think they're God's gift*. It sums them up, I think.'

'Aye, you're not wrong there. Do they give you the creeps 'an all, because they do to me.' Vicky added a shiver to show what she thought of them.

'If only that were true,' said Pramiti with a sigh. 'Far from "giving me the creeps" as you put it, he gave me the Rapture. I have never experienced anything like it before or since.'

'It works on youse?' said Vicky with surprise.

'Youse? What is that?'

Vicky gave her a hard stare. 'The plural of *you*. I thought Rapture only worked on humans.'

'Am I not human?'

There was no answer to that. If she really thought she was human, who are we to argue?

Pramiti moved her feet around on the couch and adjusted her sari again. She was getting to the difficult bit. 'He took me in the form of a serpent. Both of us. I have never known anything like it.'

Vicky's delicately shaped eyebrows went into orbit. 'How...?'

'No matter, how. He tricked me into offering him my Mānik. He said that I wouldn't miss it and that he was suffering terribly from shifting to the Spirit realm.' She looked down. 'I never saw him again, and within an hour I was nearly dead. Our Lord answered my prayer and made this mark.' She touched the red dot, the bindi, on her forehead. 'It kept me alive, but it is not the same.'

Vicky nodded sympathetically. 'He definitely tricked you, did he?'

'As Ganesh is my witness.'

'How can I put this? Are you sure it wasn't just a gift that you regret?'

'Would you give your heart and accept a mechanical pump in its place?'

Ugh. What an image. Vicky didn't like it much, either. 'Fair enough. I asked around, and if the Mānik was tricked out of you, we can get it back under English magickal law. That might not make a difference to you, but it does to us. The only problem now is finding the creep who did it.'

'I believe that I can help you,' said Pramiti, rising like a volcano of silk from the couch. She crossed to the altar and took out a small wooden box from the chest underneath. It was a beautiful example of Indian artisanal work, intricately carved and brightly painted. On the lid, Lord Ganesh was being pulled in a chariot by a team of monkeys. She weighed the box in her hands and then placed it carefully on the coffee table. She didn't sit down again.

'One thing about him I could tell was his real name. It is written on parchment in that box.'

Vicky withdrew slightly and looked at me. I looked blankly back. She addressed our hostess. 'You mean his Quicksilver name? His true name?'

'I do. Take the box. And may Ganesh guide you.'

There was a shiver of magick, and Pramiti shouted for her servant.

I bowed my thanks and within seconds we were blinking in the daylight and reaching for our umbrellas. The rain was back.

3 — *A Fae Encounter*

'What now?' I said. 'There were large parts of that I didn't understand.'

'That makes two of us. Come on, let's get out of the rain. We'll get a black cab. There's always loads round here.'

'Where are we going?'

'Salomon's House.'

'All the way back to the City? Do we have to?'

'Yes. I do not want to spend a single second longer than I have to with this burning a hole in me bag.'

She pointed to where she had secreted the little box and then started walking quickly out of the mews court.

I caught up with her. 'Is it really so dangerous?'

'Shh.' She was right about the black cabs. One was coming towards us and she stuck out an arm to pull it over. 'No talking in the cab, alright? Not about this. Tell me more about Raven. Is she really that tall?'

'You have no idea.'

I started a monologue about the enormous Witch called Raven who was part of a mission in Cornwall that Conrad and I are on. I'd said most of it already, and it soon became clear that Vicky was scanning the traffic like a spy in a film. She got worried at one point and ordered the taxi driver to take a detour off Fleet Street. She was even beginning to worry me. Surely that box couldn't be *so* dangerous?

The taxi was still moving when she jumped out on to Ironmonger Lane and dived into the back entrance of Salomon's House, something that should not be possible in a black cab.

'Bloody hell,' said the cabbie. 'The safety locks have failed.'

I knew that Vicky had used magick, because I'd felt it. I improvised. 'I think my dress may have caught in the door when we got in and jammed the lock.'

'But...'

'She won't be long. It's been a tiring day. We're very grateful. If you don't mind waiting?'

He got the hint: shut up, there's a big tip on the way. I sat back and asked him what he thought of the England cricket team's performance this summer. I was in luck – he actually likes cricket. We were deep in conversation about whether Jimmy Anderson's days were numbered when Vicky reappeared.

She was looking much happier and told the cabbie to go to a road I had never heard of and drop us outside a pub that I had no idea existed. The City of London is a very different place to what I call real London. I think it was the biggest tip I've ever given a taxi driver.

It was quiet inside the pub. Some City of London pubs have been there since the Great Fire of 1666 (and some haven't cleaned the toilets since the Blitz. Ugh); others are temples of glass and chrome that mirror the skyscrapers which surround them. This pub was in the latter category.

'I wouldn't have thought this was your kind of place,' I said. 'I thought Mages preferred haunts were just that – haunted. The only ghosts here are the reflections in the mirrors. Do these City types really love themselves so much?'

'Yes they do. I think I need a proper drink. Merlot?'

'Please. Californian if they've got it.'

I found a table in the corner where I could keep an eye on the doors without having to look at myself in the process. Vicky came back with the drinks and relaxed another level. 'Cheers, Mina. You're right about haunted pubs. Generally speaking, the older the better for most Mages. The trouble is, we're very close to Salomon's House here. All the really nice pubs are also popular with the tutors. That can really put you off your stroke, that can. They wouldn't be seen dead in here. Another bonus, the guys are much better looking. Desi and I used to come in at six and never had to buy a drink.'

I thought of her best friend, Desirée Haynes, pillar of the evangelical church choir, and tried to imagine them being chatted up for free drinks. 'Mmm, Vicky, I am struggling with that concept. You, I can see as a cheap tart, Desi not so much.'

She roared with laughter. 'Tart I may be, but I'm never cheap. Nothing but champagne if I'm not buying.' She leaned forwards and I really tried to imagine it. I only met her once before she was formally partnered with Conrad. Before she died and grew up.

I tried to imagine a carefree, twenty year old Victoria Robson in a short skirt perching on the bar stool. 'Fair enough,' I said. 'You I can believe, but I'm still struggling with Desi.'

'Just you wait and see what happens when we get our own place.' She took in a big breath and held her hand to her right breast as she did so. 'No pain from me wound. Good. I did wonder how it would cope with being stressed.'

'Why were you so worried?' I asked. 'What was in that box and why couldn't we even talk about it in the taxi?'

She had sat next to me at the table rather than the more natural position opposite. She wanted to watch the doors as much as I did. Being around Conrad has that effect on you. She scanned the bar again and lowered her voice. 'You've met Niði, the Dwarf. Even without magick yourself, could you feel something ... I don't know. Something *wrong* about him?'

'There was very little right about Niði. Not that I didn't like him.'

She shuddered. 'Every time I think I understand you, Mina, you say something like that.' I didn't take offence. I am used to being misunderstood.

She continued, 'Dwarves have a part-silicon biology. No human really understands it, and it's the same with the Fae. Not silicon, but mercury.'

'I have heard something about it. I focused on snakes, not fairies, when I spoke to Dr Somerton.'

'Shhh! Never use the F-y word! Fae, yes, the other one, no. Never.'

She was deadly serious. And wound up. Conrad uses it when he's particularly pissed off, and I shall have to find out what the problem is. Not today, though. 'You were saying,' I said. 'About mercury.'

'Aye. Well. It's very toxic to humans. Very, very toxic. To the Fae, it's crucial. As far as we can tell, it has a place in the brain, and it definitely has a place in their magick. Being alchemists, we obviously use the old word for mercury – Quicksilver.'

'Aah. You said something about a Quicksilver name.'

'I did. And that's what's in the box. The Fae have their own language, only ever used in the sídhe, and they have secret names. That's one bit of the legends that's true: if you know a Fae's Quicksilver name, you have a hold over them.'

'So what's the problem?'

'It's dangerous. Their first reaction is usually to kill you rather than let you pass it on. I don't know, because I didn't open the box, but if Pramiti wrote that name down on Parchment, it will have sounded like a fire engine to any Fae around. We were lucky to get all the way across London without being intercepted.'

'Couldn't you hear it?'

She shook her head. 'It broadcasts on a different frequency to my magickal potential. I might be making a fuss over nothing. Anyway, it's safe in the Esoteric Library.'

'Won't they try to break in?'

'There's a vault and a treaty. I put the name in there without looking, and they leave it alone. Long story.' She took a sip of wine. More of a gulp. 'Before we go on, I just wanted to say that I thought you were brilliant in there. You had Pramiti wrapped round your little finger.'

I looked down at my wine and let my hair come forward. I don't like compliments, not even ones from Vicky, who is as genuine as anyone I know. 'I had a forked stick,' I said.

'Eh? Forked stick? What are you on about, man?'

I looked up. 'Before they invented long pincers for picking up snakes, they used a forked stick. My grandfather used to do it.'

'You what? Your grandfather was a snake charmer? I thought he was some sort of lord of the manor.'

I frowned. 'He was. He still is. He only stopped dealing with the snakes when his arthritis got bad. Someone has to deal with them. They try to come in during the monsoons, especially when you have an open house.'

Her eyes bulged. 'You are kidding me.'

'No.'

She shivered. 'I am not visiting your family. Ever. At least that explains why you weren't so scared of her as I would have been.'

'I was respectful of her. I just did what I had to and then let her go, which is what Daada-ji did. He used to throw them over the wall into the cotton fields.'

She chuckled. 'What was she talking about eunuchs for? Was that a metaphor for the uselessness of men?'

I turned my wine glass around. 'Pramiti is the servant of Lord Ganesh. My Lord. I want to pay the debt and get his blessing, but we have a problem.' I looked up. 'If we succeed, and restore her to her powers, she will be dangerous. The Nāgin keep slaves. That poor girl serving her. She will not be receiving any wages.'

'Oh.'

'Precisely. And don't forget that there are Nāgas, too. Male versions of Pramiti. They do breed.'

'Shall we cross that bridge when we get to it?'

'Yes. And tell me about the Rapture. Does it have to do with sex?'

'Usually, but not always. It's a special power of the Fae and a few other creatures. It's the magickal equivalent of heroin. Total pleasure overload. It's very addictive, or so I've heard.'

There was something in her voice. 'Have you?'

She shook her head. 'Nearly. I once knew someone who did. She was nearly lost completely. It's not without its risks to the Fae, so they don't use it a lot. I could name a very popular entertainer from our dad's era who could use it on a whole auditorium.'

I was about to push her for more details when something made us both look at the doors. A man had come in, and he was looking our way. My heart missed two beats, the first because he was drop-dead gorgeous and the second because he had a hunger in his eyes that raised hackles on my hackles. Whatever they are. It was spooky. That's the word I used when I am creeped out by magick. Spooky. And the spookiest thing of all was the man who held the door open for him: our cab driver. How????

'Incoming Fae Knight,' said Vicky. 'I thought it wouldn't be long before we had company.'

'What do we do?'

'Try not to panic.'

'Helpful.'

'Oh, and if he offers to shake hands, check your ring afterwards.'

He went to the bar and peeled off five twenty pound notes. He pointed to our table and the barman nodded. When he came over, I realised that I was holding my breath. His hair was tightly curled and jet black, his jaw was chiselled and his shoulders broad under a fine silk suit jacket. He was just too good to be true in all departments. That didn't mean that I couldn't enjoy the view, though, did it?

When he got closer, just before he was about to pull out a chair, he stopped and frowned for a second. 'This, I did not expect,' he said. 'A Captain of Nimue's Guard and her well protected friend.'

Nimue's Guard is the Fae name for the King's Watch. They don't like saying the word *King*.

I made namaste and he bowed in return. He studied us for another second and held out his hand. 'I am the Knight of the Silver Field, also known as Jon Ashford, in the service of the Duke of Ashford. It's a pleasure to meet you.'

Vicky shook and said, 'Watch Captain Robson. Vicky. Off duty at the moment.'

It was my turn. My arm tingled as his fingers wrapped around mine. I felt warmth and strength in his hand, but nothing else. 'And I am Mina Desai. Also off duty.'

He released my hand and I couldn't help checking that my engagement ring and my favourite gold bangle were still there. From now on, Vicky was definitely in charge.

The barman arrived with three champagne flutes and an ice bucket with a bottle of Taittinger, my favourite Champagne, chilling nicely. 'Will you join me?' said the Knight of the Silver Field.

Do they really go around calling themselves things like that? I was in agreement with Pramiti: they really do think they're God's gift. I shall refer to him as Jon.

'It would be a pleasure,' said Vicky. 'As we're on common ground.'

Jon hesitated with his hand over the ice bucket. Vicky had made it clear that we would only talk to him under a flag of truce. Technically that meant we were joint hosts, but there was no way I was paying for champagne at these prices.

'Very well.' With a swirl of magick, the cork was out and the glasses were full. 'Good health and long life,' he said.

We joined the toast and waited for him to make the first move. Naturally, he picked on me.

'I can't say I've heard your name before, Miss Desai, yet here you are with an Ancile on your skin and a very special ring. Your fiancé wouldn't be a Gnome by any chance, would he?'

I smiled and sipped my champagne. Vicky nearly choked on her bubbles.

'Howay, man, what do you take us for? Your boss'll tell you sharp enough. Mina is the Peculier Auditor, and she's here on her own account, not her fiancé's.'

He gave me a searching look and reluctantly turned his attention to Vicky. You might say that his reluctance was because he saw me as the weaker one and wanted to press his advantage. I prefer to think that he found me more attractive. In an exotic way, of course. I'll let you decide.

'You were lucky that I was nearby,' he said. 'Even so, I had to run to get here. Don't worry, we won't be disturbed.'

I tried to keep my mouth shut. I really did. And I failed. 'Who would disturb us?'

Vicky knows me too well to be upset. 'Other Fae,' she said. 'He's put a marker down. A bit like when Scout leaves a puddle. Unless a very big one turns up, of course.'

Jon's whole attitude changed in a second. The security cameras wouldn't show anything, but right here, round the table, I could feel the temperature drop and his charm clicked off like Vicky had thrown a switch.

'Why were you parading my master's name through the streets of London like the Lord Mayor's Show, and where is it now?'

'That answers one question,' said Vicky. 'It was definitely Enscribed on Parchment in an unprotected box.' She put her glass down. 'Cards on the table, eh? We were given your master's name by someone he once dealt with.'

'Really?'

'Really.'

He frowned. 'Does that person know what they've done? Do they realise how serious this is?'

Vicky looked at me. 'Mina?'

'I think she knows exactly what she did.'

Jon rubbed the stubbly beard that added extra mystery to his face. Stop it Mina! Focus on the job.

'Where is it now?' he said.

'In a safe place,' said Vicky. 'The Esoteric Library. Fairly and legally deposited.'

He nodded. 'And you would take an oath that you did not read it?'

'I would.'

He sat back. 'Much as I'm enjoying your company, why are we here?'

'Pour us another glass and Mina will tell you.'

It was my turn to choke on the fizz. I gave her my *you could have told me* look and tried to pull my thoughts together. A large glass of merlot, followed by Champagne, all on an empty stomach, isn't the best preparation for negotiations with supernatural creatures.

Jon poured the drinks with an effortless flick of the wrist to make sure there was no spillage. 'Would you like to make the toast?' he said to me.

Perhaps it was the wine. 'To mutual satisfaction,' I said.

'I'll always drink to that,' he said.

'Your master was in Delhi in 1903,' I said. 'He travelled under the name Lord Butler.'

'If you say so.'

'I do. And he brought back a souvenir. You know what it's like these days, all those former colonies wanting their art and treasures back. Perhaps the Duke of Ashford might consider restitution.'

'Is that so? I'm sure my lord has many souvenirs.'

'Get your phone out. I'll message you an image. I'm sure it'll jog his memory. You can go outside and bring him up to date.'

We made contact and I sent him a new-agey picture of a woman and a snake twined together. It would get the message across.

He stared at his phone. 'Are you serious? A snake?'

This young Fae knight was clearly wet behind the ears. I got the feeling that this would be the one and only time I would feel older and wiser than one of them. 'You'd better send it quickly,' I said. I also had to resist the urge to pat his arm.

When I got up this morning, I did not envisage feeling like an older woman looking for a toyboy. Tempting, though.

'Fine.' He picked up his glass and took it outside.

'We'd better take it in turns to go to the ladies,' said Vicky. 'You go first.'

We both went, and both got back. The Knight of the Silver Field was still outside. We could see him nodding and almost bowing through the smokey glass walls. 'Looks like we've hit pay dirt,' said Vicky. 'What's your next step?'

'Unlike the British government, I am a firm believer in always leaving No Deal on the table.'

'Hey! You know the rules. No Brexit discussions.'

I grinned. Vicky gets very sensitive about these things. 'It was a metaphor. If this Duke of Ashford doesn't want to play ball, we'll text the location of his sídhe to Pramiti and she can deal with him.'

'You wouldn't.'

I nodded firmly. 'You could sell tickets. It would be quite a show.'

Vicky's complexion is perfectly adapted to a climate where no sun shines from September to May. To say that she went white would be to say nothing. She did swallow hard and lick her lips nervously.

Jon came back to the table with his phone still glued to his ear. 'Is she in the country?' he said to me.

I gave him a smile and blinked at him.

'She won't say,' he said into the phone. He listened and said, 'Probably … Of course, my lord.' He held out the phone to me. 'I'll put a Silence around this corner.' he said. I accepted the phone and he stood up.

'Hello. Is that the duke?'

'Yes, I am Lord Ashford, Miss Desai. What an honour. I believe that you are not only the new star of the Cloister Court, but you're also engaged to the Dragonslayer. My congratulations.'

The voice was rich and throaty with a hard edge. If this Fae had ever gone into the movies, he would have played the gang boss in a crime story.

'The honour is mine, Lord Ashford,' I replied. 'I am only here in a private capacity, and Vicky is a personal friend. None of this need go any further.'

'Good to know. I doubt that Conrad Clarke would be happy if anything happened to you.'

'Why should it?'

'Indeed, Miss Desai, indeed. None of us wants an awkward situation to turn into a crisis, do we?'

I thought his question was rhetorical, but he clearly expected me to buy into this. 'We do not. Let's all work together to resolve it.'

'Good. I want to help, and I will help, but there's a problem. I gave the ruby away. A long time ago.'

'That really is awkward.'

'But not the end. If I remember correctly, your … friend? Client? Compatriot?'

'We'll stick with client. It's closer to the truth.'

'As you wish. If I remember correctly, your client can be quite volatile. I'm sure she hasn't changed. If you keep my identity from her until tomorrow morning, I will undertake rigorous enquiries overnight.'

'That is no problem. I have an engagement tonight anyway. Might I ask how long ago it was when you last saw the Mānik?'

'The ruby? During Edward VII's time, and that's another problem. I gave it to my Lord Prince. He mounted it in a ring so that humans could use it, and he gave it to a princess. A human princess from one of those little German places. The human princess was married to the Duke of … It doesn't matter. He was very much a member of the British royal family. Another reason for keeping this quiet. Thank you for your forbearance, Miss Desai.'

'And thank you for the time, Lord Ashford. And the champagne.'

'Give Sir Jonathan your number and I'll call you. Until tomorrow. Goodbye.'

Vicky had been listening hard. 'I don't know whether to be terrified or encouraged. Pramiti hasn't exactly hidden herself. He could be organising a pre-emptive strike against her.'

'I only promised to keep his identity secret, not his existence. I shall give Pramiti an update. I'm sure she'll take appropriate measures.'

Jon (who looks nothing like a *Sir Jonathan*) cancelled the magick and sat down. I returned his phone and gave him my number.

'If you'll excuse me,' he said, 'I need to be going. I'll leave what's left of the bottle for you. Good to meet you.'

We shook hands and he left. I started to message Pramiti, and Vicky checked her own phone.

'Look at this!' she said. 'Conrad's invited me for dinner with youse tonight, and both his sisters.'

She was right. In a separate text to me he said that Rachael was less likely to explode if Vicky were there. I couldn't argue with that and told Vicky that I thought it was a lovely idea.

'I need to get changed,' she replied. 'I can't go like this.'

'And me.' I checked the time. 'I don't think we can get to both our flats *and* the restaurant. Shall we split up, or can you lend me that dress you wore to the garden party?' I added a smile.

Vicky gave me a dark look. 'You mean the one me Mam said was too tight and too short?'

Her mother was right. I wasn't going to say that, though. 'I thought it was a lovely colour, that's all.'

'Go on. If Rachael's paying, it'll be worth going. And I want to see how she gets on with Sofía.' She poured the last of the Taittinger. 'Talking of getting on, how did you find Sir Jon? As a person.'

'Rather handsome, actually. Smoother than I'm used to, but I could be persuaded.'

'Aye, and that's the rub. He's only a knight. Barely a teenager in Fae terms, but that's what they do in person. They radiate desirability. You'll notice he turned it off sharp when he didn't get his own way.'

I thought back. 'You're right. He did.'

'Watch out, is all I'm saying. You can't stop them doing it, but you can control the way you respond.'

I tilted my head. 'And if I didn't want to control it? For argument's sake?'

She shook her head and looked down. 'You wouldn't regret it until afterwards. Shall we go?'

4 — *All Kinds of Family*

We had no idea what time Lord Ashford would get in touch, so Vicky and I agreed to meet at the Regent's café in Regent's Park. It was roughly half way between her place in Islington and ours in Notting Hill. Conrad was spending the day sorting out the flat with Sofía, ready for her moving in permanently now that she was going to be a student at Salomon's House.

It was a brighter day, but still not bright enough for Vicky's enormous shades. 'I'm out of practice,' she said.

'At drinking? Not from what I've seen in Clerkswell.'

'No. General debauchery. I'm sure there was more cream in that starter than I normally eat in a week. I need coffee. Preferably intravenously. And pastries.'

'Lightweight.'

We were deep in a discussion about why Vicky had offered a room in her potential new house to Alain Dupont when I got a three word message: *Farthingale and Daughter.* What? I showed the message to Vicky.

'Bloomsbury,' she said. 'I'll book an Uber.'

She got the driver to drop us at the back of the British Museum. I have always liked this part of London: serious and solid, unlike the chaos of the West End or the cutthroat cleanliness of the City. 'Where are we really going?' I said.

'Biggest human dealers in magickal Artefacts in Europe, that's where.'

Somewhere in the back of my brain an alarm bell was sounding. I must have been more hungover than I thought because I had no idea why it was ringing.

We headed round the corner and Vicky said, 'There's quite a few dealers round here. If I'm in town when Sofía starts at the Invisible College, I might take her on a tour. We won't be going to Farthingale's though.'

'Why not?'

'Right out of my league. When it comes to Artefacts, I'm an IKEA kind of girl. Farthingale's are like Sotheby's, Bonhams and Christie's all rolled into one. It's down here.'

This area is full of little parks and squares – Tavistock, Woburn, Russell. Vicky turned off one of them and into a short no-through road with a large house on the right. It was a stunning property, all white and pillars with a huge front door up the steps. If Conrad were here, he'd be telling me that it was neo-Georgian or post-Gothic or something. Whatever it was, I was looking at lots of zeroes in the price, and that alarm bell in my head was now ringing so loudly that I couldn't ignore it. Vicky was about to cross the road until I grabbed her by the arm.

'Vicky, would this be a good place to buy a necklace of Moondrops?'

'You what? Where did that come from? How have you even heard of Moondrops?'

'Would it?'

'Hell, aye. If they haven't got one, they'll know where to get one.'

'Then we can't go in dressed like this. I need to change.'

'What! Is my dress not good enough for you now?'

It was unfortunate. In the fug of early morning, I'd put Vicky's dress back on after last night and couldn't be bothered to change it when I woke up properly. She had taken a dim view of that when we first met.

'I need a disguise. I don't suppose you can put a spell on me?'

She shook her head. 'I keep telling you. They're not *spells*, they're *Works*, and no, I can't. Not one that would get us up the steps. What's the problem?'

I already had my phone out and was retreating down the road. 'Angels costume hire. It's only round the corner. A couple of corners. Come on.'

It was more than a couple of corners. It took more than five minutes, which is Vicky's limit for walking, and she was starting to moan like a toddler when we got there. 'For the love of Pete, will you tell me what the flamin' hell you're up to, Mina?'

I stopped outside the small shop front, currently filled with a tribute to Alice in Wonderland. 'I'm not going to tell you in case I'm wrong.'

When we emerged from the shop (or the third floor of the shop, to be accurate), Vicky announced, 'I am not walking around London with you dressed like that. We are taking a cab, and that's that.'

'Quite right,' I said. 'Princesses do not walk. And don't forget my name.'

'No, Rani.'

It had started as a joke in prison: I shared a Bollywood DVD and they got hooked. A lot of the girls started calling me *Rani*, after Rani Mukherjee, star of my favourite film. When I got out of jail, the Clerkswell girls realised that Rani also means *Princess*, and kept it up for some reason. I should point out that although the young Ms Mukherjee is the same height as me, she has a much smaller nose and much better jaw line. And a better figure. Conrad says I have nicer eyes. Aah. Bless him.

'Good,' I said. 'You call the cab.'

'You're pushing it now, pet. I'm supposed to be your friend, not your servant.'

I put on the accent. 'I am not understanding your strange English ways.'

'Give over. Talk normal or they'll twig straight away. Besides, the driver's more likely to stop for you than me on account of you being dressed in neon yellow.'

It was the most princess-y of their Indian costumes and the only one that fitted. It would do. I got the cab (she was right about that), and we were soon back outside Farthingale and Daughter.

'You do realise,' said Vicky, 'that if they have an Indian on the staff, we're up shit creek.'

'They don't. Trust me on that.'

'Fine.'

Vicky went up to the Conrad-sized double doors and pressed the bell. Underneath, a brass plate said *Farthingale House*. And that was it. The world of magick does not advertise.

A young (English) man answered the door and ushered us in. Vicky had told me that they would know straight away I had no magick of my own, but that the engagement ring should conceal my Ancile. Even though I was clearly a princess, the young man welcomed Vicky, not me. She is the Mage, and that's all they really care about.

'How can we help?' he said. He'd already taken in Vicky's street-casual outfit and decided not to call anyone important.

'My friend would like to talk about Focuses for Divination,' said Vicky.

He turned his attention to me. I made an elaborate namaste, and he bowed. 'This way, Miss…?'

'Rani Mukherjee,' I said.

'And I'm Ralph,' he replied, leading us through the most exquisitely furnished hallway and down a short corridor to a comfortable small sitting room. He pronounced his name *Rafe*. Typical. There was freshly brewed coffee waiting for us.

Conrad's father would also tell you something about the furniture in here. It looked old and valuable, which is all I can say. I miss my mother every day, even though we didn't speak for years and she only dragged me back to her death-bed to shout at me. Even so, a little part of me is soooo glad that Conrad and Alfred do not have to go round to the old family home in Ealing. It made the Indian makeover of Pramiti's mews house look the height of sophistication. When it came to interiors, my mother had no taste whatsoever. None. There. I've said it.

'How did you two become friends?' said Ralph.

'Amelia is the daughter of our London housekeeper,' I said, trying not to look at Vicky. 'We grew up together until she became a Mage.' I lowered my head modestly. 'It is thanks to her that I met my fiancé. I am lucky enough to be marrying the mundane son of a very magickal family. From Austria.'

'Oh, really?' said Ralph.

'Yes.' Before he could ask who they were, I pressed on. 'Obviously there is a big problem with the dowry gifts.'

'I see.'

'Could we start with a selection of Tarot decks? Enchanted, of course.'

'Of course. I won't be a moment. Please, help yourselves to more coffee.'

When he'd left the room, Vicky leaned towards me and whispered, 'Rani, listen.' She pointed to the other side of the room.

I leaned towards her and tilted my head. There was an explosion of pain as she flicked my ear with her fingernail. I'm sure she added magick to make it *really* hurt.

'We will finish this conversation later,' she whispered.

I haven't been flicked on the ear since primary school. Not even in prison. Ouch.

I composed myself, and Ralph returned with a tray that made me gasp. Not even my mother's family (who are much richer than my father's) could have afforded such a thing. It was hardwood, inlaid with rosewood and mother of pearl to pick out the highlights of a geometric design. It also had three wooden boxes on it. I ignored them.

'Forget the cards,' I said. 'I'll buy the tray.'

'I thought you'd like it,' said Ralph. 'I'm afraid that it's not for sale.'

'Such a shame. Amelia, would you mind looking at the cards for me?'

'Nothing would give me greater pleasure,' said Vicky. I moved my foot so that I could tread on her toes. She was way too sarcastic.

Vicky grimaced and squeezed her eyes closed. Luckily Ralph was too busy opening the boxes and spreading out the silk squares that contained the cards. 'This one is very old,' he said, pointing to a badly foxed pack of black and white woodcut cards. 'Genuine Bavarian. A real rarity.'

'Too fragile,' I said. 'They have to be robust. His little sister has only just come into magick, and needs something she can fiddle about with.'

'How about these? Enscribed in Ireland. The Celtic designs will make them a talking point in … Austria, was it?'

'The Tyrol. Yes.'

He pointed to the cards. 'Amelia, please take a closer look.'

Vicky hesitated, then picked up one of them. Then more. She took the whole pack and ran them through her fingers. They looked beautiful, if your idea of beautiful is those anaemic redheads they seem to go in for over there. There were rather too many half-naked women for my tastes.

'These have got some real heft,' said Vicky. 'A *lot* of Works in them. They should be a real challenge for little Waltrout.'

At least she was getting into the spirit of the thing. Where did *Waltrout* come from? Ralph didn't think it was unusual. 'Fine. I'll take them,' I said. 'You do understand that I'll have to settle on mundane terms.'

'Of course,' he said smoothly, wrapping the decks away. 'Obviously we don't take credit cards. How would you settle?'

'How much for the cards?'

'Twenty five thousand. Guineas.'

What???? I tried to wave it off. 'We can discuss the price later. When we've got the more important items. I got my phone out and checked one of the documents on it. I fixed Ralph with my most regal gaze and said, 'I need something for my future mother in law. I'd like to get her a Moondrop necklace, but I don't think she'd use it much.' The look on Ralph's face told me what I needed to know, and I pressed on. 'She is a Necromancer, I'm sorry to say. What do you have in the way of Triangle Censers?'

'Triangle Censers?' said Ralph. He couldn't quite believe it. Had I overplayed my hand? When you're lying, you should never go back. Press on. Double down, as they say.

'Brass, preferably,' I added. 'And while you go to check, you should give Hledjolf a call. I bank with him.'

'I'll be as quick as I can,' he said. He left the Gaelic Tarot cards on the coffee table in their box and took the tray away with the rejected ones.

Meanwhile, Vicky had been texting. She nudged me gently and pointed to my phone. A new message. From her. She clearly expected the Farthingales to be listening to everything we said. This was the message (and my reply).

Vicky: *Have you gone mad????? You'll be lucky if they don't call the King's Watch. And WTF is this about Hledjolf???? BTW, if my foot's bruised, you're in even more trouble.*

Me: *Don't panic. They've bought it. I know what I'm doing. And please address me as Your Highness.*

Her reply was full of emojis, two of which were obscene. I won't reprint them.

I was full of confidence on the surface. It's a good job that Vicky couldn't see my crossed fingers. I was starting to panic when the door opened and the senior management appeared, in the form of a woman in her thirties. Instead of a sharp suit, she wore a floaty summer dress and had her hair down. There was something about the cut of that dress…

I stood up to make namaste. 'Congratulations,' I said. 'When is it due?'

She beamed and shook hands. 'Thank you. Not until the spring. I'm Danika, also known as DeeDee.'

'Aah,' said Vicky. 'You're the Daughter's Daughter – DeeDee.'

'That's right.' She shook hands with Vicky. 'And you're Amelia?'

I could see Vicky about to dig herself a deep hole. 'That's my nursery name for her,' I said. 'I promised that I'd give her family, and my fiancé's family, complete privacy.'

She turned back to me. 'And you're Rani Mukherjee, but not *the* Rani Mukherjee.'

I nodded enthusiastically. 'Correct. My mother was an Ambani. You can ask Ralph to look us up when he's finished talking to Hledjolf.' I gave her the smile I give my opponents in bridge when I've made an outrageous bid: I dare you.

'I'll do that. You do appreciate that if you go ahead and purchase these items, they are strictly for export only.'

'Of course.'

'Then excuse me.'

We sat down again, and I said, 'Do you think a dress like that would suit me? Could I wear it to open the village fete next year?'

'No. You're too short.'

'Ouch, Amelia.'

'Shh. They're coming back.'

I uncrossed my fingers when DeeDee wafted back into the room with Ralph in her wake. He had the same tray, but this time there were three incense burners on it, made of brass. I uncrossed my fingers and breathed a sigh of relief. Vicky, meanwhile, was trying to climb over the back of the sofa and get away. Almost. She was definitely not keen on the goods. Ralph was now wearing white gloves with black Alchemical symbols stitched into them. He put the tray down very carefully and left us to it.

'Don't worry, Amelia,' I said. 'I won't be asking you to examine them.' I got out my jeweller's loupe and leaned forward.

Vicky made a little mewing noise and DeeDee drew in a sharp breath. I may not know much about architecture or European furniture, but I know my bling. I squinted at the carvings on the side of the censers (making sure not to touch them), and took in the detail. There were human figures, naked, with every hair of their locks realised in metal. There was a Dwarf with diamonds for eyes, and a Black Unicorn with rubies. I'd seen enough without looking for the Fae.

I put the magnifier slowly back in my bag and got out my business card. I made sure that DeeDee couldn't see the logo. 'What's your starting point?' I said.

'We don't negotiate on these items. The price is twelve point five. Million.'

'Interesting. How much will Clan Flint see of this?'

Her English Rose cheeks went a much angrier colour. 'Who are you? Who sent you?'

I passed her my card, holding it high over the table. I'll tell you something, posh English girls can really swear. Much better than Vicky can. Ralph slipped back into the room and looked very alarmed.

My arm started to tingle and Vicky put her hand to her chest. She pressed on her Artefacts and undid the Work she'd put about her Badge of Office. 'Easy, Miss Farthingale,' she said. 'Let's calm down, shall we?'

The magick stopped, and DeeDee stared at us.

I coughed. 'Shall we start by removing these rather dreadful things?'

'Take them away, Ralph, and tell Mother we have visitors.' She held up my card and Ralph plucked it from her fingers. He put it in his pocket and took away the tray. Both DeeDee and Vicky relaxed a little. I wonder if Conrad would have felt anything.

If you're wondering, those little censers – Triangle Censers – are a set used in the summoning of more powerful Spirits. I have no idea what they do, but they are one of the items that went missing as part of the Flint Hoard case which is currently before the Cloister Court.

'I'm not saying anything until Mother has called our attorney,' said DeeDee.

'This is not an official visit,' I said. 'I can't ignore what I've just seen, of course, but it's a question of whether I call Iain Drummond now or later. You will have to give up a lot of what you've got, I'm afraid.'

'What about the Triangle Censers?' she said, staring at Vicky rather than me.

'What Triangle Censers?' said Vicky. 'I didn't examine them closely enough to swear in court.'

'I did,' I said, 'but I don't think that Judge Bracewell will take my word for it.'

'Then what do you want?' said DeeDee. 'I presume this pantomime was staged for a reason.'

'The Ashford Ruby. Where is it?'

DeeDee put her hands on where her bump will be in a few weeks. 'Now that I was not expecting. You really will need to see my mother.'

Right on cue, an older version of DeeDee joined us. Her mobile phone was out, ready for action. Her daughter rose gracefully and left the chair vacant. 'Panic over, Mum. They're not going to call in Drummond over the goods I showed them.'

'But they are going to call him?'

DeeDee patted her mother's arm. 'The balloon's gone up, as Gran would say. I told you we should have shipped the whole lot to America.'

'What do they want?'

'To know about the Ashford Ruby. I'll go and start a stocktake, shall I?'

Mrs Farthingale didn't answer. She looked at us, and I bowed. She didn't return the gesture or offer to shake hands.

'Is that Chanel?' I asked. She was wearing what I can only describe as a formal peasant outfit, all layers with a big belt. I think she should have covered up her arms, but the rest of it worked well enough.

'Dior. Let's sit down, shall we? What's your interest in the Ashford Ruby, Watch Captain?'

'Best not to ask,' said Vicky. 'This is Mina's mission, not mine. I'm just here as a consultant. And bodyguard. Your daughter was going to use magick *after* Mina had identified herself. You don't want that going in a report to Merlyn's Tower either, do you?'

151

She looked from Vicky to me and back again. 'I can't work out whether this is a double-bluff by Lord Ashford with Miss Desai as a decoy or whether you're working for the creature who originally owned the jewel.'

I gave a nod. 'A good question, Mrs Farthingale. As I said to Conrad last week, a Nāgin does not own her Māṇik, any more than I own my own liver. It was part of her. It still is.'

She barked a laugh. 'I don't know whether to be relieved that Ashford has nothing to do with this or whether to alarmed about having a … what did you call her?'

'A Nāgin.'

'About having a Nāgin on our case. Very well. Did Lord Ashford tell you about the ring?'

'He did. He said it went to a human princess.'

'That's right. She left the mortal realm when the Prince of Richmond became the Queen of Richmond.'

'She's a Fae,' said Vicky. 'Lord Ashford is of her family.'

'I see. I think.'

Mrs Farthingale waited for me to process that before continuing. 'The human princess left it to a cousin on her mother's side. That cousin was a Pike.'

'A pike? A fish?'

Vicky leaned in. 'The Pikes of Norfolk are an old family. A bit like a poor man's Hawkins or Mowbray.'

Mrs Farthingale was finding this amusing. If it helped her relax, so much the better. 'The Pikes were big fish in those days,' she said. 'If you'll forgive the pun.'

'No, but carry on anyway.'

'They fell on hard times in the 1920s, and the ring came into our possession.'

'Something similar happened to my father's family.'

She smiled. 'Would that be the Mukherjees?'

I frowned. 'No. The Desais. My actual family. They had to sell off the jewels. They kept the land, though.'

'As did the Pikes. That's why they're still around. We kept the ring for a few years and then my grandmother swapped it in 1932. For this place.'

She looked around her. I wonder if Pramiti would consider it a fair exchange: her Māṇik for the majesty and location of Farthingale House. It was not a question I planned to ask her. 'You swapped it with …?'

'The Easterbrooks of Suffolk.'

'That must have hurt,' said Vicky. 'The Easterbrooks?'

Mrs Farthingale nodded. Vicky said to me, 'The Easterbrooks replaced the Pikes as the big noise in Anglia.'

Mrs Farthingale stood up. 'And the Easterbrooks still have the ring. I don't know if they use it or not.'

I stood up and bowed. 'You have been a most gracious hostess, Mrs Farthingale. I hope that when we meet again, you will understand how much I appreciate that.'

'Why should we meet again, Miss Desai?'

'May I?' I held out my phone, open at the list I'd consulted earlier. She took it and frowned. Then she got some reading glasses from a pouch at her side. A pouch I hadn't even noticed existed. She scanned the list and scrolled it.

'Where did you get this, and what is it?'

'The Clan Flint appendix to the report I wrote for the Cloister Court. It's a public document now. I'm sure you'll be going through it with your lawyer. And Iain Drummond. We shall no doubt meet at the Old Temple.'

She stared again. One of the items highlighted on the list was: *Three Censers in Triangle Configuration. Dwarven make (Niði). Fae, Dwarf, human & Hellhorse carvings. Jewelled. Unique.* She passed the phone back to me.

'You have been kinder than we deserve,' she said. 'Safe journey.'

We managed to hold it together until we got out of the street dominated by Farthingale House. Then Vicky took a swing at me and I tried to stamp on her foot again. We both missed because we were too busy laughing. The taxi driver nearly didn't stop, because he thought we were drunk.

'Angel's costume hire,' I said.

'Then take me to the Boards,' added Vicky. 'I'll get the drinks in while you get your deposit back. It's not far.'

5 — The Things we do for Love

The Boards is 100% a haunted pub. Of this I have no doubt. It was late on a Friday lunchtime, during a warm September, and the place felt like a winter chill was about to reach down and pinch your arm. I shivered in the sleeveless dress and was very glad I'd added leggings before leaving the house. Vicky already had two glasses of wine on the table and was looking at the menu. 'Hungry?' she said.

I shook my head and picked up my glass. 'Thank you Amelia. You were brilliant.'

She lifted her hand and made to point her finger at me, then she swatted the air and laughed. 'Where did Amelia come from?'

'When I was four, my best friend at nursery – who was called Faith – announced that her name was Amelia. Funny how things stick in your mind.'

'A bit of warning would have been nice. And talking of warnings, if you ever cast me as your servant's daughter again, I will do a damn sight more than flick your ear.'

I put on a serene face. 'What can I say? I was in role. It came naturally.'

'A bit too flippin' naturally. I'll forgive you this once on account of you were awesome. On a serious note, I know you hadn't planned this, 'cos you had to hire the outfit, but how did you convince Hledjolf to lie for you?'

I buried my nose in my glass. 'I didn't and he wouldn't. I really do have an account with him in the name of Rani Mukherjee, but for Ganesh's sake, don't tell anyone. Please. And before you ask, Conrad already knows.'

'Why?'

I flicked through my phone until I found an old picture that was taken by my late husband, Miles Finch. It was a side view of my left, unmangled side and full length. In it I was wearing a thick rollneck jumper, body con dress, leggings and boots. Every stitch was black. I showed it to Mina.

'Your hair's even longer,' she said. 'Almost to your waist. When was this?'

'During my money-laundering phase. I've changed since then, Vicky. A bit. I'm still good at hiding money, though. Before that, don't forget I was an accountant.'

She zoomed the picture. 'Wedding ring. Why did you stop wearing it? If you don't mind me asking.'

I weighed her up. I put down my glass. 'The Mina who married Miles died with him in the snow. I was reborn, thanks to Lord Ganesh. And Conrad. I will never forget Miles, but this person you see is not Miles's widow.'

She locked the phone and passed it back. 'I know what you mean, pet. It took me a while to figure out that the Vicky who woke up in hospital wasn't the one who'd died on the hillside.'

We gave the moment the silence it deserved. The pub door banged open and we both jerked our heads automatically to look. It was nothing. Time ticked again, and we moved on.

'What is this place?' I said. 'And why is it called the Boards?'

The street door was squeezed between two shops on the edge of Soho. From there, you went downstairs into the dark and the gloom. A few lucky customers were near the fire.

'It's what's left of a Mage theatre. It was outside the old London city walls. Mages are welcome, so long as we behave ourselves. You could call it a safe place. And it's a bit too far from Salomon's House for tutors to come.'

'Perfect, if slightly creepy. Where do we go from here?'

'I have no idea. The Easterbrooks are big in Cambridge and Suffolk, I know that. Nowhere near on the same scale as the Mowbrays or the Hawkins, but big enough.'

'Do you think that Mrs Farthingale will tip them off?'

'No way. The Farthingales will want to keep their involvement strictly off the record. That's our only advantage.'

'And you don't know the area?'

'Sorry. I know the Watch Captain for Anglia, obviously. Guy called Fergus Macarthur. He was too new for me to learn much from him before I met Conrad, so Hannah sent me elsewhere for training. I can start asking around this afternoon.' She looked uncomfortable. 'Do you get the impression that we might not have much time?'

'I do. Pramiti will do anything to get her Mānik back. If she doesn't think that we're making progress, she'll start to interfere. She was happy to wait while Conrad plucked up the courage to propose, but now the game is afoot…'

'She's got the patience of a five year old on Christmas Eve.'

'Quite. I could try dropping a few questions in tonight.'

'Why where are you going?'

'The rearranged dinner with Chris and Tamsin Kelly.'

Vicky sat back and gave me that look again. The same look that everyone gives me – or Conrad – when the issue of Chris Kelly's domestic arrangements comes up. Even Chris's mother stopped speaking to him until Conrad intervened (Conrad and Vicky met Oma Bridget on a case that was nothing to do with Chris; I believe they're speaking again).

'What is it, Vicky?'

She didn't answer directly. 'Did the Dean know you were going when she asked Conrad to endorse her election campaign?'

'She did.'

Vicky shrugged. 'Fair enough. I'm sure you'll have a nice time.' She tried to lighten the mood. 'Are you going as Mina or Rani?'

'Mina. What is it, Vicky?'

She looked away. 'None of my business. It's probably just a rumour put about by Heidi Marston. She'd enjoy that sort of thing. I'll get us another glass, shall I?'

I left it there. We'd grown closer over the last few days, but Vicky clearly has some sort of line about this, a line she didn't want to cross. What could it possibly be about Chris and Tamsin that everyone frowned on? That she was a criminal? That she was born a man? Maybe even that she was a Fae? It does happen, though where they would get three children under five from is another matter.

Vicky came back with the wine and shared the picture she'd taken of me in my Rani Mukherjee costume. 'Is that the sort of thing I'll be wearing at the Bollywood party?'

'Sort of. Cheers.'

Chris and Tamsin Kelly live four miles south of where I grew up in Ealing, and a whole world away. That's London for you.

The district of Richmond is rich indeed, in all sorts of ways. The world famous Kew Gardens is there, to the north, and to the south is Richmond Park, home of the Queen of Richmond, the Fae to whom our friend Lord Ashford owes allegiance. Chris and Tamsin live between the two in a mansion on the river. I asked Conrad how they could afford it, and he said that it came with the job.

'Which job?'

'The Earth Master of Salomon's House isn't just a teacher. He's also the Inspector of Ley lines for England and Wales. There's a massive junction under his back garden and a tunnel under the Thames that goes back to pre-Roman days. Hledjolf dug it, apparently. The Earth Master sits on top of it to protect it and keep an eye on the flux.'

'I'll take your word for it.'

It was a lovely evening. We'd caught the train to Richmond and we didn't want to be early, so Conrad had asked the taxi driver to drop us on Water Lane. The clouds had blown away, and we were sauntering along the River Thames like many other couples. We even had a dog: Scout was on his lead for once.

A couple of runners swerved round us and I checked their height. Conrad saw me and said, 'Chris won't be out tonight. He'll be chained to the kitchen sink. Or bathing the kids. Probably the latter. From what I can tell, he's very much a hands-on dad in the evenings.'

I had been bringing Conrad up to date on our quest for Pramiti's gem. He was being very good: he'd promised to stay out of it, and apart from a few (sensible) questions, he'd done just that.

He leaned on the railings, worked out which way the wind was blowing and lit a cigarette. 'Do you know East Anglia?' he said.

'No. Do you?'

'Spiritual home of the RAF. Thousands of my predecessors made their last flight from East Anglian airfields during the last war. Tens of thousands. There's a huge American base still at Lakenheath. I've been there a few times, and the RAF one at Mildenhall. And Cambridge, of course, for fun.' He smiled. 'And don't forget that Spectre Thomas was born there and ran the Esoteric Library. Shall we go, before this champagne gets warm and the flowers wilt?'

We held hands and cut through an alleyway to a private road that curved away from the river. Earth House (boring name) was behind a high brick wall with heavy iron gates. In true Mage style, there was a shrubbery behind the gates to hide the house itself.

While Conrad sent a text (no entryphones here, and he doesn't have the magick to open it himself), I looked across the road. The houses opposite were red brick and nice. I am going to guess Victorian. A middle-aged couple were gardening in front of one of them and I'm sure that the wife was trying not to stare at us. I'm used to that.

The gates clanged unlocked. Conrad pushed them open slightly and let me through before closing them behind us. We could have gone left or right, but Conrad didn't even think about it. He went left and I followed. Navigation is his thing. I'm still working out what mine might be. If I have a thing at all.

Chris had told us that Scout was more than welcome to explore the grounds and catch up with us later, so I slipped his lead and let him run off in search of smells.

'Go on,' I said. 'What sort of house is that?'

'Georgian. You can tell by the windows, the plain brick and the symmetry. Very nice. These shrubs could do with a trim.'

'You're an expert on gardening all of a sudden?'

'I'm an expert garden owner. There's Chris.'

There are two features about Chris Kelly that everyone notices – his height and his gleaming bald head. He is even taller than Conrad. He also runs everywhere and is whip thin. He has kind blue eyes and a tanned face that make it hard to judge his age. Late forties?

He shook hands with Conrad and beat me to an alarming namaste. When someone bows at you from such a height, it can be scary. 'Come in. Let me take those. Ooh, Champagne. Nice.'

The hallway was as elegant as the exterior, with Farrow and Ball painted panels and chessboard tiles. Conrad loves Gothic, which is convenient because his house is Gothic. I love Elvenham, too, but I could be seduced by this.

Chris put the gifts on a table by the door and closed it quietly. 'Kids have just gone to sleep,' he said. 'I hope you didn't mind coming later. Much less hassle that way.'

I heard the sound of high heels on floorboards approaching, changing to a percussive click on the tiles, and the secret of Tamsin Kelly's position became obvious: Chris had married the au pair. Or a student from Salomon's House. I was wrong, as it turns out, but forgive me if the real answer wasn't as obvious as Tamsin's extreme youth.

She had long, light brown hair down her back and a sparkly black dress over black tights and killer patent heels. I wouldn't last all evening in those, and it was an outfit much better suited to a Christmas party than a summer supper.

Her smile was as broad as her makeup was thick. I wouldn't say *plastered*, but certainly the product of much labour, a labour designed to make her look older than twenty-one, which is the oldest she could possibly be. The children asleep upstairs couldn't possibly be hers, could they?

'Tammy, this is Conrad and Mina.' He was clearly worried and devoted in equal measure. 'You guessed that, didn't you?'

I was nearest, and went to bow until Tamsin came and gave me a most familiar hug and kiss. 'It's so good of you to do this,' she said. I could feel the unspoken agenda hovering over us like Conrad in a helicopter.

She felt the material in my kurti. 'Your dress is gorgeous,' she said. 'Is it silk? That blue really suits you.'

'How do you do,' said Conrad, offering a hand to shake and offering nothing by way of social support. This was getting heavy, and it was about to get heavier. In the distance, I heard a bark, then the skitter of doggy claws. Scout bounded into the hallway from the back of the house and started barking at Tamsin. Conrad put a hand to his temple. He was getting Scoutgram about something.

I reached down and grabbed his collar. 'Hush boy. You'll wake the children.'

He stopped barking but didn't look happy. 'I'm sorry,' I said. 'He doesn't usually react like that.'

Tamsin was looking very uneasy. Chris stepped in. 'To be expected, I suppose. In the circumstances.'

Conrad was giving Tamsin a very strange look. A Scoutgram is non-verbal, but it gives something to Conrad's magickal senses.

'What circumstances?' I said.

Suddenly it went very quiet. Tamsin looked very distressed and started to wring her hands. Chris looked from Conrad to me and back again. 'Don't you know?' he said.

'No,' I said.

'Shit!' said Tamsin. 'You told me they knew!' She gave her husband a shove that didn't move him at all and pushed her backwards. She turned and ran deeper into the house, tears already flooding down her face.

In the stunned silence, Chris cocked an ear upstairs. When he didn't hear toddler screams, he shook his shoulders and went to the door. 'Shall we step outside?'

Conrad lit a cigarette as soon as Chris had closed the doors behind him. 'Did no one say anything?' said Chris.

'Too polite,' said Conrad. 'And we're talking Mages here. They don't share as a rule.'

Chris blew out his cheeks. 'Tammy was a rare thing. An Imprint Healer. Sort of like a psychiatrist,' he added for my benefit. I don't think Conrad had much more of a clue. 'She helped young – really young – Mages to adapt to their powers. You were lucky, Conrad. You got your Gift in one fell swoop from the Allfather. Us born Mages have to cope with puberty *and* magick powers.'

There was a yawning gap in my head between the Tamsin he was telling us about and the near-child who'd run sobbing from the hall. Was tonight's version his *daughter*? Please, Ganesh, no. That would be unthinkable.

'She used to cycle everywhere,' he continued. 'As fanatical as my running.' He sniffed and looked away. 'We'd been married twelve years. She was thirty-seven and she'd just found out she was pregnant. She was dealing with a really horrible case, a mix of anorexia and Displacement. The girl took an overdose of the remedy Tammy had given her. A fatal overdose.

'Tammy had just left their house after a visit when the girl did it. Her parents rang Tammy, and Tammy turned straight round and pedalled furiously back to the house. She didn't see the lorry, and the lorry driver certainly didn't see her. It was instant.'

He breathed in a lungful of air that seemed to go on forever and let it out in a *whoosh*. 'In her head, Tammy was on her way to rescue the girl, and that intention carried her Spirit on. She was only round the corner. When her Spirit arrived, the girl was dead. Tammy merged herself with the girl and woke up enough to take aspirin. That was the antidote.'

Conrad and I stared at each other. In case I hadn't understood, I let him ask the questions.

'Tammy's Spirit performed a full Erase and Merge?' he said. I'm glad he asked. That question sounded right to me, but I didn't have the jargon.

'She did,' said Chris. He paused for a while. 'The big problem was the girl's parents. Her mother was a Mage, and she blamed Tammy. Brought the wrath of the law down on us. Magickal and mundane.'

'Mundane?' That was me.

'Told the police I was interested in her fourteen year old daughter. Reported Tammy to the King's Watch and to the Provost of Salomon's House.'

'What did they do?'

'Social services intervened after they had a fight. A real fight. With blood. Tammy went to a foster home and we wrote letters to each other for a year until she was sixteen. We got married on her eighteenth birthday. The mundane consequences were bad enough. The magickal ones were horrendous.'

'What happened?'

'The King's Watch weren't interested. I don't know what Hannah would have done, but she wasn't the Constable then. The Provost took a different view.'

I looked at Conrad, who explained by saying, 'Gregory Parrish is the Provost. No wonder he hated me when Chris stood up for me at the Inner Council. The Provost enforces the Statutes of Salomon's House.'

'He does,' continued Chris. 'And Tammy was banned from there for life.'

I nodded. 'What was her crime?'

'Dereliction.'

'How? The girl had taken an overdose after she left.'

Chris went quiet, and Conrad answered. 'I'm guessing that she should have discharged herself in trying to bring the patient back.'

Chris nodded. 'She told them it was too late, but that's not the point. The consequences for Tammy were not good.'

'How so?'

'A teenage new Mage needs help to master their power. Tammy was barred from Salomon's House, the Daughters of the Goddess, all the sanctuary schools. Her mother did her best, but she wasn't much of a Mage. And she died two years ago.' He could see that we still didn't get it. He tapped his head. 'Mage potential is innate. I was born a Geomancer, and so was Conrad. He just didn't have the other powers to go with it or develop it until Odin stepped in. The old Tammy was born an Imprint Healer. The new one was born a Plane Shifter. They're as different as archery and marathon running.'

It went quiet.

'I'll leave you to think it over,' said Chris. 'You know where we are.' He nodded to us and slipped back through the front doors.

Conrad pointed to a bench at the side of the house and we wandered over. From here, we could see the mighty river at the end of the back garden. Earth House was higher than its neighbours, the plot raised up about eight feet. Presumably because of the subterranean workings. Handy in a flood.

We sat down and held hands for a moment. 'Are you thinking what I'm thinking?' said Conrad.

'I rarely know what you're thinking,' I said. 'Except at mealtimes. You get more like Scout every day.'

'Arff,' said Scout when he heard his name. He looked hungry. It was getting late, and starting to get chilly in the shade.

'I'm thinking that the girl had a name,' said Conrad. 'And I'm wondering why Chris didn't use it once. That's what I'm thinking.'

'Me too.'

We sat for a moment.

'Do we stay or do we go?' he said.

'I hate to say this, my love, but it's up to you. Chris Kelly is not important in the Cloister Court. You have to work with everyone else. I don't.'

He pulled his lip. Hard. 'If Vicky had told you this afternoon what had happened, would you still have come tonight?'

Conrad is very good at difficult questions. Asking them, that is. I looked at him and made a judgement. I have serious reservations about what Tamsin Kelly had done. I would have made an excuse if Vicky had put me in the picture. Conrad wouldn't. It was time to lie. 'Elvenham is the home of freaks and outcasts,' I said. 'We could start a branch at Earth House. Cora has no problem with you being on visiting terms with Chris, and Hannah would certainly have warned you off if she wanted you to stay away. I say we go back.'

'Good. I'm starving. Scout, find Tamsin.' His Familiar gave him a funny look and shook himself, then bounded towards the river.

The back side of Earth House had a big terrace with an awning and a table already laid for food. Scout went through some modern bi-fold doors and into a huge kitchen. And I mean huge. They would never have got Listed Building consent for that in a mundane house. Tamsin was standing by a marble-topped island, drinking white wine and crying. She blinked at us, not quite believing that we had come back.

Chris appeared from the hall and we faced off, not quite sure how to defuse the emotion. I wanted to hug the poor girl/woman, but her body language was tight and defensive. Conrad looked around the kitchen as if he were an estate agent. What's he up to? He grabbed two empty glasses from a selection on the side and sloshed wine into them. Without speaking, he put them in front of Chris and stepped back.

Chris hesitated, then pushed them towards us. 'Please accept our hospitality,' he said stiffly.

We picked up our glasses and Conrad spoke. 'With pleasure, as I hope that one day you will accept ours.'

We all managed a sip before Tamsin started crying again and ran off, shedding her heels on the way. I heard footsteps on the stairs. 'Where's your room?' I said.

'Top of the stairs on the right. Tammy has a dressing room off to the west.'

I picked up her heels and climbed the stairs. The top floor was just as well appointed as the downstairs and featured soundproof carpet. I won't tell you how jealous I felt when I saw the master bedroom and Tamsin's dressing room. It was all brand new. Overcompensation by Chris? Probably. She was sitting in a big chair looking very small.

'Here's what we're going to do,' I said. 'You're going to clean your face up and find some flat shoes while I show you something.'

She blinked and didn't move. There was a pile of re-usable makeup wipes on the dressing table. Home-made by someone. I picked two up, along with the cleanser that I couldn't afford, and put them in her hands. 'Go on,' I said.

She started to wipe the thick foundation off and I turned my back to slip out of my kurti. I am going to have to stop doing this. Or start wearing blouses with buttons. I don't mind showing off my swastika tattoo, but it means I have to show off everything else as well. Or *lack* of everything else. If you see what I mean.

I could see from the mirror that she was well on with the job and turned around. 'My scars are on the surface,' I said.

She did what no one else has dared to do. Not even Conrad. She reached out a finger and touched my skin, tracing the lines of the swastika. I couldn't feel it, because that skin is mostly scar tissue.

'Thank you so much,' she said.

I got dressed and she finished cleaning herself up. Underneath, she looked even younger. She put on some mascara and eye shadow, and lipstick, while I asked a few questions about the house and her children (a three year old and eighteen month old twins, all girls). I also discovered that she will never ride a bicycle again. Ever.

'I'm keeping the heels,' she said. 'Sod the pain. I barely come up to his chest without them.'

We went back down the stairs together and found the boys admiring a load of coats of arms that I hadn't noticed before because they were hidden by magick. Believe me, they added nothing to the room and I was going to ignore them until Conrad insisted that I admire the last pair. Because Tamsin is a Mage, she gets to have hers up as well as her husband's. There has never been a female Earth Master.

'Have a look at what's in Chief,' said Conrad.

'What are you on about now? What chief?'

'The Chief is the top part of the shield. It's a homage to Tamsin's family.'

'The fish? It looks evil.'

'It is. Pike are a very evil fish. Tamsin grew up in Norfolk.'

I looked at her. 'Have you heard of the Ashford jewel?'

'Have I ever. The Easterbrooks haven't stopped crowing about that since 1932.'

I tilted my head. 'Would you like to get one over on them?'

'Not half.'

I nodded. 'Make sure I get your number later, and don't tell Chris.'

'Oy,' said Chris. 'I'm standing next to you.'

'I noticed. You're a hard man to miss. Is there food anywhere?'

We sat with boys on one side of the table, girls on the other. Unusual, I know. Their choice. When I saw them in the kitchen, working to stop the dinner being irretrievably ruined, it hit home that they couldn't have a mundane *or* a magickal social life. Tamsin acts like she's Conrad's age, but she looks the same age as his half-sister. Together, Chris and Tamsin look like father and daughter. That's why they didn't sit together at dinner, or afterwards when we were all very drunk and lounging on the sitting room sofas.

This beautiful house was a safe space for them. Either of them on their own wouldn't attract attention outside, but together, heads would turn. Especially if they kissed each other.

It was well after midnight when the cab arrived. We'd been there about four hours altogether. The Richardsons must have been waiting all that time.

Chris and Tamsin came to wave us off from a side gate near their garage. It led on to a short lane and Chris said the cab would be waiting at the end. When we emerged, flashbulbs went off and cameras sounded.

Conrad shoved me back and took a position in front of me, in a squat with his gun already in his hand. He had drunk a *lot* less than me. A woman screamed. Scout started barking and dancing around.

Chris was standing dumbstruck, but not Tamsin. She raced as fast as the alcohol and her heels would let her towards the source of the lights.

'Fuck off. Fuck off and leave me alone,' she screamed. And those were the least offensive things she said.

Now my eyes had adjusted, I could see a middle-aged couple across the road. The husband was filming Tamsin as she shouted and screamed at his wife. Chris shook himself and loped across the road. He didn't touch his wife, nor talk to her. Instead, he used his loud voice to shout, 'Where's Conrad and Mina's taxi?'

The use of our names stopped Tamsin in her tracks. She looked back and saw Conrad still covering the couple with his gun. Her hand flew to her mouth and she looked horrified. She started walking backwards, away from the couple, and Conrad holstered his gun. He also called Scout to heel. The woman saw that, and used it as a signal to counter-attack.

'You murdering bitch! You murdered my Melody and now you're flaunting yourself like the cheap tart you are.' Then she said something about Conrad and me. Something I won't repeat here because it was as offensive to the

Pakistani community as the Indian one. It made my blood boil and I pushed past Conrad to intervene. Tamsin was about six feet from her at this point, and still trying to back away. What happened next happened very quickly.

The woman slashed at Tamsin's face with a knife. Chris grabbed the husband's arm. Tamsin dodged the knife and fell over on the cobbles, twisting her ankle as the high heels took their toll. I started running and did what I'd do in a close cricket match where we'd gone for a dodgy second run – I dived forward, stretching myself out and landing on top of Tamsin. While I was in the air, Scout shot past, aiming for the woman's ankles.

I landed as the knife came down. Scout made contact and the knife tore through my kurti, striking the cobbles. I owe that dog a big treat.

By the time I rolled off Tamsin, Conrad had the woman face down on the ground with her right hand up her back and Scout baring his teeth at her face. Chris had taken the husband's phone and shoved him over. 'Tamsin? Are you OK?' I said.

By way of an answer, she threw up. Well, I had just landed on her stomach, hadn't I? I checked myself for blood, and then checked Tamsin. Finally, I picked up the knife.

'Meet the Richardsons,' said Chris. 'Everyone's favourite stalkers.' He looked at Conrad. 'Were you seen coming in?'

'The couple opposite the gates saw us,' I replied.

Chris swore. 'They must have told them we had visitors.'

'What do we do now?' said Conrad, ever the practical one.

'I've got their phones,' said Chris. He was frowning, as if trying to think of two things at once. 'We'll just let them go. Don't worry, you won't have to face videos of you surfacing on YouTube.'

'Too late for that,' said Mrs Richardson. 'It's backed up to the cloud already.'

'No it isn't,' said Chris. 'I blocked the signal when the flash went off. I still am.'

Aah. Only now did I realise that a very low level of magick was in operation.

Conrad lifted the woman to her feet. Her eyes had glazed over as if her brain had overloaded.

'Where *is* the taxi?' I said.

'We sent him away,' mumbled Mr Richardson.

'I'll get Tamsin back inside,' I said. I wasn't retreating and leaving the men to sort it out, but so long as Tamsin was still on the scene, a peaceful resolution was unlikely, especially now that she'd finished vomiting and looked like she might still be up for a fight.

I took off her other shoe and helped her to her feet. Foot – she'd definitely twisted her ankle. 'Lean on me, Tamsin,' I said, pulling her arm over my shoulder and encouraging her to move. She started to turn back for a last word. 'Don't,' I whispered. 'They didn't deserve Melody. Racists like that don't deserve to be parents.'

She nodded and we hobbled down the alley to Earth House. I installed her in the downstairs cloakroom and went to see the boys. I could just make out Conrad, down by the river with Scout. The glowing end of his cigarette was a giveaway.

'We're staying the night,' he said. 'What with one thing and another, it's easiest. That was a brilliant jump, love. You timed it to perfection.'

I passed Scout a large piece of venison from the fridge. 'You saved my life, you little horror,' I told him.

'Arff.'

'What shall I do with this?' I held up the knife.

Conrad passed me the sheath. 'Keep it or chuck it in the river. I'd keep it. It's a good one. None of your Chinese rubbish.'

I took the sheath and made the knife safe for now. 'I think it's knocked you more than it knocked me,' I said.

He took a deep breath. 'The last time I saw hatred like that was on the face of a failed suicide bomber. The regular Taliban were soldiers, more or less, fighting for what they saw as the best interests of their country. I wouldn't want to live in that country, especially if I were a woman, but it was their country in the end. That hatred, though…' He shuddered. 'She must have seen Melody – Tamsin – growing over the last five years. When she slashed at her face, she was slashing at the image of her own daughter.'

'It explains a lot,' I said. 'No wonder they are ostracised. Cora Hardisty wouldn't want to confront the Richardsons, would she?'

'No, she wouldn't.' He looked as if he were about to say something else and changed his mind. 'A nightcap and then we'll sample the guest suite.'

'They have a guest suite?'

'Oh yes. Lord Mowbray has stayed there. Chris told me that he's the only Mage who doesn't give a fuck about the Richardsons.'

'Then we're in good company. Come on, Conrad. It's freezing out here.'

He put his arm round my shoulders and we turned to go back. 'I put Mrs Richardson right about one thing,' he said. 'I made sure she knew your family are from India, not Pakistan.'

For once, I let him have the last word.

6 — *Ladies in Waiting*

The big bed was empty when I finally decided that I could face the day. Conrad has always been an early riser, and now that he has Scout to look after, he's even worse. I dimly remembered him saying, 'There's been a delivery for you.'

There was a delivery – of clothes. A selection of Tamsin's athletic leisure wear, to be precise, with brand new underwear and a brand new pair of trainers from the local supermarket. In my size. Impressive. All on top of several fluffy towels and directions to the big bathroom. There was also a pack of aspirin and a bottle of water. Most welcome.

A strange sight greeted me from the windows. There were to-die-for views of the Thames and a lot of lawn. All beautiful. The strange part was a toddler and two barely walking infants playing hide-and-seek in the shrubbery with Scout. Does that dog have no end to his talents? I went to run a bath (epic) and checked my phone.

At some point last night, when full of a very fruity Chateauneuf du Pape, I'd messaged Vicky a picture of Chris and Tamsin posing by their kitchen island. I'd also told her that Tamsin had inside knowledge of the Easterbrooks. She'd replied this morning, while I was asleep: *I may need to hold my nose about this. Not happy seeing that picture. Is it just me???????? Call me when you're sober. Vic. XX.*

No, it wasn't just her, but Conrad and I had crossed a line. There was no going back. I would have to find a way to make it work. It wouldn't be the first time.

The twins had got bored of playing hide-and-seek when I got downstairs and they'd wandered back into the kitchen for juice and were now playing with blocks in the nursery. Outside, their older sister was trying to drag a hairbrush through Scout's coat in the way that only truly determined three year olds can do. He was putting up with it so far. Tamsin was sitting on a sofa with her foot in the air and an elastic bandage round her ankle.

'Thank you for the clean clothes,' I said. 'How's the foot?'

'Not too bad. I heal quickly. They fit then?'

'Lycra covers a multitude of sins. Not my first choice, but better than wearing that kurti. Where is it?'

'At the dry cleaners and menders. It'll come back like new.' She sat up properly. 'I don't want to keep going on, but thank you for last night. All of it.'

She was so pathetically grateful that all I could do was smile.

She stood up and tested her ankle. 'Getting there. I can cook sitting on a stool. Is an omelette okay?'

'That would be lovely. Where are the boys?'

'Downstairs in the Junction. Chris is showing off.'

We made the omelette together, with me passing the ingredients while Tamsin cooked. It was delicious. 'You have to excuse me,' I said. 'I am like a blind woman in the world of magick. I have to go by hearsay. Conrad said that Lord Mowbray is both a Geomancer and a Plane Shifter. Are they related, and can Chris do it, too?'

She looked very sad. 'They're not related. Mowbray is twice-gifted, that's all.'

'Conrad's half-sister is your biological age,' I said. 'She's just enrolled at Salomon's House. It's not too late for you to get further instruction, is it?'

She looked away. 'The window closes a bit more every day.'

I cleaned my plate with some home-made sourdough bread and said, 'Where's the dishwasher?'

While I stacked for her, I wondered how to approach Tamsin. She clearly hadn't opened up to anyone other than Chris for a while. I was going to mention losing my own mother when my phone buzzed. I glanced at the screen and grabbed it quickly before it went to voicemail. When the Duke of Ashford calls, you take it. If you know what's good for you.

'Good morning, Miss Desai. Can you talk?'

'I can, my lord.'

'I've been straight with you. It's time for you to be straight with me. Why are you helping Pramiti?'

He knew her name. There was an edge to his voice that would have had Conrad reaching for his gun even over the phone. 'I am repaying a debt,' I said. 'A personal one that means a great deal to me. That is my only connection to Pramiti.'

'Good to know. One other question: why have you teamed up with Victoria Robson and not your fiancé? Not that Miss Robson doesn't know what she's doing.'

'Captain Robson was awarded the Military Cross for a good reason. Conrad is staying out of this one, and Vicky is only doing it as a friend. Nothing official.'

'Also good to know. You need to know something. Pramiti has crawled out from under her rock in Knightsbridge and has started asking around. She's figured out that I'm not in the Queen of Oxford's line.'

'Sorry. You've lost me.'

'We are very loyal to our Queen. And vice versa. Otherwise, we Fae are as territorial and competitive as humans. Now that she knows whose line I'm not in, she'll work on the Queen of Oxford's nobles to find out who Lord Butler has become. It makes me nervous. It makes me wonder if the world wouldn't be a better place without her.'

'You may be right, Lord Ashford, but there's something you should know. Until she is reunited with her Mānik, she is under the protection of my lord. Ganesh. On that basis, she will refrain from making the first move against you, and I would strongly advise you to do the same.'

'I'm glad I called, Miss Desai. This has been a most informative conversation. I don't forget people who help me.'

'Nor I, my lord.'

'Then good luck in your search.'

'Was that who I think it was?' said Tamsin.

'If you think it was the Duke of Ashford, then you were right. We have a problem. Excuse me one moment.'

I sent a message to Vicky: *Things more complicated. Can you face Earth House? I promise to tell no one you've been here. Pretty please? XXX.*

I got a message back straight away: *Uber ordered. See you in an hour. I expect lunch as an absolute minimum.*

'You might need to send out for more food,' I said to Tamsin. 'Vicky Robson is coming over for a conference.'

'There is so much food in that fridge, we could feed all the joggers for a week. Unless you'd rather go out. There's a great riverside pub that's family friendly.'

I looked down at my black vest, pink top and union jack leggings. 'Like this? I don't think so. Nor am I keen to meet the Richardsons again.'

She went red. 'They don't bother us in mundane locations. There's a court injunction to prevent her coming near me. They only pester us if they think we have magickal guests, and only if they think we're vulnerable.'

There was a cry from the nursery. One of the twins had hit the other one with a brick. 'Who's the victim?' said Tamsin.

It hadn't escaped me that she rarely used her children's names. Instead, it was *The Tank* for the older girl and *The Fighter* and *The Blonde* for the twins.

'Charlotte,' I said. That would be The Blonde.

'Can you get her before she screams the house down and bring her here?'

Charlotte wailed even louder when the strange dark woman picked her up and dumped her on the couch. Tamsin wrapped her daughter in her arms and kissed her head. No lack of maternal feeling there.

'What about Beth?' I said.

'She'll be fine for a bit. Worst case scenario, she goes looking for Daddy and doesn't find him.' She ruffled Charlotte's hair. 'The fighter gets jealous when she's been naughty, doesn't she?'

I made myself comfortable in an oversized armchair. 'Tell me something, Tamsin. Do you feel like a different person, or just the same but in a younger body?'

I had a right to ask, and she knew it. Her daughter had become quiet, and Tamsin stared out of the doors at the sunlit garden. 'I am a different person.

That's why I made Chris call me Tammy, not Tamsin. I see the world differently. Literally. I'm a much better cook, for some reason. Stupid stuff.' She turned to look at me. 'The biggest difference is inside. I have never, ever been this hormonal or cried so much for no reason.'

I did wonder if there might not be a trace of post-partum depression in there, too. Who am I to say? I was choosing a different approach when the inevitable happened outside: Amanda tried to ride Scout like a horse and he objected. At least I didn't have to collect her: she ran to Mummy complaining loudly about the Bad Doggy. Tamsin went up in the Mina Rankings when she said, 'He's not a bad doggy. You were mean to him. You can say sorry in a minute.'

Amanda looked outside and suddenly her face lit up. 'Daddyyyyy!'

By common consent, we steered clear of Pramiti and all her doings until after lunch. Vicky was very uneasy in their company, despite Conrad being the one who greeted her. I could see him giving her a pep talk as he escorted her to the house. I had forgotten that she had been Chris's student less than two years ago, and not a very good one at that. Geomancy is not Vicky's speciality. She called him *sir* twice when she wasn't thinking about it.

She was better with Tamsin than I'd anticipated. I found out why when we were setting up the patio furniture for a conference.

'I always worried that she might be a hybrid,' said Vicky. 'But there's no trace of that lass in there.'

'Melody,' I said. 'Her name was Melody.'

'Aye, well. Not anymore. Identity is a complex business, and I think she's got it about right. There is no Melody any more, but what we see coming out with a stick, right now, is not Tamsin either. She's Tammy. Maybe Chris loves her so much because she doesn't have any of Tamsin's irritating habits.'

'How do you know Tamsin had irritating habits?'

'Bound to.'

As I said, you can always rely on Vicky to see the negative potential in any situation.

Chris settled his wife on the couch and took the children (and Scout) to play in Richmond Park. 'We might not get any more days like this,' he said. I think he wanted to give Tamsin the space to be herself and to have some plausible deniability if we planned anything naughty. Naughty? Why am I saying that? I've clearly spent too long around small children.

Conrad had no qualms about joining us. Up to a point. He sat well away with his ashtray and listened carefully.

I brought Tamsin fully up to speed with the situation and what had happened so far. 'So you see,' I concluded. 'We have a stand-off. So long as Pramiti is separated from her Mānik, no one gets hurt. At the same time, she is denied her true nature, and I am denied Ganesh's blessing. We have to upset this balance and run the risk of triggering a war.'

'And of upsetting the Easterbrooks,' said Tamsin. 'They may not be able to take you – us – to court, but they won't be happy if we nick their prized possession.'

'Let's start with the obvious,' I said. 'Where is their place of power, and where is the ring likely to be?'

'Tuddenham Grange,' said Tamsin. 'Not far from Bury St Edmunds. It's completely integrated into the mundane world, and they have open days four times a year. The rest of the time, it's pretty well Warded, as you'd expect. That's not where they keep the ring, though.'

'Oh? Why not?'

'It's not stable. Hasn't been for fifty years. If it's not being used by a person, it starts to disappear unless it's in a strong flow of Lux. They only bring it out for special occasions. To show off.'

'So where is it?'

'Angel House.'

'Bloody hell,' said Vicky.

I had heard of Angel House. It was in a footnote to the Flint Hoard papers. 'Where is that?' I said. 'What is that?'

'Cambridge. It's the home of the Cambridge Collective.'

I sat back and grinned. 'Then I have a plan. If you're up for it. We will have to act quickly. Before someone at Farthingales lets slip some gossip.'

Vicky looked at me. 'Like now? Well, you're certainly dressed for action, Mina.'

I gave her a hard stare. Like Conrad, I think she may be developing an immunity, because she burst out laughing. She turned to Tamsin and said, 'Do Indian superheroes wear Lycra, do you reckon?'

Tamsin wisely ignored that and said, 'Do you want me in on this, Mina? Can I help?'

'You are crucial to the plans. As are you, Vicky. And Conrad has a supporting role. We will act on Monday, because today is Shabbos and I need to talk to someone. Also, I must find Mr Joshi.'

Vicky became alarmed. 'You're not gonna rope the Boss in, are you? That's never gonna happen.'

'Not Hannah. Her sister. I need Ruth on the case. Another reason is that it's mid-afternoon and I need to go home to change. I will be appearing as a superhero on Monday, but not in Lycra.'

Vicky looked at Tamsin again. 'Has Tammy met Rani Mukherjee?'

'Who?' said Tamsin.

'Mina's alter-ego. A real Indian princess. That's how she got into Farthingale House. She didn't tell you that bit, did she? Do you want to see a picture?'

'Careful, Vicky,' I said. 'I have pictures of you as well.'

It was too late. 'It suits her,' said Tamsin.

'Too well,' said Vicky. 'You don't know the half of it. So? Is it Bollywood time?'

'Oh no,' I told them severely. 'I shall be dressed as the most powerful character of all. A part I was born to play. I shall be going as an auditor.'

Vicky snorted and laughed, until she saw the look on my face. 'You're joking, aren't you?'

'She's not,' said Tamsin. 'That's her scary face. I saw it last night, right before she saved my life.'

'Right,' said Vicky. I wasn't finished with her yet.

'And an auditor needs an escort,' I said. 'Who will be wearing her uniform. Dress or combat. Your choice.'

'No,' said Vicky.

'Yes,' I shot back. 'I shall be on official court business and you will be my escort and magickal resource.'

'Eh? No way. What about Fergus Macarthur? It's his patch.'

'Precisely. He may be implicated.'

Vicky levered herself upright and turned to round to face Conrad. 'Here, you, is this your idea? Do I have to?'

He glanced up from the newspaper. 'No and yes. You're representing the King's Watch to the Cloister Court. Call Saffron and talk to her about it.'

I stood up. 'Come on Vicky. I want to show you Tamsin's dressing room and walk in wardrobe.'

'Ooh,' said Vicky.

'What!' said Tamsin.

I pushed her gently back down. 'You rest your ankle. Vicky and I will choose something suitable for my intern to wear.'

'Intern?'

'The perfect disguise. You are my intern who dropped out of the Daughters at Glastonbury to study accountancy.'

When we caught the train back to Waterloo, Conrad had one suggestion that I was reluctant to accept at first.

'Look on it as a circuit breaker,' he said. 'If it looks like Vicky might have to compromise her office, you might need a way out. Don't forget why Vicky's doing this.'

I stopped the answer I had ready and thought about it. Vicky has become a good friend. I think. And then I thought about the uniform she was going to don on Monday, to play a part I had stopped Conrad from playing. I was now going to put her in a position where her career might be threatened.

He saw the uncertainty on my face and said, 'What do you think the real reason I got her promoted was?'

'Didn't she deserve it on her own account?'

'Yes. But probably not quite yet. I wanted her away from me. Ever since I brought her back from the dead, she's wanted to balance the scales. I was afraid she'd do something stupid trying to save my life. Or yours, given how much you mean to me.'

'Oh.'

I sort-of knew that. What I hadn't done was put it in such brutal, basic terms. He was right. He often is. Especially when he listens to me. It was time to do the same. 'Make the call,' I said.

7 — Into the Lion's Fen

'That car is too grand for an intern,' I announced. 'Vicky can drive it. Let me see your outfit.'

Tamsin got out of the jet black Volvo XC90 and pursed her lips. Black trousers, white blouse, black jacket, flat black shoes. All present and correct.

'Good. Have you got my briefcase?'

Tamsin nodded nervously and cheered up a great deal when Vicky emerged from the station with a tray of coffees and she saw the uniform. Vicky had opted for combat over dress, because who would wear that skirt if you had a choice?

'Nice beret,' said Tamsin.

'Don't you flaming start,' said Vicky. 'Rani's already had a go at us. She says that Saffron bleedin' Hawkins has had her combats custom tailored. I ask you.'

'You should consider it,' I said. 'And don't call me Rani again until we're finished.'

Tamsin finally turned her attention to me. 'Nice suit. If a little severe.'

Vic and I had caught the train to Cambridge while Tamsin drove from Richmond. Trying to meet up would have added an hour to the journeys. We were in one of the parking spots at the station reserved for police officers. I did see a Transport Police officer look our way, then change his mind when he saw Vicky's uniform and the fact that we were three women.

We stood round the car for a couple of minutes, drinking our coffee and running through the details again. I finished with a warning. 'Remember, the priority is to make sure we do nothing, and I mean *nothing* that the Cambridge Collective can complain about. The only injured party must be the Easterbrooks. It's a shame that Flora Easterbrook is the Treasurer.'

'Stuck up cow,' said Tamsin. 'She'll be even worse if she gets to be Chair.'

'Says the woman who lives in a mansion by the Thames.' That was Vicky.

I looked down my nose at Tamsin. This was only possible because I was standing on the curb and wearing heels. 'Remember, Amelia, you are not a sophisticated mother of three from Richmond any more. You are Amelia Ryan from Bristol and you are a geek with no social skills.'

'Hey,' said Vicky. 'That's Geekist.'

'Do I look like I care? Put her hair in a Goddess braid and let's get going.'

Cambridge is not very car-friendly. At least the university term hadn't started yet, so we weren't swamped by cyclists. I had been cruel to Tamsin for a reason. She grew up near here. The first time, I wanted her in the moment, not regressing, and that's why I gave directions.

'Are you sure you know where you're going?' said Vicky when I hesitated at a junction.

'Of course. I came to Cambridge on a university open day.'

'Did you not fancy it then?' There was a smile behind the words, challenging me that my exam results hadn't been good enough.

'No,' I said. 'I got the feeling they were eyeing me up for their diversity statistics not my enormous potential as a financial genius. Besides, I got sponsored to go to London and train on the job. Turn left by that church. It's a very narrow lane.'

'Little St Mary's,' murmured Tamsin.

Our target (as Conrad would no doubt say) was down a typically Cambridge lane between the church and Peterhouse College. The lane was a dead end, and devoid of parking, which was why I'd insisted that Angel House reserve me a spot. 'Turn through those gates.' Vicky edged the car carefully through a tight turn. 'Over there, where the traffic cone is. Amelia, get out and move it, will you?'

As soon as the door slammed, Vicky said, 'Go easy on her, will you? This must be hard for the poor bairn. Woman.'

'She needs a bit of ordering around. It'll do her good.'

We gathered in front of what looked like an old chapel, because that's what it was. Part of the inside was still consecrated, but most of the building was now given over to an exclusive Mage's club called Angel House, owned and operated by the Cambridge Collective, an organisation even older than Salomon's House and the King's Watch.

'You go first,' I said to Vicky. 'I'm sure the door will be locked or something.'

It was both locked and Warded. A young woman dressed like a waitress answered the door. 'Oh! Erm, it's Watch Captain Robson, isn't it? I've seen you around the House.'

And that's what all my elaborate plans were for. This girl was a student at the Invisible College, doing a summer job. Even though Vicky's never been to Cambridge, the world of magick is very small. Today, Vicky and I had to play ourselves.

'That's right,' said Vicky. 'Sorry, I don't know your name, but this is Mina Desai, the Peculier Auditor and Amelia Ryan. We have an appointment with Flora Easterbrook.'

'Sorry. Come in, come in.'

The ground floor of Angel House is offices and assorted rooms, lit by magickal light. After all, they do have a surplus of Lux here, and that's the reason for their existence. She took us along a very masculine corridor (all red walls and portraits) and up a grand staircase to the Club room.

This was a different matter entirely, still masculine but worth it because the Club room used the airy, open space of the old chapel and was flooded with light from the Gothic windows. They had kept the decoration to a minimum but gone overboard on the soft furnishings. You could choose from leather club chairs, chintzy sofas or ladder backed dining chairs round games tables. Today it was almost empty, with only four Mages in residence.

Two were sitting by a fire, reading the paper. They were both very old men and looked like they came here to get some peace and quiet. The back wall of the room was its biggest feature, given over to bookshelves with gleaming leather spines. A short, stocky woman in a maternity top was surrounded by books at one of the library tables. She wasn't *that* pregnant. Not really. She probably just wanted to cover up.

The fourth Mage had already got up to greet us. Flora Easterbrook was dressed like a Lady of the Manor rather than an executive. I think the dress may even have been hand-made. You can't get three-quarter sleeves very easily, and the length was perfect. She was in her early forties and had sharp blue eyes in a rather guarded face. Then again, she had a lot to be guarded about.

There was a quick round of handshakes, and she wasn't even looking at Tamsin when they shook. I relaxed my shoulders a little and Tamsin faded into the background behind us. 'It's a lovely room,' I said. 'I haven't had the privilege of visiting the Invisible College yet, but I have been to Newton's House. I think this is much more elegant.'

'Thank you. We're very lucky here. Have a seat. Coffee?'

'Perhaps later,' I said. 'We had one not long ago.'

Flora had been staring at Vicky. I'm sure she was itching to ask why she was in uniform. She resisted the temptation and smiled at me when we'd sat down. 'What brings you to Angel House?' she said. 'Not that you're not welcome, of course, but this isn't a social visit, is it? Oh, and you do know that Watch Captain Clarke is a hereditary member?'

I gave her a smile and a nod. 'I had heard that. He's looking forward to coming with me next time. Vicky is here today because I need a magickal adviser and she was free. Have you been following the Flint Hoard case in the Cloister Court?'

She didn't flinch. What she did do was adjust the skirt on her dress. 'As Collective Treasurer, it's very much part of my job. I confess that I haven't gone too deeply into your report yet. It's rather dense, I'm afraid.'

'Perhaps you should take advice.'

I left it hanging there, to see how she'd respond.

'Do we need to?' she said.

'I would recommend it. There are a lot of loose ends in the report. I am here to follow some of them up. To see where they lead.'

'Oh. Why?'

I rested my elbow on the sofa's arm. 'I'm due back in Cornwall this week to finish a job with the Wessex court.'

'Yes. I heard about that. Quite a drama, wasn't there? Something about the Eldest Daughter being flown to hospital by Conrad Clarke.'

'Yes. She's recovering well, I believe. While I was there, I had a long talk to Lord Mowbray.'

Her eyes narrowed. She didn't like the sound of this. Quite right, too. Especially as I was lying – all this information had come from Chris Kelly, but I wanted to keep his name out of it.

I nodded to her. 'Lord Mowbray has nothing to do with the Flint Hoard. Too big a fish. What he told me was that the only place in England where Isaac Fisher, also known as Ivan Rybakov, could have operated was here, using the Cambridge Collector.'

She blinked unconsciously and straightened herself up on the sofa. 'It's a shame he isn't here to deny it. Ivan did superb work for the Collective, and especially on maintaining the Collector for many years. As far as we know, everything he ever did was above board. We consider his loss a regrettable tragedy.'

'I was there when he died. If you'd like the details.' She looked away. 'Fisher had a lot of questions to answer, which is why the King's Watch arrested him. He may have gone, but the questions remain.'

'What do you want?'

'Two things. To inspect the Collector floor and to take an inventory of any secure storage lockers you have here.'

'Out of the question. We are an independent, chartered company. Our members expect us to maintain the highest standards of privacy. Besides, Fergus emptied Ivan's lockers the day after he died.'

Tamsin was out of Flora's eye line with my briefcase. Exactly where I wanted her. I didn't need the case now, because the one piece of paper I needed had been couriered to King's Cross Station this morning. I took it out of my bag and passed it over.

'This is a warrant from the Cloister Court. It allows me to check the names of all the registered keepers of lockers against your membership list and open those specifically named in the warrant.'

'I see.'

She scanned the warrant. I could tell from her face when she'd got to the list of names. Her eyebrows shot up. 'I have never heard of these people. They aren't members.'

'Then they won't have lockers, will they?'

She could feel the net closing. She decided to stop struggling. 'Very well. What do you want on the Collector floor?'

'Captain Robson wants to conduct a forensic examination.'

'It's at your own risk, Miss Desai.'

I half stood up and snatched the warrant off her lap. 'You'll be with us, Mrs Easterbrook. I can't have you sneaking off and changing your records, can I?'

'It won't take long,' said Vicky, standing up and adjusting the belt on her uniform.

Flora stood up as well. 'Why don't you do the lockers first, then I can leave you to it?'

We couldn't do that because my plan wouldn't work if we did. I had to improvise. 'Because Fisher might have left his stash in the Collector. Then we won't need to see the lockers.'

'Then let's get on with it.'

We returned to the ground floor and then took the staircase down to the old crypt. The modern door at the top was locked with a mundane key, and the ancient one at the bottom was secured with three layers of magick (according to Vicky). Tamsin trailed along behind everyone with her head down. I hadn't seen a single person give her a first glance, never mind a second one. Except the pregnant woman in the library.

The Cambridge Collective exists to manage and maintain the Cambridge Collector. If you've ever wondered where the Lux comes from that flows through Ley lines, the answer is Collectors. Lux is everywhere – like electricity. And like electricity, it can be concentrated. It is produced in certain chemical reactions, especially ones in living creatures and most of all by human brains. The function of a Collector is to siphon off just a little of that Lux, and where else do you get a bigger concentration of human creativity than a university? The Cambridge Collector was the first to be built after the Romans left.

Like most magickal institutions, the Collective Council is proud of its history and independence. In other words, they didn't admit women until they were absolutely forced to.

Flora Easterbrook heaved back the door, with some difficulty, and held out her hand to let us in first. 'After you,' I said.

She was miffed that I didn't trust her not to lock us in. Her problem. She stepped into the old crypt and stood to the side.

What can I say? At this point, Conrad would give you a description of the intricate flow and web of Lux that seethed in the room. I can't, because I couldn't feel a thing. Zip. Zero. Nothing. All I could see was an empty church crypt with pillars, Lightsticks and a lot of painted marks on the stone floor.

The scar on my arm doesn't sense Lux as such. What it senses is humans making magick, so it didn't react until Vicky started scanning the floor with her Sorcerer's Sight and her sPad, an enhanced iPad. She also took out a torch. When she tried to juggle the two, she nearly dropped them and said, 'Amelia, could you hold the torch for us, pet.'

Tamsin walked over and put the briefcase down, seemingly at random, and took the torch. There were a lot of pillars in the crypt (which was much bigger than the footprint of the old chapel), and when they disappeared, I said to Flora, 'We need to keep them in sight.'

'What for?'

'So that you can give evidence in the Cloister Court that Vicky didn't use magick to plant evidence.'

'And why would I do that?'

I moved to keep an eye on them and lowered my voice. 'Because Isaac Fisher was a criminal. His associates, his partners, tried to kill my fiancé. One of them ran over a Watch Captain. They sacrificed their mundane helpers. Another one stabbed Vicky in the chest. And next week Fisher was going to contract a bigamous marriage. I'd start distancing myself if I were you.'

Of all of Fisher's crimes, she picked on the least important. 'A bigamous marriage? Who to?'

'Carole Thewlis. She had a lucky escape. I can let you have a copy of the wedding licence application if you like.'

Her eyes flicked from me to Vicky and Tamsin. 'Did he really create all that Alchemical Gold?'

'He energised it. Here.'

She licked her lips. 'Do you know if he had any help from Angel House?'

'Not to my knowledge. I can add it to Conrad's to-do list if you want.'

'We'll handle it,' she said. 'I'm glad I didn't send that letter now.'

'Oh?'

'Irina Ispahbudhan's lawyers wanted Angel House to say that Isaac was a pillar of the magickal community.'

'Over here!' said Vicky.

We gathered in the dimmest, darkest corner of the crypt, something that puzzled Flora. 'Why are the Lightsticks not working?' she said.

'He turned them off,' said Vicky. 'And there was a Glamour to make it look like there was a wall here. That's faded since he last came. Have a look at the floor.'

She took the torch from Tamsin and shone it at an angle on the stone floor. Flecks of gold glittered in the LED light. 'Use your Sight,' said Vicky to Flora.

The Angel House Treasurer held out her hands, as if she were warming them at a fire and went white with anger. 'The duplicitous bastard. Right under our noses. I'll swear to that in court. No problem.'

I had no idea what they were on about, nor did I care. I made sure that photographs of the gold were taken, and swept some into an envelope with a makeup brush to keep as evidence. When I said we were done, Flora Easterbrook turned and marched out, court shoes clattering.

'Have you got what you need, Amelia?' I said.

She nodded and grinned at Flora's back. Good.

We went straight from the Collector to the safe deposit suite. Flora was now very eager to co-operate. Through another locked door on the ground floor, a twisting set of short, narrow corridors wound round like a maze. They were like this to maximise exposure to the Lux leaking up from a deliberate fault in the Collector. A bit like having a private tap at a reservoir.

The corridors were lined with doors, some full size, some just the size of a standard locker. None of them had numbers. Some had coats of arms, some had names printed on card.

'I will personally guarantee most of these,' said Flora in the first couple of corridors. 'They are all well-established members whom I know. In fact, I know all the members.'

'That's good,' I said. 'Lead the way.'

On the second turn, Tamsin dropped the torch and put the briefcase down to pick it up. Flora was already round the next corner and didn't notice that Tamsin had left the case behind when she re-joined us and passed the torch to Vicky.

Flora quickly found a small door with a card and said, 'Never heard of this person. I think they were on your list.'

I double checked it against the warrant. She was right. 'Vicky?'

Vicky tried the door. 'It's a non-linear lock. No chance without a key.'

'Flora? Angel House must have a master key.'

'Not as such. We *do* have a process, but it takes time. Quite a lot of time.'

'Seal it, Vicky,' I said. 'We can come back with more help and do them all together.'

'Right.'

Vicky took a roll of tape from her pocket and sealed the door. It wouldn't stop someone with a key, but it would do something magickal that would record evidence of tampering. We pressed on. We found two more round the corner, and I looked in my bag. 'Amelia? Where's the Jepson report?'

'In the case. Sorry. It was heavy.'

'Go and get it, please.'

Tamsin scurried off and I started to waffle. 'We think these lockers contain goods purchased with credit from the Flint Hoard. A sort of money laundering. You may not have heard, but Farthingale and Daughter were in touch with the court this morning. They want to make a statement at the next hearing in October.'

Flora drew in a breath and started asking questions. It took Tamsin less than two minutes to reappear with a report and announce, 'I've found it.'

Yes!

'Shall we move on?' I said.

We did, and found most of the lockers I was after. I would need to come back and do the job properly in the near future, but for now it was enough.

'Would you like to stay for lunch?' said Flora, our new fan.

'Next time,' I said. 'If we hurry, we can get this back to Judge Bracewell. She'll need to issue new warrants. Thank you so much for your co-operation. Damn. I've left my scarf somewhere.'

'I'll nip upstairs and check the sofa,' said Tamsin. She passed the briefcase to Vicky and we walked slowly to the front door, chatting about Cambridge. Flora had only just opened the door when Tamsin rushed back. 'Did you even have a scarf?'

'I don't think you did, you know,' said Vicky.

'Come to think of it, you didn't,' said Flora. 'I remember admiring your jacket. And your engagement ring. It's a beauty.'

As we were saying a cordial goodbye, we moved aside to let the pregnant woman from the library get past. When the doors closed behind us, everyone's phone pinged at once. They're old-school in Angel House: strictly no Wi-Fi or mobile signals allowed. We started checking them as Vicky unlocked the Volvo.

'Grantchester,' I said. 'At the cricket club. Turn right at the end of the lane, Vicky. They're waiting for us.'

'Gotcha.'

She waited until she was on the main road, and until I'd finished putting the destination into the Satnav before she asked. 'Go on then, Amelia, how did you do it?'

Tamsin was sitting in the back, cradling my briefcase. She leaned forward and pulled my hair. Hard.

'Ow! What was that for?'

'Vicky's driving, so I can't do it to her. If she calls me *Amelia* again, I will do it even harder. I learnt that trick from my daughter.'

Vicky snorted with laughter. 'It's 'cos you played the part so well, Tammy. I still can't see why you didn't tell us what you were doing.'

'That's because you needed to look innocent,' I said. 'Conrad is right: you are a terrible liar, Vicky.'

All we had told Vicky was that she had to drop the torch in the Collector and ask for help. And to otherwise ignore *Amelia*. 'Do you want to tell her?' I said to Tamsin.

'It was your plan,' she replied. 'And I need to monitor this case.'

'Very well. Tamsin has talent as a Plane Shifter.'

'Ooh. Neat,' said Vicky. 'Go on.'

'I discovered from research that Pramiti's Mānik exists on two planes simultaneously. That's why it's so powerful.'

'I'll go to the foot of our stairs. Wow. No wonder the Duke of Ashford wanted to nick it in the first place.'

'Quite. Once I knew that, I just asked Tamsin how we could get it out. She went to Chris and got that briefcase.'

'I wondered why I hadn't seen you with it before. Not stylish enough for you, Rani.'

I ignored that remark. 'It has an Alchemical cage of some sort. Proper Geomancers use them in the field.'

'I know that. No wonder she kept leaving it around, and that explains why it weighs a ton.'

'It does,' said Tamsin. 'And I had to charge it in the Collector.'

I took over again. 'When we got to the safety deposit suite, Tamsin stopped outside the Easterbrook's room. She knows their crest. Then, when I sent her back, she used the stored Lux to go onto the next plane.'

'And walk through the door. Brilliant. Is it in the case now?'

'Oh yes. That was the only way of disguising it from Flora.'

In case you're wondering why Plane Shifters haven't stolen the Crown Jewels from the Tower of London, that's because the Crown Jewels only exist on *this* plane. They, and most of the Tower, are invisible on a higher plane. But not the Mānik. Tamsin was able to pluck it out of its box, and all it took was a little manipulation to bring it back through the door and drop it into the case.

I had a feeling that recovering the gem was going to be the easy part. A feeling confirmed when we left the city and my phone rang. The number was programmed into my phone, but I hadn't spoken to this person before.

'You're definitely being followed,' she said. 'Black Mercedes 4x4 with tinted windows. Can't miss it.'

'Thanks.'

I disconnected and told the others.

'Who the flip was that?' said Vicky.

'One of the Merlyn's Tower Irregulars. Roberta Woodhouse. The Peculier Necromancer. That was her in the Club room.'

'No! You're joking. She looked pregnant.'

'She is. That business with the scarf was so that Tamsin could tip her off that we were leaving with mission accomplished.' I checked the Satnav: only five minutes to Grantchester. 'Pull in to that car park and swap places. From here it gets very tricky.'

8 — Not Cricket

Vicky swerved into the car park and swapped places with Tamsin. I noticed that she didn't cradle the briefcase with quite the same enthusiasm. Tamsin pulled out on to the main road, helpfully waved on by a flash of headlights from a big black Mercedes with tinted windows.

'Everyone ready?' I asked. Vicky was very much clued in to the next part of the plan.

'Aye.'

'Yes.'

'Go.'

Tamsin is a terrible driver. Perhaps she always was, or perhaps Melody was destined to be one. She screeched round the turning to Grantchester and nearly crashed into a tractor on the smaller road. As if my nerves weren't shredded enough already.

'In two hundred yards, turn right. Your destination is on your left,' said the Satnav.

The car rocked on its suspension as Tamsin threw it into the turn. It's a good job that the cricket club wasn't hosting a conference or something. She did a big U-turn and stopped in the middle. Conrad was already half way to our vehicle. Tamsin clicked the central locking and I jumped out. While we were driving, I'd take the chance to swap my shoes for trainers. I held the door for Conrad and he jumped in. Vicky was also out and closed her door. Tamsin accelerated away and disappeared.

'Where is she?' said Vicky. 'And by the way, this briefcase really is heavy. How did she carry it?'

'She has three children. You develop muscles. Pramiti will be sitting in the shade, and that *must* be her car round there.'

'You're not joking. A Bentley. Well, what else?'

We walked over to the sleek black luxury car. The back of my neck prickled and I had to fight the urge to look round. No doubt the Mercedes was now in a position to watch us.

Pramiti uncoiled herself from the Bentley as if she were already a snake. For all she's dangerous, she is a remarkable creature. I would love to see her dance one day. From a safe distance, obviously.

'Do you have it? I can't feel it?'

She was desperate. You could tell that because she had ignored Vicky's uniform and my tights-and-trainers combo, something a relaxed Pramiti would not let pass.

'We do,' I said. 'It is sealed in this case.'

'Let me feel.'

Vicky held up the case, and Pramiti brushed her hair back to lean down and sniff it. When she did so, I could smell the spices and gin on her breath. Conrad had taken her for an early lunch while they waited for us to turn up.

A beatific smile came over Pramiti's face. 'Yes. At last. Take it out.'

'We have company,' I said. 'That car on the road. The Duke of Ashford is inside it.'

'All the better. I am reunited with my Mānik and I can take revenge on the creature who stole it.'

Vicky looked alarmed at that prospect. I don't blame her. I was feeling alarmed, too. It was my job not to show it.

'Would that be wise?' I said. 'You will be weakened. Severely weakened while you adjust. The Duke of Ashford is far more powerful than he was when you last met.'

Her eyes flicked over my shoulder. Uncertainty crossed her face. Not an expression she was practised at. Her race are used to certainty and command, not doubt and dependency. I gave it a couple of seconds more to sink in.

'We need to get to a safe place,' I said. 'We can take you there if you let me deal with him.'

She narrowed her eyes. Something yellow flickered in them. The Mānik was affecting her already. 'How will you do that? Are you in league with him?'

'My debt is to you and Lord Ganesh. I could discharge it by leaving the case and walking away.'

Vicky put the case down. 'I need to get to the gym more,' she said.

Pramiti looked at the case. The doubt was back. 'Go.'

'Would you mind, Vicky?' I took my jacket off and folded it carefully before placing it on the case. Then I jogged across the car park and out on to the road where the Mercedes was waiting. I went to the back because Dukes rarely drive themselves, and he wouldn't be alone. The tinted window was descending before I got close.

'Namaste, my lord.' I had to suppress a shudder when the aristocratic power of Lord Ashford hit me.

He looked like a film star and had a film star's presence and aura, all wrapped in a mature, silver haired craggy-jawed ruggedness. Imagine James Bond two years after retirement. It is a long time since I've gone weak at the knees like that, and I wanted to faint into his strong arms. I planted my feet firmly on to the ground and tried to stiffen my spine.

'Miss Desai,' he said. 'A pleasure to meet you. I believe that congratulations are in order.'

I had to work hard to swallow before I spoke. 'Thank you, my lord.'

'Captain Robson is a better Sorcerer than I gave her credit for if she spotted us. I thought this car was well shielded.'

'Alas no, my lord. Vicky and I are not the only ones on this job. Your vehicle may be magickally shielded, but it does stick out rather. The rest of the team were tracking you. And Sir Jon. He could at least have worn a Glamour.'

Lord Ashford is tipped for big things amongst the Fae, according to my sources. I could see why when he laughed. A lot of Fae would have stamped their feet at what I'd just said and scorched me in a petulant temper.

'It seems we have something to learn from Nimue's Guard after all. And you, Miss Desai. Would one of your team be the elusive Squadron Leader Clarke? And his famous gun.'

I bowed again. 'Conrad has done me the honour of supporting me in my little venture. As have others. He was rather alarmed when his bullets didn't work on one of your kind, so he's brought that great menace of a sword the Gnomes gave him. Just in case.' I gave him my best Indian nod. 'All of that is a detail, my lord. Surely no one actually *wants* a confrontation.'

He nodded graciously in return. 'If only that were true. Pramiti definitely wants one.'

'She wants her Mānik more. Sadly, one cannot trust the word of a serpent under any circumstances, so a promise to leave you alone would be worthless. What if I could get her both out of the way *and* get her to lose interest in you? Would that not be a better outcome? I would be happy to perform that service.'

'A service, eh?'

I have had a crash course on the Fae, and not just their innate desirability. Unlike the Nāgin, their word can be trusted in certain circumstances. And they never forget a favour. Owed or given. The key word was *service*, which was why Lord Ashford had repeated it.

'Yes, my lord. If my service is satisfactory, everyone will be content. If not… I'm sure you can handle yourself. Away from the limelight.'

He rubbed his stubbly jaw and I felt something rubbing inside me. The power in those hands…

'I doubt the Easterbrooks will be content. I'm surprised they aren't even hotter on your tail than I was.'

'They don't know the jewel is gone. When they do find out, they won't have a clue who took it.'

I was keeping my fingers crossed when I said that. I had left Flora Easterbrook with enough paperwork and headaches to keep her well away from her storeroom for a long while.

'What's your plan?' he said suddenly.

I bowed again. 'An old Indian trick, my lord. I shall use a forked stick and throw her over the wall into the cotton fields.'

He grinned. A very carnivorous grin. I half expected his canines to grow longer. 'That's why I like dealing with the mundane world. It shows respect without fawning.' He nodded. 'I think Pramiti is getting hungry. Very well, I shall leave you to it. May fortune smile on you, Miss Desai.'

'Thank you, my lord. I shall be in touch.'

The window rose, the engine fired and I shivered. My dress has no sleeves, and without Lord Ashford to warm me, it was very cold.

Did I just say that? Did I *really* just say that? I think I need to see someone about preventative measures before I meet Lord Ashford again. A jog back across the car park would soon warm me up.

Vicky had placed herself between Pramiti and the briefcase. 'Let's go,' I said, grabbing my jacket and bag. 'The cricket club is too public. I know a quiet place only ten minutes' drive away. I'll put the location into the Satnav.'

Pramiti dragged her gaze away from the case. 'One of you will drive.'

'With respect, Vicky must look after the case, and I must call Conrad to give him instructions on following Lord Ashford.'

'Is that where Conrad has gone?'

I already had the front passenger door open. 'The sooner we get going, the sooner you will have your Mānik.'

She bustled back into the car and started the engine. I slipped into the front seat and watched Vicky perform a quick Work at the rear of the vehicle to dissolve the Glamour that Pramiti had put on the number plates. Then she got in and sat behind me, as far from Pramiti as she could get. In a Bentley, that's quite a long way.

It's a good job they drive on the left in India. Most of the time. When they're not in the middle of the road avoiding the bicycles and the cows. It meant that Pramiti didn't think about what she was doing, she just drove north out of Grantchester, towards the motorway. All she could think about was her Mānik.

As soon as I'd finished giving a coded message to Conrad, she started to press me. 'Where was it and how did you get it?'

'There are many Fae in Cambridge. We had to do to them what Lord Butler did to you and trick them out of it. Would you like the whole story?'

'Did they rage and scream?'

'Oh yes.'

'Then tell me.'

I proceeded to give her an adapted version of a well-known Bollywood fantasy movie. She drank it in like wine as we joined the motorway. Two junctions later, she barely noticed as the Satnav sent her off again and onto the A14, a wide road but nowhere near as busy. I was now keeping the fingers of both hands crossed and constantly glancing at the wing mirror. I breathed a sigh of relief when the blue lights appeared.

Pramiti wouldn't demean herself by using her mirrors unless she had to, and she had no idea that two police cars were behind us, all lights flashing. One of them overtook us and cut in. The other one started its siren.

'What do you think they are doing?' said Pramiti, mystified.

'They want you to pull over,' I said. 'Over there. Where the big slip road is.'

'How tiresome.'

She slowed and stopped. The police cars boxed us in. My arm started to throb. Vicky dumped the briefcase and shuffled over to sit directly behind Pramiti. Front and back, I could see police officers getting out. The ones in the passenger seats had been carrying their automatic rifles.

'Sorry to bother you, pet,' said Vicky. 'Can I remind you that using magick to undermine the rule of mundane law is an offence. I will arrest you if you try it.'

'What on earth are you talking about?' said Pramiti.

'Stop using magick, or I will subdue you.' To reinforce the point, Vicky got out her Badge of office and touched the Badge itself. Pramiti wavered and nearly slumped forward. Vicky let go, and my arm stopped tingling. I leaned across and lowered first Pramiti's window, then my own.

We had a policeman each, with their hands on their sidearms. The ones with bigger guns stood back. I turned to mine and said, 'Thank goodness you're here, officer. I think the driver has been drinking. You can smell it on her.'

The other officer, the one on Pramiti's side, had heard me and sniffed the air by the window. Without taking his hand off his belt, he said, 'Is this your vehicle, madam?'

'Yes.'

'It was reported stolen on Saturday. Have you been drinking, madam?'

Pramiti started to colour, spreading up from her chest. 'Not much. Not at all, really.'

'Could I see your driving licence?'

'I don't need a driving licence. I have diplomatic immunity. Talk to your chief of police. My name is…'

She gave the name she'd travelled under. And yes, when Pramiti arrived in the UK, she was travelling on a diplomatic passport. This we found out on Sunday from Ruth and Mr Joshi. He still has connections at the Foreign Office.

She'd said her name very quickly. Slowly, the police officer called over a fifth member of their party. My my, what a response. The newcomer had a tablet computer and showed it to Pramiti.

'Forgive me, is that how you spell your name?' said the patrol leader.

'Yes. Of course. Now can we get on?'

'I'm afraid not, madam. Officers from the Metropolitan Police raided your premises this morning on suspicion of offences against the Modern Slavery Act. A young woman was rescued.'

Pramiti finally turned to me and switched to Hindi. 'What is this nonsense? What is he talking about? What is this *modern slavery*?'

'I don't think the officer's finished with you,' I replied. In English.

'You were declared *persona non grata* this morning,' he announced. 'That means you have to leave the country, and I'm afraid that I can't let you drive because you've been drinking. Would you like me to call your embassy, or would you let Squadron Leader Clarke drive you?'

Pramiti was bright red now, and my arm started to tingle again. The officer with the computer stepped well back, and Conrad replaced the leader at Pramiti's window.

'If you don't calm down, your Mānik will be buried with you, debt paid,' he said. 'Go quietly, and your Mānik goes with you.'

I was quite proud of that. I'd written his lines for him.

He reached into the car and opened the driver's door. He pulled it wide and stepped back. I did the same and held open the passenger door. After re-programming the Satnav for Heathrow Airport

Pramiti replaced me in the passenger seat, and Conrad got in to drive. We had a police escort all the way to Heathrow. There was total silence in the car for one hour and forty minutes, except when Vicky asked to stop for a comfort break. We all needed one. Even the police drivers.

We took turns, with Vicky escorting Pramiti into the ladies after Conrad and I had finished. We had an audience, so Conrad restricted himself to blowing a kiss before lighting a cigarette.

'You were brilliant,' he said. 'One hundred per cent brilliant.'

'Only a hundred?'

'A thousand. A million.'

'Better. I love you, Conrad. Have we really done it?'

'Nearly there, love. Here they come.'

I couldn't believe it when Conrad drove into the Border Force compound. That was the scene of my humiliating return from India in the summer, and I was sweating profusely when he led us to the same interview room where I had arrived in chains. Literally chained to an Indian Mage.

The timing was tight – the Air India flight to Mumbai had already been called when the police escort took up position outside the room. The plane wouldn't leave without us, but Conrad would be in serious trouble if the flight missed its slot on the runway.

Vicky heaved the briefcase on to the table with a massive thump and rubbed her arms.

'This. Is. Not. Right!' said Pramiti. 'That creature stole from me, and you are on his side. He will get away free. Where is your justice now?'

She was looking at Conrad. He and Vicky stepped back, and I moved in front of her. 'If he stole from you, lodge a complaint and follow it through the courts. I know a lot of lawyers. I could recommend one. If you gave it to him on a promise, then take your Mānik and get on the plane.'

She still wasn't happy and was winding up for another go.

'You can have it now,' I said softly. 'Right now.'

She had to have it now. If she tried it on the plane, the consequences would be fatal for everyone. We knew the Alchemical cage was discharging rapidly, and the smell of it would be driving her mad.

'Very well. Give it to me.'

Vicky stepped forwards and opened the briefcase. Inside was a robust iron cage, like a lobster pot but with gold medallions and scroll work all over it. A red glow spread out through the holes. Vicky touched one of the gold seals and stepped smartly back.

Pramiti fell on the cage and threw open the lid. She took a deep breath and grabbed the Mānik. The red glow was like a fire, blowing the lights and bathing us all with a blood-red sheen. She slowly lifted the jewel and placed it on her forehead.

Her form flickered. A woman, then a snake, then a woman, then both together. The room blacked out and there was a slap of flesh on the floor. Conrad switched on a torch and shone it down. A naked, human, Pramiti lay on the floor. The bindi on her forehead was now diamond shaped.

'Thank the gods for that,' said Vicky. 'I thought she might freeze in snake form. That would be hard to explain.'

'I'll get the stretcher,' said Conrad. 'It should be airside.'

It was. Through the door that led to the aircraft, a trolley stretcher and two security guards were waiting. We got her on to the stretcher and bundled her clothes on top of her, under the blanket. Vicky volunteered to escort her to the plane because, and I quote, 'You're carrying that effing briefcase from now on, Conrad.' My last sight of her was when they loaded her into the ambulance.

We hugged and kissed for a long while, and he told me again that I was brilliant. That's always nice to hear from the man you love. Who needs Lord Ashford when you can have Conrad Clarke all to yourself?

'We'd better go,' he said eventually. 'There are still two counter-terrorism units outside who need to be stood down. And don't mention the lights. They can figure that out for themselves.'

I let Conrad deal with the police while I got three takeout coffees and a sandwich for Vicky from the cafeteria. The coffee had improved slightly since last time.

We had to wait for Vicky in the car park. Conrad had volunteered to return the Bentley to the Met Police in London. I wasn't complaining.

'What now?' I said. Conrad being Conrad, he was leaning on the Bentley smoking.

'A few loose ends to tie up. We'll have to report all this to Hannah tomorrow. And your shoes are still in Woody's car, if you're bothered.'

'I am bothered! Those are my lucky Audit shoes, and they cost a lot of money. Do we have to go back to the fens to get them?'

'No. She's coming to town tomorrow. And we're all going out tonight to celebrate. In Richmond.'

There was something in his voice. 'What?'

'Vicky's going to make her own way to Earth House for eight. Tamsin is meeting us in the pub at seven thirty. Or just one of us.'

'What's going on?'

'I've got something to show you when we get back to the flat. Here's Vicky. Don't mention it to her. She thinks that you and I are driving to Richmond because we want to go straight to Clerkswell tomorrow. Which we do. We need to get ready to go back to Cornwall.'

Vicky almost loped across to the car. 'The plane was taxiing to the runway before they'd pulled the staircase away,' she said triumphantly. 'She's gone.'

I gave her a hug, a kiss and my deepest thanks.

'Pleasure,' she said. 'It was a bit hairy in Grantchester, but you've done it, Mina. You can get married now. When's it gonna be? Please don't tell me you want a long engagement.'

'I hope not,' said Conrad.

'Next year,' I said. 'In the spring. At Elvenham.'

'Good. Is that my sandwich? I could eat a scabby horse.'

Conrad unlocked the car and we slipped out of Heathrow with smiles on our faces.

9 — A Debt Repaid

Tamsin had got to the pub before me. She was waiting nervously with a glass of wine for me and two gin glasses for her. She'd already finished one of them. She'd chosen a table by the river, and I wondered if she'd used magick to get it. All the others were full. Maybe she's just lucky.

I had one of my big bags with me. Big enough to hold the papers inside. The ones that had been waiting for me in Notting Hill. I'd brought them because I needed them. As evidence, and for Tamsin to make a decision.

I'd collected them when Conrad had poured me a drink after we'd got back that afternoon. He'd given me my drink and pointed to the table.

'What's that?' I'd said.

'Something Chris said the other night rang alarm bells,' he replied. 'While you were comforting Tamsin, he said that he hadn't gone to the inquest.'

'So? Did he need to?'

'No, but it was the fact that Tamsin had asked him *not* to go that got me worried. I Googled the accident, and the driver was never prosecuted. I asked Ruth to get the post-mortem report. You should read the page with the tab on it.'

I picked up the folder. 'Did she really die in a crash?'

'Oh yes. Multiple injuries. Ruth also checked the driver's statement. He said that Tamsin more or less threw herself under his thirty-eight tonne articulated lorry. Another driver's dashcam footage confirmed it. Read the report. I'm going to start packing.'

Conrad had already removed the post-mortem pictures. Thankfully. I turned to the page with the tab. I had to read it twice.

Tamsin Kelly had not been pregnant when she fell under the lorry. What she did have was stage IV uterine cancer. With a lot of secondary tumours. I took it through to the bedroom in a daze, the pages still open in front of me.

'When did you get this?'

'This morning. I kept it back from you until now because people could have died if your plan hadn't worked. If that was wrong, then I'm sorry.'

'No. Thank you. I mean, thank you for following through and telling me at all. What are you going to do?'

'Chris doesn't know. He has no idea. That's why Tamsin wanted him away from the inquest, and I'll bet she kept the Richardsons busy, too. It's not my place to tell him. If you don't want to see her again, then I'll tell her tonight and leave it up to her to explain to Chris why we've suddenly gone off her. I don't like doing this, but it's up to you. Tamsin did you a massive favour today. Did us a massive favour. If you throw that in the bin and forget about it, so will I.'

I sat down on the bed and cradled the report on my lap. 'I don't know, Conrad. I really don't know. I think I'm going for a walk.'

I did go for a walk, and got some strange looks. Short Indian woman in an expensive dress and trainers, with a bright blue scar on her arm. Not surprising, really. When I'd got back to Conrad, I told him that I was going to see her on my own. He nodded and carried on folding my sari. Not an easy job. I had been going to wear it to celebrate. I chose something else instead.

Tamsin had a shopping bag with her at the pub. A sustainable, jute one with the logo of a wholefood shop. 'Your kurti,' she said, placing it on the table.

I took the bag off the table and replaced it with a totally unsustainable, non-recyclable old Tesco carrier bag. 'Your autopsy report,' I said.

She flinched and blushed and squirmed like the teenager her body was telling her to be and shivered in her short summer dress. 'How?' she said.

'Conrad. Like his dog, he follows a scent to the end. No matter where it leads. He is very good at that. Deadly, in fact.'

'Where was Scout this morning?' She must have been in shock if that was the first thing that came into her head.

'He is too volatile near non-human creatures. We put him in doggy-daycare. What happened, Tamsin? I'm giving you a chance to explain.'

She started shaking her head and crying. Sobbing. I took a gulp of my wine, just to give me something to do while I waited. I'd wait until closing time if I had to.

She'd gone easy on the makeup tonight, so there weren't too many streaks when she got the tears under control. 'It wasn't murder,' she said eventually. 'I couldn't do that. I wouldn't do that.'

'Then what was it?'

'Double suicide. Of sorts. She called me first. I kept her talking while I turned the bike round. Then I told her to shout out to her parents. I don't think she had the energy left, so they found her with the empty bottle and called me. I was already on my way back by then, and I knew it was too late for her.' She took a deep breath. 'Too late for Melody. There. I've said her name. Melody was already dead when I threw myself under that lorry. Yes, I knew what I was doing, but Melody was already gone when my Spirit found her.'

Did I believe her? I don't know. Was it my place to act as judge and jury? No.

'What are you going to do?' she asked.

I pushed the carrier bag over the table. 'Take that. I want to enjoy tonight, Tamsin. I want to say thank you properly to you, to Chris and to Vicky. I owe you all a debt. I will repay you tomorrow morning, and after that it will be up to you. Tonight, I can look at you and Chris and forget what I know. I've had a lot of practice at that. Tomorrow, I will not. You tell him after we've gone or you'll never see me again. Or Conrad.'

'Thank you. I think. I'm not sure I can do this.'

'Yes you can. Drink your gin while I get us more drinks.'

She knocked back the second gin while I was at the bar. When I got back, I leaned in and said, 'You've been doing it every day for five years, Tamsin. One more night won't be a struggle. Let me tell you about Scout. He's barred from doggy-daycare.'

'How? Why?'

'He herded all the other dogs and made them jump over things. One of the owners described their little Pooh Bear as being traumatised.'

'No! You're kidding!'

'I wish I was. I am only grateful that he hasn't hit puberty yet. The consequences could have been disastrous. Drink up.'

My headache next morning was epic, especially as it was only eight o'clock when we left Earth House to go to Richmond Park. Vicky was still asleep, Conrad was on breakfast duty and Chris was looking after the kids. Tamsin, resplendent in neon Lycra, was itching to run until I told her that I only run in twenty-two yard bursts.

'Why?'

'That's the distance between the wickets. Any further is pointless.'

She slowed down then, but there was no slowing Scout. He was off and away. Far enough away that any park wardens wouldn't think he was with us.

'Why do we have to come here?' said Tamsin after a few minutes of gossip about last night.

We had arrived at one of the woods after a steep climb. I whistled Scout and whispered into his ear. He shot off into the trees and Tamsin gave me a worried look when I set off after him.

'You know where we're going, don't you?' she said.

'I do.'

We walked in silence, following a barely visible path through the trees, egged on by Scout. In the densest part of the wood, my arm started to itch, and Tamsin came to a full stop. We were there.

'Why?' she said.

'I couldn't have got the Mānik back without you, Tamsin. Or only at a great cost. The Duke of Ashford was also grateful, as was his Queen. She is willing to take you as a student. One of her Counts will teach you. No one is better at Plane Shifting than the Fae. Apart from the gods, and they don't give lessons.'

She was terrified. I could see her eyes starting to fill again. 'What if I don't come back?'

'You can study as a day-pupil. You will only meet the Queen twice, I should think.'

'I haven't got a gift to give them. I can't walk into the sídhe without a present.'

I fished a Jiffy bag out of my back pocket. 'Here. Conrad accumulates Artefacts that he can't sell on to the Dwarves.'

'Accumulates?'

'Plunder. This one should tickle her royal fancy.' I thrust the bag into her hand. 'And there's a Merlyn's Tower Irregulars badge in there. Conrad insisted you have it.'

'But what about Chris and the kids?'

'Conrad is telling him where you are now. You can decide what to tell him about Melody tonight, when we're long gone.'

I gave her a big hug, and the waterworks really started.

'I don't know,' she said.

'I do. I really hope to see you again, Tamsin. There's a Bollywood party in three weeks, if you fancy it. You could combine it with a visit to Chris's mother. She's only half an hour up the road. Now go.'

I gave her a symbolic push into the woods. She put her hand to her chest and started to shimmer. She took two steps forward and disappeared into the Fae realm.

I turned round and started to walk down the hill. When I got to the edge of the wood, I gave Scout a whistle. He bounced up and barked, and I grabbed his collar to slip on the lead.

'Come on, boy. It's time to go home.'

Mark Hayden

French Leave

This story was originally published in June 2020. The action takes place partly at the beginning **Seventh Star***, the Seventh Book of the King's Watch, but mostly afterwards.*

1 — *Judgement Day*

Let me take you back.

Back before the Battle of Brookford Farm, when Clan Salz had been founded and I'd picked up a pack of Mannwolves.

Back before my inauguration as Deputy Constable and Lord Guardian of the North, when I'd nearly died of blood loss and hypothermia.

Back before Tara Doyle/Princess Birkdale had sashayed into my little world.

Back before the Bollywood party, when so much of our lives had changed. Especially Myfanwy's – it was after the party that she and Ben threw caution to the winds and Myfanwy conceived.

The day before the party, her fate had been at the crossroads for a totally different reason: the first official inspection of her confinement in Clerkswell. Because Myfanwy is under a court order, she has to have a supervisor, and that would be me. The court requires that her confinement is monitored, and so the Boss had come up to cast her eye over things. Hannah had asked me a few questions, and then I'd signed a form to say that Myfanwy had not, to my knowledge, breached her conditions. Hannah had then disappeared into the library with a very nervous Myfanwy, and we'd gathered outside to wait...

'Do you think she'll pass?' asked Erin nervously.

'Why aye, of course she'll pass, pet,' said Vicky. She reached out and took Erin's hand. Vicky gave it a squeeze and kept hold of it to reassure Erin and to put a stop to Erin's Lady Macbeth impersonation. Erin had been wringing her hands for at least half an hour, and I haven't seen her this worked up since she was caught with a shotgun. By Vicky.

Erin is Myfanwy's best friend, and Vicky is Myfanwy's closest friend (there is a difference). Also waiting outside the library was my little (half) sister, Sofía. She's only nineteen, and being nineteen, she was on her phone. She was there, though, and that's what counts.

Missing from the vigil were Myfanwy's fiancé, Ben Thewlis, and my own fiancée, Mina. I still love saying that: *my fiancée*. Ben was at work and giving Myfanwy some space, while Mina was outside supervising the workmen.

FRENCH LEAVE

Sofía looked up from her phone. 'She is very scary, your boss. In the car, she says nothing and stares out of the window all the time. She nearly bites Vicky's head off when Vicky puts the radio on.'

'You get used to her,' said Vicky. 'She doesn't believe there's actually a real world outside London. Bringing her to deepest Gloucestershire was always going to be stressful.' Vicky glanced at me and shook her head slightly, unseen by the others. We know the Boss best, and we know the real reason that Hannah is in a foul mood. I nodded back: *we'll keep this to ourselves*.

'It must be bad news,' said Erin. 'They're taking so long.'

'This is Myfanwy we're on about,' said Vicky. 'She can talk the hind leg off a donkey at the best of times. When she's flustered, she's like a tap with no handle.'

'Si,' agreed Sofía. 'She talks more than Mamá.'

At that moment, the double doors were thrown open and a beaming Myfanwy waved a piece of paper like someone who's just passed their driving test at the fourth attempt.

Erin and Vicky piled in for a group hug, with Sofía joining the queue. Being two heads taller than all of them, I got a good view of the Boss slipping out behind the scrum. She nodded towards the back door and I shouted a loud Well Done to Myfanwy before following Hannah outside.

'I've come out for some quiet, and now this!' said Hannah when the noise of pneumatic hammers shattered the air.

A team of burly men were putting the finishing touches to a giant marquee, overseen by the diminutive form of Mina, who knows nothing about tents but is an expert on motivation by surveillance. She saw us and came over.

'How did it go?' she said.

'No issues,' said Hannah. 'All good. How's the pavilion coming along?'

Mina *tsked*. 'The marquee is on schedule, but the floor is behind.' Her phone rang and she checked the screen. 'That's the caterers. Excuse me.'

'Come on,' I said to Hannah. 'Let's escape. There's a couple of things I need to show you.' I leaned into the scullery to grab a couple of coats, mine and one of Erin's (she leaves clothes *everywhere*. Nightmare). The sun was shining, but this was late September in the countryside, and the Boss was dressed for a London office; I didn't want her moaning about the cold.

She accepted the coat with some reluctance. 'Where's this thing been?'

'Mostly on the peg since Erin bought it. Over here.'

I led Hannah away from the formal gardens to the stables, one of which houses Erin's scriptorium and another is for my new horse. Evenstar is a magnificent grey filly, a gift from the Mowbrays of Cornwall. Hannah was suitably impressed. From a distance.

I took a carrot out of the sack. 'Give her this. She really doesn't bite.'

Hannah looked from me to the horse. This may be the closest she's been to one in her life. She wasn't happy, but the Mage who'd taken down a Revenant wasn't going to pass the challenge of feeding a horse. Before I could stop her, she offered the carrot on her palm, and a rather hungry Evenstar went in for the full nuzzle-slurp-lick-crunch. The Boss's eyes bulged with shock, and for the second time today I reached into my pocket for the specially purchased wet wipes.

While Hannah wiped her hands, I gave Evenstar's nose a rub. 'There's an enchanted saddle, too, but Eseld Mowbray wouldn't tell me what it does, and I'm a bit nervous to try it for myself. Myfanwy has no clue, either.'

'Don't ask me. I wouldn't know one end of a saddle from the other.' She threw the wipes in a rubbish bag and grinned. 'I hear that Eseld was a bit of a tease in more ways than one. Rumour has it that she tried to chat up both you *and* Saffron.'

This was 100% true. I gave her a blank look and said, 'You shouldn't listen to rumours, ma'am.'

She laughed, 'Good advice,' and then held her finger and thumb together. 'Do you know, I was *that* close to hitting Myfanwy with a Silence. She wittered on so much that she nearly confessed to growing cannabis with your sister.'

I snorted like Evenstar. 'Don't. I have to close my ears to that rumour as well. Sofía has adopted Vicky, Myvvy and Erin as surrogate magickal big sisters, to go with her real life big sister.'

'She could do worse. A lot worse. How's it going for Sofía at Salomon's House? She's been studying there for, what, three weeks?'

'Yes. It's going well, I think. Sofía's good at changing the subject when I bring it up. I'm sure that if there were a problem, Cora would have tipped me off. I'll ask her tomorrow.'

When I said Dean Cora's name, Hannah looked away, staring at the top of the marquee. 'Cora's had a lot on her mind with the election. You're right, though. Conrad Clarke's little sister won't be getting a free pass at the Invisible College.'

I walked out of the stable towards the south-east corner of the Elvenham gardens, demarcated by a neatly trimmed hawthorn hedge. I led her to a gate and showed her the five acre pasture on the other side. In case you're wondering, five acres is two and a half international sized football pitches.

'This is all that's left of the original Elvenham Grange Farm,' I said. 'We own it, but we've leased it out for grazing since forever.'

'Good for you,' she said, giving me a sideways look. 'Tell me what's so impressive, because to me it looks like a field.' She pushed herself onto her toes. 'A field with sheep.'

'The sheep are the important part. Mind your ears.' I whistled loudly. A special whistle. Then I opened the gate and my dog, Scout, bounded up.

FRENCH LEAVE

Scout used to be the vessel for my Familiar Spirit, but that bond was violently severed by a homicidal Witch. Hannah had been very solicitous about my loss when she arrived earlier; she knows a lot about losing people. She'd even let Scout lick her, and that had been the first use of the wet wipes.

Having already met Hannah, Scout ignored her and bounded into the field. He's still an adolescent in dog years, and full of energy, even by Border Collie standards. Too full. We have to amuse him in relays, and now we were about to play his favourite game.

'Watch this,' I said to Hannah. 'Away, Scout!'

He shot off to the right, a black and white sheep-seeking missile. They were munching happily at the far side, and Scout and I spent a couple of minutes working the small flock until he had corralled them in the corner near the gate.

Admiration and amused mystification were competing on Hannah's face. 'Impressive. Pointless, but impressive, unless you're thinking of a career change. Does the farmer mind you boys playing games with his livestock?'

I pretended to be offended. 'First of all, Scout shouldn't be able to work like that without years of practice. The Familiar Bond has left a mark, and I think he can smell some types of magick, too.'

'Now that is interesting. You should get it checked out. You also said *firstly*, and I know you, Conrad Clarke. What else?'

'Those aren't Bridge Farm sheep. They belong to the King's Watch.'

She does know me well. She didn't flinch. She gave me her death stare and said, 'Explain.'

I took an envelope from my jacket. 'They're not just any sheep. They're Badger Faced Welsh Mountain sheep. Hardy lot. I bought them last week. Here's the bill.'

She made no move to take the envelope. 'And why do I need a flock of Welsh Faced Badgers?'

'Anna from Lunar Hall has named the blood price for her sister. Thirteen ewes and a ram. The ram is elsewhere for obvious reasons.'

She sucked air through her teeth. 'Oy vey, Conrad. Are you sure about this?'

Let me take you back even further – right to the beginning. To join the Watch, I'd saved one Witch and arrested another, a woman called Keira Faulkner. During the operation, Sister Lika had been murdered, and Keira had been complicit.

According to Keira, her partner in crime had murdered Lika, and I was willing to accept that Keira would have let Lika live. However, that didn't absolve Keira from aiding and abetting a murderous Summoner, and for that I'd always said she had to pay.

Keira was in exile for life, but she wanted to come home. Only the Cloister Court could shorten the sentence, and Keira's mother had come to me. Augusta Faulkner is one of the most tenacious and highly regarded barristers in the Court, and she wanted me to intercede on her daughter's behalf.

Lika's twin, Anna, had been asked to name the wergild, the blood price for settling the feud, and only when that debt was paid would I negotiate with Keira. The sheep in the field were what Anna had demanded, and soon they would be delivered.

Once Anna had been satisfied, I'd said that Keira should go looking for a fugitive called Adaryn ap Owain. In case you'd forgotten, Adaryn was one of the Brotherhood of the Dragon.

From that Brotherhood, three are dead, Gwyddno is in prison on a Scottish island and Myfanwy is living in confinement in my house. That left Adaryn. She had fled to France, but her last act had been to stop Vicky's heart.

I still get flashbacks to that moment, and I know that Vicky does, too. Adaryn had placed her hand on Vicky's chest and used magick. Vicky looked it up afterwards, and if you want to be medical about it, Adaryn had frozen the Sinoatrial Node, a bunch of cells in the heart. I knew when Adaryn dropped Vicky's lifeless body on to the wet grass was that I had a tiny window to get that heart beating again. I also knew that I had no idea how to do it.

And that's the reason Myfanwy lives here: she knew what to do, and she did it. Vicky lived, without any physical damage, and Adaryn got away.

If Hannah accepted the bill from me, she'd be knocking over the first domino in a chain reaction that could be violent: I was not going to let Adaryn walk the earth as a free woman one second longer than I could.

She was doing what a good CO should do: check that I fully understand something. I nodded and took a deep breath. 'I'm sure about this, Hannah. I know the risks.'

'Very well.' She took the envelope and peered inside. 'Is that all? No wonder farmers are always moaning if this is all they get for fourteen sheep. What's this?' She held up a scrappy piece of yellow paper.

'Quote for transportation. They need to move soon. Keira has said that her mother will pay, so send the bill to Augusta.'

'Fine.' She put the bill in the pocket of Erin's coat. I'd have to remind her about that. 'You can let the sheep go now. That dog looks hungry.'

'He's a teenage boy. He's always hungry. To me, Scout!'

He trotted over and I closed the gate before giving him a treat. Hannah made no move to leave and looked across the pasture. When she looked back, her eyes only met mine for a fraction of a second before dropping to her boots. She moved one foot in a circle around a clump of grass.

'You did a good thing by taking in Myfanwy when no one else would. I couldn't have done it, and it's worked out well for everyone. Now that the inspection's over, I've got it worked out. There's a train at five o'clock that will get me home before Shabbos begins. If you could run me to the station, you can get on with planning for tomorrow.'

This was what Vicky had meant when she shook her head at me. We're hosting a charity Bollywood party tomorrow, hence the marquee. Hannah had only accepted the invitation reluctantly, and now she was trying to bail out.

'What about tonight?' I said. 'Myfanwy has put a lot of time and effort into making a kosher dinner, and she can't wait for you to meet Ben. He wants to see you as well.'

She looked up. 'And that's killing me, Conrad, but if I stay tonight, I shall have to stay tomorrow. I can't do it. Mina won't miss me.'

'She will, but that's not the big issue. I'll mind even more, and believe me, the person who'll mind the most is you.'

'And now you're my Rabbi all of a sudden?'

'When you get to Ruth's house tonight, she'll give you grief and you'll hate yourself. Tomorrow you'll go to synagogue and hate yourself even more.'

And then she did something she only does in extremis – she took off her black headscarf and exposed the scarring and depression in her head where there's a titanium plate standing in for a missing piece of her skull. She rubbed some scar tissue vigorously and winced in pain when she hit a nerve.

Her eyes watered in response to the pain and then she started crying properly. 'Do you know what, Conrad? Since I lost Mikhi, I have been to Windsor Castle and met the Queen; I have attended Salomon's House banquets and made speeches; I have gone to Cora's Halloween parties. I have done all of those things, but not once have I been to a mundane social event. Not once.'

She held up her hand. She often does that, as if she knows what I'm going to say. She's usually right. 'And don't tell me that there will be magickal guests tomorrow. That's not the point. The point is that I will be a freak on show to the mundane world. Your world.'

I pulled my lip and checked the wind direction before getting out my cigarettes. I lit one quickly and looked at the heavy mascara trickling down her face. She'd bared her soul to me, showing the damage underneath, both physical and mental.

'Answer me one question. Honestly.' I pointed up at the sky. 'The Lord is watching.'

She burst out laughing. 'Did you practise saying that with a straight face, because as Hashem is indeed my witness, I couldn't have said it.'

I raised my eyebrows and waited.

'He may or may not be watching,' she said, 'but I know that he sent you to test me and torment me. Go on. Ask.'

'Will you feel worse going to Mina's party or going home knowing that you let everyone down?'

'Curse you, Conrad. I should never have let Ruth invite you to Friday night dinner. I don't want people knowing I can be almost human.' She looked away again and stuffed her hands into the pockets of Erin's coat. 'I don't want to sit in the shadows with Miss Parkes. It's the thought of anyone seeing just how badly damaged I am.'

I nodded. 'When Mina was deported from India, you saw her arrive in handcuffs. She took her dress off to show you the swastika on her chest. She's going to do your fitting personally. Just the two of you, in private. And she'll never breathe a word to anyone. The secrets of the changing room are as sacrosanct as the confessional. And yes, I did practise that one.'

'I surrender. And besides, it'll save you a trip to London.' She raised her hands in submission and realised that she was still holding her headscarf. 'Tie this on, will you?'

I obliged. 'How the hell do you know Miss Parkes?'

She groaned. 'Myfanwy told me the names of everyone in the village, what they're like and who they're related to. Miss Parkes is one of her referees.'

I stepped back, and she took out her phone to check herself in the mirror app. 'You have to smuggle me in. I can't be seen like this. I mean it.'

'I guessed.'

We started walking. 'I've been trying not to think about the party, hoping it would go away,' she said. 'Tell me what's happening exactly. And why are you having a marquee when your house is massive?'

'Dancing. And numbers. And the risk of damage. And the big screen.'

'Big screen?'

'You'll see. That one's a surprise.'

'And Mina organised all this?'

'It was her vision. She, Myfanwy and Erin turned it into reality as a joint effort.'

We had arrived at the morning room, one of the three entrances to Elvenham House. I checked that the coast was clear and showed her the old servants' staircase. 'Why would I have to go to London?' I asked.

She started climbing the steep, bare stairs. 'Like the big screen, you'll see. It's my surprise.'

2 — Sisters. Who'd have 'em?

The house was a maelstrom of (mostly) women – the Clerkswell Coven running about organising, guests coming to try on the Indian fashions and Mike from the Inkwell setting up the bar. Me? I was on point duty in the hall.

We'd thrown open the front doors for the afternoon and a steady flow of village residents were wandering in and looking lost. And then I heard my sister's voice outside. Not my *little* sister, my original sister. Rachael. She was telling someone about the dragon over the doorway and that they had to salute it. I froze to the tiles.

She came into the house, but she was looking over her shoulder. Who the hell? Rachael wasn't even supposed to be coming, never mind bringing guests.

She turned to me. 'Hello, brother. Look who's come to see you.'

Two figures stepped out of the light. 'Hello, Conrad,' said Eseld Mowbray. 'What a lovely house.' Her brother, Cador, nodded a quick hello.

Who to hug first? I'm afraid that detail wasn't covered in RAF officers' protocol training.

I moved in their general direction, and my silence allowed Rachael to get a dig in. 'Elvenham's not as big as Pellacombe,' she said to Eseld. 'Or so they say. I've never been invited.'

That made my mind up, and I opted to shake Cador's hand first, then hug Eseld.

'Elvenham is smaller, but it's a lot older,' said Eseld. 'It's got so much character! Good to see you again, Conrad.'

'And you. How's things?'

The relationships between Rachael, the two Mowbrays and me are complicated, to say the least, and they form the story of the Eight Kings. For now, I'll just say this: that the Mowbrays are very rich, that Rachael looks after their investments, that Cador is trying to sleep with Rachael and that Eseld had tried to sleep with me. And Saffron.

Another figure appeared – Alain Dupont. He stood on the threshold looking terrified until I leaned over and shook his hand, dragging him into the hall and bringing him properly into the group. Alain is a postgraduate intern at Rachael's firm and noteworthy for being French, charming, dependable, useful and broke.

Rachael was enjoying every second of my unease. How the hell was I going to manage this? Eseld had noticed and tried to pour oil on family waters. 'Rachael said you wouldn't mind her coming.'

'Why would he mind?' said Raitch. 'I'm his sister!'

Cador laughed and looked at Eseld. 'Isn't that enough to make him mind? Why do you think I've kept Eseld locked away in Cornwall?'

Eseld ignored him. 'I spoke to Mina the other day, and she told me how busy you are. I booked us a big AirBnB in the village to keep out of your way. Now shall we get fitted? We can catch up later.'

Rachael was torn between winding me up and the risk of upsetting her biggest clients; in this instance, Mammon claimed the point. She glanced into the dining room and had her back to the hall when Sofía appeared. My little sister saw Alain first and gave him a friendly, '¡Hola!', and then she saw Eseld and gave a slight bow. 'Doctora Mowbray.'

'Whoah!' said Rachael. 'How do you two know each other?'

Sofía flinched, caught between several worlds at once. She frowned and put her foot right in it. 'She is my tutor, of course.'

Rachael's impeccable eyebrows shot up? 'Tutor? Of what?'

'Riding,' I jumped in, trying to stop the magickal and mundane worlds colliding.

'That's right,' said Eseld smoothly. 'We go to Hyde Park on Wednesdays. Favour to Conrad.'

Rachael was having none of that. She opened her mouth to object, and I was only saved by the dog.

Scout had smelt someone familiar (small 'f') and bounded in to say hello – to Eseld. He's not daft. He knows exactly which humans are most likely to have treats, and this put Rachael's nose even further out of joint.

'Scram,' I said to Sofía. She scrammed. 'Girls in the dining room,' I announced rather loudly. 'Boys with me.' I turned and went into the library, leaving Cador and Alain to follow me for their fittings.

Cador was dispatched in no time, and he looked like a Mughal prince. Even Hannah thinks he's hot.

Alain was taking a lot longer, until I realised he was spending more time looking at the price list than the clothes. 'Put M Dupont's outfit on the Elvenham account,' I said to the lad.

'Certainly, sir. No problem.'

Alain's shoulders relaxed. 'Thank you, mon ami.' He gathered his outfit and added a bold red sash. We moved towards the door and he saw Cador and Rachael together. 'Help me, Conrad. What is happening here?'

'You what?' I said. 'Have you been having elocution lessons?'

He went bright red. 'Your sister is a bully. She says I *have* to pronounce my aspidistras.'

'Aspirates. "H" sounds.'

'I know that. I call them *aspidistras* to annoy 'er. I mean *her*. What is going on, mon ami?'

'Alain, my friend, you do not want to know. Why are you even here? I would have invited you if I thought you'd come.'

'She has brought me to watch the Mowbrays. Now that their father has died, she is frightened of losing them. There are five trusts to deal with, not just one.'

That sounded exactly like Rachael. 'What would you say if I told Mike on the bar to put all your drinks on my tab?'

'I would say *merci*, and I would say *what are my orders?*'

'Keep Rachael away from Sofía, simple as that.'

He grinned. 'After the first two bottles of Champagne, that will be easy. See you later, Conrad. Oh, and Mademoiselle Mowbray was right: your hhhhhouse is beautiful. *Au revoir.*'

He left with the Mowbrays, and I scrammed like Sofía before Rachael could grab me.

I took a trip outside to check on Mina, and she pronounced herself as satisfied as she could be, a situation I promptly spoilt by telling her about Rachael's surprise appearance.

Mina pursed her lips. 'Do you think she will cause trouble?'

It's not that Rachael and Mina dislike each other. Far from it. It's just that they're both, in their way, Alpha Females. I think there's a tiny part of both of them that thinks the other should know their place. Occasionally. Just a little bit.

'Of course she'll cause trouble,' I replied, trying to soften it with a grin. 'It's just a question of when and who for.'

I thought Mina was going to hit me, then a wave of sympathy came over her. 'I hope she doesn't cause trouble for herself. That would be the worst outcome.'

I sighed. 'It would. I've bribed Alain to keep an eye on her.'

'Good.'

Eseld appeared from the morning room, looking around and smiling. She had managed to charm Mike into letting her buy a bottle of champagne a day early, and brought it out with a clutch of glasses.

'You managed to escape from Rachael,' I said.

'Yeah. She's talking to someone called ... Carole?'

'Her oldest friend. Yes. I won't bore you with the details.'

'I get it: it's a village thing. Right. Where's the designated smoking area? I know there is one, somewhere. And do either of you want a glass to steady your nerves? I do.'

'Is that OK?' I asked Mina

'Go,' she said. 'I need to organise Hannah's private fitting.' She looked at Eseld for a moment before pointing a finger. 'I would love a glass, thank you. Under no circumstances are you to let Conrad have more than one. Understand?'

Eseld held up her arms in surrender and poured three glasses with practised ease.

'This way,' I said, and led her to the stables. We put our glasses down for a moment, and I put on the light so that she could check on Evenstar. 'How's things?' I said, leaving it open for her to choose which topic to address.

'Early days,' she said. She had a good look at Evenstar, checked her coat and hooves and fed her a carrot. Satisfied, she wandered back to her glass and scrounged a cigarette off me. That's the *truly* rich for you. 'You know what, Conrad? I think going to Salomon's House was the best piece of advice I've ever been given. Thank you. There is a downside, though.'

'You have to behave like a responsible adult?'

She laughed. 'And that's never been my strong point. There's something worse though. I should have realised it from the way that Saffron treated me when I hit on her, but I really knew it when I saw my first class: I'm getting old, and it's no use trying to pretend I'm still in my twenties. I'm not.' She paused to empty her glass. 'And then one of the kids – the students – said something gobby to me, and I realised that I'm the authority figure. I'm part of the system she's rebelling against. I went home and cried into a whole bottle of chardonnay.'

'Because you don't have anyone to rebel against any more?'

She looked at the marquee. 'Yeah. That was the first time that I really missed my dad. The next morning, I dyed my hair black and I'm growing it out.'

'It's not so bad being an authority figure. You haven't met Vicky yet. She calls me *Uncle Conrad.*'

She managed a smile. 'Suits you.'

'And *Doctor Mowbray* suits you. I didn't know you'd done postgraduate study.'

She gave me her dirty grin. 'I hadn't. A point that was made very forcefully when the Inner Council met to ratify my appointment.'

'Ouch. I've been there and it wasn't a pleasant experience.'

'So I heard. Cora was brilliant, though. She reminded the Council that they could award a doctorate on prior attainment.'

'Let me guess: bloody Oldcastle kicked up a stink.'

She grimaced. 'He did. What a mouldy old fart he is. He tipped me right over the edge.'

I raised my eyebrows. 'Go on.'

'You know that dome-thing they sit under? Well, I used the Ley lines to put Wards all round it and stood outside. Then I challenged them to get out.'

'I'll bet that went down a storm. Did anyone take up the challenge?'

'Oldcastle proposed that I be barred, and then Heidi Marston pointed out that I'd just walk off and leave them. She proposed that if she couldn't get out, I could have the doctorate.'

Heidi Marston is not someone I trust, particularly, even if she is Saffron's cousin. 'She always likes a challenge,' I said. 'Did she get out?'

Eseld poured herself more Champagne. I put my hand over my still half-full glass. 'No,' she said. 'And now I'm Doctor Mowbray. Over tea, you'll be pleased to know that I heard the Proctor say, "She's worse than Conrad Bloody Clarke, and I didn't think that was possible." So there you go.'

'Congratulations. How come this is the first I've heard that you're Sofía's tutor?'

'Because I asked her not to say anything in case it didn't work out and we could pretend it never happened. It's complicated. Selena Bannister's been brilliant with me, but I've had to have a crash course in Salomon's House politics. Can I have a look at this well of yours?'

'Of course. It's this way.'

We walked away from the stables, towards the edge of Elvenham, where the gardens turn into woods and the original Clerk's Well is located. It used to be a Fae gateway and still has magick. As we crossed the gardens, she picked up on what she'd been saying. 'Being Sofía's tutor was Cora Hardisty's idea. She said I was the only person in the college who wouldn't look on the Dragonslayer's half-sister as a pawn.'

That was troubling, to say the least. 'Is she doing okay?'

'You might find out tonight.'

We arrived at the well and sat on the stone rim. 'The Allfather enhanced you here, didn't he?' asked Eseld. I nodded. 'And you proposed to Mina.'

'I did.'

She pointed down the slope a little, to where a staff of wood was sticking out of the ground. It was protected by a Scout-proof fence. 'You've got magickal bits and pieces all over this house and grounds. The well, that staff, the dragon-stone, your King's Bounty. It needs proper protection, Conrad.'

She was right. 'Yes, and it does worry me. Mina wants the wedding to be here next year, and I don't want to be a gun to be part of my outfit.'

'No, you don't. You've certainly got the space for a wedding here. Wise move.'

'It's not just the space. It's Myfanwy. Mina wouldn't exclude her by getting married outside the parish. I don't suppose there's any chance you could help?'

'Of course.' She pointed to the champagne. 'I'll do it tomorrow morning.'

'We'll have to pay you.'

She was shaking her head. 'I owe you, Conrad. I'll never be able to repay that debt.'

'Don't think that, Eseld. Vicky owes Myfanwy her life. There's no bigger debt than that. The only way to repay it is to become friends and forget it.'

'Can we be friends?' she said. 'Vicky and Saffron are too young to be a threat to Mina, but I'm older. She won't be happy if I'm your friend long-term.'

'I know. Be friends with Rachael, if you can stomach her. Then I'll be in *your* debt.'

'Deal.' She looked at me with a grin. 'Can we have just the one proper snog? Just so I know what I'm missing?'

As Mina won't see this story for a long time, I'll be honest: I was sorely tempted. Very sorely tempted. Responsible-Adult-Eseld was even more attractive than the fancy dress version. 'Better to leave it to the imagination,' I said. 'Let's go.'

We paused at the fence around the staff. Eseld walked round the fence and looked at the well. All Wards need a source of energy. 'Have you ever drawn a Ley line, Conrad?'

'Way beyond me. I can barely sense them without a dowsing rod.'

She nodded. 'I'll knock something up tomorrow that should last a few weeks. We'll have to see about something more permanent before winter bites.'

'Thanks.'

3 — *Smoke and Mirrors*

Slowly, the chaos wound down and the contractors left us in peace. Eseld and her party had left for the AirBnB, and I was able to lock the doors. I breathed a deep sigh of relief and found Mina watching me with a smile.

'That's about how I feel.' She came over and rested herself against me. I bent down and kissed the top of her head.

I looked around. We were alone. 'How did it go with Hannah?'

She gave my waist a squeeze. 'Good. I think I understand her a lot better now. You're all in for a shock tomorrow.'

'Oh?'

'And a surprise. My lips are sealed. Come on, I'm starving.'

Everyone else was already in the kitchen for Friday Night Dinner – or Shabbos Supper if you prefer. The minute she'd been released from the inspection, Myfanwy had locked herself in the kitchen with Erin, Sofía and Vicky to produce a combination kosher/Hindu feast.

I found Hannah talking earnestly to Ben Thewlis at one end of the table while the others served steaming platters of food that we'd be eating for a week, and Vicky immediately grabbed Mina to give them a hand.

I plonked myself next to Ben, and found that Hannah had been explaining the law on marketing magickally enhanced products. 'An interesting topic,' I observed.

'An important one,' said Hannah. 'Ben is Entangled in our world, and he told me that Myfanwy wants to help him. Professionally.'

Poor bloke looked a bit lost, and I don't blame him. We men are simple creatures, really. Ben knows only three things with confidence: how to grow cereal crops, how to play cricket and that he loves Myfanwy. None of those prepared him for England's Peculiar Constable rattling on about the Cloister Court. He was trying to keep up, but the look in his eyes told me that he needed rescuing.

'Hannah, your glass is empty,' I said, reaching for the wine.

'I'm fine, Conrad,' she said, sitting back.

'You'll need it for Kiddush,' I said, filling the glass.

'I ...'

'You didn't think we'd sit down without it, did you?'

She stared at the folded hands in her lap and said nothing.

I leaned over and whispered, 'We're expecting it, Hannah. You won't be happy unless it's done, and we won't be happy unless you're happy.'

She looked up and smiled. 'Putting the guilt on me? Are you sure you're not Jewish, Conrad? That's exactly what my mother would say.' She realised that everyone was watching her and laughed. 'You're relentless, aren't you? All of you.'

Mina bowed. 'Relentless is our middle name, Hannah-ji.'

Hannah stood up. 'Then let us begin.'

Since that night, we've argued a lot about who was to blame for what happened after dinner. A lot of people wanted to take a share, mainly to protect Sofía. I kept my counsel, mostly because I was busy dealing with the fallout. It started innocently enough, with Sofía sending a text to Eseld:

Do you want to come and watch my show?

Nothing wrong with that, but because Sofía only knows Eseld as her tutor, she didn't think through what might happen next.

Eseld's party were having dinner at the Inkwell when she got the message, and Eseld wasn't going to come on her own, was she? And when all is said and done, part of Elvenham will always be Rachael's home.

And part of Rachael will always belong to Elvenham. Especially the part that knows which floorboards to avoid if you don't want people to hear you coming.

Sorry. I'm getting ahead of myself, and I haven't even told you what *show* Sofía was planning. The first I heard of it was when Ben and I started to clear away the meal – we were on washing up duty.

'What happens now?' asked Hannah. 'Do we sit around and demolish Conrad's cellar?'

'Sounds like a plan,' said Vicky. In case you hadn't guessed, a lot of hard work had already gone into demolishing my cellar, and Hannah had relaxed a lot during the meal.

'I could try out my *fête du feu*,' said Sofía.

'Ooh,' said Hannah.

'No!' said Vicky. 'Really?'

'You go girl,' said Erin.

'Someone please tell me what's going on?'

That was me. Of course it was me. I tell you, when it comes to magick, my ignorance is still visible from space.

Hannah waved her glass vaguely in Sofía's direction. 'Your sister clearly has a talent you didn't tell me about.' She waited for Sofía to explain, but first year Aspirants don't generally interrupt the Peculier Constable, so Hannah pressed on. 'It's a *Fire Party* in English, but that doesn't tell you anything. It started in Victorian parlours, a lot like the one you've got here, Conrad.'

'It's a drawing room, Boss. Parlours are for the lower middle classes.'

Hannah paused, then burst out laughing. 'I love it! I knew there was something about being your CO that I really liked, and it's the chance to order you around even though you have a separate staircase for servants.'

'Go on, Hannah-ji,' said Mina. 'Tell us about the *fête du feu*.' She was by far the most sober of us, because it was her turn in the spotlight tomorrow.

'Well. It's a game, of sorts, played by Mages. The artiste – that would be Sofía – performs magic tricks, like a conjurer, but some of them use real magick and some use sleight of hand. The audience form teams and bet money on whether they can guess which tricks have magick.'

I frowned. 'Gambling?' I didn't like the sound of that. Sofía is partly my responsibility over here, and it sounded like Eseld had something to do with her new-found side-hustle. If Sofía got fleeced, I wouldn't be very happy.

'Calm down, big brother,' said Vicky. She knows me too well. 'The rules mean that the artiste has no stake. The worst that can happen is that they perform for nothing.' She looked far too excited for my liking. 'I haven't seen one since I last went to one of Cora Hardisty's parties. Go on, lass, I'd really love it.'

Sofía beamed. 'I shall get ready.'

'And I shall wait in the *drawing room*,' said Hannah. 'Who's joining me?'

We split up – or they did. Ben and I knew our place.

Hannah, Myfanwy, Vicky and Erin went to the drawing room; Mina went to the library to go through her lists for tomorrow, and Sofía went to her room.

We got stuck into the washing up and were chatting amiably until I tried to get the fish kettle into the sink and splashed dirty water over one of my better shirts.

'Damn. I'll have to take this next door and give it a proper scrub.'

'Bit of a come down for the Dragonslayer,' said Ben. 'Defeated by a fish kettle.'

'Says the man putting potato salad into Tupperware boxes while wearing a National Trust pinny.'

'You mean the man who wore proper protective clothing.'

'Ha ha.'

I took the copper monstrosity into the scullery and Rachael appeared from nowhere. It took all my training not to drop the pan on my leg.

'Hello. I wasn't expecting to see you again tonight,' I said.

Rachael waited until I'd put the pan down and came over. 'I wasn't expecting to be here until our sister invited *her tutor* to a special performance of some sort. And when I get here, Ben calls you *Dragonslayer*, like it's a name everyone uses.' She came a step closer and grabbed my arm.

When Rachael's had a few drinks, she can very quickly revert to being fourteen, when she was at the peak of her meanness and her tennis playing. She knows exactly where the scar is on my arm and twisted. Hard.

'What the hell is going on at Ironmonger's College, Conrad? Because I'm certain it's not business studies.' She twisted even harder. 'And every time I ask Eseld, she changes the subject.'

Ironmonger's College is the cover name for the Invisible College at Salomon's House. It even has a website.

I carefully selected her ring finger and pulled it back until she had to let go of my arm. 'You're right. Sofía isn't doing business studies. It's not my place to tell you what she *is* studying. Nor is it Eseld's. You could try Hannah.'

'Your CO? No thanks. I don't mind torturing you, but I'm not going to rock the boat tonight. Mina and Myfanwy would never forgive me.'

See? She can be very understanding when she wants to. She can also lie for England – she is a Clarke, after all.

'Where are the others?' I asked.

'Cador drank water with the meal and went back to prep a court brief. Eseld's gone to the drawing room and Alain went for a smoke. I'll grab him, then Mina can introduce me to Hannah.'

I started cleaning the pan. 'Mina's in the library, working on the party.'

'Sofía, then. She's family, too.'

'Upstairs rehearsing.'

She rolled her eyes. 'Fine. Myfanwy can do it. She'll tell me at least three things about Hannah that I'm not supposed to know. See you soon.'

It was that little detail that lulled me into a false sense of security – the fact that Myfanwy *would* spill Hannah's secrets if no one stopped her. Because of that, I assumed Rachael would go straight to the drawing room with Alain, and once there, Eseld would ensure that any performance from Sofía would be entirely mundane. Wrong.

As soon as she was away from the kitchen, Rachael ordered Alain to stand watch at the foot of the main stairs, then she crept up them like a Ninja.

The first I knew about it was the screams.

Sofía's room is an old store room, right next to the servants' staircase, which naturally leads from the scullery. I was half way up the stairs before anyone else had even registered that there was a problem.

I emerged on to the landing to find Rachael leaning against the wall opposite Sofía's door, screaming and pointing and hyperventilating all at the same time. And then I smelled the smoke.

I ignored Rachael and dived through the door, smack into Sofía. She was waving her arms and trying to perform some kind of magick to put out the burning quilt cover, but all she did was fan the flames with a hot wind. Bugger.

I grabbed her, pinning her arms to her side, and swung her round and out of the doorway, then pushed her at Rachael for a soft landing. At that moment, Alain appeared, with Vicky on his heels.

'Vic! Open the bathroom door!' I shouted, then did the only thing I could see that would stop the house burning down.

I dropped to my knees and grabbed the as-yet-unburnt corner of the duvet, then dragged it off the bed, full of flames. Sofía had the sense to push

Rachael out of the way, and I ran to the bathroom, coughing and spluttering. Luckily it was only three doors down.

I took a deep breath and took the blazing duvet with me into the bathroom, thus painting myself into a fiery corner. It's a good job I know my own house, though: that bathroom has an on-bath shower attachment that actually works. Out in the corridor, Vicky had entered Sofía's room to check for further fire, and Alain was stamping on sparks that had landed on the carpet. The fire was out in seconds, but the mess was going to take a lot of clearing up, and I don't mean the charred, wet duvet.

Everyone in the house was now gathered in the upstairs corridor – behind Hannah. They couldn't decide whether to look at the bathroom or at Rachael, who was cowering in the dead-end of the corridor and pointing at Sofía.

'She's a monster! A monster! She had flames coming out of her! And she roasted the rabbit!'

Rabbit? What rabbit?

Oh. That rabbit.

Vicky appeared from Sofía's room with a beautiful white rabbit that was clearly in shock but otherwise unhurt. 'No fire in there,' she said.

'And none out 'ere,' added Alain, momentarily forgetting his aspirate.

I turned to the Boss: what had happened was not mine to pass judgement on.

She shook her head and grimaced. 'It's up to you, Conrad. They're your people.'

She was giving me a choice, because Entanglement is a tangled issue. That's what we call it: Entanglement – bringing a mundane person into the world of magick. It's not illegal as such. I'd done it to Mina without consequences, but that was before I joined the King's Watch. It's very much against King's Regulations for me to Entangle people without permission, and I'd walked a tightrope on several missions, given how much I rely on the help of the Merlyn's Tower Irregulars. You have to remember, as well, that all this happened *before* Tom Morton and Elaine Fraser had a rude awakening courtesy of the Darkwood pack.

There are three choices when someone encounters magick. The most common is to use a small Work of Alchemy, followed by isolation from magick, and that would make Rachael and Alain forget the truth of what they'd seen. If that's not enough, there is a more serious potion with more serious side effects.

Or there's Entanglement. The Boss had left it up to me. I took a deep breath and walked over to Rachael, grabbing Alain on the way.

I put my hands on my sister's shoulders and she calmed down a little. Her eyes regained their focus and met mine. 'What's going on, Conrad?'

'Welcome to my new world. The one I've been living in since last Christmas.'

That helped settle her, because she could now blame me for what went wrong, something she's had a lot of practice at. She swallowed hard. 'What is this?'

'Magick. With a *k*,' I replied.

'I don't understand,' said Rachael.

I held her close. There was still an emptiness in her voice. She hadn't tuned back in fully – perhaps she'd reject it all, like our father had. His brain simply couldn't process it and he'd blotted it all out.

Behind me, Hannah spoke up. 'We should leave. Rachael will need support, Conrad. Who should I ask to remain? Mina? Vicky? Myfanwy?'

I shook my head without turning round. 'Eseld.'

'As you wish. Come on, you lot. Let's leave them to it. I think you'd better stay behind as well, Sofía.'

Rachael blinked. 'Eseld? Is she one of them, too? And Cador?'

'Not Cador, but Eseld is. How do you think they got all that money without having a profile the size of Prince Charles? They own almost as much of Cornwall as he does.'

I told you Rachael is a good person. She is, but she didn't get where she is today without having an eye on the prize. 'You mean there's more like that? Filthy rich, I mean. Lots of them?'

I grinned at her. 'Saffron's mother. The Hawkins estate is almost in the same league as the Mowbrays. And that's just the ones I know personally.'

I turned round and saw Eseld waiting. Beyond her, Alain was comforting Sofía. 'You don't have to do this,' I said to Eseld.

'I owe you, Conrad,' she said gently. 'And you did ask me to be Rachael's friend. I'll take her and Alain to the well.'

I stood back and Eseld held out her hand. I passed her my packet of cigarettes and she led them away. It was time to comfort my other sister, but first I needed to collect a drink. 'Come on, Sofía, let's get out of the way.'

We went down the main staircase, and I said, 'See you at the stables. I'll get a bottle.'

I put my head in the drawing room and everyone went quiet. Except Vicky. She burst out laughing.

'You are in so much shit, Conrad,' she said.

Harsh. Harsh but true. She was still cradling the rabbit. It wasn't quite like stroking a white cat, but did look very strange. I grabbed the bottle, two glasses and headed for the stables.

4 — *Everything Happens for a Reason*

'It was too soon,' said Sofía. 'I have not been practising long enough.' She shook her head. 'I am so sorry, Conrad. Forgive me.'

I rolled the wine round in my glass. I'd struck lucky with the wine – Alain had brought a bottle of Bordeaux as a gift. 'I don't do forgiveness, Sofía.'

She looked startled. 'Even for your sister? Am I still your sister? You don't want to …' Her English failed her and she said something in Spanish, forgetting that I only speak the language to restaurant standards. I think she meant, *Am I dead to you?*

'No. You will always be my sister. You always were, even if we didn't know it until the summer. Tell me what went wrong and then clean up the mess. Then it's done. Finished.'

She looked miserable. She was a long way from home, staying in a house full of scary old people and she'd nearly set fire to the place. She had a right to look miserable and want Mamá to comfort her. She pulled herself together and gave me a cigarette.

'The *fête du feu* starts with a *pas de feu*. It's a play on words in French that I don't understand.'

'Me neither. That's what Alain is for. You can ask him to explain it.'

She managed a smile. Of sorts. Alain has something of a reputation. 'He is very good to me when I see him. He say I remind him of his own sister. He has not hit on me, as you say.'

The sting was unspoken: *He's nice to me. You're not*. She didn't know that I'd dangle Alain over the well by the balls if he did hit on her.

'Go on. *Pas de feu*.'

'Si. You have to light three things, one with magick and two without. We use candles. You saw me in San Vicente, didn't you? You saw how much effort it takes me to make fire.'

She was right. Sofía's magick is much stronger than mine, but only in certain areas. Vicky or Myfanwy could light a candle with a wink of the eye; Sofía not so much.

'Also there is a Glamour, you must make flames come from your body while you perform the *pas de feu*. Doctora Mowbray, she says it is like patting your head and rubbing your tummy at the same time. She is right.'

'Or flying a helicopter, I imagine. Let me guess: that's when Rachael started screaming.'

She looked down. 'Si. She was outside the door all the time. I had no idea she was here. I was putting so much power into the Work that I jumped when she screamed and I set fire to the bed.'

I nodded. It wasn't all her fault. Some of it, yes. And it could have been a lot, lot worse. 'Just one question, Sofía. Why the rabbit?'

This time she smiled properly. 'It is an English joke, no? The magician and the rabbit? He is very distracting for the audience for later in the show. In a good way. They look at the rabbit while I make the trick.' She shrugged. 'I give him a carrot and he sits still while I put on a Glamour of flames.'

No wonder Rachael was freaked out. Seeing a rabbit burst into flames would unsettle anyone.

I had one more question, and it had to do with Sofía's talents as a Mage. We knew she wasn't a Diviner like her mother and that she had strengths in Herbalism. One of the main reasons for going to Salomon's House was to discover what she was really good at. 'This is a part-time thing, isn't it? It's not your magickal major subject, surely?'

'No, but it is connected. I am still not sure about it, though. Doctora Mowbray wants to wait a little longer.'

'I understand. How about this? When you're *really* ready, I'll organise a proper *fête de feu*, with some big guests, and you can knock 'em dead. How about that?'

'Thank you, Conrad. I will go and clean up the mess now.'

It was time for a hug. If you think I'd been treating her like a junior officer and not my little sister, you'd be right. That's partly because, for all our good intentions, we're still getting to know each other. She'd nearly burnt down my house, to say nothing of putting lives at risk. I only had one model for dealing with a situation like this, so I used it. And, yes, you could also say I was acting more like my Dad. Then again, I am old enough to be her father. Just.

We went back inside and she disappeared into the scullery to get binliners and cleaning materials. 'Can you fetch Pedro, and I will swap with you?' she said.

'Pedro?'

'Pedro is a good name for a rabbit.'

Peter Rabbit. D'oh.

'Very funny. Swap him for what?'

She held up my phone. 'Picking the pocket is part of my act.'

'Well done, Sofía. That was neat.'

She shoved my phone in her pocket and grinned. Yes. She's definitely a Clarke.

And so is Rachael, and the difference is that Rachael would have read the messages first. Would Sofía grow to be like Rachael? No, because at nineteen Rachael was already devious, tricky and unpredictable; Sofía is a mere beginner.

I found Pedro in the corner of the drawing room and returned him to Sofía before settling down to update the others. Mina had been watching carefully up to now; her instinct had been to let me deal with things and support me by looking after the others – we did have a houseful, after all. I'd just finished being scolded by Myfanwy for dereliction of duty when the doors burst open and Rachael strode into the room. And stopped dead.

'Where is she? Where's Sofía?'

'He made her clean up the fire. On her own,' said Myfanwy accusingly.

'Quite right, too,' said Rachael. See? It's the Clarke Way.'

She pivoted and headed for the staircase, leaving room for Alain and Eseld to make an appearance. Alain looked around the room, searching for something.

'If you're looking for the St Émilion, it's over here,' I said.

'*Merci, mon ami*,' said Alain, grabbing a chair and a glass.

The rest of the room were focused on Eseld and her story; having known Rachael all her life, I could fill in the blanks for myself, so I turned away and looked at Alain.

He blew out a breath he seemed to have been holding for hours and drank some wine. '*Salut.*' He wiped his lips and continued, 'Upstairs. Before.' He waved his hand to encompass the near-disaster. 'I had seen nothing. You could have lied to me. Why did you bring me into this? I am glad you did, but…?'

'You keep my secrets, Alain. I can trust you, and that's rare. Two other reasons – first, it wouldn't be fair on you, because Rachael would sack you.'

'What!'

'She's a Clarke, remember?'

'So?'

'Her word is binding. Correct me if I'm wrong, but didn't she just promise not to tell *anyone*?'

'Yessss?'

'So, she wants a slice of the magickal money, doesn't she?'

He burst out laughing. 'She does, and she wants me to help. I am to resign in one month and open a new office: Occult Estate Management Ltd. She has to work three months' notice, so our firm can try to stop clients going with her. Eseld has already promised to move her investments and to push Kenver to do the same. He is the bigger prize.'

I stuck out my hand. 'Congratulations.'

We shook. 'Thank you, Conrad. I may regret this, but thanks to you, in six months I have gone from intern at a bank to founding a company with the legendary Rachael Clarke. *Salut.*' We clinked glasses and he leaned back. 'Now tell me the real reason.'

'Can't there be two real reasons?'

He gave a Gallic shrug of epic proportions. 'Like sister, like brother, like sister. Tell me.'

'There might be some business coming up in France. I might need a translator. Strictly translation only. No combat duties.'

He snorted. 'You said that once before and I ended up with a gun pointed at me. Now that Rachael will be paying me a proper salary, perhaps I don't need the job.' He waited a beat. 'Of course I'll do it. Rachael would never forgive me if I turned it down.'

'Thanks. I need to make a delivery, then it's down to my agent in France to find our target. It may not even happen.'

'I will be ready.'

'Good.'

Rachael was like a whirlwind for the rest of the evening, and was still going strong when Mina said that she was going to bed. It was a massive day for her tomorrow, and I said I'd be up in a minute after a quick Clarke Conference. I grabbed my sisters and headed outside. It was the first time I'd spoken to Rachael since I'd found her screaming.

'You're going to be quiet tomorrow, aren't you?' I said to her. 'And remember whose day it is.'

'Ahead of you, bro,' she shot back. 'I've already arranged for Eseld's driver to take Hannah into Cheltenham for synagogue. Frees up more of us to help Mina.'

See? I told you she was a good person, really.

'Thanks.'

She flashed a quick smile. 'Is it true, what Eseld said? That Dad can't accept magick?'

'It is true. He saw worse things than you did and blotted out the magick completely. It could hurt him if we try and force it on him.'

She nodded. 'And Mum? Eseld only knows what you told her in Cornwall, and that wasn't a lot.'

'For her, magick is like me,' said Sofía. Raitch and I looked at her, perplexed.

'Mary knows it exists, like she knows I exist, but she prefers to ignore it, like she ignores me.'

'Sounds about right,' said Rachael. 'Maybe you should learn bridge, like Mina did. Perhaps she'd talk to you then.'

I didn't think that was entirely fair on Mum, but now was not the time. 'I'll see you in the morning,' I said, and kissed my sisters goodnight.

As I walked up the stairs, I really thought we'd be continuing that conversation soon. How wrong can you be.

The next day, at the party, I got swept off to a new life in the North and Rachael went back to London. I told Alain who to talk to about Keira, Adaryn and the Dragon, and a few days later he called me.

'Do you really think this Keira will find the Dragon lady? I have seen how these Witches hide now, and no one can find them.'

FRENCH LEAVE

'You don't know Adaryn. She's incapable of hiding, and I think Keira will find her – it's just a question of when.'

5 — Blessings

Keira Faulkner

'It'll soon be over. Don't worry. She won't be long.'

Keira Faulkner didn't reply. She'd last spoken four hours ago when she made an oath on the London Stone, an oath that would keep her from Britain for the rest of her life. She was saving her last, tiny reserve of strength for something important, and talking to the Bailiff was not important.

She could feel it inside her, a flickering, dying flame of life, and she curled up to protect it. As much as you can curl up when you're strapped into a wheelchair and locked in the back of a prison van.

It was a very nice prison van, to be sure, with carpet and wooden walls, but the wood was there to hide the Wards and the metal frames that were keeping her locked in, the Lux locked out, and that turned the van into a mobile Limbo Chamber.

Limbo. Why Limbo? They should call it a travelling pocket of Hell, because that's where she was, and that's where she'd been since Lunar Hall. Her own, personal, luxury, five star, customised zone of Damnation.

She brought her hand to her face and felt nothing, because both were covered in bandages, and had been since she picked her face raw in the second week. She'd been supposed to eat when they changed the bandages, but she couldn't stop scratching, so for a week they fed her with a spoon. Not that she was eating much anyway.

Keira barely registered the thump on the side door or the Bailiff getting up to open it. Only when a blast of freezing, rain-soaked air blew in did she make an effort to sit up. Funny, she'd always imagined France as being bathed in sunshine, not freezing and wet like England. She was facing the roller-shutters at the back that led to the hydraulic lift, and had to turn to see the side door. An umbrella came in first, furled and tossed casually on to the floor, followed by … what?

The woman was wearing a black raincoat, hood up, and a pair of bright red leather boots. When she took the coat off, Keira saw that the boots went all the way up to her thigh, where they met a black leather dress. What the fuck? Was she on her way to a fetish party and got lost? The woman shook out her blonde hair and leaned into the Bailiff for a kiss. Two kisses. And she held him by the elbows. Was that for balance on those heels?

'Septimus! It's been too long,' she said. Her pronunciation was clear, even though her accent was strong and her voice gravelly.

Septimus Morgan, Bailiff to the Cloister Court, took a good look at her. 'Elodie. You didn't need to get dressed up on my account.'

'Pfft. No French woman makes an effort for an Englishman. You wouldn't notice. Could you get my bag?'

'Of course.'

Morgan ducked through the door and came back with a piece of hand luggage, rainwater running down the plastic sides. The woman – Elodie – had a *proper* bag, of course. A Chanel clutch. Well, what else would she have? Keira saw all that, and a glimpse of thigh, when Elodie took a chair opposite her and studied her with a *tsking* sound. When Morgan put the case down, she turned away and spoke to him.

'The Russians are having a party tonight. Only they would have a party on a Tuesday. Still, it means I don't have to take my husband. Do you have the medical file?'

Morgan loosened the clips on his rucksack and passed over a folder. Elodie skimmed the contents, alternately nodding and shaking her head. Under the stronger lights at the back of the van, the lines around her eyes were more prominent.

Keira made an effort to clear her throat. 'I can hear you, you know. And see you.'

Elodie lifted her hand in a gesture of dismissal. '*Un moment, ma petite.*' She carried on reading for a moment. '*Bon.*' She opened her flight case and shoved the folder inside before rummaging around and picking out a couple of items. When her hands (complete with red talons) emerged, Keira pulled hard on the straps that bound her to the wheelchair.

Lux. Elodie had a clear glass bottle of liquid that sparkled and shimmered with magick. Liquid Lux. Keira couldn't keep her eyes off it as Elodie stood up and walked in front of her.

'Hello, Keira. I am Elodie Guerin, Préfet de sorcellerie étrangère, Sûreté de magie.'

Whatever. Just hand over the Lux.

'Before you can seek sanctuary in France, you must agree to be bound by our laws.'

'Fine,' said Keira. Suddenly, from bone-dry, her mouth had become a lake of saliva.

'*Non*,' said Elodie, shaking her head. 'To get this *bénédiction*, this *Blessing*, you would agree to have both legs cut off, wouldn't you?'

Keira nodded her head. If that was the price…

'And your mother would be in the court in five minutes. I know all about her. I am going to give you some Lux, and then a little more, and when I have your attention, we will talk again.'

Keira finally noticed what was in Elodie's other hand – a small silver chalice. The French woman poured a little of the Blessing into the chalice and brought it to Keira's lips.

Keira drank. Sweet Goddess. Thank you.

Life trickled down her throat and spread through her body. In seconds, her head was pounding as the magickal parts of her brain tried to kick in again, like a runner who tried to sprint after two months in bed. Like Keira, in fact.

She registered cold fingers on her neck: Elodie was taking her pulse and feeling her magick. Keira tried to slow her breathing and closed her eyes.

'A little more,' said Elodie.

Gradually, over the next ten minutes, the world, the real world of magick, restored itself inside Keira's head. She couldn't see beyond the Wards and barriers, but she could feel the patterns of magick that were locking her in. She could sense the powerful presence of Elodie in front of her. And she could feel her own power. Elodie sat down and started talking to Morgan. Keira slumped back in the chair and let the power of life flow through her limbs.

'Keira? Wake up.'

What? How had she fallen asleep? How could she?

'Your brain needs to repair itself,' said Morgan. 'You'll be doing a lot of sleeping in the near future. Have some water.'

Keira managed to cradle the water bottle in her bandaged fists and wet her mouth. Morgan sat down, and Elodie took his place in front of her, one red boot crossed over the other and her hands on her hips.

'Keira Faulkner, you have been exiled from Albion. Do you wish to seek Sanctuary in France?'

'Yes.'

'Will you be bound by the laws of Witchcraft and respect the Council of Magick?'

'Yes.'

'Good. By the authority of the Republic, I admit you for one month. Welcome to France.'

'Is that it? I thought I was supposed to understand what I'm agreeing to.'

'You have agreed to be bound for one month. In one month, you will be back on your feet and we can talk again, and someone will come to give you advice.' She turned her head. 'Septimus, we are done here.'

Morgan took a variety of items out of his rucksack – Keira's passport, her phone, her mundane jewellery, her credit cards. He passed them all over to

Elodie and used the handle to pull up the roller-shutter. When the seal was broken, the Sympathetic Echo was revealed in all its glory.

Every Mage experiences the Echo differently: some by sight, some by sound, some by temperature. To Keira, the Echo was wind moving on her skin and the smell of magick in her nose. She'd clocked Elodie's mundane perfume as soon as she came into the van, a heavy musk, but now the currents of Lux could flow around her, she smelt Elodie's magick, a hot combination of … *kwrshereff.*

Since childhood, she'd struggled to put the smell of magick into words, and words had never been her strong point. Fire has no smell. Smoke does, but fire doesn't. To Keira, Elodie smelt of burning, boiling water. None of those three ideas has a mundane smell, but that's what Keira had in her nose. She'd learnt to live with it.

The hydraulic ramp was horizontal, and Morgan unfastened her chair from the floor clamps. He placed her suitcase on the ramp, then pushed her forward and pressed the button to lower it. The Sympathetic Echo was glorious, but her mundane surroundings were anything but.

A great wire fence, topped with barbed wire, surrounded an almost empty car park. Monstrously bright LEDs on tall polls shut out the last of the afternoon light and illuminated the no-man's land on the other side of the fence. The only vehicle anywhere near them was the ambulance that had backed its rear up to theirs. Before the rain blurred her vision, a pair of paramedics jumped out of the front and walked towards them.

Elodie, umbrella raised, appeared from the side and directed operations in French as the paramedics got the stretcher out. 'We're going to lie you down for the journey,' she said to Keira. 'Safer and more comfortable. The straps are no more than a seat-belt. You are not a prisoner anymore.'

Keira nodded and let them get on with it. No one had bothered to put a coat on her, though Elodie made a half-hearted attempt to shield her with the umbrella. Within minutes, she was in place, her suitcase had been loaded and the doors slammed shut with Elodie sitting next to her. Keira had let all this wash over her because she was so busy drinking in the tiny eddies of Lux that flow all around the world and enjoying the feel of magick in her hands again.

The ambulance engine started, and Elodie spoke. 'Was he that bad?'

'Sorry. Who? What?'

'Septimus. He wished you *Bon Voyage* and you ignored him.'

'Because I didn't hear him.' She shrugged. 'He was okay. He tried his best, I suppose. I'll send him a postcard.' It seemed like the right thing to say, but she had no intention of contacting Bailiff Septimus Morgan again. Ever. 'Where are we going?'

'The Forêt de Compiègne. North-East of Paris. There is a spa and rehab centre with a sacred spring. Your mother insisted on the best, and paid for it.' She gave Keira an amused smile. 'Your mother has been very insistent.'

'Sounds about right.'

Keira's mother was Augusta Faulkner QC, former top barrister in the Cloister Court. She'd come out of retirement to represent Keira after her arrest. Not that she'd done anything to get her out of the Limbo Chamber. Not really.

Elodie made herself comfortable and grabbed some of the blue cleaning paper to wipe the water and flecks of mud off her boots, frowning at the dirt's impudence. Satisfied, she threw the paper in a biohazard bag and folded her hands. 'So, Keira, what is he like? The Dragonslayer?'

Keira slumped back and stared down at the bandages on her hands. She'd nearly committed suicide in the Undercroft. She'd had a breakdown and just been exiled from her homeland, and this woman asks about Conrad Bloody Clarke? Unbidden, her mother's words came into her head: *Be nice to the French authorities. If they kick you out, you've got nowhere to go.*

'Tall. Very tall,' she said. 'And sneaky. Determined. Remorseless. No wonder Odin chose him.' She shuddered. 'When he pointed the gun at me, his eyes were like winter in the Arctic Circle.'

'He sounds interesting. Very interesting.'

Keira lapsed into silence, because she was having the first real flashback to Lunar Hall. Before now, the memory had been sealed, and now the Lux had unlocked it.

Moles ... bombs ... blood ... and Clarke's gun pointing at my face, not wavering by a millimetre. And then the spit, thick and phlegmy, landing on my cheek. The gun barrel, black and getting bigger and bigger ... falling. Falling down the barrel of the gun...

She woke up with a scream. Elodie was holding her arms and shushing her with the French equivalent of *there, there*. Keira had never thought she'd say it, but she really missed her mother.

6 — *A Body at Rest*

The next four weeks were oceans of bliss, interrupted by islands of torment. And French. Lots of French. A small number of the staff spoke English, but most either didn't or didn't want to admit to it. Keira spoke no real French at all. Not beyond what you need for a weekend in Cannes.

Angelique understood her. Sort of.

The Hotel Compiègne Spa de Source was a very exclusive, mundane retreat for the rich and famous who had addiction issues and for their children who had eating disorders. Set in and around an old chateau, it also boasted a sacred spring, and the keeper of the spring was Angelique.

Keira knew a lot of Mages who dedicated their lives to ancient sources of magick, but Angelique was the first she'd come across who'd started as a nun from the Ivory Coast. Under Angelique's care, the bandages came off, the weight went back on and most of the scars healed. Slowly.

There was one scar that would never heal: the burn on her right hand where Conrad Bloody Clarke had first stood up to her and forced her to run away, her hand seared by mageburn as her Ancile overheated. When she went to shake hands, people felt it and often tried to look, but it was easy to keep her hand hidden because she was left-handed. It was a bit like her new life, really. She was clearly marked out as different, and all she could hope for was that in exile she could keep the truth hidden.

The first bump in the road was when Keira unpacked her case after a week spent mostly asleep in bed (with daily wheelchair trips to the spring). Her passport was missing, replaced with a miraculously created French Identity Card. Of course – part of Sanctuary meant that she couldn't leave France for at least two years.

There were other bumps. When she found that she was broke, for example. 'Why is there no money in my bank account?' she'd asked her mother.

'Because you had to pay for your keep in the Undercroft. I did tell you.'

'What! They nearly killed me and made me pay for the privilege? How is that possible?'

'Because that's what they've always done, and no one's going to vote to change it.' There was an audible sigh. 'I've taken on a few cases again. Just to keep me ticking over. I'll be able to pay you an allowance until you get settled. I've spent most of my savings on your treatment at the Spa.'

Keira bit her tongue and didn't speak the words in her head. *You shouldn't have given all your money to Lunar Hall then, should you?*

And that wasn't the last time her mother had to remind her of things she'd been told in the Undercroft. Keira's mind had become a blank between Lunar

Hall and Calais, presumably as a way of not thinking about the Limbo Chamber.

The first week she had slept and ate (the food was superb). The second week she walked, tentatively, around the grounds. The third week she spent in the gym. Only in the fourth week did she start running again.

She began at dawn. She'd walked most of the trails in the park, and knew one that should stretch her without crippling her. She was wrong.

Half way round, she had to pull up, head pounding and breathless. The mist around the bushes shimmered, and she was back in the Heart of the Grove at Lunar Hall, her arms outstretched and the perfection of Dodgson's Mirror surrounding them.

Them. Plural. Behind her stood Debs, and in front of her, Deb's daughter Abbi lay on the altar. Above them, the Imprint of Helen of Troy was slowly taking shape, ready to merge with Abbi. The Mirror reflected everything – light, power, matter, energy. Everything was turned back by its reflective brilliance. The Mirror was open at the top (to allow Helen and air to enter), and its roots were deep in the ground, but not deep enough.

Keira tried to stop it, to stop the vision proceeding and to focus on the here and now of the Forest of Compiègne. No good. The ground boiled and six black shapes thrust their snouts out of the earth. Moles. Enhanced moles, each the size of a large dog, and all coming for her…

She collapsed on to the wet grass of France and forced the vision out of her head. With help from a translation app on her phone, Angelique told her that she was using Lux to aid her running, because it was too soon, and the depleted level in her body had allowed the trauma to re-surface. No running for a while yet. And *definitely* no magick.

The vision of Lunar Hall had been bad, but it wasn't the worst thing to happen that day. The very worst thing was her visitor.

They called her from the gym in the afternoon, and she found a fat man sitting in the lounge, salivating at the English Afternoon Tea that the waiter had just deposited in front of him. He stood up to greet her and looked even bigger round the waist. Keira shuddered inside and prayed that he wouldn't try to kiss her. He didn't, and offered a hand to shake.

'Ms Faulkner. Pleased to meet you. I'm Jeremy Tyson, but you can call me Gertie.'

His voice was cultured, English and camp. Very camp.

'Why would I want to call you Gertie?' It was the first thing that popped into her head. 'Sorry. I've had a bad day.'

'You've had a bad few days, dear. Take the weight off and tuck in. My treat. I do *love* the tea here. One of the best in France.'

He was older than he looked at first, and his sleek hair had dye-job written all over it. She sat down and forced herself to smile. 'Thank you. How did you know I was here?'

'You mean, *Who sent you?*' he said, arching his eyebrows. 'Well, dear, I sent myself, because I'm the chair of PEST, the Parisian Expatriate Society. Welcome to France. Have an eclair, they're divine.'

Keira had never had a sweet tooth, and after an hour in the gym, the sight of the eclair revolted her. 'In a minute. I'll start with some carbs and protein.'

Tyson looked at her as if she'd sworn in church. 'As you wish. Let me be mother.'

He poured two cups of tea and devoured an eclair, closing his eyes and savouring the flavour. 'Mmm. Divine. Now, how are you, dear?'

It was the third time he'd called her *dear*, and normally that was a cue for a verbal (or physical) riposte. But this was not normal. She chewed a sandwich and realised that a real-life Englishman, be he ever so revolting, was better than nothing, and soon she was unburdening herself to him. He was a very good listener.

With the patisserie all gone (and all eaten by Tyson), he put his cup down and put on a very different smile. 'How did you get on with our Head Girl?'

'Who?'

'Elodie. The Prefect. I call her the Head Girl because it annoys her. She's coming to see you on Friday.'

'Oh. First I've heard of it.'

'She's a busy woman. It's my job to introduce you to some of the expatriate Mages and help you orient yourself in the big city. She'll slap an order on you requiring you to live in Paris at first. Nothing personal.'

Keira shrugged. Paris was as good as anywhere.

'First some dos and don'ts,' he continued. 'For the first two years, you can't engage in magick outside your house unless you're under the supervision of a registered French Mage. Got that? The Head Girl will come to see you every six months, and do not get on her wrong side. If she has to make even one extra visit, even if you're totally innocent, things can go badly.'

At full strength, Elodie would be no pushover, and Keira had barely any strength at all. 'I understand. My barrister said that there were five other British Mages in exile. What did they do?'

His lips twitched. 'You mean your mother told you. Well, two of them did their two years and left the country. One died of natural causes, and the other two have left Paris and buried themselves in the countryside.'

She frowned. 'How am I supposed to make money?'

He grinned. 'Work for a French Mage is the obvious answer. If not, get a mundane job or live off your mother. Now, tell me what he's really like. Is it true he's got an artificial leg?'

She flinched back. Not again. 'I thought you'd come to talk about me, not Conrad Bloody Clarke. You do know he's a got a talent *this* big?' She shoved her finger and thumb in Tyson's face. 'He's just lucky, that's all.'

Tyson brushed crumbs off his shirt. 'It's not the size of his talent I'm interested in, dear. He may not be magickally gifted, but he's just put one over on those sheep botherers in the Lakeland Particular. You may have more magick, but who's the one in exile, hmm?'

Keira bit her lip. 'Sorry, Jeremy. It was good of you to drive all the way out here.'

Tyson reached out and patted her knee. 'It's tough, I know. I've brought you a copy of the regulations – in English. The Head Girl will make you sign the French version, and that's my top tip: learn French. Have you given any thought to where you might live in Paris?'

'I have. I'll stay in a hotel until the sale of my Guildford home goes through then look for somewhere to buy.'

'Oh dear. No property allowed for two years, I'm afraid. There's loads to rent, though.'

'Oh. Is there like, a proper social scene for ex-pat Mages?'

'There are a few places we gather. I'll take you on a tour when you're settled in.'

'Thanks. If you don't mind me asking, why do you live here, Jeremy?'

'I told you: it's Gertie. No one calls me Jeremy except my dear mother. I've been in Paris since forever. I just find it more congenial.' He tipped his head on one side. 'You're looking tired, if you don't mind me saying, so I'll love you and leave you. Just one more thing – I'm the only one who knows the whole story of Lunar Hall. Apart from the Head Girl, of course. I'd keep quiet about the human sacrifice, if I were you.'

'What! We weren't sacrificing anyone! Abbi had agreed to it.'

'There's not many who would see it your way. You might not want to test your theory. Take care.'

Keira had never been big on baths before: a quick shower after a run and she was good to go, so why waste time soaking in water? And then she met Marcus.

She still had the shower when she got back from her run along the Seine in the morning, but now she put aside an hour in the afternoon for a proper soak and to get ready for him coming round, or for going out to one of their favourite restaurants. Now that the weather was better, they might even just take a walk through the park. So long as they were together. That was the main thing.

The afternoon sun had already warmed the balcony, so she poured herself a glass and wandered out in her robe and slippers. There was plenty of time to get ready later. Especially if he had to work late again.

Marcus had wanted her to take a *proper* apartment, with old furniture and high ceilings. No chance. Keira was a modern woman with modern tastes, and for her the priority was clean lines, clean surfaces and space, both inside and out. From here, she could see all the way to Les Invalides over the rooftops, and more to the point, she could smell magick on the breeze. She closed her eyes and drank it in.

It was daytime, of course, so not much was going on. The serious business of magick is mostly carried on at night, but there are some things that don't need darkness. Like Divination. *There*. She caught the whiff of flowering paper that told her someone was using an enchanted deck of Tarot cards. She raised her glass and gave a small toast to Conrad Bloody Clarke, her nemesis and her inspiration.

When she'd gone to her first PEST social, all the sad losers wanted to talk about was Conrad Bloody Clarke. *What's the Dragonslayer Like? Could you sense the presence of Odin?* Not a single person asked about Keira's magickal accomplishments, and most of them talked in French. To each other. What was that all about?

The inspiration for her job came with the bad news from her mother: after paying off the mortgage on her house, there was barely enough to cover a year of living in Paris at the sort of rents she'd seen, and the so-called allowance that Augusta had started to pay would barely cover her running shoes. Just to have something to talk about, she'd asked her mother for the latest on the Dragonslayer's doings, and hadn't he only gone and broken the Golden Triangle? All of magickal Paris was agog with the news, and she'd even had a dinner invitation from one of the better families.

After a few bottles of wine, they'd started treating her like a normal person, and she'd realised that Clarke might be on to something. He had no talent, so why were they talking about him? Because he sniffed out people's weaknesses and exploited them, using his Badge of Office as a fig leaf to cover up naked appropriation. Why couldn't she do the same?

Her hosts were only too happy to tell her where the hotspots for magick were in Paris, so Keira worked out a plan. Her magickal nose was returning now, as was her stamina, so she had wandered around sniffing for running soil. Well, that's what she called it. You have running water, and this is what soil would smell like if it ran in rivers. It's also the distinctive odour of Necromancy.

Armed with a list of licensed Necromancers (they do love their licences in France), she found one who was holding very, very illegal séances. She waited outside until the Mage left, then followed her back to her apartment. The next morning, she followed her again as the woman went to get breakfast. It was a risk, of course, but she left the café with a wad of Euros and the promise of the same every week. Well, the Necromancer was hardly going to complain to the Head Girl, was she?

Keira now had a number of clients, as she called them, and that Tarot reader would be a nice juicy addition. When she could be bothered to track them down. Tonight was a Marcus night, so they could wait.

Marcus was the first mundane man she'd had a relationship with since she was a teenager. Why had she waited so long? She sipped her drink and snuggled into her robe, thinking back to that night in the Bristol.

Her mother had scolded her for booking into one of Paris's most expensive hotels, but she'd deserved it. And it was only a single room. At the back. With a view of the air-con units. What it also had was a sumptuous bar full of rich men eager to buy her dinner. She wouldn't touch most of them with a ten foot pole, but Marcus was different. For one thing, he was English. For another, he was polite. For a third, he listened. For a fourth, he was married.

He was there for a conference, and lived out towards the financial district where he worked for a British bank. On the second night of the conference, she gave him a smartphone loaded with her number. And some pictures. He sent one of himself an hour later.

They'd been together for three months now, and she knew she was in love when he turned up at her new apartment at seven o'clock one morning to join her for a run. He'd lasted half a kilometre before he had to stop, but he'd come back the next morning. And the next. Not the one after, obviously, because it was the weekend and he had to go back to the Bitch in Kent.

And then there was Zurich: one whole week of Marcus. He'd been even more excited when she told him the reason he couldn't find anything about her in the UK was that she was in witness protection. Just for fun, she'd knocked up a fake passport to get into Switzerland.

The sound of her phone dragged her back to the present, and it was Marcus's special Skype ringtone. Probably working late. Never mind. She waltzed back into the apartment and picked up her phone, sliding to accept the call.

It was a woman. A curvy, blonde woman.

'So that's what you look like,' she said. 'A scrawny tart if ever I saw one.'

Oh My God, it's the Bitch. Keira was transfixed.

The woman continued. 'Clever idea to give him a special phone so he could leave his real one behind. Made it much harder to track you down, but I did. Well, it's over now, so fuck off and crawl back into the sewer you came from. Goodbye, ferret-face, I've got a husband to punish.'

Keira was still staring at the phone a full minute later. How had this happened? Surely he wasn't going to let the Bitch get away with that? No, of course he wouldn't. He'd be back in touch soon. Once the dust had settled.

Over the next three days, she kept checking to see if Marcus's phone came online. Nothing. The Bitch must have destroyed it. No worries. He'd get a new one soon. When he'd sent the Bitch back to Kent.

And then she got an Internet Alert: Marcus had taken a promotion. In London. Effective immediately.

FRENCH LEAVE

She cried herself to sleep that night, for the first time since the Undercroft. Things got even worse two nights later.

7 — When acted on by Outside Forces

Smoke. Fire. What? She woke coughing, with smoke in the room. Cigarette smoke. The only person she knew who smoked was Conrad Bloody Clarke. He hadn't followed her here, had he? And what the fuck was he doing in her bedroom?

As well as the sledgehammer smell of tobacco on her mundane senses, she caught a magickal whiff of the intruder, and it wasn't the Dragonslayer: it was the acrid stench of rotten concrete. A Gnome. Now she was really scared.

Her bed had a wooden headboard that she'd enchanted in a moment of boredom. When Marcus came round, she used magick to make it glow, saying it was a new nano-LED system. She quickly gave it a pulse and the light revealed a horrible little Gnome sitting on the bedroom couch and using a plant pot as an ashtray.

'You speak no French?' he said.

Keira said nothing.

'Well, the message is simple. Stop your protection racket now, or the next time I come, you won't wake up. Clear?'

'Who told you?' she said.

The Gnome crushed out his cigarette. 'Doesn't matter. You stop with all of them. Today. And think yourself lucky that we do not ask for a refund.'

He got up and left her shivering in the bed. When the front door slammed, she rushed to open the windows and let the smoke out. If her landlord got a whiff of this, she'd be out on her ear. Never mind that, how was she going to pay her rent?

She stayed, shivering at the open window until dawn started to peel away the night. The bedroom faced east, so she got a good view of the sun's halo as it rose into sight. The growing light took her back to the Grove. Again. Every time something bad happened, she went straight back to the Grove, and the moles…

Not this time. No.

She forced herself to think about the moment *before* the moles, when they'd had their own evening sunrise – Helen of Troy manifesting herself in a golden glow over the secure walls of Dodgson's Mirror. They'd been so close, so nearly there. And they could do it again. She could do it again.

Helen was still out there, and Helen had been given a big dose of Lux before the rite was interrupted. Yes, she'd need another Summoner and another volunteer, but Keira had a copy of the Rite, locked in a safe place. All she had to do was get back to England and retrieve it. Without being killed, of course.

Energised, she pulled on her running gear and got ready to head out. Keira didn't think while she was running. Not as such. She focused on the process, and let the process do the work. Yes, she often found that ideas popped into her head when she got out of the shower afterwards, but while her feet pounded the streets of Paris, her head was focused only on rhythm, breathing, stride and pace.

She didn't go too far this morning. Partly because she hadn't slept much, and partly to save her energy for when she got back: there was cleaning to do.

She put all the bedding in the wash and polished every surface before nipping out to the shops and buying some carpet shampoo. By the time she'd finished, there wasn't a trace of tobacco or Gnome in the bedroom. Now for the living room, and while she was at it, every last trace of Marcus could go in the trash, too.

The pounding on the door made her freeze and raise her magickal guard. She killed the music and relaxed when she realised that it was probably a neighbour, complaining about the noise. Anyone wishing her serious harm wouldn't have knocked.

Just to be on the safe side, she opened her magickal sight and panicked again: there was a Mage on the other side of the door. At least they were human. There was no point asking who it was, because the door was too thick, so she risked a quick peek at the spy hole. Jeremy Tyson, in all his Hawaiian shirted glory. What?

She opened the door. Soon, the likes of Gertie would be in her past, so she didn't bother to be polite. 'What are you doing here?'

He gave her his public smile. 'And a good morning to you, too, Keira. We need to have a chat. A serious one. We can do it here or we can do it in comfort at the Hotel du Mars.' He looked her up and down. 'But only if you get dressed.'

She seethed. Just as she was starting to plan her future, Gertie shoves his pock-marked nose into her business. It would be too risky to just slam the door in his face. Last night's visitor had shown her that her home was *not* her castle, and anything he had to say could be said in front of mundane witnesses.

'I am dressed. They're used to me in there.' She grabbed her phone and her keys, and thought about taking the stairs, but that wouldn't faze him: he'd just take the lift and probably beat her to the front door.

What she did do was force the pace along the streets, going just fast enough to make him hurry. When they got to the hotel, the waiter gave her a quick glance and showed them to a table deep inside, only one step away from the toilets.

Tyson maintained a stony silence while they waited for the coffees to arrive, then took his time adding sugar and stirring. Keira forced herself not to start drinking. Finally, he tapped the drips off his spoon and took a sip. 'Why did you do it, Keira?'

'Do what?'

'Start a one-woman protection racket around Paris.'

There was no point trying to deny it here. 'How else was I supposed to make a living?'

He looked genuinely nonplussed. 'Get a job. You're a talented Mage. Very talented, or so I hear.'

'I did try. I took details of three jobs after that social you took me to, and none of them spoke English.'

'And you've made no real effort to learn French, have you? Not properly.'

'I get by.'

'*Getting by* is a flat-share in St Denis, not a penthouse by Les Invalides. I really thought you'd opted for Exile so you could make a fresh start.'

'It was Exile, death or brain damage. Have you ever been in a Limbo Chamber?'

Tyson had the grace to look away before he continued. 'You've got one last chance, Keira. Elodie has taken pity on you and decided not to arrest you.'

Keira's blood ran cold, and she found that her hand had moved to her face of its own accord and was rubbing on the scar tissue. The scar tissue from where she'd picked her skin away.

Not again. She was not going back into a Limbo Chamber. They could try, but she'd rather die resisting arrest than go quietly.

Tyson was looking over her shoulder for some reason. She turned her head, but no one was there. He took out some papers and sighed. 'Elodie has graciously agreed to allow you to apply for residence in another *département*. Outside the Île-de-France.' He gave her a stare. 'That's the districts next to Paris, if you didn't know. I'd suggest one a long way away.'

'I … She … She can't.'

'She can't force you, no, but it's that or the Bastille.'

She laughed. As far as she could tell, the French had only a residual sense of humour; calling the magickal prison *La Bastille* was about as funny as it got.

Tyson glanced over her shoulder again, and then quickly added insult to injury. 'Elodie has spoken to your landlord. He won't hold you to your lease. You can go at the end of the month. I really am sorry, Keira.'

Her response was automatic. 'No, you're not.' Now that it had sunk in, the sheer absurdity of the situation came into focus. 'But they were all breaking the law! They get off Scott free and I get rusticated! That's not fair.'

'One didn't get off, and that's what made Elodie so lenient. That Herbalist is now in the Bastille.'

'Why aren't the other criminals in jail?'

Tyson waved over the waiter and ordered more coffee. He looked disappointed. In her. Well, he could fuck off. He was not her keeper.

'Do I need to spell it out?' he said.

'Clearly.'

'I imagine you met the Peculier Constable?' Keira nodded. She was not going to say anything else about her time in the Undercroft. 'Well,' he continued, 'Elodie Guerin is not Hannah Rothman. Constable Rothman would have shoved you and the suspects all in the Bastille without batting an eyelid, but Elodie was mortified that you found more illegal Mages in a month than her Parisian colleagues did in a year. Not good for the Bureau's image. They couldn't overlook what the Herbalist was doing, so she's in jail and you're not. Elodie has had a quiet word with the others, and she used the Gnomes to warn you off. Nothing on the record.'

Keira had thought that she had a grip on magickal politics. Clearly she hadn't.

'Aah,' said Tyson. 'Here comes the coffee and your other visitor.'

Keira whipped round and her heart, already in her boots, dropped through the floor when she saw her mother coming.

'I'm sure you've got a lot to talk about. I'll leave the paperwork here.' He stood up. 'Thank you for coming, Ms Faulkner. I'm just finished.'

'Thank you for telling me, Mr Tyson,' her mother replied.

Tyson edged around Augusta and left Keira trapped in the corner with her mother. This was now officially the worst day of her life.

They kept it civil but strained until they got back to the apartment.

'I've been up since before dawn,' said Keira. 'Never been this clean. What do you think?'

Instead of complimenting her domestic skills, Augusta said, 'How could you?'

Keira could feel her lip going. 'How could I what, Mum?'

'How could you rent something as ostentatious as this? It was that man, wasn't it?'

For the fifth or sixth time since her mother had swept into the café, Keira coloured up. 'My choice of apartment had nothing to do with Marcus.'

Her mother moved to the terrace door. 'Let me guess: he wanted you to have a bijou shag pad.' Keira was stunned into silence. Her mother turned round and turned the knife. 'How could you be a married man's plaything, Keira? And a mundane one at that? How could you?'

'I loved him! He loved me!'

'No he didn't.'

'How would you know? Have you ever loved anyone?'

Her mother looked away. 'I love you, Keira. I will always love you.' She looked slowly around the sitting room. 'At least you've taken his pictures down. I presume you had them everywhere.'

Keira wondered if there were a course in motherhood, a course where they teach you to be perpetually in the right and simultaneously always wrong. She had taken down Marcus's pictures only an hour ago. They were still under the sink. She decided to change the subject, because there was only pain and no future in talking about Marcus.

She flopped onto the couch and stared at her mother. 'So what am I going to do, then? Any words of wisdom?'

Augusta lifted her hands and dropped them to her side. Her mother was fit, healthy and active, but she didn't have the stamina she used to. After all, she'd been up before dawn to catch the Eurostar. She made a face and sat in a leather and metal recliner. It was either that or sit next to her daughter, and that wasn't happening yet.

'You'll do what you want to do, Keira. You always have and you always will. I'm frightened to suggest anything because you'll only do the opposite just to spite me.'

'Is that what you think?' said Keira. She heard a wobble in her own voice and hated herself for it. Oh God, no. Here come the tears. 'You think I do things just to wind you up?' She dropped her voice to a whisper. 'You couldn't be more wrong.' She lapsed into silence, because she didn't want to say what came next: *All I ever wanted to do was make you proud of me.*

Her grandmother had been a powerful Mage, but a powerful Mage who lived in a reclusive order of Witches and didn't engage with the world. Except for having children, and Grandmother had been very disappointed that Augusta was only technically a Mage, and that she'd opted for law school instead of a lifetime's servitude at Lunar Hall.

Keira was sorry, very sorry, that everything had blown up at the sacred grove, the sacred grove where her grandmother was First Sister. She'd died on the same night that it had all gone pear-shaped, and who had laid her grandmother's body on the altar? Conrad Bloody Clarke, that's who.

It was Augusta who broke the silence, and Keira looked up when she heard an olive branch in her mother's tone. 'I'm getting more work,' she said. 'Your favourite Watch Captain has dropped a bomb in a very muddy pond. It could take years to sort out.'

'Oh?'

'Have you heard of the Flint Hoard?'

'Yeah. A bit. Isn't it mega-huge?'

'It is. Four hundred thousand Troy ounces huge.'

Keira looked up. 'Who owns it?'

Her mother smiled the lawyer smile. 'That's the question. It'll keep me in refreshers for a long time. I can increase your allowance a little, but not enough for anything like this place. I just wanted you to know that I won't let you actually starve.'

FRENCH LEAVE

Augusta was trying to be nice, and when it came down to it, her mother really was the only person who was still talking to her. Keira looked around the room. Without Marcus's photos, it did look sterile. And alien. And uncomfortable.

Without warning, the tears came properly, and she blurted out, 'I want to go home. Is there nothing you can do?'

Augusta's answer came quickly, as if she'd thought about it, and as if there was more to come. 'In the short term, no,' she said.

Keira took her time to reply. Her mother had something up her sleeve for the future, and there would be a price. There was always a price with Augusta.

'I'm a lot better than I was,' said Keira. 'I'm doing 5K regularly, now, and doing it all with the body.'

'And it did me the world of good to see you,' said Augusta, with something close to sincerity. There was a "but" coming. Sure enough. 'But it's not your physical health that worries me.'

'You need physical health first,' said Keira. Her mother hadn't done a day's exercise this century, as far as she knew. 'And long-term mental health is boosted by having goals. And a purpose.'

Augusta smiled. 'Did you get that from a book?'

'So what if I did? You read a fair few books to be a lawyer, didn't you?'

'Fair point. I take it you don't want to return as a fugitive.'

Mages live off the mundane grid as a matter of course. Hiding wouldn't be difficult in that sense, which is why her Imprint had been stamped on the London Stone. As soon as Keira set foot on British soil, the Stone would glow and she would be pronounced an outlaw. There would probably be a price on her head, but that wasn't the big worry.

'No, Mum, I do not. Conrad Bloody Clarke would drop everything and hunt me down. I'm not a psychopath, you know. I know it's not his fault I'm here, and I know that even if I got the drop on him, his girlfriends would all queue up to avenge him. I don't want to die, I want to live.'

Augusta levered herself out of the recliner and came to sit next to her daughter. 'I know you do, love. And Clarke is in a relationship. A monogamous one. His actual girlfriend is a mundane accountant, you know, and she shattered the right knee of one of my clients. The others would have to form their queue behind Mina Desai.'

'An accountant? And is she, like, Indian?'

Augusta's lips twitched. 'Are you jealous? Did you want him for yourself?'

Keira shuddered. 'Mum! That would be like shacking up with Angel of Death! I just didn't picture him holding hands, that's all. What's she like?'

'I don't know. I'll find out soon, though. She's a crown witness. Anyway, the long and short of it is this: the only way the Cloister Court will commute your life sentence is if Clarke petitions on your behalf.'

Keira exploded with a laugh. 'Right. As if that's gonna happen.'

'You won't know until you try. I'm seeing him later this week. In court. I'll ask. I'll beg. I'll do whatever I can to give you some hope, Keira. I can't bear to see you like this.'

Augusta paused. Keira had wondered how long it would be before her mother turned it round to being about *her*. Augusta was quite content for Keira to suffer, so long as she didn't have to watch. Typical. Then again, Augusta was willing to go out on a limb and prostrate herself. That took a lot. It was more than she'd ever done before. Keira supposed that she should be grateful.

'I don't like being like this, Mum. I don't fit in, and I never will.'

'I expect there will be a price,' said Augusta cautiously.

'Whatever. I'll do anything except go back to the Undercroft.'

'I won't tell him that. Leave it up to me. Now, can I buy my daughter some lunch? Somewhere nice. I'm afraid I have to go back this evening.'

Keira stood up. 'I'd love that. I'll get changed.'

'Good.'

Her mother phoned a couple of days later, and wonder of wonders, she insisted on a video call. When they connected, Keira saw her mother still in her court blouse, the neck open where she'd removed her barrister's bands, and her hair pinned into submission for the wig.

'Do you want the good news or the bad news?' said Augusta.

The fact that there was good news at all made Keira sit up, and a little brace of fireworks went off in her heart. 'The bad, obviously. No one ever wants the good news first.'

'Before he even thinks about it, he wants you to pay the blood price for Sister Lika.'

Oh. Oh shit.

Before they'd entered the grove at Lunar Hall, Debs had killed a young Polish Sister, only a kid really, to stop her raising the alarm. There'd been a bloodlust in Deborah's eyes that Keira had never felt, not even when she'd tried (and failed) to kill Clarke.

After Clarke had beaten her, Keira had had the weirdest feeling when Lika's identical twin sister had walked up. Keira could spot a real ghost from a mile away, but all Mages have a mundane childhood, and memories of haunted house films had gripped her insides and squeezed when she saw a dead woman walking towards her.

And then the very-much-alive Sister Anna had spat in her face and cursed her while Clarke held that gun pointed at her heart. That experience was very much part of her recurring nightmare.

Legally, paying the blood price didn't mean admitting guilt. It just meant paying the debt on Deborah's behalf. In theory.

FRENCH LEAVE

In the reality of Keira's life, and Clarke's, it meant totally admitting it. Like 100% admitting it. And that was before Clarke had named his own price. But he was willing to talk. Willing to consider it. That had to mean something, right?

'What does Sister Anna want?' she asked her mother.

'I don't know. He's going to find out and get back to me.'

Keira took a deep breath. 'I'll pay it. Whatever it is, I'll pay.'

Her mother's shoulders slumped. 'Thank you. It means a lot to me.'

Why should it mean anything to her mother? What business was it of hers? Whatever.

'Did he say what his own price was?' she asked tentatively. This was the real issue.

'He does have a sense of humour, does Watch Captain Clarke,' observed her mother dryly. 'He said that he wants to believe that you've turned over a new leaf, and to prove it, you've to find a fugitive in France.' She peered down her nose, like she did at a recalcitrant witness. 'Given your recent career choice, sniffing out a Bard should be right up your street, dear.'

'A Bard? Here?'

'Adaryn ap Owain, fugitive from the Dragon business. Believed to be in Brittany. I'll bring you the files when I come to help you pack at the weekend.'

Keira nearly said that she didn't need any help to pack a suitcase. Then she realised that seeing her mother would be really good. Seeing those files would be even better.

'I'll book a table at that place in the Marais I told you about.'

8 — Will gain Momentum

Vicky Robson

'Vicky, we have a problem with the Jones file.'

'I'm fine, thanks Conrad. How are you?'

He didn't even miss a beat. 'I know you're fine, and you know I'm fine because you were on the phone to Mina for half an hour last night. Don't be grumpy. That's my job.'

Okay, I admit it: I was feeling a *bit* grumpy.

'Aye, well, I suppose it is a bit unrealistic to expect a man to care about these things, not when he can subcontract the social heavy lifting to his girlfriend.'

That got a rise out of him. 'You were talking about a Halloween party! Odin give me strength, Vicky. I was going to see you tomorrow and I was looking forward to it. Really looking forward to it.'

I didn't miss the point. 'You *were* looking forward to it? What's happened? Where are you going?'

'Not me, we. We are going to France.'

He couldn't see me, of course, but I sat up anyway. 'What? When?'

'Pack your bag. Your lift's on the way.'

'You're joking, aren't you?'

'Oh yes, I frequently send people to foreign countries for a laugh. Sometimes I even book them on ferries and arrange accommodation just to see the look on their faces.'

'Alright, alright, no need to gan over the top. What ferry? Why aren't we flying, and what's this about a lift?'

'Helen Davies is on her way to pick you up. We're going to Brittany, and the ferry from Portsmouth to St Malo is both overnight and sensible. That way, Helen will have a car.'

Once Conrad has gone into command mode, you have to join in. He's like a tidal wave of authority that sweeps you along. Doesn't mean I can't dig me feet in a little bit.

'Is this a private mission or on the books?'

I'm as fully committed to the King's Watch as Conrad is. After all, I have died once for the cause. You can't get more committed than that, can you? On the other hand, for Conrad it's a matter of service, and for me it's a career. Most of the time, there's no difference, and in this case I'd go anyway, but I wanted to know if my job was on the line as well as my life.

'Bit of both,' he replied. 'The Boss has authorised our trip to France. What happens after that may be ... open to interpretation. A lot's happened, Vic. I'll explain it all when we meet.'

'Are you not going with us?'

'Alain is already on the Eurostar to set a few things up. I'll be on my way to London shortly. I need to see a couple of people before I follow him.'

'Alain's going? Has the Boss approved that, too?'

'As a non-combatant translator, yes. I'll send all the travel details to you in a minute. Helen should be with you in an hour.'

It hurt. Just a little bit. He'd mobilised Helen and Alain before asking me, and I was the one who'd died on that Welsh hillside. I decided not to be a wimp and said it out loud. 'Why am I the last one to know, Conrad?'

His voice softened a little. 'Because you're the most important one, that's why. If I had to call the others back, they'd be annoyed, but they'd get over it. If I'd phoned you before I'd got permission from the Boss, you'd have got wound up for no reason.'

I could see his point. I'm not saying I agreed with it, but if I'd been pacing the house for half the day wondering what was going on, it wouldn't have helped my blood pressure.

'What about Myfanwy?'

'She's another reason I put off telling you. She's known it might happen. I'll call, if you like.'

'Don't be daft. She's in the next room. I'll tell her.'

He exhaled heavily. 'Thanks.'

'Just two quick questions, Uncle C. Two questions you won't have thought of. First, would you have gone without Hannah's permission?'

'Yes. And so would Alain. Not Helen, though. What's the second question?'

'What's the dress code, of course?'

'Ha ha.' He paused for a second. 'Don't pack your combat uniform. If things do get tasty, I doubt we'll be representing Queen and country officially.'

I took a deep breath. 'Right. Gotcha. When will I see you?'

'Tomorrow lunchtime. In Locky Reck. Thanks, Vic.'

Helen Davies waited until we were sitting down in the bar of the ferry before asking the Big Question. 'How do you think you'll feel if you see her?'

When she said *her*, she meant Adaryn ap Owain, also known as Imogen Jones (which was why Conrad called this mission the Jones File). Helen had the right to ask that question because she was one of the three who'd brought me back from the dead.

I don't remember dying. I was already unconscious when Adaryn stopped my heart, and I didn't get any visions of angels or see glowing lights. Nothing. I just woke up in the A&E department of Swansea Hospital feeling like Death warmed up, which wasn't surprising, really, given that I had been dead and that I now had hypothermia.

That journey had begun with Conrad taking me down from the hillside. He and Myfanwy had used magick to re-start my heart, then Helen had used her powers as a detective sergeant to rush me to hospital before I relapsed. Not only that, she knew Adaryn from before. As a fan. She's not a fan any more.

'I don't know,' I replied. 'Is this between you and me?'

She nodded. Conrad has described Helen as a maternal powerhouse, which is very much a man's perspective. I'd describe her as a powerful woman. She's not a detective sergeant any more – she's now the Watch Captain for Wales, and is doing a good job.

I placed my hands on the table for inner strength. I don't revisit this very often, if I can help it. 'The whole dying thing was like … I don't know. Like it was all part of the Dragon thing, not Adaryn herself. I haven't forgiven her for the way she treated me, though. No one calls me a "horse-faced Pikey" and gets away with it.'

She leaned back, stunned. 'She called you that?'

'And other stuff. And she orchestrated so much death, Helen. Orchestrated being the operative word.'

Helen smiled and took a big slurp of her espresso martini. Adaryn ap Owain is a gifted musician in any setting, and she's also a Bard – capital "B". She can use her enchanted harp and other gifts to amplify magick in all sorts of ways that are as alien to me as the Welsh language.

We'd spent most of the journey from Clerkswell to Portsmouth sorting things out. I had a load of calls to make, mostly to Saffron Hawkins. Since Conrad went up north, Saff and I have been working to cover two Watches, Mercia and the Marches. I had a load of notes to pass on, and I had to ring me Mam, too. Now we were on the ferry, we had time to think about what the hell we were letting ourselves in for.

I unfolded the printout that Myfanwy had run off while I packed. I now knew that *Locky Reck* was really *Locquirec*, a coastal village west of St Malo on the northern coast of Brittany. The hotel looked good.

'I hope you don't mind me asking, Helen,' I said, 'but why did Conrad ask you to come? For me, it's personal, but for you…'

'It's just as personal for me, Vicky, now I'm a foster mother. And it's political, too.'

'How are the twins?'

'Running me ragged. That's why I've lost all this weight.'

'I thought you looked thinner. How are they settling into the high school?'

In all the fallout from the Dragon were two young victims, twin children of a Zoogenist, Surwen. When she'd been pregnant with twins, Surwen had used *in utero* magick to try to turn her son into a daughter, and she bodged it, something that Guinevere would have to live with all her life, poor bairn.

'They're fine. Gwen keeps her head down and gets on with it. Easy to do when you're only eleven. It's Elowen who's having problems. The nightmares have started already.'

We Mages come into our magick around puberty, and it can be messy. Elowen was lucky in one respect: she was living with a magickal family. When I'd started having hallucinations, I kept quiet because I didn't want to get sent to St Nicks. At the same time as nightmares/hallucinations, emerging Mages also act like psychic beacons. Any grown-up Mage with a heart will step in and get help, which is what had happened to me. I could have done without the all-girls boarding school, but at least I have all me faculties.

'Bad are they?' I asked.

'Hywel is brilliant with her – that's my husband – I think he may have latent powers as a Healer, and she's seeing the senior Druid, of course.' She paused, then smiled and brought herself back to the present. 'Who's this Alain chap who's coming?'

'He's canny, is Alain. Friend of Conrad's originally, and he's now our lodger. Me and Desirée bought a flat. Alain works for Conrad's sister Rachael.'

'But he's not a Mage, right?'

I shook my head. 'Alain's in the team because Conrad trusts him and because he's French. You don't speak it, do you?'

She snorted. 'Learning Welsh *and* English was hard enough. Fancy another martini before dinner? It's not bad this ship, is it?'

It wasn't. Quite nice, really, and quite quiet, which meant that Conrad could afford to get us an en-suite cabin each on expenses, something I was very glad of the next morning.

'I think I'd better drive today,' I said when I saw Helen. I'd had to go searching for her when she didn't appear for breakfast. One look at her face told me she'd not had a good night.

'You better had,' said a rather green Helen. 'Can I have another hour throwing up before you get me?'

'Be my guest. Are you regretting that fourth gin now?'

'Grrurp,' said Helen, before shutting the door gently in my face.

'Sorry I couldn't get four rooms,' said Conrad after we'd hugged in reception. 'I've put you in with Helen, if that's okay.'

'So long as it's a twin room. I'm not surprised you couldn't afford it; this place is awesome, Uncle C.' I wasn't exaggerating. The *Grand Hotel des Bains* is pretty much your ultimate health hotel and hydrotherapy spa, perched on the cliffs and all pine and clean smells. 'Why are we here, in this hotel specifically?'

He shrugged. 'Recommendation. I'll explain later. How's Helen?'

'Gone for a walk round. She's a lot better than she was. Where's Alain?'

'Sorting out a meeting room and lunch. The clock's ticking on this one, Vic.'

'Isn't it always?'

'Usually. Here's your key. I'll go and give Helen hers. Meet back here in half an hour?'

As well as giving Helen her key, Conrad was going for a crafty smoke outside. 'No problem,' I said. I held out the car keys. 'Fetch the bags while you're at it, will you?'

He took the keys. 'Yes, ma'am. Anything else, ma'am?'

'That'll be all for now.'

I changed my top before lunch and forced myself to look at the scars that Adaryn had left me. The visible ones, anyway. When Myfanwy had brought me back, the electricity had burnt me, and it had been the NHS who finished the job, so no special Mage Healing. Mostly, I ignore them. I didn't take a holiday this year (for reasons that had nothing to do with Adaryn), so the question of bikinis didn't rear its ugly head. It will soon, though.

When we met up again and found the room, lunch turned out to be a healthy buffet. Stuff that. I broke off half a crusty baguette and made meself a sandwich. Then I made another for Helen, who was feeling a lot better.

After food, Helen cleared away the mess and poured coffee. Okay, perhaps Conrad was right about the maternal thing. The man himself started passing out papers, and left them face down. He had not just one, but a stack of four shiny new passports as well, but he kept them to himself.

'Here's what happened,' he began. 'Keira Faulkner's mother called me on Wednesday morning, two days ago. Augusta said that Keira had gone missing suddenly on Tuesday night. Her phone is out of service and Augusta has reason to believe she is in danger.'

We looked at each other uncomfortably. Helen spoke first. 'Why is this our problem, not the … What do they call their King's Watch over here?'

'It's the *Sûreté de magie*,' said Conrad, 'and the reason it's our problem is that Keira told her mother that she'd found Adaryn.' He paused. 'Even then, it should still be a Sûreté problem. However, it won't surprise Vicky to hear that Keira's been a naughty girl.'

I groaned. 'What's she done?'

'She got kicked out of Paris, for one thing. That's what prompted her to beg for mercy.'

'Is she stupid or what? How'd she get kicked out of one of the most magickally permissive cities in Europe?'

Conrad shook his head. 'Officially, she simply left. Unofficially, she pissed off *Les Fils de Pierre*. The Gnomes. And she embarrassed the Sûreté.'

'Bet that went down like a lead balloon,' said Helen.

'It did. She gave her official residence as the city of Saint-Brieuc, which is why we're here.' He sighed. 'And this is where it gets complicated. I spoke to my opposite number in the Sûreté, a lady called Elodie Guerin, and she sent the mundane Gendarmes around to check the address. It was a short-term rental property, and Keira hasn't been there for weeks. Madame Guerin isn't interested in looking for Keira, and is quite happy for us to do so. That's our official mission.'

'Do the Sûreté know about Adaryn?' asked Helen.

'They do, and they did look for her when she first came to France. They don't know that Keira was looking for her, too.'

I know Conrad, and I know when he's getting to the tricky bit, because he pulls at his lip. 'Augusta Faulkner has told me the rest. I saw her yesterday afternoon, and she's hopping mad.'

'Let me guess,' I said. 'She blames us for all this.'

Conrad made eye contact with me. 'You know what, I don't think she does. Yes, she expects us to find her daughter, because that's why we've been put on this earth, but no, she admits that whatever hole Keira's in was entirely of Keira's digging.'

'Go on then. Tell us.'

'Keira's crimes against the King's Peace were enough to make her stand out in Paris, but not out here,' he continued. 'She created a new mundane identity for herself and pretended to be on sabbatical. Got herself a job with a Mage called Avril Ménard down the road in Pont Menou. That's where we're off to now.'

'Let me get this straight,' said Helen. 'The Sûreté know nothing of Avril Ménard's connection to Keira?' Conrad nodded. 'Who is Avril? Is she dangerous? Do you think she's been shielding Adaryn?'

'All I know is what Augusta could tell me. Avril Ménard is a Necromancer, she's not local and she's not a Druid – a *Druiz* in Breton. Keira took the first job she could get that would utilise her talents, and Mme Ménard has no connection to Adaryn.'

'So what's the plan?'

'Have a look at the printouts. Mme Ménard's house has a ring round it.'

I turned over the papers and discovered a printout from Google Earth of a tiny village surrounded by fields and with a wood to the north. The Mage lived in the wood. Don't they always? I also noticed that the passports had disappeared into one of Conrad's many pockets. I looked around the group and guessed what was coming. Alain would be going, of course. That's why he was here. Conrad would leave Helen out of it to protect her, and although he does have a big ego, it's also true that he has an international reputation. There is only one 6'4" English Mage with a limp who wears a ring from Odin. It was too much of a risk.

'What's my cover story?' I said.

Conrad grinned. 'Keira would have mentioned a younger sister, so you can be an old friend or a cousin. Up to you. And Alain can be a colleague or your boyfriend, whichever comes most naturally.'

When I first met Conrad he tried to set me up with Alain. He is a good looking bloke, in a suave kind of way, and great fun. He's also poorer than me and quite scared of Conrad, so the moment passed and that's why we're friends. What? You think I'm shallow? Guilty.

'Cousin,' I said. 'And Alain is a friend of my brother who's doing me a favour.' I looked further. 'Who's this Eleanor Weyland and what's she got to do with anything.'

'Eleanor is your cover name.'

I looked at him mutinously. 'Why Eleanor? I hate that name. There was a lass at school called Eleanor who made my life a misery.'

'Sorry. Too late now. That other sheet also has Satnav details for the supermarket in Plestin-les-Grèves, two kilometres from Pont Menou. I'll go to Pont Menou with Helen and reconnoitre; you two wait in the car park.'

Alain had followed everything intently and now spoke. 'Good. Come on, *Elinor*.'

It sounded even worse when he said it like that. I pointed the finger at him. 'Less of that, you. Eleanor Pickett was not a Mage and I got my revenge on her back in the day. Don't tempt me.'

He shrugged. 'What am I supposed to call you, then?'

I didn't dignify that with an answer.

9 — *Acceleration*

'I thought the French were supposed to be mad drivers,' I said as we drove out of the little village.

'They are,' said Alain. 'Unless they drive a rental car, like this. I have signed all the papers in my own name. When we get to Mme Ménard's house, shall I speak first?'

'You'll get used to this, Alain,' I replied carefully. 'When you're with a Mage and you meet another Mage, they won't care about you, no matter how good looking you are. She'll know that I have magick before she answers the door. Can you teach me something to say so I stop her slamming the door in our faces?'

Alain still can't get his head around the fact that I don't speak a word of French. Not one. I did Spanish for two years at mundane school and was excused languages at boarding school for "special lessons". Magick, in other words. I still had to do games, though. Urgh. He also can't believe that this was my first visit.

He thought for a moment, then said something in French.

'You what?'

He said it again, more slowly. I still didn't get it.

'Never mind, I'll stick to Latin.'

'You speak Latin?'

'Of course not, but every Mage in Europe understands *in pacem*. In peace.'

'Let's have another go. Just five words, and you know the first two already. *Bonjour Madame*.'

Okay, so maybe I did know two words of French. '*Bonjour Madame*,' I repeated.

A pained look came over his face. He kept his eyes on the road and sighed.

'What?'

'The word *Bonjour* has a *zh* sound not a *j* sound. Never mind. Just listen to the noises I make.'

'Hey! Have I ever complained that you call me *Veekee*, not Vicky? No, so wind your neck in.'

He shook his head again. 'Forget about the words. Just listen, OK? Right. *Zhevey Anne*.'

'*Zhevey Anne.*'

'*On Pay.*'

'*On Pay.*'

'*Zhevey Anne on Pay.*'

'*Zhevey Anne on Pay.*'

'Good. We will quit while we are ahead, as Rachael says at the casino.'

That was ever so slightly alarming. 'Do you go often?'

He realised what he'd said. Alain is very good at Chinese Walls – keeping his relationships with Conrad and Rachael apart.

He shrugged. He does that a lot. 'Only one time. I was her guest with a potential client. He lost 20K in the evening while Rachael made two. He is not a very good client.'

He was lying. His accent may be dodgy, but his English is too good. He said *Rachael says*, meaning more than once. I left it there, and we were soon at the Super-U.

'We have a while, no?' said Alain.

'Aye.'

'Good. Excuse me.'

He was half way out of the car with a holdall before I could say, 'Howay, man, where are you going?'

'There is a *Tabac* here. Conrad and I need supplies. I won't be long.'

'You're a bad influence on each other,' I called out to his retreating back. You'd think it would be warmer in Brittany. Perhaps it was, but it was also damp and windy. Autumn was well under way here. I looked around the car park, and the lights were different, but that was about the only way of telling that I was in a foreign country. At least we'd have a proper French meal in a proper French hotel tonight. Unless Conrad dragged us off on a night-time assault. It's been known. I could picture the future conversation with me mother now:

How was France, pet? What was it like?

Well, Mam, I saw a car park and got shot at in the dark. That's it.

I got me phone out and checked the WhatsApp group we'd called *Halloween* in case someone looked. It included me, Mina, Myfanwy, Erin and Saffron. What? You didn't think Mina would let me out of the country without a solemn oath to tell her everything, did you?

And Myfanwy has a right to know. Conrad would go absolutely mental if he thought Myfanwy was in the loop, because of the Dragon. Yes, I know he trusts her with his life. He wouldn't let her live in his house if he didn't, and he wouldn't be best man at her wedding to Ben if he was worried, but she'd been part of the Brotherhood. She used to hang off Adaryn's every word. He'd rather lose her and Ben as friends than put the operation in jeopardy. Not for his sake, mind, but for Helen and Alain. And me. It must be lonely at the top.

Which is why it's a good job he has Mina. If he allowed himself to think about it, Conrad would understand that Mina would eviscerate Myfanwy if she betrayed the mission. Good word that, *eviscerate*. Mina taught it to me, and she was using it in the true, original sense. It was also Mina who set up the WhatsApp group, and Mina who insisted on Myfanwy being involved. She can take risks with Conrad that I can't.

Erin and Saffron? If they weren't in the group, they'd sulk and Myfanwy would have to tell them anyway. I'd left them a short voicenote from the hotel while Alain was sorting the car.

Mina: *Is there something Conrad's not telling you?*
Saffron: *It would be a first if there wasn't.*
Mina: *Hey! That's my job.*
Saffron: *Just sayin*
Me: *He's got some dodgy passports for some reason. Erin…*
Erin: *Don't look at me! I'm not the only Enscriber in England. Or France.*
Myfanwy: *Take care.*

It didn't take long for Alain to reappear. Helen and Conrad weren't far behind, and we climbed into the back of Helen's Range Rover.

'She's at home,' said Conrad. 'Lights are on in the house. It is a bit gloomy out there. There's just her car in the drive.'

I took a deep breath. 'We're on then?'

'We are. You're not going to like the next bit: Keira's cover name. Augusta thinks she may have issues, because she called herself Mina Leclerc.'

'What! You're having me on, Conrad.'

'I wish I was.'

'For flip's sake, why?'

'Augusta asked the same question. Apparently Keira said, "If you can't beat them, join them." And yes, Augusta wasn't happy telling me, but that's the name her daughter used with Avril Ménard, so that's who you're looking for.'

He paused to let that sink in, then turned his attention to Alain. 'These are your orders. One, do everything that Vicky tells you and do it without question. Got that?'

'Of course,' said Alain. He said like he meant it, which was quite reassuring.

Conrad wasn't finished. 'Two, stand or sit behind her at all times. Three, translate everything that's said after Mme Ménard welcomes you. Four, accept any hospitality graciously.' He waited for Alain to nod, and handed me a Harrods bag. A proper hessian one. 'This gift will prove you know "Mina". We'll be close. Take care.'

Helen added, 'Good luck, you two.'

We slipped out of the car and looked at each other. There was a twinkle in Alain's eyes. He was up for this.

It wasn't a big house, but it was much bigger than a cottage. That's all I can tell you. It also looked very French, and I couldn't work out why. Then it hit me: the shutters. Do all French houses have them, or only old ones? And lots of twiddly ironwork around the place. No, I have no idea how old it was. I took a picture before we got out of the car and sent it quickly to the Halloween group.

Alain led the way and knocked confidently on the door, before stepping back and standing behind me. Good boy.

Madame Ménard was older than I expected, well into her late sixties or early seventies in Mage years. I looked at the hand holding the door, and her grip was firm: no trace of the Mage's Curse. She was the first private French citizen I've met (hotel staff were all in uniform), and yes she was very chic, from her elegant silver hair to her tailored dress to her posh shoes. I'm not a shoe expert, by the way. More of a handbag girl. Comes from having big feet, I suppose. She raised a sculpted eyebrow when she saw us, and that was my cue.

'Zhevay Anne on Pay, Madame Maynard.'

She started using her Sight to scope me out, and I returned the favour. I had to hold my nose, magickally speaking, because I do not like Necromancers as a rule. All that hanging around with Spirits is a bit creepy if you ask me. She didn't give a lot away, and I could feel power held in check.

She spoke, and that was Alain's cue. I even understood his first two words in reply. 'Merci, Madame.' Then he switched to translating. 'Madame Ménard welcomes us and politely asks our business.'

'Thank you, madame. I am Eleanor Weyland, and this is my friend Alain Dupont.'

'I understand,' she said evenly and in English.

'I am a cousin of Mina Leclerc. We are worried about her.'

She frowned and rattled off something very quick to Alain. He responded in his best trust-me-I'm-honest voice and finished with, 'Eleanor, the gift?'

I offered her the Harrods bag and she took it gingerly before peering inside. When she saw the box of Yorkshire Gold teabags, her face lit up. With relief and worry in equal amounts, I reckon. 'Welcome in peace,' she said. 'Please come inside.'

Her heels tapped across the tile floor, and she led us to a sitting room that can only be described as elegant and uncomfortable. No wonder French women all have straight backs.

'I will make tea,' she announced.

Alain translated the next bit for her. 'All my life I have wondered why the English like tea, and it was only when Mina made it that I understood. Please sit down. I will not be a long time.'

'This is so wrong,' I whispered when she'd gone. 'Keira is not Mina.'

There was a book and a pair of glasses on a side table next to the settee, so I sat in an armchair opposite her place and Alain pulled a chair from the wall to sit behind me. When you ignored the high ceiling and the draughty windows and the dark furniture, I suppose it was quite cosy.

Mme Ménard wasn't long, and placed a tray with teapot on a console table to the side. I couldn't suppress a smile when I saw that the teapot had a knitted cottage teacosy. I wonder where she got that from?

'Forgive me,' she said. 'I am alone today. Marie does not work today. Do you speak any French, *mamzell?*'

Alain coughed. 'That's you. Mademoiselle is you.'

'I'm sorry. No. That's why Alain is here.'

She nodded and switched to French. Alain coughed again. 'She wants to know why you speak English with a Danish accent, because Mina never spoke about Danish relatives.'

'Danish????'

'I will explain.'

I have no idea how Alain explained the concept of Geordie to her. That bit never did get translated. She gave me a funny look and nodded, then poured the tea.

To keep things simple, can you just assume from now on that everything she says had to go through Alain? She asked him for clarification a few times, but mostly she understood me.

'Mina didn't talk much about her family,' said Mme Ménard. I was ready for that one.

'We're third cousins or something,' I replied. 'My mother was very close to her mother. I'm sure she talked about her mother.'

Mme Ménard gave a wry smile. 'She did. So you are here for Julie?'

Who the hell's Julie? Oh. Right. The Mother at Lunar Hall is Julia, and as Keira's real mother is *August*, the fake one might as well be *July*. The fact that Keira had blown the real Julia's arm off is neither here nor there to Keira.

'That's right. For Julie. She is very worried. I came as soon as I could. She would have called you, but Mina never gave her your number.'

'And I tried to find Julie Leclerc in England. There is the famous one, of course.'

'Is there?'

Alain added, 'There is a French TV host called Julie Leclerc.'

'And a New Zealand Cook!' said Mme Ménard. 'I did wonder if Mina had made up her mother's name, but as she never watched French TV, how could she know?'

I put on my best smile. 'Believe me, madame, Aunt Julie is very real.'

'So, Eleanor, how can I help? I am very worried about Mina. She said she was going out on Tuesday afternoon and I have heard nothing since. And before you ask, she did not say where she was going or who she was seeing.'

'Could she have been seeing any of your clients? Has anything happened that might make her a target?'

She shook her head. 'She barely saw my clients. Her role was to secure the perimeter. She would say hello and pass refreshments and then retire to keep the site secure.'

I did baulk a little at the thought of Keira Faulkner passing refreshments to anyone. It just didn't compute somehow. It was time to add a bit of extra detail.

'Well, apart from going running, what else did she do?'

'Pfft.'

Yes, she really did say that. I thought it was only on bad films that French people said *Pfft*.

'Always running. Running in the morning, running in the evenings. Obviously we work at night, so her time off was in the day. After a week, she started going out occasionally with my granddaughter, which was very strange. Mia is only eighteen.'

'Where did they go?'

'Mia took her to some of the main sites of magick, something I would have been happy to do myself, but they seemed to get on well. They went out one night last week and stayed out. My daughter was not happy, but nothing happened.' She looked conflicted, as if she couldn't decide whether to feel guilty about not caring for Keira or for introducing Keira to her granddaughter. 'Mina went out on her own on Tuesday. Mia was home safe, so I thought nothing. I started to get really worried about Mina last night.'

Dammit! Why in the name of the Goddess did Keira have to pick that name? It was doing my head in.

'Go on.'

Mme Ménard shifted her position and drank some tea. 'I called my daughter, but Mia would not tell her anything and she said that she wasn't worried. Children.' She looked at Alain properly. 'Monsieur, could you get the phone from the hall?'

He jumped up and jogged out of the room. A shiver was running down my spine. The last time that Keira had made friends with a teenage Witch, it had ended with Abbi on the altar, ready to sacrifice herself to Helen of Troy.

Alain returned with a cordless landline phone that must have been state of the art in the last century. And it still worked. Mme Ménard made a call and spoke ninety miles an hour to someone. She looked up and spoke to Alain.

'She wants to know where we're staying,' he translated.

That wasn't in the briefing from Conrad. I had to make the decision instantly: any hesitation would give it away. I told the truth mostly because the Grand Hotel des Bains is the only hotel I know of.

Mme Ménard relayed it to her daughter (I'm guessing), then drummed her fingers on the side table. '*Bon.*' She put the phone down. 'They will come to see you tonight at six.'

'Thank you Madame Ménard,' I said.

Having done her bit, she looked at me more carefully. I was ready to get up and go, but something stopped me. The next time she spoke, it was in English. 'Mina has many troubles, I think. That is why she left England, *non?*'

'Aye.'

'Yes,' said Alain, and I'm not sure if he was agreeing with me or translating.

'She talked about a married man who broke her heart in Paris. Foolish girl. And many *dettes*. *Dettes?*'

'*Oui*,' said Alain. 'Debts.'

'Thank you. Many debts in England.'

You can say that again, I muttered to myself. 'Can you be honest with us?' I said out loud.

Mme Ménard frowned and switched back to French. 'I have been nothing but honest. It is you and Mina who are keeping secrets.'

'I know,' I replied with a smile. 'And you have been very helpful, madame. Did Mina take anything valuable with her when she left?'

Mme Ménard gave a bitter smile. 'Tell me, has she done this before?'

'Yes.'

'Then I am pleased to tell you that your cousin has changed her ways. She *did* take something, but I lent it to her, and she left more valuable things in her room here. I know, because I checked. I also found another mobile phone, a much more expensive one. It is locked. You may see her room before you go.'

'What did you lend her?'

'The three …' Alain's translation ground to a halt. Mme Ménard had said something magickal. I had a good idea, though.

'May I, Madame?' I said, reaching into my bag. I don't carry pictures of magickal Artefacts on my phone, but I knew what to Google. I searched and showed her the image.

'Yes.'

'We call them *The Candles of Delphi*. Did you show her how to use them?'

'She knew the basics. I helped her practise a little. I do not think she had a future in my Art, but she wanted to learn.'

'Thank you very much, madame. Could we see her room, please?'

She led us up a moderately grand staircase with more ironwork and then round to a dusty part of the house. 'I gave her the room far from me. Privacy and quiet for both of us. I will wait for you downstairs.'

We pushed open the door and Alain's first thought pretty much summed it up.

'She lives like a nun.'

'Aye, but without the crucifix over the bed.'

We found a lot of running gear, some jeans and tops, and then a load of expensive dresses pushed to the back of the wardrobe: relics of her time with

Marcus, I suppose. Augusta had mentioned that part briefly, just in case Keira had done something stupid. The good stuff was under the bed.

'What is this?' said Alain, staring at the pile of crystal balls, mirrors and brass disks.

'Avril wasn't lying,' I replied. 'This stuff is worth way more than a spare set of candlesticks. Come on, we'd better go.'

We ignored the phone on the nightstand and thanked Mme Ménard.

'I hope she is safe, and please tell her that her position with me is still open.' She passed Alain a piece of paper. 'My number, if you have any questions. Or if you have news.'

'Is it me or do we spend a disproportionate amount of time in car parks? Just asking,' I grumbled.

Conrad likes his comforts. I'm living in his house during the week, remember, so I know all about his luxuries. But when he's on duty, he seems totally oblivious of rain/cold/howling gales. He looked at Alain and they shrugged at each other.

'Beats back alleys,' said Helen. 'I've spent more of my life in the dirty alleys of Swansea than I care to remember. Right, I've got one cappuccino, two Americanos and one Rocket Fuel. Come on then, Vicky, spill the beans.'

I nearly snorted my coffee. 'Did you ever say that to a real suspect?'

She tilted her head to one side. 'A few times. You'd be amazed at people's expectations of police stations. Unless they've grown up with them, of course.' She looked into her coffee cup. 'Too many kids saw more of our nick than they did of any school. What you got?'

'I've got a wannabe Necromancer on the loose with a set of Delphic Candlesticks, a teenage girl who might be being lined up as the next incarnation of Helen of Troy and a meeting at six o'clock in the hotel. Our hotel.'

Alain and I gave our report, pausing only to explain the significance of the candles to Alain.

'You know that Spirits float about invisible most of the time?' I asked, to check how much lore he'd picked up.

'So Eseld told me. I have to take her word for it.'

'Well, they do. And most of the time, they can only see our world dimly. You use the candlesticks to make a Delphic Triangle. That's like a combined lighthouse and charging station. The Spirits come up, and if you want, you can let one of them into the triangle. They get enough Lux to achieve a partial manifestation. I've done it meself a few times. Just to pass the module at the Invisible College.'

'That's more than I have,' said Helen. 'Way beyond me, that.'

'Me too,' said Conrad. 'And just to be clear, Keira couldn't use the triangle to summon Helen?'

FRENCH LEAVE

'Why naa.' I wagged my finger at him. 'Remember, Conrad, the word *summon* should only be used with a capital letter, and it's a whole other ballgame compared to Calling the Dead, which is what I'm talking about. Could you, personally, do a full service on a Chinook with a motor vehicle toolkit?'

'No.'

'Neither could Keira Summon Helen. However, she might have Called her. I'd be surprised, though. Very risky.'

He nodded and pulled his lip. 'Excellent work, Vic. You, too, Alain.'

Alain pointed to me. 'She was brilliant. She had Avril eating out of her hand. I did not believe how quickly she trusted you, Vicky.'

I shook my head. 'Once she knew we weren't with the Sûreté, she didn't care. Her business is illegal, or she wouldn't have hired Keira. Once we'd shown up, it was in her interest to give full disclosure.'

He looked at the three of us. 'Will you tell the Prefect?'

As one, we shook our heads.

'We'd better go,' said Conrad. 'You'll need time to prep before the meeting.'

'What are you trying to say? Is it me hair? I hate this weather.' I reached for my phone to check.

Conrad looked like butter wouldn't melt. 'I assumed you'd be messaging Mina. At least, I hope you will, because I need to have difficult conversations with Hannah and Augusta. Swap, if you like?'

'Go away, Conrad. I take it you'll both be there.'

He looked at Helen. 'You take the bar and I'll watch from the terrace.' Helen nodded. 'Okay, you two head back. I need to get something from the supermarket.'

I gave him a dark look. 'I thought Alain had already stocked up on fags for you.'

'Oh, it's not for me, it's for you, Vic. See you later.'

When Saffron was working with Conrad, he made her do a disguise, physical and magickal. She showed me one night when we'd had a bottle, and it's very good. If Conrad tried the same with me, he'd be wearing it himself on the Eurostar going home. So there.

10 — *Lounging Around*

'I 'ave told you before, Vicky, your 'air does not like being straightened.'
  The longer we spent in France, the thicker Alain's accent had got. He was dropping his aitches again.

'It's hair, with a "h", and it's none of your business.'

He smirked. 'That means I'm right, and you know it. I shall order for us an invigorating hhhhherbal tea.'

I never did find out Avril's daughter's name. Not even her last name. She marched Mia into reception at ten past six with a face like thunder, and everyone in the hotel turned to look. The mother looked like she'd come straight from a lawyer's office, so sharp was the suit, and Mia looked like she'd come straight from a 1960s folk festival.

The mother clocked us in seconds and came over. We stood up, and she stopped outside hand-shaking distance. Her English was much better than Avril's, and I could sense very little magick in her. Perhaps she really was a lawyer.

'My daughter would only talk to you on her own. For some reason she thinks that I will tell all her secrets to the Gendarmes or the Prefect of Magick.' She softened for a second. 'She is very worried about Mina, and I am glad that someone is here to stop her running into danger.' She thought about what she'd said. 'Promise me that you will not take her with you looking for that woman.'

She'd made as much eye contact with Alain as she had with me, something she wouldn't do if she had notable magick. She looked to Alain for the promise, and he pointed to me.

'I don't want to get all legal with you,' I responded carefully, 'but she is eighteen.'

The woman snorted. 'I know that, which is why I want your promise or I will drag her out by the dressdress.'

'Sorry?'

Alain said, '*Tresse d'Déesse*. Goddess Braid.'

Aah. My eye went to the woman's neck, something I should have checked before. Yes. A tiny gold crucifix on a chain. Oooh. Big family differences.

'I promise not to do anything without your permission,' I said.

'Good. And do not buy her alcohol.' She gave us a nod and went to find a seat on the other side of the lounge.

You have to remember that the Hotel des Bains is a health spa. Yes, they do corporate stuff, but they are not used to tense discussions happening in a public place. The manager had appeared and was giving us the eye. When the two Ménard women swapped places, he followed the mother to take care of her personally.

We stayed standing while Mia came over, the skirts of her velvet ensemble skimming the floor. Somewhere in my genetic memory, a song started playing: the chorus of *Lady Eleanor*. Being a Geordie, you grow up with certain cultural values that are not just unique to Newcastle but totally bonkers. Newcastle United is the obvious example, as are stotty cakes and the Blaydon Races. Fading a little but still there is the Lindisfarne Christmas Concert. That's Lindisfarne the band, not Lindisfarne the island. What with my cover name and Mia's outfit, one of their three hits just popped into me head.

'Hello, Mia, my name's Lady Eleanor.'

Did I just say that? Alain's mouth dropped open. Yes, I did just say that.

'Sorry, I mean Eleanor Weyland.' And then I felt it: Mia had psychic powers.

Now that is very, very rare. Thankfully, they were undeveloped or she'd have caught me on the hop, and as it was they'd worked in my favour, because the first thing she said was. 'That is nice. Your parents name you for the song?'

'Yes, they did, as it happens.'

While I was regrouping my mental powers, Alain leaned over and shook Mia's hand, giving her an even better chance to dig into his head. I wasn't too worried, though. Believe it or not, being mundane gives you protection. The lecturer in mind magick had told us that for a psychic, trying to probe a mundane mind is like trying to navigate a swamp in the dark. Oh, bit of trivia; if you're wondering why psychics don't have a capital letter (like we Sorcerers do), it's because the real name is in German, begins with an "M" and has ten syllables. No doubt Conrad will use it at some point.

Defending against psychic powers is something they don't teach you at Salomon's House because there aren't enough psychics to practise with. Even though the magick inside us makes it easier to be probed in theory, in reality most Mages have built-in defences. My subconscious mind had shunted her query about my false identity into a genuine memory. One day she'll learn to find her way round that. Hopefully, she'll also learn some manners.

'Have a seat, Mia. I don't know what the rules are in France, but where I come from we don't scan people without asking first. Not unless we want a fat lip.'

Mia went red, darted her eyes around the room and said something to Alain in French. He replied, then said to me. 'I was explaining the *fat lip*. I think she has the message. Also, she says her English is not as good as her mother's.'

We sat down, and I took another look at her. She was a young eighteen and would definitely get carded if she tried to buy alcohol for herself. The half peasant/half goth outfit was mostly green and she'd extended it to her hair.

Either by magick or a precision dye job, one of the three braids of her long brown hair was actually green. I'll go for magick.

The Goddess Braid didn't rule out her being at the College of St Raphael, but it would be unusual, so I asked her where she was studying, trying to change the subject away from psychic probes. Her answer was a real test of my poker face.

'With the Druids.'

She pronounced it sort of like *Druieeze*. No wonder Keira had latched on to her – a real shortcut to finding Adaryn. I left that there for the moment and said, 'Your mother told you that I'm Mina's cousin, right?'

'Yes.'

'Well, Mina's mother is very worried about her, which is why she asked us to come and look for her. She'd have come herself, but she doesn't have the power I do.'

'You mean she can't be bothered.'

Whoa! Where did that come from? Augusta Faulkner is like a total lioness when it comes to her daughter. Clearly Keira didn't have the same opinion and had shared it with Mia.

I looked over at Mia's mother, and I realised that Keira had played Mia like a fiddle. Mia had grown up with at least one strict but loving parent in a protected environment. Now, I don't want you to think that I lived on the mean streets of Newcastle. I didn't. What I did have was a long rein. I am only seven years older than Mia; it felt like seventy right then.

She saw me looking at her mother. I decided to reverse the psychology. 'If you went totally missing for three days, like Mina has, what would your mother do? Seriously.'

'She would look in every henhouse, outhouse and doghouse for me.' There was a nervous smile. 'That was one of Mina's favourite films. She told me about when she told me the truth about who she was and why she left Albion.'

This was a crunch moment, and I wasn't sure how to play it. I sat back and looked at Alain. He lifted his chin fractionally, and I nodded.

'Mia,' he said, very softly. She'd been giving him little looks since she sat down, and now she turned to look at him properly. He asked a question in French and left it hanging. I had to trust him on this one.

She flashed him a flirty smile and looked at me. 'He asked me which version of the truth she told me. The second time we met, I made the ... *sonde?*'

'Probe. Sounding works, too.'

'I made the sounding and she blocked me totally without noticing. When I tried again, she took my hand in hers, like this.' She leaned over and took Alain's hand, much to his embarrassment. After a second, embarrassment turned to shock.

He swore in French. I think. 'How do your hands become like marble? Solid as stone?'

Mia let him go. 'Mina told me that she has to wear armour all the time, and that I had to trust her to tell the truth in time. That day she said that she had stolen gold from the Dwarves.'

'This is serious?' said Alain.

Mia is a very touchy-feely person. For good reason. She gripped Alain's fingers and gave them a light squeeze. 'It is a story. A legend,' she told him. 'Anyone who says they steal gold from the Dwarves is dead or a liar.'

'Did she ever tell you the truth?' I asked.

Mia shook her head. 'It didn't matter.'

'And if she's not in danger, what will she say when we find her?'

'She will use some of the English swear words she would not teach me.'

'So let's start looking, shall we? What did you do together?'

'I showed her the large sites. The Loci Lucis? Good. Yes, I showed her them. She had never been to Wales and wanted to know about Druid magick. We went to an open meeting and she was very respectful. We went to one site a couple of times and she showed me some of her magick. She is a very good teacher.'

'Why that site?' I asked, not wanting to jump straight in with a *where* question.

'It had deep Ley lines. Very few people can tap them. She can. I know she went back to practise Necromancy, but she wouldn't let me go. My grandmother had forbidden it, and she would do nothing to upset grand-maman.'

'Where was it, pet?'

'Pet?'

Alain said something equivalent, and Mia smiled.

'Dol-de-Bretagne. In the east of the land. It's where we went to the concert, as well.'

Yes! Bullseye! 'Oh, aye? Was it contemporary or traditional music?'

She shook her head. 'I cannot tell you. I should not have said. It does not matter.'

Mia could wait. Helen was going to follow them when they left, and it clearly wasn't far.

'Thank you so much,' I said. I took out my "present" from Conrad and passed it over. He'd been to the little repair shop at the supermarket and come back with half a dozen business cards, giving me a choice of being *Eleanor Weyland: Private Imprimatist* or *Eleanor Weyland: Independent Financial Adviser*. Having seen Mia's mother, I opted for the magickal cover story. 'Text me your number, Mia. We might need your help again.'

She took the card and dealt with it immediately, pulling her phone from a well-concealed pocket in her skirt and messaging me.

We all stood up, and I risked a handshake. Alain went for the double kiss, and she had words for him.

'Goodbye, Alain.' A mischievous grin spread on her face. 'Good luck with that girl. Sophie, is it? *Au revoir*, Eleanor. And good luck. Please find her.'

We watched them go. Helen had slipped out ahead of them as soon as we stood up, and she'd be waiting in her car in the village to put a tail on them, as she no doubt never said. When they were through the swing doors, I turned to Alain.

'You are in so much shit if Conrad ever finds out about Sofía.'

He was horrified. 'Non. It is not true!'

'Don't lie, Alain.'

'Well, yes, I like her very much, but no, I wouldn't dare. You should have heard what he said to me.'

'I can guess.' I could see Conrad moving towards the doors and lowered my voice. 'If you do ask her out, remember that it has to be exclusive and you are not allowed to chuck her under any circumstances. Clear?'

'Believe me, I will *never* ask Sofía out. End of.'

Conrad sat in the chair that Mia had just vacated. 'Excellent work. Both of you.'

'How do you know that?' said Alain.

'Because I can read Vicky like a book. She hit gold. Go on, spill the beans. You know you're dying to.'

'On one condition: you promise that we follow it up in the morning. I want me dinner.'

'Is Keira in imminent danger?'

'How the hell should I know?'

He grinned. 'If she dies horribly tonight, can you live with that on your conscience?'

Alain looked alarmed. I know better.

'Totally.'

'The table's booked for eight. Should give Helen time to get back and get changed. Right. Let's go for a proper drink and you can tell me all about it.'

A quick phone call to Mme Ménard established that Mia was probably telling the truth and that the Locus Lucis was also a mundane tourist attraction: Le Menhir de Champ-Dolent (which means Big Rock in the Field of Tears). And then something amazing happened.

'Alain and I will reconnoitre tomorrow. You and Helen can have a spa day.'

'So the boys go out to play and the girlies have a spa? What books have you been reading?'

FRENCH LEAVE

He shrugged. 'Come and look at the rock if you want. No skin off my nose. If I wanted you out of the way, I'd just order you to stay put or disappear in the night. You do know it's a two hour drive don't you?'

Helen had just got back (Mia lived in a large house not two minutes from that supermarket car park). She had no idea what we'd been discussing, but she heard what Conrad said and turned to me.

'Are you mad, girl? Have you seen the spa menu?' She rummaged in her bag and took out her keys. 'There you go, boys. The Range Rover's much comfier. No smoking in the car. Now, Vicky, spill the beans.'

We groaned and I started again.

Dinner was excellent. I'm not a connoisseur of fine dining, but this was right up there with the best I've had. Alain chose the wine and Helen told stories about her time in Swansea CID. After what she's been through, being a Watch Captain must be light relief most of the time.

The boys had gone by the time we got to breakfast, and the spa lived up to its billing. Except for one thing. With no Alain to translate, I accidentally found myself standing naked at the end of a tiled room while a big lass with a powerful hose sprayed me with cold sea water. I kid you not. She also clocked my scars.

When I emerged from that, tingling and slightly dazed, we'd had a message: *Get yourselves something to eat and be ready to leave at 18:00.*

Ah well, dinner two nights running would have been a bit too much. 'What are you going to wear?' asked Helen.

'Something comfortable, dark, warm and waterproof.'

She sighed. The reality of life in Team Conrad was starting to bite. 'And there's me paying twenty Euros to have me hair styled.'

I cast an eye over it. 'You were robbed.'

'Vicky, that doesn't make me feel any better. I need carbs and I need them now.'

'You and me both.'

11 — *Enemies, Old and New*

'Well, what have you been up to?' I asked Alain when we set off. Conrad had said that Alain could fill me in rather than waste time having a collective discussion.

'It is very strange watching Conrad walk round a menhir. To me it looks like radical theatre. Or exercise time in the prison. He was most distracted and made a lot of calls. I have a report.'

'You what?'

'A moment.' I waited while Alain checked carefully for traffic and joined the main road east. 'Good. He said I had to remember this and tell you.'

'Why didn't he call me? I thought that's what I was here for.'

'He said you'd ask that. He didn't want to disturb you, and that he needed to talk to Eseld and someone called Chris Kelly.'

'Oh. Right. Fair enough. They know more about Wards and Ley lines than I do.' Would I have been more pleased or annoyed if he'd dragged me out of a whole-body replenishing massage? On reflection, more annoyed. 'Go on then.'

'He says that the menhir is a very old gateway. It sits in the middle of an ancient aeroplane.' He paused. 'He didn't say that, did he?'

'No, I don't think he did. I think he said that it was a Grove of the Old Gods and that it exists on an *elevated plane*.'

He thought about it. 'He did say all of that. I shall have to have lessons. I do remember the next part. It has a sun-cap and we can do nothing until after dark.'

All creatures have strengths in magick. Amongst other things, the Fae are experts on curating spaces on higher planes and creating access points, but they don't have a monopoly. The Fae spread through Europe in the late Bronze Age. We think. There was already magick here, and the native humans had relationships with higher creatures who have since disappeared. They don't like it at Salomon's House, but everyone calls them the Old Gods. Nimue, the guardian Nymph of Britain may or may not be one of them.

Either way, some of those sites of ancient magick still exist, mostly very well hidden. It looked like the Menhir de Champ Dolent was better known, and a sun-cap suppresses the magick during the day, pushing it underground, which is where the real action is. Conrad has told you about his adventure at Draxholt, when he sank under the earth, and something similar would exist here. I sincerely hoped that we wouldn't have to go there; my claustrophobia is much better than it used to be, but the thought of actually moving through the earth made me shiver.

'You can't have been on that all day,' I said to change the subject.

'No. We spent an hour at the menhir, then went to Dol. While Conrad made his calls, he sent me looking for Druids.'

'What!'

He couldn't do that. He wouldn't do that. Yet he had. I tried to think it through from Conrad's perspective. Alain has no magick. Alain is French. On his own, Alain wouldn't be able to find the Palace of Rhiannon if he walked past it. But Druids, like most Circles of magick have a religious dimension and a mundane membership, too. Got it.

'Let me guess,' I said. 'He told you to find all the cultural heritage places and museums and go chat up the girls.'

The smile gave it away. 'Close, Vicky. He said I should talk to all the women and girls in Breton costume.'

I might have known. Still, I had once gone to see a Gnome wearing a short dress, and that's just since I met Conrad. You don't need to know about before. 'And how did you get on?'

'They are very passionate about their culture. In St Emilion, we are passionate about wine. Here, they are passionate about their language and their dreadful music. Morane has such a beautiful voice, it is a shame to waste it.'

'Morane? Even by your standards, that was fast work.'

He shrugged modestly. One day he'll get the message that his ability to charm women out of their knickers is not the best thing about him.

'Morane. It means *Sea*, and yes, she is a Druid.'

'How the hell do you know that?'

'It is October. There are very few tourists. We had time to talk. I asked lots of questions about art, history, politics … and Druids. It was the only time she changed the subject. She works in a cultural centre and shop. There is not a single mention of Druids anywhere. Strange, non?'

I had to ask. I really had to know. 'What did you say about yourself, Alain? How did you explain why you were here on a wet Saturday?'

'Simple. I told her that I am a civil servant in the tax office, but really I want to be a writer, and I need to do lots of research. If you say you are in the finance office, no one ever cares.'

And the moral of today's story, boys and girls, is that if you want to get someone's attention, tell them that you're a writer. Actually, that's Alain's real attraction to women. When he fixes you with those blue eyes, you get the feeling that he really wants to hear what you have to say. I have good evidence that all he's thinking about is what you look like naked, but that's not the point.

'Anything else about the day?'

'We had a nice lunch, then went back to the menhir. We practised some French. He is a good learner, unlike some people. Nothing else, really.'

And there it was. Conrad *was* up to something, and Alain either didn't know or had been sworn to secrecy. 'I'll just message the girls, Alain.'

Me: *Conrad is up to something.*

Saffron: *I asked around about this Elodie Guerin. She has a bad reputation with other women's husbands.*

Mina: *I don't worry about those ones.*

Saffron: *Not even Eseld??????*

Mina: *No, but we do need to find Eseld a man. Or a woman. I think you should volunteer, Erin.*

Erin: *Eurgh. That's deffo Saffron's job. I think they're well suited. Both rich, both …*

Saffron: *Oy! No!*

Myfanwy: *Shut up, you lot. Erin, get on with the tea. We'll be round at eight.*

Which was nine o'clock, French time. We'd probably be going into action around then.

'Which supermarket are we meeting in?'

'We are not. The railway station is nearer. It has a huge car park.'

It did, and it wasn't deserted. 'The TGV stops here,' said Alain. 'All these cars will be people who 'ave gone to Paris for *Le Weekend*. That means *weekend*, in English.'

He thought that was hilarious and I haven't got a flippin' clue why. I don't want to know, either. The one good thing about these briefings is that Conrad always provides coffee. I huddled into the Range Rover while the boys stood outside smoking.

'What do you reckon, Helen? Did he give anything away?'

'Our leader was noticeably unforthcoming on his movements at certain parts of the day, Vicky.'

'Snap. Did he tell you Alain scored with a Druid?'

'Yes, but he put it in more romantic terms. He is a big softie, really, isn't he?'

I gave it some thought. 'Mebbees. Officer and a gentleman. That sort of thing.'

'Nothing wrong with that. Hang on a sec.' She got out her phone and pressed a button. When it was answered, she whispered something in Welsh, waited a second and hung up. 'I was just telling Hywel I loved him. Just in case. We split up once, you know. He was being a total dickhead about me working nights, and then I got shot at. We both realised we needed to change. Him more, obviously.'

'Of course.'

'And since then, I've never gone into an operation without telling him I love him. Just in case it's the last thing I say to him. Do you know what he said the first time? He said, "Helen, one day you will call me a useless waste of space and then die crossing the road." So I told him it wasn't about making him feel better, it was about me. Here they come.'

Conrad got out his notebook and dripped rainwater on the leather seats. 'According to French social media, the menhir is a popular meeting place for teenagers, but not at night in the freezing rain. You can never discount thrill-seekers, though. What are your suggestions for approaching it, Vic?'

I knew that was coming, and I had my answer ready. I'd even looked at the map. 'You and I drive past once. If it's clear of mundane activity, we go past a second time and I'll activate the Discouragement Ward. I can do that from the car. Then we park up and approach on foot.'

'I agree. That's the plan, then. We'll take the Renault. Don't want to risk damaging the Range Rover.'

Alain didn't look happy. The car was on his credit card.

'What about us?' said Helen.

'Hold position here. It's only two minutes away if you put your foot down.'

'Why have you really brought me, Conrad? It's not that I haven't enjoyed it. Well, apart from the sea-sickness. I didn't enjoy that.' She shivered. 'But what am I doing here?'

He was reaching for his pocket, and I thought he might light up. 'Witness,' he said. 'And backup. You're the cavalry and you've got Elodie Guerin's number. Mostly you're here to protect Alain.' He grinned at Alain. 'Not saying you need protecting or anything.'

I got the strange feeling that, for once, protecting Alain wasn't top of the list. I think Helen is here to act as a witness. A witness for Elodie, for Hannah and for the Druid Council. He'd skipped over that one.

His hand emerged from his pocket with four bits of technology. 'High powered Bluetooth ear and voice sets.' In his other hand he had medical tape and make-up wipes. 'You need to tape the mike to your cheek. Vicky, you call Helen, I'll call Alain. I've already checked, and mobile coverage is good by the menhir. Any questions?'

'Do we have a code word?' said Helen, untangling the lead. 'In case you need to summon us without giving the game away.'

'Good thinking.' He pulled his lip. 'Horlicks. As in, "This is a right Horlicks." That do?'

'Urgh,' said Helen. 'Good job I hate the stuff.'

'I have no idea what you are talking about,' said Alain. 'For once, I am glad. *Bon chance, mes amis.*'

We got in the Renault and Conrad adjusted the seat to cope with his enormous legs. I noticed it was an automatic, so he'd been planning this for a while. We established phone contact, and Conrad drove off.

'What the fuck are you doing?' I asked when he switched his headlamps off. We'd just left the main road, following the road sign into a narrow lane. 'You'll kill us.'

'I'm testing my night vision.'

I gripped the dashboard and kept quiet. He slowed right down as we passsed between some hedges, then the view opened out across dead looking farmer's fields. He drove slightly faster, then switched the lights back on. I breathed out.

'It's getting better, but still not good enough to drive on a foul and wet night like this. About twenty seconds.'

We turned through a couple of bends, past some bungalows and on to a straight road. I took a sharp inbreath.

'By the Goddess, it's huge,' I said. 'Is it as big to look at with mundane vision?'

'Yes. What can you see?'

'Power. Lots of power.'

That's how I put it to Conrad. What I actually saw, given that it was pitch black and chucking it down with rain, was a boiling mass of darkness. Like looking into a well and seeing two octopuses fighting under the water. And when I say darkness, I don't mean Evil. Or do I? There was definitely more than just power there, and then we were past it and I couldn't see.

'Any human activity?'

'No.'

'I'll do a circuit. Quicker than trying to reverse in the dark.'

'No, turn round, please. I need to be on the same side. I can't work magick across you.'

There was a big T junction ahead, and Conrad swung the small car round easily. I wound down the window and got ready. He slowed right down this time, and I reached out with my hand, praying he didn't go too close to a road sign. I grasped one of the tendrils of Lux streaming out of the menhir and tugged. Then I thought of the # sign and sent it down the wire of light.

A lot of public places with magick have Discouragement Wards that use a Work of magick shaped like the # symbol as the key to trigger them. I felt a wave of magick wash over me, telling me that dinner in the Hotel des Bains was much better than walking through the rain.

'That's a strong one,' said Conrad. 'Okay, Alain, we're parking up now.'

The road was wide enough to leave the car on the verge with enough room for a lorry to get past. I pulled up the hood of my waterproof and squeezed out of the door. Conrad already had his gun out.

'Aren't you worried that those Gnomes in Cheshire had Anciles that were proof against your ammo?' I asked, quickening my pace to catch up.

'Not yet. Not here. I've got Lloyd looking into where they got them from, but they won't be standard issue in France.'

When we got to the entrance, he could clearly see much better than me. 'Can I use me torch?'

'Yes.'

FRENCH LEAVE

I shone the light on an information board and a picnic bench. Between them, a path ran down to the menhir. It was huge. Four or five times the height of a man. Or woman, like the woman standing at the base. The naked woman.

'We have a reception committee,' said Conrad for Alain's benefit. 'Not obviously hostile yet.'

'We have a naked woman in the rain,' I added for Helen. 'Nothing suspicious about that.'

'Is she blue?' said Helen. 'I would be.'

I didn't answer, and we spread out to walk down the path. When I got closer, I recognised her, and so did Conrad: it was Keira Faulkner.

Or rather, it was a version of Keira. Probably the idea of herself she has in her head. I've only met her once, when I arrested her and I had to manhandle her. It was like handling a bag of sinews. This woman had Keira's sharp features, but she had more curves, rounder hips and bigger, perkier tits. And totally salon hair instead of the trademark ponytail. Not a real person then.

Conrad bowed. 'My lady, may I present Watch Captain Victoria Robson. Vicky, this is Helen of Troy.'

...Erm? What? OK.

My legs were telling me to run. My right leg even managed to turn itself round before I grabbed it and forced myself to bow. 'My lady.'

'I thought you'd never turn up,' said Keira/Helen. The voice was cultured and rounded, like a good actress playing a Jane Austen character. Keira herself sounds like a whiny brat. 'I was going to give it until midnight and let her go.'

'You have Ms Faulkner?' said Conrad with more calm than I felt.

Helen rolled her eyes. 'I have her on life support. In the menhir. Her body is in a coma in the hospital at Dinan.'

'Alain, could you get on to that?' said Conrad.

Helen peered at his cheek. 'Clever. You are a resourceful man.'

He holstered his gun and reached for his cigarettes. Sometimes that man can be totally infuriating. 'Vicky, is there any way of verifying her statement?'

'Only if I let her,' said Helen. 'And don't talk about me as if I'm not here, Conny.'

He flicked his lighter. 'Sorry. Why have you got Ms Faulkner trapped in a menhir, if you don't mind me asking?'

'She's not trapped. She's on life support. I saved her when she was attacked.'

'You just happened to be around? Like a big sister?'

'Don't flirt with me unless you mean it.' She'd been leaning against the rock, and stood up straight, moving and flexing her hips to draw the eye down. She even ran her hand down her waist to emphasise it. It was only a projection, of course, but she'd gone to the trouble of diverting the rain around it to preserve the illusion. When she ran her hand back up her body to her right breast, she let out a wave of magick that set my nerve ends tingling. If Alain had been next to me, instead of down the phone, I'd have jumped his bones there and then.

Conrad sucked on his cigarette and stood there, impervious, like a lighthouse in a storm.

Helen – Helen Davies – whispered in my ear, 'Alain is through to the hospital.'

'Forgive me,' said Conrad. 'I meant no insult, I was just curious.'

'Apology accepted.' Helen T flicked her hair away from her shoulders. 'She called me here and helped me anchor on this lovely piece of power.' She stroked the menhir and smiled like a cat. 'She said she had a plan. The next time we met, she said she was going to see a man about a harp. The next thing I knew, her Spirit was wailing over the countryside like a banshee. I went and found that she'd been attacked. I scooped her up and brought her here.'

Conrad looked at me. 'How does that work?'

'The Bridge of Orpheus,' I replied, more to Helen T than to him.

She rewarded me with a smile. 'Correct. The stupid idiots who attacked her didn't check.'

I turned to Conrad. 'It's like a tiny, tiny Ley line all the way to the hospital. If it's severed, her mundane body will die.' I turned back to Helen T. 'I take it that Keira's Spirit isn't in any shape to go it alone?'

Helen shook her head sadly. 'No. I can carry her, but I need help, which is why I've been waiting here. You should be able to manage it, if your friend drives.'

'Good,' said Conrad. 'Now we know what the stakes are, what do you want? Bearing in mind that I don't care whether Keira lives or dies, and that we can probably find Adaryn on our own.'

I was fairly sure that Conrad did care about Keira. She'd got herself into this mess looking for Adaryn. He wouldn't walk away and let her die, would he?

She put her finger to her chin. 'Ooh. Let's see. What do I want? Nothing, Conny. Nothing at all.'

He pulled at his ear, a sign he's annoyed. I wouldn't dream of calling him *Conny*. 'Which tells me two things,' he observed. 'First, that Keira has a copy of the Rite of Delphi, and second, that she still wants to Summon you in the future to get the Bowl of Cassandra. If I let her die, it'll save the soul of some poor girl. Madame Ménard's granddaughter for example.'

'I'm not interested in Mia. She'll be too old by the time Keira goes home, and I don't like *Gedankenübertragung* Mages.'

Okay, I was wrong. I thought it began with "M".

'If not her, then someone else.'

'You know better than that,' said Helen T. 'You can't punish someone for a future crime.'

FRENCH LEAVE

'True. I was just letting you know that if Keira Faulkner ever does get back to England and try to Summon you, I'll be there to stop her.'

Her eyes lit up. 'Game on, Conny. Shall we go?'

'No.' He tapped his head. 'I've been in the wars, Helen. Not like Troy, perhaps, but bad enough. If we reunite Keira's elements, she could be out of it for days. She could have head injuries. She could have blanked everything out. There's enough Lux here for you to manifest her Spirit. If she has something useful to tell us, we'll escort you to the hospital. That's the deal.'

'What if she has nothing?'

'I don't think you're bluffing, Helen. I'm certainly not.' He turned to me. 'If I walk away, Vic, what will you do?'

Damn him. Why did he have to put me on the spot? I started with the easy one. 'If you ordered me to, I'd leave without a backward glance.'

I looked at his eyes for a clue, but they were invisible in the darkness.

'And if I didn't order you?'

I thought it through. What would happen? I took a deep breath. 'I'd walk away. If I helped bring her back, Twinkletoes here would tell Keira what you'd done. The queue of psycho Mages who are after your blood is long enough without adding Keira Faulkner to it. I might cross you off me Christmas card list, though.'

The ghost of a smile flicked over his lips. He opened his mouth, then flicked his head to the left and reached into his pocket. 'Hello Alain?'

Back in the car park, Alain must have leaned his head next to Helen Davies' mike because I heard every word.

'The general hospital in Dinan have a *Jane Dupont* in critical care. She is in a coma. In French, my family name is used for unknown victims. Like Jane Doe. The nurse on the ward only talked to me because I said I was acting for someone from England. She found it funny. It must be Keira.'

'Thank you,' said Conrad. He turned to face Helen. 'Captain Robson has given you her answer. Produce Keira or we walk.'

'Fine. I'll be a few minutes.'

'We'll be here.'

She vanished, and I shivered. 'Can't we wait in the car?'

'You can. I'd better not.'

I stepped close to a big evergreen bush to get out of the wind and rain. Conrad lit another cigarette and stood his ground.

Over the earpiece, Helen Davies said, 'Should we get ready to go to the hospital?'

'Not yet,' I whispered.

'Is it as scary out there as it seems from here?'

'Yes. Hang on, here they are.'

We didn't get two Keiras, we got one Keira and ... a Mina Desai. Now that was very, very creepy. It was a perfect likeness, too, right down to the birthmark that only Conrad has seen but I've heard about. He shook his head, more in sorrow than anger. I think.

Helen/Mina was close to the menhir, a rather dazed Keira was in front of her, not far from Conrad.

'Keira?' he said. 'Can you hear me?'

This Keira was more like it. Leaner and scrawnier and with the pinched face. She still had perky tits, though. Damn her. She looked at him in awe, like I've never looked at anyone since me twelfth birthday.

'Yes, Dragonslayer, I can hear you. Helen says you will rescue me.'

His lip twitched. 'Have you found Adaryn ap Owain?'

'Found her. Seen her play the harp and sing. Bit too lush for my tastes.' She spoke breathlessly, even though she wasn't breathing. Her eyes never left his.

His lip twitched. 'Spill the beans, Keira.'

She reached out a hand and snatched it back. 'You've met Mia, yes? What did she tell you?'

I decided that this twosome needed breaking up. 'Don't worry, Mia was very loyal to you. Wouldn't give anything away about your illegal activities or the concert.'

'She's a good kid,' said Keira. She put her hand to her own face and her image shimmered, blinking out for a second.

'I told you not to touch yourself,' said Helen when Keira had stabilised.

She turned around and frowned. 'Who's that image, my lady?' she said.

Helen pointed to Conrad. 'His fiancée. It was the best I could do. If he's got the hots for anyone else, it's well hidden.'

'That's Mina?' said Keira. 'Oh.' She turned back to Conrad, whose face had gone beyond granite. Cast iron, maybe?

When Keira started her story, she changed her tone. Almost professional. 'Adaryn ap Owain has a racket going. She appears in the encore of a local group of musicians, and she uses her Bardic skills. Makes it quite obvious to any Mage in the audience. At the end of the gig, the lead singer thanks her and says that people can buy tickets to Mademoiselle Arnaude's private concerts. Arnaude means powerful eagle, by the way. I bought a ticket for Tuesday night. Her bodyguards attacked me, chased me across the fields and tried to kill me. They did kill me. The Great Helen saved me. That's it.'

'Thank you,' said Conrad. 'That's excellent. We're going to need all the details, obviously.'

'What time is it?' said Keira.

'Twenty-one fifteen. Quarter past nine.'

'The band – the mundane band – are playing at the Salle Armorique in Dol tonight. Adaryn will be on stage about half past eleven. The band are called …'

As you've discovered, I don't speak French. I speak even less Breton.

Alain's murmured in our ears. 'It means *The Minstrels from the End of the Earth*. Finisterre. They are awful.'

Conrad pulled his lip. 'Adaryn's harp. Was it on stage throughout?'

Keira tried to shake her head and flickered out of focus. 'No. They wheeled it on between the end of the set and the encore.'

'Describe the attackers, please.'

'Please? Why so formal.'

'Because you've earned it,' he said. 'It's a step up from brutal. The attackers?'

'Two men, two women. I got the impression there were more inside. One of the men was mundane. None of the Mages were particularly powerful, but I haven't been able to replace my Ancile. They were armed with handguns and I knew I was outnumbered. Funnily enough, it was the mundane one who gave me the *coup de grace*. Anything else?'

'Where was the private concert?'

'A big manor house in the middle of nowhere off a side road between La Haye and Pont Galou. Know them?'

'I know where they are.' Of course he did. 'Did it look like their house? A rental?'

'It had Wards and Alarms. They were deactivated, but permanent. It's definitely a base, but whether they live there, I couldn't tell you.'

'Vic? Anything?'

'Why you?' I asked. 'Why did they suddenly attack you?'

'I'm good at insults,' said Keira. I heard them shout when I got out of my car. *"C'est le Rosbif."* Just before I died, my last thought was *why not "La" Rosbif?*

Helen Davies spoke up. 'Ask if they attacked straight away.' I did.

'No. They stood waiting until I ran. There was a big gate behind me that had already closed, or I'd have tried to drive away. The one thing I can think is that they told me the wrong time when they sold me the ticket. Half past six is a bit early. I think they wanted to check out *le Rosbif* and as soon as I ran, they attacked. Perhaps if I'd held my nerve, like you, Dragonslayer, I could have got away with it.'

Conrad grunted, ignoring the praise. 'If this was on private land, how come you're in Dinan hospital?'

Keira looked nonplussed. Helen T supplied the answer. 'They took her phone and bag, then dumped her on the main road. I had to do flying saucer illusions to get someone to take notice and "find" her.'

Conrad nodded. 'Are we done?'

'Yes,' I said. Helen Davies agreed.

'Then we'll be back before dawn.'

'Hey! What if you're dead! What about me?'

'Don't worry. Alain will call Madame Ménard and Mia. Between them, they can manage it. I should point out, I'm not planning on dying.'

'Who's Alain, and why won't he be dead?'

'He's your ticket to life, Keira. Now, if you'll excuse us, we have a fugitive to apprehend.' He bowed. 'My lady, it's been an honour.'

Keira's mouth moved, as if she were trying to bite her lip. 'Take care, please, Dragonslayer.'

He nodded and took a step back, glancing at me.

'My lady, Ms Faulkner,' I said. Probably a bit loudly. I'm happy walking in Conrad's shadow, but I don't like being completely ignored.

Helen T nodded her head. Keira said, 'Yeah. Thanks.' We both turned and left.

When we got to the car, I let out a long whistle. 'Flipping heck, Uncle C. That was a facer and no mistake.'

'Sounded like it.' Oops. That was Helen Davies. I'd forgotten we were still connected.

'Pour us both a coffee,' said Conrad. 'Won't be long.'

We both ended our calls and got in. 'Are we gonna talk about the whole Mina thing?' I asked. 'Just so I know.'

His face relaxed into a grin. 'Of course you can tell her. But tell her that I said she's much sexier in the flesh.'

12 — Eagle's Nest

Helen Davies had not only poured the coffee, she'd run the engine to get the car warmed up. It was only when I got inside that I realised how cold and stiff I'd been. Thanks to the expensive waterproof, at least I was dry above the thighs.

'You want me to call Madame Ménard now?' said Alain. 'Before she goes to bed?'

'No,' said Conrad. 'I want Vic to call Mia and tell her to call her grandmother. Give them the headlines but don't mention the hospital or Helen of Troy. If they ask point blank, tell them that the hospital is in Rennes and that the guiding Spirit is Asterix the Gaul. No, I want Alain to call Morane and pump her for information on this Salle Armorique place. Go and do it in the other car if you want privacy.'

'Of course,' said Alain. 'What do you want to know?'

'Fundamentally, I want to know if there's a big car park or if it's in the old town.'

'OK. Why? Just so I know what we're really looking for.'

It was a fair question. Conrad thought carefully before answering. 'That harp of Adaryn's weighs a ton. If the hall is in the old town, they won't turn up until just before they need to. If it has a car park, the harp will be waiting outside in a van. And so will Adaryn.'

He passed Alain the keys, and Alain got out. When the door was closed, Conrad closed his eyes and massaged the bridge of his nose. I sipped my coffee. I was going to need a pee very soon.

His eyes snapped open and he peered through the window. Alain was in full flow, gesturing and smiling under the courtesy light of the rental car. 'Vic, make that call to Mia. Helen, let's get going. Turn right out of the car park and then left at the first roundabout.'

She started the engine and said, 'What's the rush?'

'Timing. I think they're still at the house.'

I gritted my teeth. 'Conrad, I haven't been to the loo for three hours. I can't go into an operation like this.'

'Me neither,' added Helen. She flashed me a smile of thanks.

'There's a hostel by the entrance.'

Normally he's very sensitive to comfort breaks. For some reason, this was really eating at him. He peed behind a tree. Typical man. I had to use magick to jump the queue, and I was first back. Naturally, he was standing in the rain, smoking.

'What's up, Conrad? You're not normally this rattled.'

'Lack of intelligence, Vicky. It has to be now, and it has to work first time.'

'Why can't we wait?'

He glanced over my shoulder and must have seen Helen coming. 'Keira has to be woken up tonight. Word will get round. We're in enemy territory, here. Too many lives at risk. Even Morane could be in danger.'

I had to repeat myself three times before I was sure that Mia had understood me. By then, we were deep in the countryside, and Alain had confirmed that the Salle Armorique was in an alley opposite the cathedral.

'Slow right down,' said Conrad. He had a map open on his lap. 'Vic, start feeling for Wards. I can see two likely turnoffs ahead.'

We took the first turnoff, to the right, and passed a few small houses with lights showing from the windows. Then the lane turned into a track. 'Do I keep going?' said Helen.

By way of an answer, Conrad reached round to the luggage section at the back of the Range Rover and pulled out his new sword. He laid it, still in its scabbard, on his lap and took out his gun as well. 'Yes.'

Helen drove carefully down the track as it curved then forked, with a farm track to the left and a set of gates with big stone pillars to the right. I could feel the magick. 'Here we are.'

'Helen, back up out of sight of the gates and turn off the engine. Wait here while Vic and I take a look.'

I would have complained if I were Helen. She's not much of a Mage, but with her new Badge of Office, she's got a lot of Artefact support. Maybe it's the police training, but all she said was, 'Yes, sir.' I opened the door and got out into the rain. Again.

Conrad was already standing by the gates. 'What do you reckon to the magick?' he asked.

We've been here before. Lots of times now – a stone wall with Wards and gates that are sealed and Alarmed. Except where was the wall?

'I don't think the wall is enchanted,' I said. 'If it is, I can't feel it.'

'What wall? There's only a fence. A strong one with barbed wire, but still a fence.'

There *was* a wall, but he was right: it was only decorative and ran about five metres on either side of the gates. I couldn't see any further because there were trees in the way and it was dark.

'Let's have a look at the fence,' he said. He set off up the farm track, then cut right over a ploughed field. Ugh. It was like walking through a mixture of Plasticine and manure. Thankfully there was a six foot strip of firm grass next to the fence.

'How long to cut through this with magick?' he asked.

'Half an hour. It may have mundane security on it, too. And are you gonna drive over that?'

'No. Helen has her Police Advanced Pursuit certificate. She can drive. I … Here they come.'

Two vehicles were coming through the parkland and over the slight rise that must be concealing the house from the road.

'Quick. Let's squeeze through the trees.'

Easier said than done. Conrad used his long legs to get over and around things, while I had to try to squeeze through. At least we were out of sight of the vehicles once the wall shielded us. There was a twist in their path just before the gates, and Conrad used that fraction of a second to run across the road. I was just emerging from the trees when the electric motors started to drag the gates apart. I didn't dare shout anything. What the hell was his plan?

I got an inkling when I heard Helen start the Range Rover's engine. If she had any sense, she'd get out of the car and leave it as an obstacle. A long, low black limousine glided out of the gates. I had no idea who or how many people were in it. The second vehicle was a grey Transit that accelerated to get through before the gates started to close. At that moment Helen switched on every light her car possessed.

It blinded me, and must have given the limo driver a heart attack. He/she slammed on the brakes and skidded in the rain. The van driver hadn't been blinded, but they missed their brake and slammed into the limo. I raced right to get my back to Helen's floodlights and was in position when they started to pile out.

The biggest guy got out of my side – the passenger side – and a woman in casual clothes from the rear. Two more figures got out of Conrad's side, and there were two in the van as well. Six against three if Helen joined us. One of the women on the far side was wearing a fur coat, but she had long blonde hair, so she couldn't be Adaryn.

Conrad put his French to good use, shouting at them to stand still or something. They took this as a cue to shoot at us. And the blonde woman started to sing. So she was Adaryn.

I advanced at a steady pace as four bullets bounced off my Ancile. Why hadn't Conrad shot someone himself? He'd given the bastards a fair warning. Over the singing, I heard a woman's scream and the singing doubled in volume. The guy who'd just shot at me dropped his gun and took out a mace. A very old mace with steel flanges like petals on the heavy end. If he'd hit Keira with that, I'm surprised she had any brain left. It started to glow with magick. Shit.

The other two on my side drew knives. It was time to fight back before I got my face rearranged. I had no idea what the magick was in the mace, so I started with the woman to his left, the other one who'd had a gun. I drew power and span round like a baseball pitcher. At the right moment, I loosed a scythe of compressed air at her legs.

I heard the crack of bones, and she flipped over like she'd been hit by a car. At that point the singing stopped and Adaryn shouted, 'Run for the chateau!'

The other guy, the one with the knife, turned and legged it straight away. He knew he was next. The guy with the mace clearly knew something his friend didn't, because he was coming right at me.

I feinted to the right and dodged to the left, and all that mud on me shoe skidded on the road. I did the splits and the mace whistled right past me. Owwwww. My groin muscles nearly separated, and I had to roll on my back to ease the pain. I tried a blast at the guy's mace arm. Nothing doing. He had no magick, but the mace did. He raised it for the killing blow, then collapsed forward when Conrad stuck him in the arse with his sword.

You'd think he'd been castrated, so loud was the screaming. He'd already dropped the mace, and Conrad kicked it away. He put his boot on the guy's hand and threatened to Taser him. What? He stopped screaming after that.

Conrad held out his left hand, keeping his sword pointed down in his right. I let him pull me to my feet very carefully. Ow that hurt. I saw Helen moving in the glare of light, and she brought a woman round the front of the limo, already restrained, despite the blood running down a deep cut in her arm.

'Do this one next,' said Conrad. The bloke started to chunter until Conrad pressed his boot down again. With deft, experienced fingers, Helen dragged his arms behind his back and put the restraints on. I left them to it and went to the woman with two broken legs. She was in a bad way, alright.

I knelt down and put my arm on her shoulder. 'Hey, can you understand me? It's OK.'

'The pain! My legs!'

She only wore a light coat, and it was already soaked. What the hell was I gonna do?

'Sit her up against the car,' said Conrad. 'There's nothing else we can do at the moment.'

She moaned when I helped her sit up, then her eyes sort of glazed over. She needed help, something that wouldn't be coming any time soon after Conrad took their phones and the car keys. He squatted in front of her. 'The sooner this is over, the sooner I'll call an ambulance. Who is in the house?'

She pointed to the mace guy. 'Arthur's father and grandmother. She is in charge. She is very powerful, especially with Arnaude singing.' She looked down at her legs and groaned again.

'What about the mace?' he said to me.

I patted the woman on the shoulder and turned my back on her. Well, she had just tried to shoot me. I walked over to the mace and scanned it, then picked it up. It was old, very old, and was designed to be used by Mage or mundane fighters. With an influx of Lux, the mace became both Ancile and a tool for slicing through magickal defences. Nifty. I weighed it in my hand. I could definitely use that.

Helen had finished and stood just behind the woman with the bleeding arm.

'Let's go,' said Conrad. 'Helen, you escort our prisoner. Vicky, you go right, I'll go left. Quick as we can.'

'What's your name?' said Helen.

'Eloise,' said the prisoner.

We moved at a fast walk, and you could see that this wasn't the first time that Helen had frogmarched someone. Thank goodness Eloise was wearing flat shoes. 'What happened on your side?' I called across to Conrad.

'As soon as Immi – sorry, *Adaryn* – started singing, they came at me. Same as on your side. Luckily for me, the mace was on your side. As soon as I disarmed this one, they legged it.'

'You have torn my arm,' said the prisoner. 'Let go of me! Aargh.'

'Less of your lip, girl,' said Helen. 'If you bleed on me, I'll be sending you the bill.'

In case you need a reminder, Conrad knew Adaryn ap Owain, aka Mademoiselle Arnaude, when she was just Imogen Jones, a girl at school. And yes, he did ask her out. She said no. Perhaps if she'd said yes, history would have been different. That's why he calls her *Immi*.

'And why did you threaten to Taser that bloke?' I asked.

'Pardon?'

'Arthur? You said you were gonna Taser him.'

Conrad laughed. 'No I didn't. I said *taisez-vous*. Means *shut up*. Here we go.'

The chateau came into view, and I would have said that it was a medium sized mansion, not a chateau. No turrets or battlements, see? Or moat. Mind you, it was raining enough not to need a moat. The reception committee was waiting out front.

You could see who was in charge straight away. A woman of Mme Ménard's age was in the middle. Where Avril Ménard prefers formal chic, this one had gone full Druid, robes and all. And staff. Six feet of ancient magickal wood was held in a tight grip and without thinking, I sent a pulse of Lux into the mace. It seemed to get even heavier, and I caught a whiff of something smoky. That was strange, but not as strange as seeing Adaryn hide behind the Druid matriarch.

To the woman's right was her son, Arthur's father. He had a sword that looked like the twin of the mace: another Mage/mundane weapon. The two men who'd run from the ambush were there, too, along with another two women, one of them possibly the leader's daughter. She stood at grandmother's left hand, and held the third weapon, a flail. I think. A spiked ball on a chain at the end of a stick, and she looked as if she knew how to use it.

We stopped about fifteen metres away from them, and the matriarch's eyes were drawn to the mace in my hand. 'Where is my grandson?' she said.

'Ask your Bard,' said Conrad, pointing to Adaryn with his sword.

'Arnaude ran away!' shouted our prisoner. 'She ran away and left Arthur to die. They all did.'

The matriarch lifted her staff and magick pulsed.

'He's alive,' said Conrad. 'Wounded but alive. Eloise, tell them what happened.'

There was rapid fire French. The matriarch asked a question that included *Arthur*, and Eloise answered. When she asked another question, Conrad said, 'Enough!' Helen reinforced the point with a tug on the restraints.

'Who speaks the best magickal English?' said Conrad.

'I do,' said the Mage with the flail.

'Good. Just for the record, I am Conrad Clarke, this is Victoria Robson and Helen Davies has your friend.' He paused.

The matriarch lowered her staff and dialled down the magick. 'This is Chateau *Tonguey* – T-A-N-G-I. The traditional spelling of Brittany.'

Fair enough. Chateau Tangi it is.

'This is my son, Armel Tangi and my daughter, Maëlys Tangi. The others are members of our Druidic Circle. Do you want to see their ID?' The smile on her lips said she had all the time in the world for this; the twitch in Armel's weapon hand said that he'd rather be looking for his son.

'They have no authority here,' said Adaryn. 'He didn't use his title, did he?'

'You are the Dragonslayer, non?' said Mme Tangi.

'Also Lord Guardian of the North. Elodie Guerin knows we're here. She told me to get on with it.' He lifted his gun hand, and dangled the Hammer by the trigger guard. 'Mademoiselle Maëlys? Tell your mother what a Disruptor Round is. I didn't use them at the gate because I want no deaths.'

He does love a bit of theatre, does Conrad. He got down on one knee, laid down the sword, and took a proper, two handed grip on the gun, resting his left arm on his knee.

Maëlys whispered in her mother's ear, and she flinched. The gun was now pointing right at Mme Tangi.

'I am too old to stand in the rain,' she said. 'I would ask you in, where the fire is warm, but Arthur is badly injured.'

'No he isn't,' said Conrad, 'but the woman is. How about this.' He used his head to point to the two men on our left, one mundane, one Mage. 'You two take the Mercedes and get them to hospital. Call it a gesture of peace. They must go to a hospital for broken legs.'

One of the other women burst out. 'Rennes.'

'Oui,' said Mme Tangi. 'Go.'

'What about me!' said Eloise.

'You need a neurosurgeon,' said Conrad. 'They don't work weekends. One of the others can give you a dressing in a minute.'

The two men moved forwards, and Helen chucked some keys on the ground. They picked them up and ran off, giving us a wide berth.

'What now?' said Mme Tangi. Her shoulders had visibly relaxed once the Druids were off on their mission. 'I cannot offer you hospitality. Not after this.'

'We don't want it,' said Conrad. 'Your family and Adaryn only. The others go somewhere else. And Armel lays down his weapon. He will be our hostage. We will offer no violence against your family except in self-defence, as we did before.'

Adaryn heard *your family* and knew which way the wind was blowing. 'You can't trust him!' she said. 'He lies and lies.'

'I give you my word,' said Conrad. He lifted his right hand and showed Odin's ring.

'It is done,' said Mme Tangi. 'Armel, put down the sword and go to them.'

Adaryn grabbed the matriarch's arm, and then let go as if she'd had an electric shock. The fear was growing in her eyes. Good.

'My son will recover fully?' said Armel.

'He will,' said Conrad.

Armel was tall and beefy and definitely knew how to use that sword. He laid it carefully down and walked towards us with his hands raised.

'Off you go, Eloise,' said Helen, giving her a nudge in the back. One of the men rushed to help her, and all the others followed, leaving Team Conrad and the Tangis alone. Plus Adaryn, who looked *very* alone.

Without a word, Mme Armel walked into the house, followed by Maëlys and Adaryn. 'After you,' said Helen to Armel. And she really did have a Taser. They walked forwards, and I heard a cough.

I turned to Conrad. 'Help me up, Vic. This posture does my leg no good.'

'Come here, you great lump.' I hauled him up and he did his little dance where he shakes his leg and hops around. I picked up his sword and dropped it straight away. 'Did that thing just growl at me? You have a dog sword?'

'Wolf. It's called Great Fang and it protects my new pack of Mannwolves. Amongst other things.' He stooped, somehow, and retrieved it. 'Come on, we don't want to miss the party.'

I hurried after his great legs. 'You have a sword called Great Fang? You get worse, Uncle Conrad, you really do.'

13 — It's always Unlucky for Someone

Behind the opulent front doors was a gobsmacking great hall.

'Wow,' I said.

'You're not wrong,' said Helen.

'Too Baroque for me,' said Conrad. 'Never been keen on pink marble in private houses.'

'Not a lot of marble in Swansea,' said Helen.

'Nor Heaton,' I added.

There was a lot, mind you. Columns and panels and staircases, all covered in it. And frescoes on the ceiling. What it had above all was warmth. Physical warmth. As one, we gravitated to the fireplace and its roaring fire. You could actually have a stand-up barbecue in that fireplace.

I took a proper look round, for magick and other threats. There was definitely magick in the little dais below the gallery, and I'm guessing that's where Adaryn did her stuff at private parties. No, that's not being fair to her. She may be 100% a poisonous worm, but she's also a premier Bard. She can use her voice and her harp to amplify all sorts of magick. Want a straighter blade on your sword? Ask Adaryn to warble in the corner of your smithy. Want a more powerful Dæmon in your Summoning circle? Ask Adaryn to sing its name.

Okay, I can't see her in a smithy, and now that we were inside, I took a good look at the changes she'd made in her appearance.

She has naturally dark, naturally wavy hair that goes well with her wide eyes. The (expensive) blonde dye job made her face look pinched, and she'd lost a fair bit of weight off her curves, as if she were going for the elfin look and failing. She'd opened the fur coat to reveal a burgundy velvet gown that finished just above her ankles. I'm guessing she planned to change out of her trainers at the Salle Armorique.

Mme Tangi had taken a hard chair and rested the staff between her knees. The rest of us stood, with two Tangis and Adaryn to the left of the fireplace and Team Conrad plus Armel to the right. Mme Tangi spoke first.

'You want Arnaude, yes?' she said.

'Yes. Nothing else. Just her and we'll leave you alone.'

'There is just one problem, monsieur. She owes us a great deal of treasure, both Lux and Euros. We have invested a lot in her. We would want compensation for our loss.'

'What about the project?' said Adaryn, wildness in her eyes and desperation in her voice. 'You can't sell me like a slave after all we've started to build here. You can't trust him. He's just a tool of the old enemy. He sacrificed to Lord of the Gallows, and used Odin to slay one of *our* Dragons.'

Since we'd got to the fireplace, my eyes had never left Adaryn's face. Not once. And not once had she looked at me. When Conrad said nothing, I knew he was waiting for me, and I was ready.

I lifted the mace and pointed it at her. 'What's a cow?'

Maëlys gave me a crafty smile. 'A cow? *Une vache.*'

I kept the mace steady, anger burning in my biceps. 'That woman is a cheap, cowardly cow. A great big *vache*. She ran off and left the other Druids in Wales. She left Rhein to die, and no, Conrad earned the title of *Dragonslayer* all on his own. She left your grandson to die, Madame Tangi. Ran away and left him to die. Be thankful for our mercy.'

I lowered the mace.

'How much?' said Conrad. 'Never mind. Whatever it is, I suggest that Adaryn's harp and your son's life will clear the debt.'

Armel Tangi looked relaxed. He glanced at his mother and raised his eyebrows and gave the faintest of shrugs. He was a good boy.

Adaryn took a step to her right, away from Mme Tangi and Maëlys. 'Not the harp. That's priceless. I'll gift it to you and lease it back. Together, we're worth far, far more.'

She was staring at Mme Tangi as she spoke, and didn't notice that Conrad had given a hand signal. Helen moved away from Armel, taking a couple of steps into the room. I stepped right, and lifted the mace on to my shoulder.

Mme Tangi returned Adaryn's glare. 'My son is worth more than all the harps in the world. He is worth infinitely more than you.' She turned away. 'We have a deal, monsieur.'

Adaryn lifted her dress and sprinted, right into the path of Helen Davies. There was a loud *pop*, and Adaryn ap Owain collapsed on to the stone flags, rigid from the electric shock. That'll teach her to leave off her Artefacts to wear a low-cut dress.

We did have one problem: over here in France, we couldn't use the power of Nimue to arrest Adaryn and suppress her magick. Conrad stayed near Armel and the fireplace, just in case, and I moved to Adaryn. When I got close, Mme Tangi had something to say.

'Be careful with the fur coat. It's mine.' It's a good job for Adaryn that she didn't hear that. It's one thing to be worth less than a mother's only son; it's quite another to be worth less than her fur coat.

I covered Adaryn and let Helen detach the Taser, slip the coat off and check her pulse. Satisfied, she put the restraints on, then used her Badge of Office to scan Adaryn for Artefacts. She removed a loose-fitting ring and chucked it across the floor to Mme Tangi. Maëlys put down her flail and picked up the ring.

My best friend is training to use choral magick – only Druids call them Bards. Desi is nowhere near Adaryn's league, but I've picked up some useful tips. 'Conrad, a gag would be a really good idea.'

'Cut one off her dress.'

Helen had a pocket knife and made short work of the hem. Adaryn was shaky, but coming round. It would need both of us to hold her upright. I looked at Conrad, and he nodded then shouted over to the gallery. 'Go and get Monsieur Tangi a coat. We're taking him to the gates and then releasing him. Alone.'

'What about the massed arm?' said Madame. Eh?

'The mace?' said Conrad. 'It can be a lesson for Arthur. He did try to kill my partner. Unprovoked.' One of the women appeared with a big coat and stood by the doors. 'Leave it there, thank you.'

He got out his phone and placed a call while we got Adaryn to her feet. 'Alain? Success. Get the tickets and go to the rendezvous point. Ten minutes.' He turned back to Madame and bowed. 'To me, this is done. *Fini*. I will say nothing to Elodie Guerin. Goodbye.'

Mme Tangi inclined her head. 'Goodbye, Dragonslayer.'

Conrad ushered Armel Tangi to the door and used his foot to check the pockets of the coat on the floor before allowing Armel to pick it up. Armel brushed the dust off first and put it on. He didn't look back once, but I did. His mother was staring at her son, worry clearly visible, but his sister was staring at Adaryn with a smile on her face. Good.

We left the warmth of the hall and found that the rain and wind were worse, if anything. I am so gonna need a bath, but when? Conrad clearly had a plan for smuggling a Druid out of the country, but I didn't ask.

'Monsieur, help with Arnaude. Vicky, take the lead. Fast as we can, everyone.'

When I let go of Adaryn's arm, she struggled and moaned and tried to push Helen over. Fat chance. Helen squeezed a painful nerve, and Adaryn squealed behind the gag. Armel took the other arm, carefully, and we set off.

I toyed with getting my torch out, but the path was light enough to follow. I glanced behind, and Conrad was walking backwards at the rear. I opened my Sight and felt no one near. It didn't take long to get to the bashed van, and when Adaryn realised she was near her harp for the last time, she had another futile go at escaping. At least she was soaked through now, and that would soon take the fight out of her.

'Watch her,' said Helen, 'and I'll check the car. Just in case.'

'Turn it round as well,' added Conrad.

We backed away from the gates to the shelter of the wall, and Helen climbed in to the Range Rover. Some of the tension left me when the engine started first time, and she soon had it facing the way we came.

'Monsieur, face the wall, hands on your head,' said Conrad. 'I won't make you lie down, but...'

'I understand,' replied Armel.

He did what he was told, and Conrad told me to get in first. He half pushed, half hoisted Adaryn into the middle, almost throwing her into the car. I grabbed her and hauled her upright, and Helen put her foot down as soon as Conrad had closed his door.

'Are we going to the station?' asked Helen. 'Or straight to Calais and the Eurostar?'

Calais would be safer, I reckoned.

'Neither,' said Conrad. 'Left at the end of the track.'

We got off the side road on to the country lane, and Helen went even faster.

'Left at the main road,' said Conrad. Hang on, that was heading away into nowhere. Even I knew that. Dol-de-Bretagne, the TGV station, the motorway and all points of civilisation were to the right. As soon as Helen had made the turn, he said, 'Fast as you can for one mile. Get ready to turn right, signposted *La Durantais*. Vicky, text Mia and tell her to get moving. Urgently.'

He moved his sword, and brought the edge up to Adaryn' neck while I got my phone out. I opted for the simplest message: *Go now. Urgent.*

With the swaying of the car, it took me two goes, and I only hit *Send* just before Helen nearly put us into a ditch turning right.

'Half a mile on the left. You'll know it when you get there.'

Conrad pushed Adaryn right on to me so that he could sheathe his sword, then put his arm through hers, ready to pull her out. What the hell was going on? Had he done a trade of some sort? Were the Sûreté de magie waiting for us in a random field? I only caught a glimpse of the sign as Helen swung through a wide gateway and bounced on to a grass field. And then it all made sense: in front of us, all lit up, was Conrad's helicopter, the Smurf.

'You crafty bugger,' I said. 'So that's what you were doing yesterday: moving the Smurf.'

'And training Alain to start her up. You get out first and open my door.'

Helen stopped a good way from the helicopter, and I got out. The grass was firm, but slippery, and I got round as quickly as I could. The Smurf's lights dimmed for a second, and the engines started to whine. I pulled the door open, and Conrad slid out, using brute strength to drag Adaryn like a sack of spuds. Helen joined us, and he handed her over just as the whine went up a notch in pitch and volume. Then a bass note got added, and the rotors started to move slowly. Conrad raised his voice.

'Alain is staying here to sort everything out and get your stuff. We'll be in London in less than an hour. I'll finish the checks and come back to help you get her inside.'

Alain climbed out of the cockpit, and Conrad took his place. Alain jogged over and gave us a big grin.

'You're very naughty,' I told him. 'Isn't this a bit OTT?'

'Conrad says that every Druid in Brittany will be looking for us. It is the only safe way. For all of us.'

I felt rather than heard my phone ringing. It was Mia. This could be important, and I showed the screen to Helen before stepping back a bit, away from the noise. It made no difference, and I shoved my finger in my other ear. 'Speak up, Mia.'

'Grand-maman asks what *sorcellerie* we need.'

There was no point lying now. 'Tell her that the spirit is Helen of Troy.'

'Common?'

Oh, right. *Comment?* 'Helen of Troy!'

'Merde!' I understood that. 'A moment.'

At that point, I'd realised that I'd closed my eyes to concentrate on the sound. I opened them just as Adaryn headbutted Helen Davies full on the nose and punched her in the stomach.

I dropped my phone and ran round the car. How the hell had she escaped? I got the answer when I smelled burning plastic and saw the raw burns on her wrists. She'd actually used magick to set the restraints on fire.

Alain did the only sensible thing and ran to the Smurf, where Conrad was staring at the instruments, totally oblivious. Adaryn wrenched out the gag and spat.

'I am not going to die in that cesspit!' she screamed before jumping in the car. I got out the mace and tried to work out how to stop a Range Rover with it.

I didn't need to try, because the keys were in Helen's pocket, not the ignition, and I was standing over Helen to protect her. Adaryn got out and started to sing, then she looked over my shoulder and her voice dried up. That would be Conrad, then, but I was in the way.

With no warning, Adaryn charged me, screaming magick and growing talons of fire from her fingers. I sent a pulse of Lux into the mace and swung it at her head. Thank the Goddess for those engines, because if I'd heard the sound her skull made when it popped open, I think I'd have thrown up on the spot and had nightmares.

I stood, staring at Imogen Jones, aka Adaryn ap Owain, aka Mlle Arnaude, aka Immi, while Helen got to her feet with Conrad's assistance. The first thing she did was put her arm round me and whisper in my ear.

'Suicide by cop. Not your fault. Nothing to do with you. Suicide.'

Yeah. I suppose it was, really. Even if she'd killed me by some miracle, Conrad would have put her down in a second. I don't know whether to feel flattered that she chose to die at my hand rather than his.

Conrad eased the mace out of my hand and wiped it on the grass before tearing off more of Immi's dress and wrapping it round the weapon. He chucked it in the back of the car and said to Helen, 'I'm going to turn off the engines, but they need to warm up fully first. Get Vicky in the car and give her some coffee with lots of extra sugar. How's the nose, by the way?'

Helen was feeling it gingerly and looking at the blood on her fingers. 'Not broken, I don't think, but it hurts like hell. Come on, Vicky. Let's get you in the warm.'

Helen – and Alain – made me keep talking for some reason. Not that we had much to say. The coffee was nice, though. In a couple of minutes, it started to get quieter, then all I could hear was the rain on the car roof until Conrad knocked on my window. What?

Helen used the master control to lower the windows and passed him a coffee. He lit a cigarette, and Helen said, 'Organised crime?'

'Got to be,' he replied.

'Sorry?' I asked.

'Madame Tangi may well be an Archdruidess, but her family are also running an organised criminal network.'

'I think Arthur was banging Adaryn as well,' added Helen. 'Why else would he try so hard to stop you at the gates?'

'Could be,' mused Conrad.

That was a horrible thought, and the shiver that followed it woke me up a bit. 'Can't you start those engines again, Conrad? Can't we go home?'

He shook his head. 'I'm not technically licensed for bad weather night flying. I could have gotten away with it in an emergency, but not now.'

'What!' said Helen. 'You were gonna fly me without a licence?'

He shrugged. 'A technicality, that's all. I think we'd better rendezvous with the Ménards now.'

'Me phone!' I said. 'They were on the phone when Immi went apeshit. I'd better call her.'

'I'll get your phone,' said Alain. 'And I'll talk to Mia. I must call someone else, too.'

Conrad leaned right in to me. 'Are you up to calling Mina? I'd do it myself, but there's a loose end out here.'

'What are you gonna do with her?' I saw the look on his face and added, 'You can tell me. I'm not gonna faint or nothing.'

By way of an answer, he went round and opened the back of the car. Yes, I'm afraid that Watch Captains do carry heavy duty body bags in the field.

'We'll take her in Alain's car and leave her at the hospital. Elodie Guerin can sort out the paperwork. Let's relocate to the menhir. We can sit there with the engines running and no one will complain.'

Alain passed me my phone and I dialled Mina before my courage ran out.

14 — French Left

There was one more surprise and one more confrontation before we left Dol-de-Bretagne. The surprise was waiting for us in the lane near the menhir – a young woman in a long padded jacket with the hood up.

'Ooh, I wonder if that's Morane,' said Helen, peering through the rain. I'd been promoted to riding shotgun now that Conrad was with Alain. He was already out of the car and taking her hands in a very intimate gesture.

'You know what, I'm so glad these seats aren't cream,' said Helen as she opened the door. 'I don't know which is worse, the mud or the blood.'

I reluctantly joined her outside, and added, 'I'd like to say it gets easier, but it doesn't. Not for me.'

'I'm not sure I want it to get easier. Right, what have we got?'

It was Morane, and she lowered her hood to reveal a very intense face, long brown hair and bad skin with no makeup. It was the eyes that got you, big blue ones behind huge glasses. Conrad was not looking happy.

'We need her, mon ami,' said Alain. 'Her mother is a *tea-druizze* … a minor Mage. More than that, she is a big nurse at Dinan Hospital.'

'She is not big,' said Morane. Alain was right, she had a lovely voice that sounded like it came from someone older and taller. 'She is a senior staff nurse. She will let you in to the hospital, but only if you tell me what you need her for.'

Conrad raised an eyebrow in my direction and I smiled at him. We were both thinking it: *he only met her yesterday. How does he know about her mother already?*

'Let's get in the Range Rover,' said Alain.

I pointed at Conrad. 'Fine, but you get in the back.'

We discovered that Morane was in a different order of Druids to the Tengis, so Conrad gave the signal to tell her a bit more, and then the Ménards arrived, and that's what provoked the confrontation.

It happened outside, and it happened as soon as Mme Tengi's name was mentioned. Avril Ménard went off on one with her daughter, then Alain joined in, then Morane, and the Anglophones stepped back until they'd slugged it out. When Mia Ménard had stomped off into the rain, and then stomped back again, and finally bowed her head in submission, Alain came over and whispered, 'Mesdames Ménard and Tangi are old rivals. I think there will be a lot of shaking up in Breton magick after tonight. They are ready to go.'

After the drama of death, near-death and GBH, the next stage nearly brought on hysterical laughter. Are you a fan of logic puzzles? I'm not. See if you can work out how we got to Dinan.

- Morane had been dropped off by her mother, so we had three cars.

- The Ménards had to travel together and sit at least one foot apart to escort Helen of Troy, so neither of them could drive.
- I was too shattered to drive.
- The Ménards had to go with a Mage.
- I would not go in Alain's car on account of the dead body in the boot.
- Alain would not let Morane go in his car for the same reason.

When we approached the menhir, Helen of Troy emerged in what I think may have been her original form, and by the Goddess, she was beautiful. Barely an adult, she had gorgeous golden skin, black hair and bright blue eyes. Her face was a perfect oval, and only her little snub nose stopped her being a checklist of ideal features, and that made her even more attractive. Her arms were slender and her hands curved protectively round a nine-month baby bump. That would be Keira in there, I'm guessing. She didn't speak and didn't even pretend to walk. She waited for the Ménards to flank her, then floated gracefully above the ground with pointed toes.

'You'll catch flies,' I said to Morane.

'Pardon?'

'Close your mouth, hinny.'

She snapped it closed (she had very white, very even teeth), and after a tense drive, she directed us to the service entrance of the hospital. It was three o'clock on a Sunday morning, and I have never been in a city so dead. Not a soul about. No cars, nothing. Made our job easier. It looked lovely, especially the old town, but we passed that by and settled for the sodium lights of the hospital.

Morane's mother was waiting, a thin coat over her uniform top. She was wearing jeans, so I'm guessing she wasn't on duty. She spoke to her daughter for a couple of minutes, then waved us in (after getting the fly catching message). Alain kept watch on the vehicles.

We took the lift up one floor, and thankfully Keira had a private room. Just before we went in, I thought I saw a white shadow down the corridor. I opened my Sight, but got nothing, so I closed the door behind me and shut the blinds on the observation window.

Helen of Troy floated down to the floor and became less shimmery, more solid. 'Pull back the sheets,' she said.

Morane's mother did the honours, and Helen T raised a graceful leg to climb on top of the comatose Keira. I gritted my teeth, ready for something gruesome. Some magickal procedures are very, *very* graphic. Think *Alien*. This was mercifully quick and only marginally gross. Before Helen could dismount, alarms were going off all over Keira's monitors.

The senior staff nurse leapt into action, silencing noises and cancelling alarms. 'It has worked!' she said. 'A miracle. See? There is activity all across the brain.'

'Excuse me,' said Helen. 'I've got to demanifest now and get back to the menhir for a rest.' She reached out delicate fingers and ran them along Conrad's sleeve. 'Until we meet again, Conrad.'

He didn't flinch. 'Thank you, my lady. Go well.'

She gave an enormous wink at Alain and patted Mia on the shoulder. And then she was gone.

'You must go, too,' said Morane's mother. 'The duty nurse will be here soon.'

We slipped out, shook hands and said goodbye in a cloud of Conrad and Alain's illegal smoke outside the hospital boiler rooms; the boys had already deposited their package outside the mortuary. The Ménards left first, with a promise from Avril to let Keira convalesce at her house in Pont Menou. She looked really happy that we'd got her lodger/assistant back, and she also promised to keep her out of trouble. If she could.

Alain and Morane went together. She'd offered him a spare bed, and the poor lad did look rather green, which left us three, the King's Watch.

'Have we got to drive to Locquirec?' I asked wearily.

'No,' said Conrad. 'Alain's got us a special rate on a three bed family room at the Auberge Centrale. Strictly cash to the night porter. You and I need to go see Keira in the morning, Vicky.'

'Only after a big breakfast. Or two. Two breakfasts minimum.'

'Done.'

By heaven, that bed felt good. And there was a proper bath. I didn't even mind that I had to put on the same clothes after it. Other people might have minded the smell, but they were too polite to say.

And the rain had stopped, so it didn't matter that I'd thrown my blood-stained waterproof in the garbage when we went for breakfast. I only had one breakfast in the end, but it was a big one. Conrad suggested that we take the scenic route to the hospital, and we wandered round soaking up the atmosphere for a bit before he asked me whether I wanted to fly home with him this afternoon.

'I'm going to stay in Dinan,' he explained. 'Elodie Guerin is on her way, and there's a lot to sort out. Alain will take me to the Smurf in Dol. Helen's got to catch the ferry in the morning.'

'I'll go with Helen. If there's a repeat of the last crossing, she might need help. And besides, I can score for another night in the Grand Hotel des Bains.'

His mouth twitched. 'So it's not my flying you're worried about?'

'No. If you say it's good to fly, then I'm happy. Or at least not too unhappy.'

'Fair enough.'

'I've got to ask, Conrad. Would you have left Keira to die in that menhir if Helen of Troy hadn't manifested her for questioning.'

He smiled and said, 'Captain Robson, that is a serious allegation. Of course I wouldn't have left her. And what about you? You made the same declaration.'

I laughed. 'Shame on you, sir, for questioning my judgement.' We locked eyes and stopped smiling. I don't think that either of us knew the true answer. Good job we hadn't had to find out.

Morane's mother met us in reception. She was now on duty, and I peered at her ID badge. *Guivarc'h*, it said. So that made her daughter Morane Guivarc'h. Has a nice ring to it, in a French kind of way. She said that "The English Patient" was awake and had been pretending otherwise, especially when the Police Nationale stuck their heads in. That was one of the many things that Conrad had to sort out.

'How did you know she was English?' I asked.

Mme Guivarc'h was a typical senior nurse – very professional, with a big heart and a hard carapace. 'I didn't, and I don't work critical care. She had no ID, nothing, when she was brought in, but one of the scientists, young Jean-Guy, thinks that he is Sherlock Holmes. Before the police took her clothes for evidence, he looked at them. He said that her running shoes were custom made in England and that her underwear was English.' She paused to let us know what she thought of Jean-Guy looking through a comatose woman's smalls. 'He called her the English Patient, like the film, non?' We went to the ward, and a white-coated figure disappeared out of the other end. 'That's him,' she whispered.

'Please,' she said after talking to the duty nurse. 'The patient is very tired, and can barely speak. The feeding tube, you know? I have told them that you are her cousin, Vicky. Please show your ID first. Au revoir.'

We thanked her, and Conrad took out a passport. He opened it to the bio page and gave it to me. It had my picture and Eleanor Weyland's details. The bastard had even aged me three years, a point I made forcefully if quietly.

'It matches the picture,' he said.

'I'll so get you back for this,' I hissed.

Keira did look ill, and her voice sounded terrible. She also looked *whole*. No matter how good the projection that Helen of Troy had made, the real, sick, Keira Faulkner looked much better than the image.

'Thank you, Dragonslayer,' she croaked. 'And you, Watch Captain. Standing up to a Bard like that was a brave thing.'

'I am in your debt,' said Conrad. 'It's us who should thank you. I will keep my promise, but I could do more. I could make a statement to the Court now, and again in three years.'

'Two and a half,' said Keira. 'What's the snag?' By the Lord, she sounded bad.

'Shh,' said Conrad. 'Just nod. Elodie Guerin's coming. She doesn't care what you do, so long as you keep a low profile, so stick with Avril Ménard, OK?' She nodded. 'And you can't keep this *nom de guerre*, is that absolutely clear? You are not any form of Mina Clarke.'

'I'm sorry,' she whispered.

'Good. Here is your new cover name. Stick with it or the deal's off.'

He passed her another of those new passports. She took it and peered at the name, then tried to laugh.

'What's up?' I said.

She passed it to me. From now on, Keira Faulkner would have to call herself Elizabeth Oswaldtwistle

'Hey, Conrad,' I said. 'No taking the piss out of Northern names, okay? Not funny.'

He kept his face straight. 'I wanted to make it something that French people would remember.'

He took the passport back and said, 'I'm giving this to the Police Nationale so they can clear up your mugging. See you in two and a half years, Lizzy. And thanks again.'

He shook her hand, and so did I.

'Can you find your way back to the hotel?' he asked. 'I doubt they'll let me out of the hospital for a while.'

'Aye, course.'

'See you at the Halloween party, then. Or the night before.'

We had a long hug.

'Take care, Uncle Conrad.'

'And you, Vic.'

I walked out of the hospital with a spring in my step, something I hadn't expected. I reckon that old proverb needs updating: *Revenge is a dish best served sprinkled with mace.* We hadn't heard the last of Helen of Troy and Keira – sorry, *Liz* – but we could forget about them for now.

Time to meet Helen Davies for that second breakfast, I reckon.

FRENCH LEAVE

Keira

It took him until Tuesday to pluck up the courage to come into the room. By then, she could speak properly and eat solid food. And her magick had stabilised. Keira wasn't exactly back to her old self, but she was on the road.

The shadow in the white coat had been lurking ever since Sunday, at least four times a day, casting glances while he pretended to talk to the nurses, and looking very worried when the police were escorted to her room for interviews on Monday.

Avril and Mia Ménard came on Tuesday morning, and he finally came in not long after they had gone. Avril had a new respect in her eyes, and had left with a promise to upgrade Keira's room and status. Mia was agog with the news about those Tangi psychos, and all-in-all, things were looking up. Keira even kept her promise and forced Avril to stop calling her *Mina*. They settled on a very French *Lizabet* for her new name, and Keira heard Avril practising it while she put clean clothes in Keira's hospital wardrobe.

It had been a mistake to call herself *Mina*, especially after seeing Lady Helen pull that stunt. By all Hell's Dæmon's, Mina Desai was tiny. Keira's respect for Conrad Bloody Clarke had grown further, of course, but she had to focus on herself now. She could do this. She could make a good life here.

The white coat man came in at that point, with a portion of freshly squeezed orange, her favourite. 'Excuse me, Elizabeth. Can I come in?'

'Of course. Is that for me?'

He passed her the drink. 'You are not too tired?'

'No. Thank you.'

'I would have brought flowers, but they are banned. I am Jean-Guy, the senior scientist in the laboratory.'

His English was flawless, and although he looked like he'd been cast from a mould stamped *geek*, he wasn't that bad. No magick, though. 'Aren't you very young to be a senior scientist?'

'Yes, but I am good. I do not run the laboratory, that is the manager, but I am still senior in science. Can I sit down?' She pointed to the chair, and he sat on it, pulling it closer. 'It was me who worked out you were English, did they tell you?'

They hadn't, and he looked eager, so she let him tell the story. He had the grace to blush and apologise about the underwear, and for watching over her while she was unconscious. Aah. Bless him. Then he leaned forward. 'You were abducted, were you not? By them? I saw them come back here. The golden one with the anti-gravity shoes. It's okay, Elizabeth, you can tell me. I have always known we are not alone in the universe.'

Aliens? Poor lad. If only he knew the truth.

'I wish I could tell you, Jean-Guy, but I think they wiped my memory. Did you see the tall English one on Sunday? The one with the limp?' Jean-Guy nodded. 'He was from the British Government. He said that they understood, and they'd support me.'

He took her hand impulsively, and his fingers were warm, comforting. 'Please, Elizabeth, I would like to get to know the real you. The girl in the coma, it is a joke, non? The young man watches her and falls in love with a picture. Then you wake up and the young man does not like the real person. I want to get to know you.' He released her fingers. 'My little sister says there are no visitors from other planets, but she says there is magic. How stupid.'

'You have a sister?'

'Danielle. She is still at school. Would you like to see her picture?'

He was a bit too quick to take out his phone, and he noticed the look in her eyes. 'I promise I have not taken pictures of you while you slept. That would be … horrible. Nothing.'

'Show me Danielle.'

He swiped to his photos and let her check the recent ones. Nothing suspicious. Then he showed her a girl of no more than sixteen or seventeen, with a wide smile and happy eyes. And very good bone structure under the puppy fat. She might make an excellent candidate for Helen in a couple of years, once Keira had run a check on her magickal potential.

'Yes, Jean-Guy, I would like to get to know you. The French police won't let me leave the country for months. Perhaps years. It gets very lonely, carrying a secret like mine. Very lonely. And I'd like to get to know your family, too.'

This time, she took his hand, and he smiled.

'Danielle would love to meet you,' he said. 'I have told her all about you, Elizabeth.'

She gave Jean-Guy's hand a squeeze, and the smile of pure happiness spread over his face.

'I look forward to it,' said Keira.

Author's Note

I sincerely hope you enjoyed this collection of King's Watch Stories and that you can see why they needed to be told. Not all of Conrad and the gang's adventures are epic (though French Leave comes close – it's as long as some novels).

I put this collection together just after publishing *Six Furlongs* but before starting to write the next novella – *Fire Games*. I may not wait as long before publishing the next collection.

And why not join Conrad's elite group of supporters:

The Merlyn's Tower Irregulars

Visit the Paw Press website and sign up for the Irregulars to receive news of new books, or visit the Facebook page for Mark Hayden Author and Like it.

Printed in Great Britain
by Amazon